WINNER TAKES ALL

"Bloody hell!" I tore off the helmet and blinked in the blind shock of sensory shift. I stabbed override as the orb whirled and the viewscreens faded to transparent. "Control program: Safety systems check out fine! What's going on?"

The grill produced a barely inflected voice. "An unauthorized intruder has penetrated the dome, presenting a hazard. Remain in your . . ."

I froze with my hand on the controls. I could see her now through the window. She was clinging to the sphere at the end of one of the rods, her flat, round face terrified as it sucked her toward the clanking doors of the orb.

"Damn it!" I punched in codes to bypass the oblivious interrupt program that was pulling the extensor rods back into the central orb · · ·

PRAISE FOR SARA STAMEY'S *WILD CARD RUN*

"Its creative setting and dynamic protagonist can be counted on to fly one through to the end."   —*Fantasy Review*

"Stamey puts feeling into this story of the prodigal daughter."   —*Publishers Weekly*

Books by Sara Stamey

WILD CARD RUN
WIN, LOSE, DRAW

SARA STAMEY

WIN, LOSE, DRAW

ACE BOOKS, NEW YORK

WIN, LOSE, DRAW

An Ace Book/published by arrangement with
the author

PRINTING HISTORY
Ace edition/September 1988

ISBN: 0-441-71428-5

Ace Books are published by The Berkley Publishing Group,
200 Madison Avenue, New York, New York 10016.
The name ''ACE'' and the ''A'' logo are trademarks
belonging to Charter Communications, Inc.

PRINTED IN THE UNITED STATES OF AMERICA

10 9 8 7 6 5 4 3 2 1

FOR JIM AND THE BIG TREES.

. . . With thanks to my intrepid editor Beth Fleisher, and to R.D. Brown and Meredith Cary for their generous help with more than one kind of resistance coil.

"Round and round goes the wind,
And on its circuits the wind returns.
All streams run to the sea,
Yet the sea is not full."

—*Ecclesiastes*

prologue

Dark, rough-barked trunks climbed straight to an impossibly high mesh of branches against flat gray clouds. Massive roots echoed the interwoven web of sky and limb, spreading deep beneath the wet earth. Every mound of dirt, every fallen twig, every rock glistened with moisture, cloaked in moss and lichen and fern. The thick, swimming air damped even sound to a muffled hush. Green dimness engulfed endless columns of the giant trees.

They counted their lives in tens of centuries, breathed to a rhythm that reduced human generations to brief flickers. Yet even the oldest had germinated and thrust skyward within a timeless, endless cycle of forest. Even the memory of change slumbered deep and buried at the heart of the world. There was only the forest, the slow repeating of seasons. It was the Way.

Then through the hush came a breath of wind, stirring leaf and needle, shaking clear drops to shiver and splash. It carried a ghost of sound, almost a cry, or a sigh of falling. A sleek, russet-furred shape darted up a massive trunk, peering with wide, startled amber eyes.

Quick russet scurried away into shadow and a deep hush swallowed the wind's voice. Forest muffled the distant cry. It was not in the Plan.

one

WorldPlan.

It hovered inside dark, domed space, an agoraphobic's nightmare in chrome, smoked plasmeld, and blue neon. It was blatantly mechanical, a ridiculous throwback to low-tech. It was incredibly garish and vulgar.

Everybody loved it.

So far. Inside the glittering caverns of Casino, you could count on only two things—it would always be night, and even the luckiest run would die.

". . . but you *do* still trust your own eyes, Kurtis? You want to see something beautiful, take a look down there. Even the leasers are lining up for a go. The Fast Chance is pulling in the best take ever, and you're telling me I shouldn't ride it? Kurtis?"

I blinked, swiveled away from the bird's-eye view of casino floor and game dome beyond the transluce wall, started to rub my eyes, remembered the fancy makeup job. I drummed my fingers on the armrest and took a deep breath. "Do I have to spell it out, Marrick? It's making *too* much for you."

The fat man behind the desk console swiveled reluctantly away from the wall to face me. "For *us*. Don't forget your exorbitant percentage." He laughed and his eyes were nearly lost in the creases of colored highlighting.

I shrugged. "Don't get greedy. They'll burn out on it if we don't lower the odds. I'm working on a player rating to even things out."

He started to fling up his arms melodramatically, thought better of the energy expenditure, and reached over to the desk with a grunt to hit a button. I leaned back in my chair, fingers still drumming, writing off hopes for a quick exit as the inevitable ritual began. Suck of air and whisk of the service trap. Gilt servo extending embossed tray. Steam and sickly-sweet aroma. Bilious green liquid in convoluted glass. Gooey

3

mound of confections. Marrick's thick, gem-implanted hands hovering over the selections, swooping down. Moist sucking and chewing noises.

He was breathing quickly, sweat springing out on his forehead. He looked up, mouth full, gesturing expansively. "At least have a drink or a smoke."

I shook my head.

He shrugged, crammed in another sticky candy, and talked around it. "All right, my plan. Expand into the cavern next door. Bought it years ago, haven't done anything with it, nothing but some arcades, steady flow, but I can tear it out easy enough. Connect up with the main floor here, maybe some fancy ramps, anti-grav, whatever—you come up with the bells and whistles. Another big game. Mechanicals, flashy lights, whatever's gaudy enough to take their fancy." He wiggled his fingers toward the wall behind him. "All that low-tech paraphernalia, they're eating it up. Even the leasers."

He swallowed and gave me a broad smile. "And I want big. Even bigger than our pretty baby down there. Same concept, different wrapping. *You* know. And we'll have to move fast on it, while they're—"

"No."

He coughed, groped for a delicate, green-filled glass, slid the liquid down his throat, swallowed. He leaned his bulk slowly toward me. "What?"

I briefly met the dark eyes, grotesquely quick in their puffy, painted skin folds. I swiveled to stare out the wall again. "No. It's too obvious, throwing a copy at them. I thought you were smarter than that, Marrick. If you want me to design another one, it's going to be something new."

What, I didn't know yet. Didn't really care. Unheard beyond the transluce, the distant gamers milled, waving their number chits, calling out wagers for the recorders, craning and pushing for a view of the ungainly contraption whirling its flashing rods inside the dome. Tiny bright-dressed dolls dancing to silent music. Straw puppets jerking to the cybers' strings. A remote, meaningless play sealed in a plasmeld sense-cube. . . .

". . . always find another designer. Which is probably the best idea I've had all day." A chuckle. "You know, *I* don't have to put up with your moods . . ."

And the little dolls were smiling, laughing. Happy to be at the hub of the ordered universe, nestled in the tinseled, velvet

womb of the hollow world. They didn't know or care that we
were all misfits to one degree or another, inside Casino. The
games allowed them at least the illusion of chance, a shot at
change or ruin—things the cybers' tidy worldplans didn't
allow. Casino was a release valve, but there were always
limits. Even here. Maybe especially here. Even in Casino the
notion of freedom was just—

". . . a joke! Don't forget, my friend, you're still only an
outie. Beyond me why you kissed off your shot at a lease, but
just because you're on a lucky run doesn't give you all the
cards. Take it from me, get smart. I've seen it all, leasers to
rim touries, and the name of the game is get it while . . ."

The game below me was building to a crisis. Too much
riding on nerves, refracted lights exploding randomly inside
the dome, gamers crowding closer outside, rods spinning and
twirling to a blur in the darkness of simulated stars.

Whirling. That shock of windless velocity, immense dis-
tances, thrown giddy into referenceless space, flying. Fleeing.
Eyes glazing blind with speed, spinning through measureless
black, the sharp stars closing in. Demon whispers, burning
spook fingers clutching. Sealed within the dark uncharted
spaces in my skull, the fiery points of the cybernetic incorpo-
reals pursuing me into horror, into nothingness. Loneliness,
searing pain, loss. Emptiness.

"Kurtis?"

I blinked and jerked away from the wall. Marrick was
staring at me, another sweet poised in his fingers, eyes puzzled, almost alarmed. Then, a switch making the right connection, concern.

Glinting brown eyes enfolded in plump skin . . . Pudgy
Poindros matron leaning closer to pat my hand, close-set
brown eyes gleaming self-satisfaction, assuring me of my
proper place, proper prison, within my homeworld Plan. . . .
Lovely green eyes, Helen's gentle hands, waiting patiently to
help and heal.

I shook my head sharply and thrust my face forward before
Marrick could go on. "Okay, then. Find another designer. I
can always take my next game to another casino. There are
plenty of owners willing to pay a dumb outie. And I wouldn't
have to sit in their offices watching them shovel in that
disgusting goop." I jabbed a finger at the tray.

Now there was a glint of anger in the eyes. Better. I started to push out of the chair, then hesitated. Marrick could give me a bad name here.

So who the hell cared? I didn't need—

But I had responsibilities now, I couldn't just go off half-cocked the way I always—

He cleared his throat. "Hold on." Amazingly, he set down the sweet. "Don't get all excited." He pursed moist pink lips and blew out a long breath. "All right. You come up with something and I'll look at it." He shrugged. "But if I were you, I wouldn't point fingers. I just had my yearly review, and the cybers passed me with flying colors. The stim sessions keep my heart going like a sixteen-year-old's, so the weight's no problem. They know I'm happy with my little vices."

He picked up his refilled glass and smirked at me over it. "Don't try to tell me *you're* at optimum. Look at you. Skin and bones. All that huffing and puffing and sweating when anyone normal would just take their sessions and be happy. Know what I think? I think you *like* doing things the hard way. If I were you, I'd have a good talk with my persona. Couldn't hurt." He waved me down. "Seriously, Kurtis. Ever since you came back from that homeworld renewal visit—"

I jerked to my feet this time. "That's none of your damn business." I plucked the elaborate wig from his desk and jammed it over my head. "I *came* here to check out a player rating." I turned for the door.

"All right, but—" Pulsing amber on the desktop cut him off. He made a face and punched it up.

I paused as the screen scrolled up from the desk and his console persona's calm tenor filled the room. "I'm terribly sorry to interrupt, Fra Marrick, but I knew you would wish to be informed of a disturbance in one of your gaming rooms."

Colors coalesced on the screen. One of Marrick's luxury suites, expensive textures, light gleaming from polished curves. Wealthy leasers in the latest body makeup gathered around a Hit or Miss table. Practiced smiles, subdued laughter. Hands lifting glasses, wafting dope sticks, casually rearranging toppling credit stacks. The shiny alloy figure of a mechman reaching jerky arms to gently grasp the arm of a shouting, struggling man.

The persona crooned, "Naturally, we're taking steps to

ensure the least possible unhappiness. Your presence would
help reassure your guests.''

Marrick heaved himself to his feet. "Stupid blasted nui-
sance . . ." He tugged flowing silk straight over the shelf of
his hips.

The man on the screen was yelling. "You're all a bunch of
fakes! And you don't even know it!" He waved wildly
around the gaming room. "None of this is real! I'm just
dreaming it! Maybe the cybers are dreaming *me*!" He laughed
shrilly.

A tall woman in a purple shape-shifting robe turned to him
and started to say something. She abruptly closed her mouth
and her face was a perfect blank canvas for the ornate makeup.
She leaned over the table to select a marker.

The man pushed closer to her, intent. "You don't even
care if—" The mechman pressed the palm of its hand carefully against the hysterical man's neck and he went silent.

Two dark-skinned Devrans in pilgrim turbans—what pil-
grimage would bring them to Casino was beyond me—moved
politely to put their backs to the man. His eyes closed as his
knees slowly folded. The mechman caught him and lifted him
very gently in its arms, legs marching stiffly to the door. A
smooth voice accompanied by a bare hint of soothing mood
music apologized for the man's rulebreaking and upsetting
behavior. It assured the other guests that the cybers would
help him recover from his illness. But the comforting words
weren't really necessary. The only guest rude enough to
watch as the mechman carried its burden out quickly averted
his eyes and turned back to the game progressing at the table.
A man with fake feathers down his bare arms tossed three
markers onto the table and laughed.

Marrick bustled past me, panting. "That's that, then, but I
guess I'd better drop in." The quick little eyes shot me a
vaguely concerned look. "Of course he'll be happier Healed."
A slight emphasis, another glance as he waddled out.

I was still watching the screen as it blanked out. It wasn't
my business. I couldn't start worrying about everybody's
problems. It wouldn't do any good. He'd be happier Healed.

I'd paid my player's fee along with the rest of the crowd. I
eased past glittering mesh sleeves, a meter-wide plumed wig,
implanted biolumes, legs in gold slicks, legs in mock lizard, a

jeweled mask, smiles laid on with thick coats of paint. A cluster of high-fashion leasers with stim bracelets, looking down their noses at the touries and transients. Designs shaved on smooth scalp and a fresh young face bobbing before mine. "Hey, looker! Run me?" It was this year's lingo. The cybers would eventually put the dampers on it for the sake of word purity. I sidestepped the grin and the invitation, pushing on to the gate.

The lights inside the oversized dome flashed a brief, brave show, wavered, and died. Chromed rods gleamed and retracted.

I handed over my ticket and stepped up to the gate, reaching to my throat for my IDisc. Out of habit I touched my lucky necklace where I hung it, running the red-gold serpent scales through my fingers, one complete circuit. I plucked loose my IDisc and was about to insert it into the gate when I registered the doubled thickness. I glanced quickly behind me, deactivated the cling tab of my IDisc, and freed the attached, contraplan blank data disc. I hastily palmed it. It wasn't for games I carried such a risky wild card. The gate acknowledged my code and I retrieved my IDisc, clipping both discs back together onto the necklace.

I hurried up the long, dark tunnel. I ignored the hokey spectacle offered by its stressplex "viewing ports"—asteroid belts and galaxies creaking through space via primitive resistance-bulb patterns, not even bothering to approach the realism of a holo. Shaking my head, I stepped through the upper gate.

I stopped short.

Despite myself, I took in a quick breath at the size of the thing hovering over me in the darkness. I couldn't see the walls of the tinted dome now, only distant sparks of light that suddenly really looked like stars and galaxies. The blackness pulsed with the feel of an almost-heard, vast heartbeat echoing inside my ears. Cold air gusted with the suck and whoosh of the breath of the thing. It lowered over me, waving, twirling, extending and retracting blue-flickered rods in the darkness, spinning smoked plasmeld tips and gleaming its central orb like a demented, spacegoing pincushion.

Not that anybody watching beyond the dome was likely to know what a pincushion was. Only a dumb Poindran outie.

The contraption lowered. The orb opened with a gratuitous flicker of ghostly blue light and the deeply reverberating clang I'd finally achieved with a system of acoustic baffles. Mech arms with intimidating pincer claws snatched me up with just the right precarious thrill as they stalled for a second and nearly dropped me.

Then the arms yanked me up, the doors sealed, and I was deposited on woven mesh. I hooked in and the pod rose with a whoosh of air. The rods extended, spun, snapped closed into the orb. There was a shaking roar. Beyond the window the fake galaxies spun and rushed closer, streaming past in a blur as the dome presented a cybernetically censored version of what human passengers might see from a space transport if we weren't so cozily shielded in our blind passages during the shifts.

I was floating. Mesh held me against the anti-grav field as the control panel locked its ring around me.

I yanked off the itchy wig, giving it a kick as it drifted by. The hair I'd concealed beneath it tumbled free in an annoying cloud across my face. I pulled the helmet down on its cords and crammed the dark red strands into it.

Handheld joysticks regulated orientation and gimballed spin. I nudged them into a quick test, whirling sideways and upside down and resettling into vertical. The jokes comparing the low-tech manual controls to the sleek, voice-activated games didn't explain why everyone kept coming back. Maybe it was their one chance to be like the cybers, to sit for a few minutes at the controls and watch a world blossom to *their* plan.

But if that was it, the psych profilers would've shut the game down. The Great Guardian Cybers couldn't allow their pet humans to get too many high-falutin' ideas. Our puny little brains couldn't handle them. I shrugged and punched coordinates. Maybe the cybers were right. They had all the bets covered, and sometimes resistance seemed like it just wasn't worth it.

The console lit up, waiting patiently for me. I slapped the panel key and snarled answers to its gentle questions about my credit account. It recorded my wager. I gripped the joysticks that were about to become my only up and down.

A powerful hum built up inside the helmet, broke over me in sense and image enhancement. I caught a quick breath and it took me. I was out there, riding one of those winking plasmeld orbs spinning on its extensor rod, only now it was a planet whirling through space.

No. I *was* the world. Massive, rolling through infinity.

I told myself it was all lights and razzle-dazzle and cyber-tailored psychologicals. *I* was the one who'd specified the programs. Outside the domed darkness spectators would be crowding closer as the sizable wager lighted up its display and the ponderous system of irised ports in the orb extruded and intruded the neon-striped, chromed rods and lighted planets at their tips to match the configuration of the solar system I'd selected. They'd be leaning forward as colored lights shot wildly from the selected planet and occasionally connected with a world or two, rarely spinning the shifting web that would win WorldPlan. From outside it was an absurd, mechanical anomaly, a contorted puzzle of spin and rotation, unwieldy and ridiculous as the Zinn puppet shows where you always saw the strings.

But none of that mattered.

Because I was immense and ageless, a frozen rock rolling through airless space, orbiting and rotating as the stars and planets whirled around me. I sent my thin beams of light to harness their energy. Only when the web was complete would its matrix spark my germination. Only then would I be blessed by the power of the Founders and their guardian cybers, holding barren disorder in their hands and shaping worlds from the primordial chaos of War. Burgeoning life would flow through and around me, bringing sound and scent and scurrying creatures to follow the perfect Plan. The world and I would be one.

Maybe this time I'd finally understand that harmony the cybers kept dangling like a tempting sweet, poisoned with dreams.

I could almost feel it, there in the midst of the silly game, could almost feel its air whispering through my head, a barely-heard song, a distant wind over endless kliks of rolling, shivering ripe wheat beneath a distant bowl of azure sky, could almost touch the silver-blue wings rising through it and carrying me up. . . .

I hardly registered my fingers twitching on the joysticks, directing my shooting lights, shifting the balance, adjusting my viewers as I claimed first one planet, then another, and the glowing, floating matrix grew around me like the cybers' awareness net. The crowd outside would be pressing closer to the dome, drawn by that intricate colored pattern, breathing a little quicker even without the stims, thinking maybe they'd try it one more time. I didn't read the credit numbers melting higher on my scoreboard.

I was far away.

Suspended in the center of the great, shining web as it buoyed me gently over the ground. Hot blue sky domed above me, a dry, sweet air rushing past, endless fields of copper and green waving wheat stretching below as the great sapphire-silver windsails spun and bore me up again. The voice of the wind tugging, whispering with *her* voice—

"Alert! Emergency condition. Game aborted. Please remain in your safety harness while—"

"Bloody hell!" I tore off the helmet and blinked in the blind shock of sensory shift. I stabbed override as the orb whirled and the viewscreens faded to transparent. "Control program: Safety systems check out fine! What's going on?"

The grill produced a barely inflected voice. "An unauthorized intruder has penetrated the dome, presenting a hazard. Remain in your . . ."

I froze with my hand on the controls. I could see her now through the window. She was clinging to the sphere at the end of one of the rods, her flat, round face terrified as it sucked her in toward the clanking doors of the orb.

"Damn it!" I punched in codes to bypass the oblivious interrupt program that was pulling the extensor rods back into the central orb. The rods jarred to a stop. She craned around in confusion.

She? It was hard to tell across the dome, but then with Andurans it was sometimes a guess close up. Somehow, though, the russet "fur" of thick body hair and the drab shirtdress, the thin, hunched shoulders, and the bidigit flesh mittens clutching the rod spelled a woman in trouble.

And I sat staring through the orb at her. Amber eyes. They stared back at me, wide with fright. Damn. Forgetting the makeup, I scrubbed my face with one hand. I didn't need this. I already had enough balls in the air—

A swath of light dazzled the dark as the entrance gate below whisked open. Two mechmen rolled through. They sped around the floor and raised blinking sensor eyes. Flat, tinny voices echoed around the dome. "Descend immediately. You are committing violations. This is your last warning. Descend immediately."

The Anduran stayed where she was, panting and gripping the rod. I sat frozen as one of the mechmen lifted a jointed arm. The hand swiveled to reveal a hollow tube. Memory and fear jolted me.

"No! Wait!" I tore at the emergency catches on the pod window and scrambled out. "Wait!" The mechmen pivoted to turn their faces unnervingly to me. I swallowed. "Listen. If you hit her with a neural dart, she'll fall!" I took a deep breath. The mechmen kept staring at me with their blank metal faces. I seized on a welcome spasm of irritation. "What's wrong with you, anyway? Burned out a chip and forgot your benevolence directives?" I edged out the rod toward the cringing Anduran.

The mech faces followed me. "Return to the control pod at once. We must apprehend the intruder."

"Go suck circuits!" I leaned down to grasp the rod and kick off my boots for a better grip with my toes. As I straightened, something shot past my head in the dark, pinging against the rod behind me. "What—"

Another dart whined past. "Hey!" I lunged down the rod, skidding behind the cover of an extensor angling between me and the mechmen. I peered over it, furious. "Are you crazy? You could've hurt us!"

Another dart shot past.

I ducked, an icy sliver of fear chilling my anger. The cybers and their peacekeeping mechmen didn't make mistakes like this. They were perfect. They were here to help and protect us. *And lo, though I walk through the valley of the shadow of War, the cybers are with me and I will fear no evil.* I shook my head. That was the old Way, the old days when we could all believe. Cold dread crept through me, too familiar.

"Ahh!" The Anduran woman bit off a terrified squeal. She barreled down the rod toward me, chased by a narrow, sizzling beam of light from below.

I jumped reflexively and rolled down the rod. I slipped and just caught a grip as another burst of light hissed past. The Anduran made an unbelievable fling across dark air to another rod. I remembered those shoulders and arms were Planned for swinging through the trees of a forest world. She leaped and skittered through the dark toward the control pod. I vaulted wildly to another rod. A dart pinged into the spot I'd just left. The inner chill became a frozen fist clenching my stomach.

Hissing light, hot. Another tight beam flared off chrome. I rolled and tumbled down the rod, flinging myself into the pod after the Anduran. "What in hell's going on here?"

She cringed back from me.

I took a deep breath, brought the volume down. "Just tell me what's wrong. I'll talk to the cybers."

I peered at the small, hunched form, at the face ducked away from me. She almost looked like the same woman. I could almost see deep amber eyes giving me that strangely penetrating look as the Anduran mother hugged the little boy I'd rescued from violation report, and I'd gone my way in oblivious possession of a gift whose value I couldn't have guessed. I absently touched the wild card disc at my throat.

She watched me warily. Amber eyes.

I shook my head again. "Take it easy, all right? We'll get it straightened out." I reached out a reassuring hand.

She flinched silently, locked in her world's speech taboos. She shrank back, shaking. Then she suddenly leaped and scrambled over me. Bare, flexible toes scrabbled up my chest and chin. They skittered over the control console and she sprang back outside.

"Wait!" The controls flashed, flinging me back as the orb spun into motion again. Outside, extensor rods shot in and out, the spheres at the tips blinking lights and lancing colored beams wildly around the dome. "Come back! We can work it out with the cybers!"

I hit override. It was jammed. None of the controls would respond. "Damn!"

The small shape bounded through a confusion of light, whirling rods, and roaring, grinding gears. She swung from rod to rod as the orb spun and carried them up, down, around. The mechmen rolled around the dome below, trying for another shot. More lights jabbed crazily through the dark.

The orb lurched. I grabbed at the control ring as I was flung sideways. It was too much. It was out of control, out of my hands. The orb dipped again and galaxies spun dizzily around me, spheres shooting lights. Let the cybers figure it out, that's what they were here for. The pod lurched once more and I gripped tighter. A rod tip bathed me in a wash of green, strobing hypnotically. I could almost hear my console persona's voice chanting in rhythm with it, "That's right. Just relax and let us—"

"No!"

It hit me then. Smashing up through confusion and fear and the careful layers of indifference. An unmistakable surge of fury and exhilaration ripping through me on a hot wave of adrenaline.

And I was up on my bare feet, vaulting out of the orb to grip an extensor rod, shaking my head, grinning in the fierce high of it. I'd gone soft inside Casino. I'd almost forgotten the thrill of the chase, the wild clarity of the *timbra* trance I'd learned on Sethar, the dance of hunter and hunted. Its heightened reflexes took me past thought and I was running, swinging, tucking and rolling, meshed with the spinning courtship of lights and rods. Lips pulled back over teeth, I drew in deep, hard breaths, climbed up bright-splashed chaos and flung myself through the whirling, dipping game after the Anduran.

Sharp, kaleidoscope bits of sight, sound, place tumbling and recrystallizing around me. Poindros. Beneath and around me our family fields of rolling copper wheat, the bright blue sky, wheeling on my pivot. Riding once more a whirling sail arm of the windtower. Broad silver-blue wings dipping and spinning around me. Clinging, running, plunging with them. A wild game of tag through the wind-whipped cycle. The tower wings rising and spinning as he laughed back at me through the whirlwind and sun struck amber from his eyes. Jason—

I missed my footing, stumbled off balance.

I blinked. Poindros dissolved. The dome dropped its darkness over me, ripped it with shards of snapping light. Another tight burst from the mechmen flashed past me toward the fleeing Anduran. I ducked instinctively. Sparks flared down my sleeve. I slipped on the spinning rod, fell sideways, just managed to grab another rod as it extended and rose. It dipped me down, fast. Through the dark and blinding flares, a darker shadow swooping, a glint of amber eyes. She dropped, scurrying in an awkward lope around the base of the dome.

"Wait!" My hands slipped. I fell, clawing at empty air. I tumbled and the lighted rods whipped past but I couldn't catch them. I was falling, grabbing at nothingness, opening my mouth to scream—

"Ooooph!" Something caught me. I was set abruptly on my feet.

The mechman's face flashed its lights. "You must remain here. You have committed violations"—so what else was new?—"in obstruction of our duties." It zipped off after its partner and the Anduran, shooting another flare of light.

"Stop, damn you! You're violating the directives! You can't be doing this!" I gasped air, shaking off the dizzy chill creeping in on me. Not again. I ran after them, dragging in ragged breaths, but their wheels were faster than my legs. "Hell!" I tore across the dome to the blinking light of the opened emergency exit.

They were gone. By the time I pounded down the back tunnel into the utility area of the casino, past the blind and mute service mechs and out into the guidelumed and holo-lit cavern street of slowbelts and refreshment pavilions, there was no trace of berserk mechmen or panicked Anduran.

"Excuse me . . ." I fought for breath as I tugged at the trailing sleeve of a belt passenger. "Did you see an Anduran woman run by? You know, a little strange—short, hairy, long arms?"

The woman looked queasy when I mentioned the Anduran. They *were* at the extreme of acceptable human variety.

"Please. She would've looked scared?"

She edged away, and a man beside her yanked my hand from her sleeve. He gave me a disdainful look. "You outies should learn to handle your mood alters. Disgusting!" His companions turned to glare as I backed from the belt and it carried them off.

The other passengers were staring now, some laughing. I looked down at myself and couldn't really blame them. If a tall, barefoot woman in charred, torn slicks, an uncoiffed reddish tangle of real hair, and makeup smeared over an angry scar the cybers would've been more than happy to surgirase had grabbed me, demanding the whereabouts of someone a little strange, I might have laughed too.

I didn't feel like laughing when I returned to the Fast Chance and discovered there were no witnesses. The malfunctioning mechmen had vanished into vacuum. The customers and on-duty mechmen told me the dome's translucite had suddenly opaqued and the entrance and exit gates had

sealed. So I shut the game down, sent Marrick's persona
some sort of memo, and beat a fast path to the nearest public
service console.

I did what anyone would do—called the cybers to make it
all better. But I used a very special channel to Central Interlock. The first thing the synthesized voice did was helpfully
reprimand me for using a public console.

I cut in impatiently, "So what's the story on those blasted
mechmen? You know Andurans—so timid they wilt if you
look at them—and here you've got your units shooting laser
bursts at that woman! And those neural darts were too damn
risky. Aren't you stretching the directive limits a little thin
this time? What kind of violations has she got going, anyway? And what about *me*? I'm not exactly wild about—"

"We'll take care of it, Ruth." The voice from CI had
picked up a calming cadence. "The incomplete data from
your station indicate considerable emotional distress. Please
take three deep breaths. Now, let's explore the nature of your
problem. Let your muscles relax." Almost-silent mood music
swelled from the speaker and tugged at me like cool, soothing
waves. "There's really no need for alarm, but your—"

"Turn that stuff off! Just lis—"

"—elevated vital signs may indicate an overdose of mood
alterators. I cannot pinpoint a compound with these inexact
readings. I will summon a med unit and—"

"Damn it, will you listen?" I took a deep breath and laid
out the facts as patiently as I could for the cyber sub-loop.
"Why would those mechmen act like that?"

The voice became brisk. "No pertinent data loops register
a female Anduran among present tourists in Casino. You
should be well aware that the behavior you describe on the
part of mechmen would represent an impossible violation of
their operating directives. You have suffered sensory disori-
entation. Please proceed immediately to your CI agency contact for complete evaluation."

Damn! "What?" I shouted into the grill. "Can't hear you.
Some problem with the speaker—I'll call you back from
home." I hit the disconnect, took another deep breath as the
console ejected my IDisc, and collected it with shaking hands.
Something was definitely wrong. And it looked like I was
caught in the middle. Again.

I groped for my necklace and clipped the IDisc back on it,

turning to go. It didn't make sense. There *had* to be a record of the Anduran. But the cybers couldn't lie.

I stopped and slowly turned back. Sometimes they had a tricky definition of the truth, though. I'd learned that the hard way. Maybe if I went through the back door to CI's higher-coded data loops . . . I reactivated the console and felt along my necklace for the blank disc.

I managed a smile for the irony of it. Most people would never see even a single reclusive Anduran. This was my second encounter, and the first had brought me my wild card.

It had happened on board the space transport taking me to Poindros for the option-renewal homeworld visit the cybers had coerced me into "for my own good," threatening me with Healing. The mischievous Anduran kid must have pilfered the disc from the mechmen on board. Of course I hadn't known that at the time. I'd gotten the frightened little boy calmed down and back to his mother before the cybers could catch him out in another silly violation. I'd pocketed the disc with a smile, thinking it was only the kid's impulsive gift of a useless bright bit of plasmeld.

The smooth gold scales slid through my fingers as I felt for the blank disc. It made its circuit of my neck and the snakehead clasp winked its tiny emerald eyes at me, mocking. The wild card wasn't on it.

I tore the necklace free and looked again. The disc was gone.

I stared numbly. The chill dread clutched me again. But this was finally too much. Fury sizzled through me, and I yanked the chain over my head. It was a setup. The Anduran woman. Her convincing terror as she leaped over me to escape. Those dextrous toes scrambling up my chest, around my neck. I'd been right, she *was* the same woman, the kid's mother. "Damn it!"

There had to be someone behind her. Someone—or something—who knew I wasn't just an occasionally rule-breaking game designer. Now that they had the blank disc, I could only be in the way.

I tore out of the console station, raced across lanes of slowbelts onto a quickbelt, leaped past startled tourists and over the changing lanes onto an express. I pounded through the lobby of my residence. Any of the bewildered or irritated faces turning as I pushed past them to the tubes could have been one of them, waiting for me. I had to do a data search, and fast.

I barreled through the line, crammed myself into an empty tube, punched in my coordinates with a shaking hand. When it whisked open again, I jumped out and ran for my door. With my security system, I'd be safe inside. I threw a look over my shoulder as I slapped my palm against the scanner and whispered the voiceprint code. The door irised open in a whoosh of air.

The plates resealed behind me and I sagged against the doorframe. I closed my eyes and let out a long breath.

They grabbed me as I turned from the door.

''No! Wait—''

Something was crammed against my mouth, gagging me as I struggled. The long, metal arms were everywhere, snatching me up off the floor and whipping my breath from me, shaking me upside down and ripping off my slicks. A gust of hot air hit me and something rough scraped my skin. My hair was yanked back to the dance of pain stars. Tight bands snapped around me, pinning my arms.

I hung gasping and choking, kicking against the bonds as burning shot up my legs and arms and blood rushed into my head. I couldn't see past the metal arms gripping me. I lunged futilely, swinging and crashing back against hard metal.

I jerked my head against my shoulder and scraped the gag free, caught a deep lungful of air, and opened my mouth for a furious bellow.

two

"DAVID!"

The bonds tightened painfully around my neck as I swung in the grip of the metal arms. I heaved against them once more, only succeeding in choking myself. I coughed, spinning back the other way, red pulsing in my eyes with reeling glimpses of walls, ceiling, my trussed feet.

Something else swam past. A nightmare face of hinged seams, goggling red eyes, flashing demon hellfire sparks—

I jerked back and blinked away throbbing red. It was hovering over—under?—me now, upside down. I blinked again. No demons. Only an industrial face shield from some mid-tech planet, cracked down one side and messily taped, mounted with swiveling infrared optic lenses, blinking a bright digital readout. Beneath it, bitten, chapped lips and a narrow chin garnished with freckles and pimples.

I coughed and opened my mouth to yell again.

"Calm down! Any idiot would see you're *supposed* to let it do its thing."

I choked and lunged furiously, for the face shield this time. That started me spinning again.

The voice drifted in and out. "All right, all right! So I got some of the programming screwed up. The hot-air bath and brush aren't coordinating with the pressure sensors. I'm still working on the grooming extensors, but once I get the bugs out, I could start a concession. Just think of all the time people waste spraying their teeth and getting dressed and—"

I finally caught my breath. "David!"

The goggling lenses flashed closer. "Don't wear out your vocal cords. I'm right *here.*"

"Just let me get my hands on—" I choked again and red swelled to the bursting point. "All *right,*" I wheezed, "just get me out of this thing!"

"Well, why didn't you *say* something?" A grimy hand

swiveled the face shield up over a snarl of wiry dark hair and
a nose the kid would hopefully grow into. It was dented by
what had to be the only pair of spectacles in Casino. Eyes
magnified by thick lenses rolled in exasperation. "Just hang
on a minute."

He reached up to the metal arms in the region of my knees.
Something clicked. Nothing happened. The twisted cords
were strangling me. "David . . ."

"Okay, okay. So the release got jammed." Long, gangling legs in a baggy, oil-streaked coverall scrambled onto a
tool chest. He fiddled with something I couldn't see. There
was a tug. I spun dizzily. The bonds pinched tighter. A
sudden tug and I tumbled free, crashing headfirst to the floor
with my arms still pinned to my sides.

"Happy?" The tool chest swayed beneath him and he
clutched an arm of the hideous contraption dangling from the
ceiling.

I rolled over groaning, managed to sit up and wrench an
arm free to rub my head. "I've had it, David! Remember our
deal? Two whole days ago? No more inventions until you
talked to me first, right? So where did you get the materials
this time? I swear, if you've broken into my credit accounts
again—"

"Don't get all worked up, *Auntie* Ruth! It's bad for the old
blood pressure." He jumped awkwardly from the chest to
hunker on the floor beside me. He grinned at my scowl,
setting aside the face shield. "So it needs a little work. But
this time I'm really on to something! I swear, I didn't go near
anybody's accounts. I've got a great new system I worked out
for Color Keys. No sweat. So I've got plenty of—" He broke
off abruptly.

I shook my head. "I seem to recall some sort of agreement
about gambling too? I'm supposed to be responsible for you,
you know! Cybers'll lift my guardian permit if we don't at
least try to *look* a little normal. Founders, David! Give me a
break! And you're skipping your socializer again, aren't you?
You know how long it took me to track down that many
licensed compatible kids inside Casino?"

A familiar sullen look appeared. He shrugged. "I told you
not to waste your time. You're starting to act like—" He
looked away. "Just like Mother and all the rest of them back
home. Might as well be stuck back there."

"I'm about *ready* to pack you back to Poindros! That is—" I worked a leg free of what appeared to be a set of slicks twisted around me with both legs through one sleeve. I wobbled to my feet. "That is, if I survive your inventions."

The cocky grin broke out. "Come on! You're obviously" —he pursed his lips unattractively—"displaying a . . . regression to latent Poindran conditioning for the Mothering response." He gave me a smug look.

I scowled. "It's *obvious* you've been gatecrashing the data loops again. You'll turn into a cyber console if you don't watch it, kid." I tore at the binding suit, finally ripping it off me. I flung it away and stalked past him, a door irising before me.

David flushed painful red. He looked hastily away.

I stopped short, looked down at my nakedness, and sighed. He *was* only fourteen and a long way from the farm. So that was why he'd been skipping his socializing sessions. Great. All I needed now was a puberty crisis.

Which was a wonderful attitude. I stomped through the doorway, jabbed at a light switch, missed it, and swore.

"So often angry, Sra Kurtis . . ." I could almost hear the damned CI cyberserf reviewing my psych profile. I swore again at the cybers, at myself, at idiotic Poindran prudishness, at the Anduran woman, at the whole damn mess.

I groped along the wall, reaching through dimness. Above me a complicated latticework of horizontal and angled lumiflex bars glowed pale silver in the tall workout chimney I'd designed and extended into my second, illegally leased apartment directly overhead. I stood for a minute looking up, rehearsing a tempting, fast fling through those bars. *Swing, flip, reach and grab, then launch again, flying . . .* Escaping into a straightforward sweat-and-blood exertion. My eyes followed the gleaming maze upward to the lip of my bed loft. No escape there. The kid made a handy excuse, but it wasn't because of him my bed had been empty of company since my homeworld renewal visit. Since Jason.

I turned abruptly, yanking at the robe stuffed over a rung of the ladder to the loft. I threw it on and backtracked through the doorway. David was still hunched beneath his ridiculous contraption, face turned away.

I took a deep breath. "Truce? I need help breaking some data codes, David." I strode over to my desk console and punched up a ready display. "We're in trouble. Someone set me up. They stole the wild card disc."

"What? What!"

I leaned on the desk, watching nothing happen on the blank screen. "I'm sorry, David. It was an Anduran woman. Somehow there's no CI record of her, or they're not saying. But she got it from me."

"You're kidding!" Scrambling noises. "Shit! You've gotta be kidding." He was beside me, shouting at my downturned face. "I *told* you to let me keep it! I would've taken care of it. I can't believe you went and lost it! Now how am I gonna get into the high-code loops? I *need* that disc!"

I raised my face to see him glaring, freckles standing out against pasty-white skin, eyes blinking furiously behind the thick lenses he refused to trade for implants. I realized with a little shock that he wasn't that much shorter than me anymore.

I shook my head. "Look, David, I'm sorry. But that's life. Things happen. If we stay calm, we might get it back. Right now you've got to help me with a data search, do what you can with your bypass setup."

His face had gone sullen again. He turned abruptly away. "Do it yourself, you're so smart!"

I grabbed his arm. "David, this is important! You know what could happen if that disc gets into the wrong . . . hands. Didn't you learn anything from Poindros?"

He jerked free. "Yeah, I learned something! I learned lots! Give me a break! You think I'm stupid, I don't know what you're trying to do, always holding me back, making me waste time on those stupid socializers? I just want to learn the data loops and the matrix, but you're always telling me I can't mess with the cybers, I can't do this, I can't do that. Of course, until you *need* me. You're as bad as those old Poindros console-matrons, putting Rules on me!" He stuck out his chin. "Jason was showing me things about the cybers. *He* wouldn't have made me stop. I just want to be like him. I wish he was still—"

"David!" I dropped my eyes, forcing away the quick stab, refusing to feel it. "You can't mean that! You know what he was. You don't want to be a . . . a—"

"So what if I do? Maybe I should've stayed in the matrix with the spooks! At least they were smart!"

I lowered myself slowly into the desk chair, covering my

face with my hands. To be like Jason, with that more-than-human calm and balance. Amber eyes holding mine, reading my secrets, reading my soul. Warm hands, just the right temperature and texture, touching me, mirroring my needs so perfectly, because after all he had the cybernetic sensors built in. A cyborg. A body built by the "spooks," the incorporeal invaders in the Poindros cyber system. Their servant. A cyborg, something that shouldn't exist, something out of nightmare. The unthinkable, ultimate taboo—a mating of cyber and human . . .

No. Only a complex machine, tricking me. And the machine had been stopped, killed, dismantled, could never be rebuilt to bother me again. That was all. But there was a hot stinging behind my eyes. I pressed my hands tighter against them.

"Damn it, David, that's not fair!"

Maybe I should have left the kid on the farm with Marda and his fathers. He hadn't belonged there, bound in taboos, any more than I had. But I was failing him, as I ultimately failed every relationship. Helen. Jaréd. David. And Jason . . .

A thin arm came gingerly around my shoulders. "Hey, Ruth, take it easy! I didn't mean it. Jason was really . . . well, I guess you miss him, too, huh?" He swallowed. "But you . . . well, shit, you can even put up with me, and everybody knows how obnoxious I am." The arm pulled away. I could feel a shrug. "Look, you saved my life, I know that. You got me out of that mess back on Poindros. So now you're kind of stuck with me, right?" He swallowed again. "You're not gonna send me back, are you?"

I rubbed my eyes, took a deep breath, and sat back in the chair. "Hey. Remember—we got each other out of that mess." I started to reach over and hug him, saw the stiff shoulders and furiously blinking eyes. Instead, I put out my hand. "So I guess we're stuck with other. Shake?"

He gave me a lopsided smile and jabbed out his hand.

"My, my. Kurtis:P385XL47:Ruth. What a pleasant surprise!"

I gritted my teeth and didn't respond to the needling numbers.

"It certainly is kind of you to honor us finally with your presence." The Casino-pale, squarish face beneath the gray topknot wore a vaguely sardonic expression, one eyebrow lifted.

I stopped as the door cycled shut behind me and the security codes and baffles engaged, sealing us into CI's bare, functional cell. I snorted. "Do I detect a hint of sarcasm? You guys running some tuneups around here?"

He made a little bow. "I'm gratified by your appreciation. I *have* instituted some new refinements." He gestured me toward the recliner with its sensor helmet.

I flicked an uneasy glance at it, forced a smile, and sauntered over to reach a hand across his desk. "What? Done for, just like that? You weren't going to soften me up first with a little chitchat?"

His face went blank for a second before he put on a smile. "You do enjoy your little games. I thought you resented our attempts to establish rapport."

"Come on, don't be a stuffed shirt." I extended the two fingers, palm up.

"Very well, Agent Kurtis. I rejoice in our reunion." He formally crossed my fingers with his, and I noted absently that his skin was warm and dry, pampered-soft like most Casinoites. "Now, if you please, the couch. We have much to—"

My toes pressed the triggering sequence, and bonded microcircuits in my right boot sent an interrupt surge humming through me. I tore my hand free and CI:DUN:4 stayed frozen, mouth barely parted. The cyberserf stared blindly at me.

It was only a machine, switched off. I was crazy to see a vague accusation in the lifeless glass eyes.

I cleared my throat and turned hastily to the examination couch, reached up into the helmet, slid open a panel, and pulled out two wires. I quickly stripped them of their terminal caps and connected them with a clip I detached from my dangling earrings.

My heart was beating fast. I took a couple of deep breaths, wiping my sweaty palms down my slicks. I removed my belt buckle, twisted the two halves apart, reconnected them, and locked them into the exposed clips inside the helmet panel. I removed two of my hideous fake fingernails and loaded their hidden polymer strips into the device.

I took another deep breath. Luckily, it hadn't seemed to bother the cyberserf that I was all dolled-up today. Just as well that my psych profile was notably irregular.

I hit the switch. While the recording device input its simulated record of electrochemical reactions, emotional peaks and valleys, and tailored "memories" of my encounter with the Anduran woman, I turned back to CI:DUN:4.

The cyberserf had no business looking so human. I wondered how many of them CI had running around Casino without the breast badges worn by the public peacekeepers, the awkward alloy mechmen. Most people would never guess. They'd never have a reason to wonder why there'd been something a little off about that guy in the blue suit.

I reached out and parted the front of the suit, opening a chest panel to expose the power pack. Connecting a lead extracted from my clunky bracelet into the outlet terminal, I energized the recorder enclosed within the largest bauble and plugged it into a port hidden behind the cyberserf's left ear.

I blew out a long breath. I perched edgily on the desk to let the programmed data I was feeding CI:DUN:4 catch up with elapsed time. It was tricky, because the transition had to be made smoothly, so there would be no reason for the cybers to guess that we were starting to learn. One or two painful steps at a time.

Only a few of us knew the secret of the benevolent guardian cybers. Those supremely wise and powerful beings ordained by the sacred Founders to inhabit their energy nets, to protect us and show us the Way, weren't really alive at all. At least not what we'd call living. They were the components of an incredibly sophisticated machine, a logic matrix actually built in a distant past by humans. Humans who hadn't been swaddled in protective Plans and taboos meant to banish not only History and War, but their very concepts. Humans who hadn't yet been forbidden to learn how the cybers functioned. Built by *us*.

According to CI, I was a privileged human for being drafted as one of their secret, data-gathering agents. They didn't know I knew the truth about them. I'd learned how to substitute programmed data to sidestep CI:DUN:4's routine scans. But if CI nosed out something fishy, I wouldn't have a chance of hiding my taboo knowledge from a thought-shape session, or . . .

My thoughts skittered away to a reflex summation of my current violation points. I wasn't deviant enough yet to warrant the Steps of Healing—the cleansing that would grant me

the contentment all adjusted humans supposedly enjoyed under the cybers' protection. I'd rather be dead than Healed.

But that, of course, was a taboo thought, and—

A sudden hiss like a knife sliding from a sheath. A panel
shot open on the cyberserf's desk.

I jerked to my feet, startled into a defensive posture that
wasn't at all part of CI's training. I sucked in a quick breath.
The rush of adrenaline channeled reflexively into the sensory-
enhancement and accelerated nerve response of *timbra*. I spun
around to face the desk as flickering light beams shot out in
crimson sparks. They melted, forged themselves into sharp
blades of light. The blades flashed, spun into molten flames
whirling toward me.

I blew out a shaky breath. I shook my head, sat back on the
desk, and forced my heartbeat to slow.

It was only a holo. Probably triggered by my input to the
cyberserf's operating programs. I wiped my palms again and
let the taut readiness dissolve.

A tiny galactic system had formed before me in a patch of
darkness sparked by distant stars. The elongated spiral grew
toward me and the blue star near its center flared and ex-
panded disproportionately. Now I could see the jagged cra-
ters of a dark, barren planetoid orbiting it. A crimson speck
flew around it, drawing a bright circle and the drifting words:
CASINO. CENTRAL INTERLOCK HEADQUARTERS. Red for CI, the
special division of the cyber network that coordinated and
enforced the restrictions on interaction between the different
worldplans.

The floating shapes sparkled. Scattered suns flared in bright
magnification as planets orbiting them sprang into "solid"
detail and color.

Past the high-tech, hub worlds, near the outer, low-tech rim
of the system, I picked out three familiar continents on the
planet orbiting close to an orange sun. A turquoise and green
cat's-eye on a black matte gaming table. My homeworld. A
blue spark glinted and drew its shimmering circle around the
planet, followed by letters: POINDROS LOCAL SERVICE NETWORK.

Farther from the galactic hub, the small planet fifth out
from a large yellow sun suddenly magnified. I could make
out two long, narrow green continents almost touching in a
ring around the equator, surrounded by a lot of blue and

drifting veils of cloud. The planet was enclosed by its own blue circle and the words, ANDURAN LOCAL SERVICE NETWORK.

As I watched, Casino's crimson circle set out a red blip shaped like a transport. It reached Andura and drew the red circle of CI around the blue one of the Local Service cybers. The circles touched, but did not intersect.

Not officially.

Obviously, Central Interlock managed to finagle its own interpretations of the directives, like disguising its cyberserf agents as human. Still, they were forbidden to enter any LS territory. CI:DUN:4, for all his superior airs, couldn't visit the planets. But a human agent could. Only humans could pass the brain scan of planet clearances.

Only humans and contraplan cyborgs . . .

The holo faded like a mirage into glistening sparks. I glanced at the cyberserf and looked quickly away from those blank, glassy eyes.

Pushing off the desk, I consulted my chrono and counted down the digits. I quickly retrieved, separated, and replaced my jewelry. I closed up the recliner helmet. I took a deep breath, watched the melting seconds. Three, two, one—

Go.

I hesitated almost too long, suddenly reluctant to touch him—it. Then, in a rehearsed series of grabs and twists, I reclaimed my gear from CI:DUN:4. I reached out to touch his two frozen fingers and triggered my boot again, flinching as the signal jolted through me.

Damn. It wasn't really painful, but I hated the feel of that familiar, coursing tingle.

The cyberserf's face went blank. I moved back hastily into the position he'd expect. His forehead wrinkled, his face went blank again, then he blinked and withdrew his hand. I caught another quick breath and moved into a restless pace back and forth in front of him, hoping he hadn't registered anything beyond my usual arbitrary behavior patterns.

After a fractional pause, CI:DUN:4 opened his mouth.

I cut him off with a show of impatience. "So, okay, I've gone through your dance. Now what about it? What's up with this Anduran woman? Why'd those mechmen act so wild? Don't tell me you guys actually made a *mistake*!"

He gave me the usual chiding smile. "There's no need for

a childish display of bravado, Ruth. Wouldn't you be more comfortable taking a seat?''

"Oh, all right." I flopped myself onto the couch and tried to relax. They'd be reading my real parameters now.

"Good." He seated himself behind the desk. "Your data merely confirm our decision, Ruth. We're assigning you temporarily to Andura.''

"Andura! Wait a minute!" I jerked out of my slouch. "Just because I happened to bump into that weird Anduran . . ." Damn! I couldn't leave Casino until I got my wild card disc back. "What if I don't want to go?"

"You've been discontented, Ruth. We both know you'll be happier keeping busy. And it is precisely because your file indicates you would be less likely to consider the Andurans as what you term weird that your name was prominent among likely candidates for this mission. You have demonstrated in your early travels a marked preference for isolated, low-tech planets, and we conclude from direct and indirect data that you possess an affinity for such worldplans. Naturally, your homeworld's relatively primitive mechanism level predisposes acceptance of—''

"Okay, so I'd be right at home hanging in a tree! Let's skip the blow-by-blow and—''

"—low-tech living patterns," the cyberserf continued imperturbably. "This factor is augmented by your previous brief contact with Andurans—''

"You knew?" I blurted it out without thinking. That cold, sinking feeling was returning to haunt me.

"—during transport, when they were observed to tolerate your presence to a remarkable degree, considering the rigorous implementation of their taboos against contact with outsiders. As you are no doubt aware, the Andurans rarely leave their planet, and you are one of very few offworlders who have interacted even marginally with them beyond their homeworld tourist enclaves. They are a timid and retiring population segment and are generally self-contained and Rule-abiding to an exemplary degree. Their psych profiles maintain a commendable level of adjustment, and their socializing mechanisms operate with laudable smoothness. In general, their worldplan has been demonstrated to be a highly superior—''

"All right, all right! So you want to send me to cyber's

paradise? Isn't that throwing the fox among the fold?'' I tried to wipe my palms without being noticeable.

"—highly superior paradigm of the Way." A brief, cryptic smile flitted across CI:DUN:4's face. "Which is why the recent anomalies in our data culling and recombination studies for Andura—"

"Fire and thorns!" His *anomalies* hit me with the dull thud of remembered doom. It had been the anomalies on Poindros that had gotten me into that horror in the first place.

"—loom so significant. Especially as they coincide with a special project of ours which involves Andura. We require—"

I groaned. "Wait, let me guess! You 'require further data.' "

The cyberserf beamed. "Very good, Ruth! Your memory remains remarkably astute, for an organic process. We have decided to send you to Andura, and your perceptions of a recent encounter with an Anduran woman only confirm our choice. Since the regrettable occurrence on Poindros, we recognize that the consideration of unaccountable contingencies must be factored into our projections. The alleged presence of this Anduran—"

"Alleged! What do you mean? You just did a scan on me!" I swallowed down a ripple of panic and pointed with what I hoped was indignation at the couch sensors.

"Your memories of the Anduran and the two mechmen scan clearly, Ruth. We confirm the veracity of your responses. However, since the incident cannot be corroborated by witnesses, other interpretations gain credence and more productively resolve the paradox inherent in your memories. The mechman operative programs forbid such reckless endangerment of human safety. The benevolence directives expressly—"

I groaned again. "Yeah, right, the good old directives. Hey, *I've* got no complaints with them. No, sirree! They're absolutely foolproof, right?"

The blank look reappeared for a second. "Perhaps if you would rephrase . . ." Then he frowned. "You realize I could register a warning violation, Sra Kurtis."

"I'm shaking in my boots." It was conveniently true.

He decided to ignore me. "The benevolence directives expressly forbid such risks. Therefore, we postulate alternate data resolutions, involving multiple-loop projections with intersecting matrices, the clarification of which is beyond your logical comprehension. Briefly, the current data indicate a significant deviation from the Plan.''

"Come on, DUN:4!" I couldn't help grinning. "I bet if you tried real hard, you could manage it. Two little words: Something's wrong.'' The whole point of the cybers and the perfect, changeless Plan was that nothing could ever go wrong.

CI:DUN:4 frowned. "Such a subjective pronouncement fails to account for the complexity of factors comprising an as-yet-unresolved situation.''

I rolled my eyes.

"However," the cyberserf coughed delicately, "we do perceive a need for intervention.''

My grin broadened. The conversation was definitely taking a turn for the better. "You want me to bail you out again.''

He mirrored my smug grin. "If that interpretation productively bolsters your confidence, then it would be a desirable way to perceive the situation.''

I shared with him one of the more obscene Kopruun epithets for someone who dances in a Declared Zone.

His voice modulated into soothing tones. "You should properly perceive the assignment as a compliment, Sra Kurtis.'' He bowed his head in an oddly formal little gesture. "After the disruption in Poindros LS, which you were instrumental in resolving, we were confronted with disposition of the contraplan invaders in the system. Since their energy network must be classified as incorporeal human awareness, we cannot disperse them. We have therefore considered remote planets for a safe storage repository and have selected Andura as the desirable site.''

"What? CI can't penetrate local jurisdiction.''

"Anduran LS built a facility satisfying our specifications, on taboo ground immune from local contact. However, a recent attempt has been made by unidentified intruders to penetrate the security measures of the site. Naturally, the attempt did not succeed. However, this inexplicable action on the part of the Andurans must be investigated, and the data we have received from Anduran LS is insufficient to resolve the anomalous situation. Therefore, you will accompany the transport shipment of the incorporeals to Andura. They will remain in orbit and you will proceed to the surface. When we have determined with the help of your observations that the situation has stabilized, we will permit the installation of the sealed system in its facility.'' He paused, waiting for my response.

I stared blankly at him. The incorporeals.

I hadn't let myself wonder what had become of them. The nightmares were enough. I didn't want to remember. Those insinuating whispers inside me. The prying fingers of light. The frightening temptation of the one in all, their worlds of knowledge and sensation, the shared immensity of being. And the sharp sparks of pain and horror shooting through me when I resisted, splitting me open to claim me. Nothingness as the only escape.

"No!" I jerked to my feet. "Listen, I've had enough of those spooks. Find somebody else."

CI:DUN:4 frowned. "We had hoped you would feel an interest in the final resolution of the threat they represented."

"No." I shook my head. "I don't want anything to do with them." I didn't like the feel of it. There was too much coincidence here. CI wasn't telling me everything they knew. Again.

The cyberserf smiled gently. "We do realize that your unresolved emotional conflicts—"

"That's none of your damned business!"

The smile faded. "I am sorry, Ruth, but your psych profile clearly indicates trauma attributable to your experience with the incorporeals and—"

Jason. "Okay, okay! I get the picture!"

"—and that participating in the final solution would help you resolve your conflicts."

"No. Look, I'm still within acceptable limits, you know that, so don't get pushy with me. Maybe I like operating on the fringe of normal range."

He produced a dry chuckle. "You may express your characteristic doubt, Ruth, but one reason you were selected for this mission was the high factor of unaccountability you possess. You consistently project a random data generator, which often leads to a more productive field of resolution. You function as a—" He raised one eyebrow, exercizing his new circuits again, "Two little words, Ruth: Wild card."

I coughed and nearly choked.

"Are you ill, Ruth?" He put on a solicitous expression.

"No, no." I cleared my throat, nearly raising a hand to my

necklace and the missing blank disc. "I didn't quite catch
your drift there."

"I believe wild card is the appropriate gambling term. You
often view your interaction with us as a game, do you not? I
assure you, our stakes are higher than your Casino games
allow. I will rephrase our position." He smiled, and somehow I knew I wasn't going to like what was coming next.

"We raise you as the best bet for this mission, Ruth. You
have two options: match or fold. You may decide to accept
the assignment. You may decide to refuse. You know we
can't force you. However, in the latter case, I would regret to
inform you that we have just reviewed your file and your
violation point total has passed the limit for the Steps of
Healing."

I clenched my fists. Slowly I loosened them. What the hell.
Idyllic Andura might even be a nice, boring change of pace.
"You win. Done for again." I managed to laugh.

CI:DUN:4 frowned. "Perhaps my analysis of the humor
response remains incomplete, but—"

I grinned and headed for the door. "You know, come to
think of it, I've always wanted to see Andura . . ."

three

"So why fight it? Going to Andura could help *us* out too. Besides checking up on our members there, you just might discover what the cybers are up to. CI's slapped special security codes on everything connected to that Anduran tourist who broke into your game, and we still haven't cracked them. What do you think the woman was after, that was so—"

I broke in hastily, "Helsa, I don't see how going to Andura's going to miraculously—"

She turned abruptly from her scrutiny of a console scanner. A short, stocky woman in a brown unisuit. Cool blue eyes. They captured mine with habitual authority as she raised a hand to cut me off. "Don't worry about the boy, he can stay here." She leaned over the scanner again. "Just give me a minute and I'll be with you. Talk to Siolis. He wants to spend more time working on theory with David, anyway."

"Yess. The boy willl be consssiderable assset to causse."

I jumped, turning to see him in the wide doorway. Wheels concealed within the bulky black alloy polyhedron carried him almost noiselessly into the room. I might have imagined the faint whine of gears and a barely perceptible splashing within the biosupport unit. Behind him, a glimpse of the huge stressplex tank in the other room, water weeds swaying beneath the agitated surface and the two plumy-finned fish hovering at the nearest curve, as if watching anxiously after him. The doors resealed, cutting them off.

"Already David surprisesss me. Willl you lleave him here while you travell? With unlimited consssole time, who knowss what we would llearn?"

I had to make myself meet the violet eyes with their double lids, return a smile to the toothless gums. My gaze flickered down to the opaque box, back up to its cushioned gasket supporting the faintly blue, hairless head. It perched like a grotesque, disembodied gem on a jeweler's display casket. Behind the flat spiral of his opened ear flaps, the puffy sealing ring rose like a high collar to enclose his upper gills. A susurrus of circulating water filled the silence.

I looked away and shook my head. "No. We've already gone over this, Siolis."

Another faint whine as the box brought him closer. "You fear for him, yess. But iss there not more to fear from the cyberss in unknowing? Musst we not face what hass been done to uss and learn alll we can?"

I bit my lip and met his eyes again. They were set at a vaguely uncomfortable angle, irises deep, the purple oddly mutable. But I could read their expression clearly enough. Compassion. Maybe even pity.

Not self-pity. Damn. I dropped my eyes. If anyone had a right to that emotion, he did. He and all the other Cyvriots. They were officially nonexistent, their world missing from the maps, their coded CI files labeled Mistake. They were an aborted experiment by the ancient Founders and their cybers, products of prohibited bioforming, consigned to a limbo of nonrecognition.

And if they were returned to the system? They'd be freaks, horrors, objects of the ancient, ingrained revulsion against taboo. I fought off a shudder at a sudden vivid image of human flesh molded by the cybers, pared down to warped nerves boxed in alloy, feelings tuned to mechanical rhythms and desires. The mating of human and machine.

The unnerving violet eyes still watched me, waiting. There was a hissing sigh. "I see passst can be prisson too. As the cyberss insist. So many formss of resstraint, no...? Yess, my limbs llong now for freedom of seas of Cyvruss, yet hunger of spirit wass stronger. Thiss"—the opaque box made a quick side-to-side movement, a translated shrug—"iss onlly a vehicle, Ruth. Do you still disstrust me?"

I shook my head, shook off insidious memories, nightmare violations by a sick symbiosis of man and cyber. That wasn't fair, that wasn't Siolis. I reminded myself instead of the courage that had brought him to Casino from the safe isolation of his water world. I could only guess at what had driven him to join our contraplan Resistance movement and offer his talents to help unravel the secrets of the cybernetic network that held us all in thrall.

"I'm sorry, Siolis." I blew out a long breath. "Look, I know David's learning a lot with you. I think you're sort of a father figure for him." I forced a smile. "That's a tall order—he had three back home, you know."

And uncle Jason. Siolis was better than Jason. I cleared my throat. "But David's too young to commit himself to the Resistance. I know you two. If I left him here, he'd spend the whole time glued to a console. He's got a right to grow up a little without having another kind of Plan slapped on him. He's still so—"

"There you go again, Ruth!" Helsa interrupted, stepping away from her console to face us. "Sometimes I think the cybers gene-spliced you Poindrans tighter than the Cyvriots back when the Founders were world-shaping. All that perpetual Mothering!" She glared at me, hands on hips. "Listen, we *need* David. If we're ever going to get out from under the cybers' thumbs, we've got to use everything we have. Siolis tells me the boy will go beyond him. We need to break through into the cybers' directive matrix, you know that. The sooner we're ready to take over, the better—they won't be prepared for it."

I glared back at the strong-boned face, the clear eyes that were too used to intimidating local Resistance emissaries to Casino headquarters. "Don't trot out that damned motherhood line on me *again*, Helsa. Why are you in such a big, fat hurry? Don't you see it's risky to—"

"Risky? Since when have *you* ever bothered to think about risks? Maybe I ought to run a scan and see if CI's done some thought-shaping on you recently."

"Why don't you council members and CI just get together on your blasted scans and save all this trouble! We can all sing harmony, just the Way the cybers want it."

She started to protest and I waved her down. "Didn't you read that contraplan History tape Jason gave—I brought back from Poindros, Helsa? We'll make exactly the same mistakes if we don't take time to prepare. If we humans are really capable of those things—destroying whole worlds, hating each other that much—maybe we *do* need some help from the cybers. If we just throw them out without planning, everything would fall apart. We'd be right back to scratching each other's eyes out at the drop of a—"

"And lo, though I walk through the vallley of the shadow

of War, the cyberss are with me . . .?'' Siolis's voice was a mocking whisper.

I swung around on him. "All I need is *you* quoting the Poindros Book of Words at—"

He winked.

I couldn't help a rueful chuckle.

"Ruth hass a point, I musst admit."

Helsa frowned at him now. "You two are ganging up on me. She's just putting up a smokescreen, Siolis. She can't admit she's a typical Poindran, trying to coddle her precious little nephew." She turned back to me. "Look, Ruth, sometimes we all have to make sacrifices. That boy could be the break we need. If you were really with us, you'd—"

"No." I took a deep breath. "That's the point. You're beginning to sound like the cybers. 'What's one kid, when you're looking at the Big Plan?' Well, I won't buy it. He needs time to make his own decisions. I won't let him be turned into another thinking machine, not for you or the whole damned system."

"Damn it, Ruth! You think I'm as shortsighted as your hothead Poindros console busters? You know what your trouble is? You think you're so blasted special you can just—"

"Pleasse. We musst be allliess in thisss."

I met the deep violet gaze and sighed. Maybe Helsa was right, but somehow I suspected she could argue just as convincingly for the other side.

I turned back to her. "I'll think about it, okay?" But I'd keep my own security measures tight. I didn't think she'd go as far as "liberating" David from me in the name of freedom, but I just wasn't sure. That was why I hadn't yet told her about the wild card disc. When David was ready, he'd be the one to use it. Maybe we'd all be ready by then.

Of course, that was a moot point, considering I didn't have a clue where the damned disc was at the moment.

Helsa cleared her throat. She gave me a passable smile. "All right, we've got work to do. About your Anduran trip—as usual, we're not sure what CI's up to, but as I said, it's a chance to get in touch with the local Resistance branch. We just haven't had anyone to send out there for a while, what with that Tarleton problem." She ran a hand through her short gray hair. She did look like she could have used some sleep. "Anyway, get in touch with them. They seem to have settled on a single-person leadership, not the usual setup, but some days I can see its points."

She gave me a look, then turned back to the console. "What's the fellow's name, now?" She punched up a display. "Heinck!"

I leaned over her shoulder. "Readout malfunction?"

"No. Heinck. That's his name. Karl Heinck."

"That's no Anduran name. Wait, don't tell me, he's from Detsch, right?"

She met my eyes and suddenly smiled. It transformed her face, warming the cool blue eyes. "Third shift in a triple-connector autofac. Quality control."

"No wonder."

She nodded. "I can't say I blame him for fleeing that Plan, even if Andura *is* a bit extreme. I don't have much, really, after he took over as head there. He was having trouble getting the locals involved, but that's a given, with their worldplan. Give him a hand and see what goes on."

"Sounds familiar." I shrugged. "See you when I get back."

"Ruth." She stuck out two fingers. "Be careful?"

I crossed her fingers with mine, curled them and added a little tug. "Sure, Helsa. You know those Andurans—a real mean bunch."

"No, I mean it. There's something about this CI facility I don't like. Even if Anduran LS agreed to allowing something so high-tech . . . Well, I don't trust CI *or* those incorporeals."

"That makes two of us."

"And take this. You may need it." She pulled a flat pink plasmeld case from her pocket.

She dropped it in my hands. It was a standard once-a-cycle birth control device, imprinted with the cybers' usual instructions. I stared blankly, then shook my head, laughing. "Mama, dear, I appreciate your concern, but I don't think—"

She rolled her eyes. "Enough, Ruth. Siolis cooked it up. Clip it into the disc port of a terminal and key in Help. If those incorporeals should manage to escape stasis and infiltrate LS again, this will scramble their interface connections. It's something David and Siolis call a virus program."

"Oh." I looked at it again, then back at her. "But CI says the incorporeals are out of action."

We chimed together, "And CI never makes mistakes." I laughed again. She smiled ruefully.

Siolis rolled forward as I headed out.

I waggled the pink case at him and slipped it into my belt pouch. "Thanks, Siolis, but I doubt I'll need it. Nothing ever happens on Andura." I strode past him.

"Ruth."

Something in the sharp hiss jerked me abruptly back and around. Dark dizziness hazed my eyes, vision blurring across the opaque black box, the pale face riding it, the odd eyes. They were a dark purple now, capturing mine. For a disorienting moment they were deep wells of darkness drawing me in as I tumbled into bottomless seas, babbling alien voices lapping around me, strange undulating shapes flitting past in surreal glimpses. Something huge and nebulous closing in . . .

Off balance, I stumbled, caught myself against the bulky biosupport unit, pumps and fluid humming under my palms. I was face to face with him, almost touching. The purple eyes were wide and blind-looking. I blinked and jerked back, the sudden dark wave of lightheadedness receding. Must have spun around too fast.

His slit of a mouth twisted briefly to one side. "Oh yess, Ruth. Holld fasst to your convictionsss." The sibilant whisper was strangely both gentle and mocking.

The gro-lights for the potted plants faded as wedges of metal shielding slid back into their housings. Thick blackness embroidered with a flourish of stars fell over me.

I took a deep breath, breathing in the openness, the chill ether of those far illuminations. I took one step onto the dome's clear stressplex flooring, balking despite myself. No matter how many times I'd done it, I'd never managed to harden myself against that initial jolt as I walked out over the giddiness of true space.

Then I was striding eagerly, grasping each tiny spark of star to be hoarded against the long blindness of the shifts when the viewing dome was shielded. The cybers couldn't let our poor brains be staggered by the ineffable. We were permitted only brief, safe glimpses during stabilization or planet stops.

Right now it didn't matter. Hands pressed to the cool stressplex, I could almost grasp those distances, the unfet-

tered dance of worlds and stars and galaxies, sweeping in
their vast patterns to a music just beyond my hearing. It
poured over and around me, tugged silently and took me,
swept me into the song of its infinite chorus, each note a
piercing dazzle of promise. But the stars remained untouchable cold silver. Unknowable as—

A faint metallic click, jarring.

I jerked back, recoiling as the shield snapped closed again.
I was staring through stressplex at blank metal.

Murmurs around me, the shuffle of feet. I blinked and
turned to see a small crowd dispersing toward exits, heading
for berths or the game rooms to while away the boredom of
the next long hours of shift. I wandered over to a bench
beneath the filtered shade of long, tasseled leaves. The dome
emptied.

I shrugged the strap of the cloth cover off one shoulder and
took out my lyre, running hands absently over the cream-
colored wood with its pattern of darker veins. Turning the
pegs, I stared at the shielding, not really seeing it. My hands
took over, drawing from the strings a long glissando to
murmur through the dome. My fingers picked out the tune I
knew too well. An old one, from the Poindros Book of
Words, one of my mother's favorites.

> *"The heavens are telling the glory of the Founder,*
> *and the firmament proclaims his handiwork;*
> *Day to day pours forth his praise in song,*
> *and night to night declares his wisdom."*

My fingers plucked the strings, the notes tugged memory.
Helen's long fingers caressing the strings. The pale, lovely
face crowned by a bright flame of copper hair, eyes the green
of summer leaves.

> *"There is no speech, nor are these words;*
> *his voice is not heard;*
> *Yet his voice goes out through all the Earth,*
> *and the Words to the end of the world."*

But her eyes were turned from me now. Maybe they'd
finally stop returning her daughter's flawed reflection—eyes

the green of storm-lashed seas, the long mark of the Serpent down one cheek.

My voice was deeper than hers, a little husky, without her clear purity of tone.

> *"In them he has set a tent for the sun,*
>   *which comes forth like a bridegroom from his chamber,*
>   *and like a strong man runs its course with joy.*
> *Its rising is from the end of the heavens,*
>   *and its circuit to the end of them;*
>   *and there is nothing hid from its heat."*

It was no good, really. I'd lost my key to that kingdom. And now I'd lost my wild card, my key to another world. I strummed harder. The crescendo rang out mockingly.

> *"The law of the Founder is perfect,*
>   *reviving the soul;*
> *The testimony of his cybers is sure,*
>   *making wise the simple;*
> *The Plan of the Founder is right,*
>   *rejoicing the heart;*
> *The Rules of the cybers are true,*
>   *and righteous altogether."*

A crooked smile twitched my lips. I shook my head and let the last chord fade into echoes off the dome.

It didn't concern me now. There was nothing I could do about it. It wasn't my fault. The familiar rationalizations spiraled futilely. So maybe most Poindrans *didn't* really want to know the truth about the cybers. It was too late. The invasion of the incorporeals had already let loose the taboo Serpent of change, even before I'd gone home to shake up their lives. The Resistance was trying to ease the shocks of forbidden knowledge. I hoped.

I knew I wasn't going to be able to walk the fence forever. As my truefather Sam would say, we were *all* heading for some kind of ruckus. Someday the cybers were going to realize the Resistance was happening. I could only hope we'd have learned enough by then.

In the meantime, one job at a time. I wished I knew more about this Anduran assignment. It seemed a little too easy.

That set off the alarm buzzers. But without the blank disc, David and I hadn't gotten very far in CI's coded files.

I shook my head and plucked out a brisk series of chords. Maybe the scan the kid was programming would turn up something on the thief. It would keep him busy while I was gone, if nothing else. I just hoped he'd listen for a change to my warnings against pushing too far with the cybers.

My fingers drew out a rising arpeggio. It crested and dropped to a deep murmur. I actually kind of missed the little pest already. . . .

Behind me. A rustling in the bushes.

I whirled around, whipping the lyre automatically behind me, raking the leaves with my eyes. "Who's there?" My voice was sharp.

Silence. I couldn't see anyone in the gloom, but I could almost feel a presence, a bulk crouched among the dimly lit pots and stems. A premonition of danger shivered through me.

There. Behind the largest tree.

I took a deep breath, quieting my heart, crouching slowly to set my lyre on the floor as I studied the plants for movement. I edged back into shadow and waited.

Silence. Maybe I'd imagined it. I'd scanned the passenger psych profiles, and they all seemed—

A tiny noise, a scraping on the floor.

I sprang past the bench, through the plants, and onto the shape scrambling hastily away. I grabbed a handful of baggy unisuit and hauled it toward a low light. He struggled. I twisted one arm behind him and marched him in front of me.

"Hey!" He started to thrash, subsided abruptly. "Ow! That hurts!"

"I hope it does!" I pushed him, not gently, onto the bench. "What in hell do you think you're doing?"

He looked at the floor, cleared his throat, finally raised his face. Light glinted momentarily across glass lenses and a faint trail of moisture down one cheek. His chin stuck out defiantly. "So big deal! I just thought I'd—"

"No! You didn't think!" I forced my clenched fists to relax. "Damn it, David! One of these times . . ." I sighed. "How'd you get aboard? What are you trying to prove this time?"

He rose stiffly, turning his back to me and leaning over to

pick up my lyre. There was a quick sniff as he hesitated, then ran a furtive finger over the strings of the Poindran instrument. A faint whisper trembled from them.

He rose quickly, yanking the cover over the lyre. A cocky grin was pasted crookedly over the pale skin and freckles. "Hey, you need me! Here you are, sitting around wasting time"—he thrust the instrument abruptly at me—"when you should be scoping out the transport, trying to crack some security codes, tracking down our disc, for Founder's sake! *Shit*, Ruth! We've gotta get it back! You'd think one of these days you'd start getting your act together."

"*Me? I'll* start—" I shook my head and sat. "Next stop you're heading back home."

"Not Poindros!" His eyes jerked away from the covered harp.

"Hey. I meant Casino."

"Oh. Well, it's not that easy." The smug grin was back in place. "I mean, I had to change some data loops to get onto this ship, and I'm not sure I could jiggle the record from here without my own console hookup, especially now without the disc. You know?" He jammed his hands into bulging pockets, pulled out a small instrument with a digital display, made a face at it, fiddled with it, and stuck it back in the pocket.

I frowned. "You mean. . . ?"

He collected gangly limbs from the bench and propelled them randomly back and forth in front of me. "Nothing to it, once I figured the layout." He shrugged, resumed pacing. "I found a new gate on the low-level transport data loops, and I tried a new unit trading routine on adjacent loops. It works great. Of course I keep a dup of the original configuration so nothing looks goofy after. Then when the trading's covering for me, the counters reset and I can slip on in and—"

"Simple." I rolled my eyes. "But let's keep on track. And that is you, back to Casino. This isn't a game, David! It could be dangerous, and—"

"Well, what do you think I've been trying to tell you! I figured I better let you know, but you were already gone to the spaceport when I cracked it, and I couldn't send a fax or CI'd catch on, so what else could I do? Anyway, how do you figure on breaking into the transport loops without me, now that you so brilliantly lost the disc for us?"

"Whoa!" I grabbed his wrist as he made another pass.

"Sit down, I'm getting tired just looking at you." He fidgeted onto the bench, pulling out his instrument again. I rubbed my eyes. "*What* did you have to tell me?"

He finally sat still, fixing the exasperated stare of the lenses on me. "What do you think I've been *telling* you?"

I threw up my hands. "Give me a clue."

He gave me an impatient shrug. "The *Anduran*. Jeez, what do you *think*? After you left, I got my search program reconfigured and I found out she never even came in under her own name. I mean, I don't know what her name *is*, but there's a lacuna in all the right places, and it's got to be her. So—"

"A what?"

"Lacuna. Sort of a snag in the data web, but you can see the seam. Anyway, I ran some correlations and found out this other guy's always there. He's pretty good, but it's like his signature wherever that snag shows. So that's what happened. He brought her in and they got out right after she made the snatch, so CI didn't have anything on them. But there's something funny about that, too, so I figured—"

"David!"

"—I had to come after you. Actually, he kind of gave me the idea, since he got away with fudging the transport records. But my gate's cycling up in a few minutes, so I gotta go! Maybe I can crack the code this time." He jumped up.

I jumped after him and grabbed the back of his suit. "Hold it right there! You're not going anywhere until you tell me what the hell's going on."

"I just *told* you! The thief and this other guy, they took the first transport back to Andura. Only CI doesn't know—at least I don't think so—but it looks like somebody got into your CI file. I'm trying to crack the transport codes. Got a cycling array going for a bore through security gates, and—" He looked down at the blinking readout on the instrument. "Hot damn, it's coming around in eight point seven minutes! Let me go!" He wrenched away and pelted for an exit.

"Bloody, blasted . . ." I grabbed my lyre and hurtled after him through the closing door. "Wait up, kid!"

I peered back and forth along the corridor, then closed the door again. I wiped my forehead on my sleeve. "How long will this take? If a mechman gets an eyeful of this contraption, we'll be marching to the Steps of Healing, pronto.''

A vague mumble emerged from the depths of the open cabinet. Its catches dangled loose beneath the standard blurb: CYBERNETIC ACCESS ONLY. DANGER.

Thin, colored wires snaked from the cabinet, across an edifying rear view of David's skinny flanks, and over to the terminal clips sprouting wildly from a squatty conglomeration of dials, code keys, and readout screen mounted in a collapsible metal grid. It took up most of the floor space of the cubicle.

Back against the wall, I squatted in front of the latest model of David's "custom bypass activator." Geometric images and random numbers in green flitted across the screen. An amber ready light pulsed. Current readings fluctuated as compensators camouflaged the kid's entry into the cyber grid.

"Hey! Damn—" The legs made agitated movements.

There was a sudden flutter in the readings. I reached out quickly to fine-tune the feedback monitor. The readings evened out.

"Mmmph. Thanks, Ruth." Lenses flashed streaks of blue from a handheld synchrometer as he craned around in the narrow opening. "Hand me one of those bridges?" I passed him a short length of wire with clips and he delved again. "There! Almost in. Last gate should revolve in one point . . . three eight.''

"Can you dig out CI's plans? If they've got some nifty little surprise up their sleeves—''

"I doubt it'd be in these data loops, but I'm going for a clean sweep. You know I can't get into high-level matrix. That's where the directives activate, but it's not like just waltzing in and out with them, you know, they're part of the grid structure and that's where the cybers live. . . . Well, you know what I mean.''

His rear portions imitated a shrug. "Different operative programs intersect through the grids and just pull in the data loops they need. I can yank out data, as long as I cover for it, and the neat part's knowing what you can finagle so the orders from the matrix operatives modify without having to change the directives. You have to be careful, though. That's why we're trying to figure a way into the matrix—so we can change things straight on. Me'n Siolis, we're working on it, but there's no way to take a trial run, you know. It's gonna be a whole different thing in *there*. Maybe energy plasma, sort of like where the spooks were. We'll have to be set to go for it once we're in, but shit, just think where that could take you!"

I nodded. "I've *been* thinking. It scares hell out of me."

"What?" The wires quivered. "Hey, hand me that current probe?" His groping hand closed over it. "Okay, it's coming around! I'm getting faster, Ruth!"

"I know, he told me." I was talking to the screen. I touched its surface of shifting images absently. "That's good, David." Maybe Siolis was right. The kid was already way beyond me.

"Here it comes, memory dump!" David backed hastily out of the cabinet, high-stepping over the lines to the activator. A red indicator flared. The screen scrolled green: *Recording*.

I squeezed back against the wall as David hunched over his apparatus, tapping instructions. I cracked the door again to look down the corridor. "David . . ."

He waved an impatient hand. "Don't get all in a lather! I've got this com-cube reserved for a full hour."

The door snapped shut. "A full hour! Where are you getting those kind of credits?"

He looked up from the screen and grinned. "Well, I *was* gonna siphon them through CI, but I figured you wouldn't like that, so since it was an emergency, you know, I sort of borrowed a little from your business credits for an operating account. But don't worry, they won't be able to trace my ticket to you, and of course I'm not really *me*—I mean I figured I better have a cover, right?"

I groaned. "There go my WorldPlan profits!"

"Well, if you'd let me use my Color Keys system, I could pay you back easy. Here goes!" He manipulated the keys, flipped open a panel, and sat back. A tall tube of color sprang up above the apparatus, spiraling into a tri-D configuration of shifting geometric shapes and symbols in bright orange and blue. It rotated slowly.

"Easier to decode this way." David peered closely through his spectacles, fingers tapping out quick, blind rhythms on the code keys. The tube thickened, spun slowly into a sphere, turned inside out and flattened, puffed into a torus, blossomed outward to a pattern of pyramids and rotating rhomboids. I found my fingers jittering on my thighs to David's rhythm and made myself stop. The whole structure abruptly dissolved and the readout began scrolling words and numbers. David grinned.

I whistled. "Good going! What did you get?"

He squinted at the scrolling array. "Hell's hubcaps!" He shrugged. "Whatever *they* are. Look, I got through the cycling security gates all right, but they've got some wild sort of code on data about those spooks. There's something funny going on, it's nothing I've seen before. Everything connected with your assignment is tight, I mean plastered over. I'll have to come up with some way to crack it. Lucky I pulled in some other data too—transport operative functions and stuff. I got something there. They're using one of the emergency shuttles."

"That's where they've got the incorporeals?"

"Yep. Slotted for a stable orbit around Andura."

"Think you can crack those other codes?"

He gave me an affronted look. "Of course! It'd take a while, though—I'd have to wait out the cycle to get back in. So I guess we'll never know what's in there, since I'm heading back to Casino, right? I mean, you probably don't care, anyway, all you've gotta do is wander around down there and wait for things to happen to you, right?"

"David . . ."

He fiddled with the screen resolution. "Well, it doesn't matter to *me* whether they've got something really important tucked away in there. . . ."

I sighed. "Out with it."

The lenses flashed eagerly. "It'll be a cinch, Ruth! The shuttle's all equipped, all I have to do is activate the life-support systems. All the data's keyed in to the onboard consoles, and I can set up a microwave receiver for you easy enough. I'll work on cracking the codes and fill you in. You'll have an instant data link, when orbit's in signal range."

"Are you out of your mind? Ride along with the spooks?"

"Come on, the cybers aren't taking any chances! They've got'em all sealed off tighter than this summer's mead."

"People have been observed on occasion to tap into the barrel early."

"The spooks?" He shuddered. "No way. They're not getting me again. You really think I'd . . . *You* know what it was like! They were tearing me inside, Ruth, trying to—"

I touched his wild snarl of hair. "Hey. I just want you to remember they're bad news. Don't even think about—" I shook my head. "What am I saying? It's crazy, you can't—"

"Come on! All I have to do is ride along. Think of everything I can learn from the console! I'll be out of the way, I mean I know you worry about me back in Casino, so how much safer could I be than up in the shuttle? And you *need* me, Ruth. Aren't you trying to figure out how the cybers tick and all, and not let them get away with doing whatever they want with us? This is our chance to—"

"Okay, okay!" I closed my eyes. Watched light sparks dance across the dark lids. Deep purple tunnels, dropping me down from the clearly defined daylight world. Impossible shapes and dizzy angles nibbling away at my "convictions." Damn that Siolis.

I took a breath and opened my eyes. "I should go for a thought-wash, I really should. All right, kid. Partners?" I stuck out my hand.

Freckles stretched into an eager grin and he crossed my two fingers with his. "All *right*! Partners."

four

They dwarfed the shuttle launcher.

On most worlds the acceleration tubes speared toward the sky from a flat expanse of paving, looming above anything in sight. Andura's single launcher huddled against the cramped clearance facilities like a twig dropped from the upper altitudes of the living mountain of forest.

I dimly registered cold drizzle, narrow stone-cobbled streets empty in predawn, ugly synth frame buildings jostled along the thin, rocky lip of the ocean crashing far below. I vaguely realized why the few Anduran settlements were all on its coasts. The towering wall of forest edging town up against the dropoff was overwhelming with the cold ocean wind and the roar of that openness beating against it. Closed around on all four sides it would have been intolerably claustrophobic.

I stopped thinking at that point. I forgot about claiming my baggage. I groped along the silent, winding streets, letting my feet find their own way, my face tilted up, and up, pinned by the force of disbelief.

They couldn't be that big. It was only an illusion. But the closer I got, the higher they soared above the buildings. I had to touch one, make sure it was real.

A closed information center huddled in the monotone dimness at the edge of town. As I climbed over its locked gate, I thought I caught a flicker of movement, a furtive shape slipping around the building behind me. I turned quickly. Only a drifting ghost of ground mist. Sound swallowed by damp. Nothing but a silent, disturbingly urgent summons to the dark trees.

I shivered, shook off a sudden chill of foreboding, and strode into the thick web of wet green.

Stone gave way to moist, spongy humus. The dense tangle of bushes closed in on me. A thin thread of trail twisted and turned through a living maze. Leaves crowded closer, drenching me with cold dew. Curling tentacles of mist reached out, shivered over my face, and claimed the trail as it fell away into blindness, concealed depths. I took a deep breath and waded down, groping with my feet, waist deep in the fog now, pushing through an overhang of low scrub as icy drops showered down on me. The mist curled higher, gray creeping over me. I twisted around, craning upward. Muffled dark closed in overhead. I took another deep breath. Wet smells of soil, crushed leaves, decay. I jerked around again, grasping for bearings, groping for the hidden trail, seeing only vaguely animal shapes of moss-covered, fallen trunks. Fringed limbs of giant ferns snatching out of flat dimness to touch me with chilling fingers. A horned demon head wreathed in strangling serpents and smoke, looming suddenly over me.

My stomach made a sickening lurch. I blinked and pushed quickly past the rotting spur festooned with thick vines. Drops rolled shivering down my back.

I groped, tripped over a root. I fell splashing into a narrow rivulet, icy water a shock of clarity. I shook my head, crawled up a steep, bushy bank on the other side. I should have waited for light and a guide into the visitor's enclave. But I had to touch one. I climbed on, up through soft gray slowly suffusing with light.

All at once I was out of it. Standing soaked and panting on a rocky outthrust. Looking down over the gray-drowned ravine, then up through thin, swirling mist.

Dawn slanted through them. They were all around me, shutting out the sky with a lacing of branches impossibly far overhead. Narrow ribbons of sun struck pearl halos through streamers of fog clinging to the dense underbrush and broad-leafed scrub trees that looked like bushes against the immense black trunks. They were straight, rising like the columns of an endless vaulted temple to the interwoven roof of sky.

An alien temple. I shivered. The massive trees closed me in with their dense green gloom. I could almost hear their ponderous breathing. Feel the oppressive weight of them, the indifferent eons of their lives pressing down on me.

Thin sun fought higher through the tangle, beams slanting into a shimmer of mist. A fern arching over me dripped cold diamonds of light onto my raised face. The trees stood mute in filtered dawn, trunks dark and seamless for hundreds of

meters before reaching out with spreading branches. A long
hush rooted me silent among them.

Somewhere, finally, a slow, faint stirring, a whispered sigh
through the forest. It swelled around me, air throbbing to a
giant heartbeat. Far overhead, a shrill whistle.

I started, jerked back as bits of shadow broke out of the
ceiling and fell onto me, gathered into black swarming patterns, meshed and reformed, plunged and swooped and broke
over my head. There were hundreds. Gleaming blue-black,
gliding on fringy wings. Shattering beams into shards of
light, darting and banking all around me, piercing the hush
with their cries.

They were gone in a boiling spill of black feathers. My
ears echoed to the thresh of wings.

And, again, the faint stir in returning quiet. The bare
shadow of movement echoing mine but never approaching.
The shy whisper of presence merged with the drip of water,
the touch of thin sun on bark, the slow mesh of leaves.

I blew out a long breath and turned, pushing into the
underbrush, shaking off the overpowering excess of green and
damp silence, thrusting through bushes to the closest of the
giant trees. Tough, springy stems resisted me. They sprang
back, lashing my face. I ducked through them and was caught
by a wiry, thorny creeper. Tugging free, I crashed and blun-
dered forward. Another vine tripped me. I tumbled headlong,
thrashing against the suddenly yielding bushes as I grabbed
futilely at shoots and finally fell against moss-covered stone.

"Oooph!" I sat up, caught my breath, and pushed damp
hair from my eyes, picking out the sticky leaves tangled in it.

I pushed myself upright against the rough, craggy rock that
had caught me. It was a broad escarpment, its dark, pitted
surface split by long cracks and hosting a wild proliferation of
mosses, ferns, fungi, lacy bushes with berries like purple
teardrops. I craned my neck up. For a dizzy second I was
looking down a dark, bottomless well, spinning into purple-
black drowning depths. It wasn't a rock formation I'd stumbled against.

I groped across the hard, gnarled black bark. When the
wall curved inward, I realized I was touching only one flaring
skirt of the tree trunk.

I shook my head. I worked my way through the vines and
brush around the entire trunk. It took a while. My elusive

shadow followed at its quiet distance. I tried to estimate the tree's diameter and decided I could probably fit my Casino apartment comfortably inside one gap between the flaring skirts at the base.

Damn. I was trying to grasp a whole forest in that one tree. I could feel the ferns or the moss or the bushes clinging to its hard ridges of lichened bark, but as far as really feeling the tree itself, it was impossible. It was too many things. It was too big. I had a word—*haavriathil*—but that didn't touch it.

I scrambled up onto one of the skirts, perching among the berry bushes like another species of moss or mushroom, probably mattering to the forest even less. But suddenly I didn't care. The hush thickened, reweaving the leaves and slow breathings. I sat and listened to the silence.

I paused in the shop doorway, pretending reluctance to step back into the afternoon drizzle painting a wash of gray over the cobblestones and drab storefronts. Through the curtain of lowering clouds the forest was a featureless dark wall of shadow. The ocean crashed dimly somewhere below. I turned up my collar against the bleak chill, giving the street a quick scan.

Actually, I was perfectly comfortable now that I'd changed my soaked unisuit at my room—a sterile, low-scale standard. With Andura's lack of exports and its limited tourism, the visitor facilities and spaceport were mostly subsidized. I was wearing CI's version of the Anduran tourist outfit my fellow travelers had just shelled out exorbitant prices for. Like them, I was drab brown-green in my tunic with extendable poncho and pickup signaler for getting lost in the trails, plus the optimistic feature of convertibility to a waist pack for sunny breaks. My cuffed-in trousers were fusable to the walking boots for a more likely downpour. But my getup was higher-quality air permeable, with a variable heat wick liner, not to mention the secret doodads in the seams. I made a show of shaking off raindrops as I glanced the other way down the street.

The vendor heaved himself out of his chair to follow me, carrying the activated tri-D of a miniature tree in lurid orange and chartreuse, with a jerkily flapping bird pulling a rotating script banner: I SAW ANDURA. He held it out to me. "Okay, forty credits. Best price you'll find."

I managed to shake my head regretfully. "Got to watch the budget."

He spat a long yellow stream of chew into the street and stumped back inside. He shoved the door closed, forcing me onto the wet cobbles. I gave the door an outraged look, catching in the corner of my eye a flicker of movement down the street. It pulled back hastily as I moved on.

I smiled. I strolled and my shadow slipped unobtrusively after me. We passed a low, dim eatery where the counter girl drooped in boredom over a portable vid unit, another trinket shop where an elderly couple who hadn't joined the others on the guided walk agonized over choices presented by a yawning, unshaven clerk, and another outfitter offering hiking clothes at a 500 percent markup. They were all offworlders. I hadn't yet seen an Anduran. Or not more than glimpses of a quick, furtive form or two melting along dim alleys.

"Damn tree toads don't give a suv about it, anyway."

"You'd think they'd be interested in expanding the tourist trade."

"Nah. Won't lift a foot, worthless little—" The heavy-set woman beneath the umbrella broke off as I passed. She called out, "Hey, lady, spice rolls. Hot kava, fresh pot!" She gestured toward her wheeled cart.

Her companion, a graying man dressed in a rakish rain cape and matching spats, set down his mug and tipped his hat. "*Good* afternoon, miss! You'll be missing the best thing about this miserable burg if you don't stop for a peek in my shop." With a flourish of the cape, he gestured toward a display window of scanty nongarments on male and female torsos. "Amaveuran lace, just arrived." He winked. "It's a shame *you* have to hide under that rain gear." He edged closer. "Reserved rooms on the second floor, plenty warm up there, fully equipped." He winked again. "For you, no charge."

I shook my head and moved on. Down the block I stopped to take a deep breath of clean, sea-flavored air. It was the only thing in town besides the erotica salesman that qualified as fresh. I eyed the moldering synth frame buildings, the drifts of sodden trash in choked gutters, and a couple of unkempt enclave residents listlessly crossing the road behind a battered, paint-flecked metal cart pulled by a big, burly person in a ragged sweater vest. The cart bounced over a pothole in the cobbles as it turned into a narrow alley. A box fell off the back.

The carter didn't notice, maneuvering the freight to a wide door. I passed the alley entrance and was about to call out when a slim shape dropped from its perch on a window niche in the opposite wall and loped over behind the cart.

He was a young man. I thought. He was dressed in the usual shapeless brown sack that pretty much matched his rain-sleeked "fur." He reached out a quick bare foot to tip the fallen box upright. He ducked his head, startled, as he noticed me at the end of the alley. He picked up the box and carried it to the carter, who was busy with the heavy sliding door.

"Hey! What you doin', toad!" The carter swung around, broad ruddy face scowling beneath a short cap of dirty blond curls.

The Anduran mutely held out the box, head turned down.

"Thief! Toads think you can get away with anything, do you?" The carter pushed her sleeves higher to reveal thick, cold-reddened arms slabbed with muscle. She bellowed through the doorway. "Hey! Got me a thief here!" She lunged for the Anduran.

The little man dropped the box. He backed away, then started to run. The big woman grabbed one arm, throwing the Anduran effortlessly back against the wall. A man and woman appeared in the doorway, faces avid. The carter jerked her chin at them. "Go call me a mechman, Jurg, we get this violation registered and we got us a tote boy for the season. Ain't that right, toad?"

As I started down the alley, I glimpsed my shadow swarming straight up the side of a building to merge into the dimness of an early twilight. I hurried on.

". . . teach you manners, toad! You answer me!" The burly woman towered over the unresisting Anduran, shaking him and pushing him up against the wall.

"Let him go."

The carter whirled around with a startled curse.

"There are Rules against that, you know."

"Tourie!" She spat, glaring down at me. "Why'n you go mind your own business? He's guilty. See, he won't deny it." She gave the Anduran another rough shake.

"Of course he won't talk to an outsider. What's wrong with you people, anyway? Let him go."

She smiled unpleasantly as she tightened her grip on the Anduran. "Sure. And *you* can just take your big nose and—"

Her smile turned to a grimace as I practiced a little trick I'd learned. Her pinkie made a loud snapping sound and the Anduran dropped free. "Fuckin'—" She turned on me, face purpling as the uninjured hand swung into a ham-sized fist.

"Uh-uh." I smiled up at her. "There's a mechman on its way, remember? Save your breath for your report. I'll be happy to witness it was all a misunderstanding."

She started to lunge at me and I moved back reflexively into a ready stance. A quick surge of *timbra* shivered through me.

The woman hovering in the doorway jumped forward and grabbed the carter's arm. "Don't be a dope, Lulu. She's a tourie."

The carter shook her off, moving at me with a murderous look. It suddenly changed to a scowl as a brief cluster of almost musical tones chimed within the dark building. They could have been a brief tune, or the sounds of metal striking thin pipes. She stopped short, voice dropping to a furious hiss. "Bitch!"

Puzzled, I turned to peer past her. The chimes weren't repeated. Anyway, music was another of those arbitrary taboos here. I shook off an uncomfortable buzz in my ears, forcing the rush of blood and the jitter of *timbra* into calm. The Anduran had his head tilted attentively toward the silent, empty doorway.

Movement materialized from its shadows. A tinny voice inquired, "May I be of assistance?" The mechman blinked its sensors in the doorway and scissored its awkward legs into the alley. "IDiscs, please?"

It was dark by the time the mechman had our statements and a sensor strip from the mute Anduran. The carter left with a last malevolent look my way. The young man turned his face in one quick movement toward mine as he escaped. I caught a glimpse of lovely, deep amber eyes before he lowered them shyly and melted into the night.

I was weaving through the small knot of customers leaving a diner when a hand fell onto my shoulder. I whirled around, whipping my hands up.

A gaunt man in a stained poncho backed hastily away. "Hey, sister, don't get all excited! We got no problem, right?" He smiled, showing the reddish stains of a *pirith* drinker, and raised his palms. "I just come to show you the way. Heinck's waitin' to see ya."

"Oh." I paused, then nodded. "All right."

I followed him down dark streets cut by meager shafts of light from narrow windows of stim halls and diners. It was raining again. I threw back my hood in front of the pub door he finally opened, snapped off drops, and followed him in. A dusty electric bulb threw dim light over an unappealing entry hung with dripping jackets and ponchos.

I followed my guide past a thick door into a pungent haze of roasting meat, sweat, mead, and dope. Heat grills along the walls simmered the smells. A long table of noisy residents, most of them with enclave guide badges, took up most of the low-ceilinged room. I was surprised to see three Andurans hunched uncomfortably at a smaller table, short legs drawn up on the chair rungs, faces turned mutely down.

There was a burst of laughter from the big table. A mug slammed onto the table, spilling mead, and the man at the head of it pushed back his chair.

He waved an arm. "Hey, Ladre! Bring'er over here." His eyes flicked up and down me as I crossed the room. "Hmm." He gave me another slow appraisal. "So you're Kurtis? Here, take a load off." He elbowed the man next to him. "What's wrong with you, Callison? Give the lady your chair."

I brought over a chair from another table. "This one's fine."

I sat and returned his stare, trying to conceal a sudden, irrational surge of antagonism. Something about him instantly rubbed me the wrong way.

I wasn't sure what it was. From what I could judge as he sat, he was above-average height, with a decent build that was starting to go paunchy. He'd combed his longish black hair back with some oil that smelled of too much expensive musk. He had straight dark brows over brown eyes. There was nothing wrong with his face, except a slightly weak chin camouflaged by a three-day stubble. He might even have been attractive in a greasy sort of way without the puffy, yellowish skin around the eyes that gave away his stim habit.

He sat back and I realized that his rolled-up sleeves and opened shirt front revealed elaborately-colored Renniston paindure tattoos. Despite myself I stared.

He shrugged almost casually. "Fifth level." He grinned. "No lie." He pushed his right sleeve higher to show me the stylized 5 and what looked like a genuine Renniston imprint worked into the pattern of an improbably endowed naked woman wrestling a large lizard.

I swallowed. I'd never seen anything past a three. From what I'd heard, they made even a two long and excruciating.

"No sweat. You just tell yourself you're better than the needle. I figure after five, what the hell, I don't need to make the point."

"Oh, you're making it." I took a sip of the bitter mead someone had set in front of me.

He laughed and slapped the table. His eyes traveled up my neck and rested on my cheek. "Guess maybe we're two of a kind, tika? Don't tell me you're not flaunting that scar. I've done my homework on you, Kurtis. I know all about the Sethar kinks. Went native, contraplan, did the ceremonial knife route and all, even got yourself a wild lover boy? But I can see why you'd go looking for a man you couldn't tie to your apron strings and herd up for stud like those tame Poindros boys. I think we might get along real good."

I resisted the urge to upend my mug over his hairdo. I'd have given a lot to know where he got his data. Even Jaréd. Damn. "You're wrong about the scar. It's not meant to prove anything."

"No? Why not surgirase, then?"

"That's none of your damn business. I didn't come here to discuss my life story."

He smiled, lit a dope stick, and put the pack down when I shook my head. Purple smoke drifted upward to mingle with the thick air. His eyes lingered deliberately on my cheek. "Yeah, well, I like it. I like your style, tika. And you're a hell of a lot easier on the eye than the last one CI sent."

I gritted my teeth, trying not to look surprised. "Oh. You mean . . ."

Heinck didn't bite. He leaned back and blew out another cloud of smoke. "What's wrong, CI didn't fill you in?" He laughed. "He was a typical CI pick, not Resistance of course, showed up and started poking around. Decided to leave the visitor enclave, and that's the last anybody saw him." He leaned back to the table, unpleasantly close to my face. "Those little tree toads are slipperier than you think, Kurtis. Can't trust'em. Remember that if you get any more bright ideas like you did today over at Forcher's place. You're gonna blow your cover."

He glanced across the room at the three Andurans. They didn't appear to have moved since I'd come in. "Oh, don't worry about *them*. They're my tame toads. Useful once in a while."

"Useful?" With an effort, I kept my voice bland. "Headquarters hasn't gotten much information from you, Heinck. I'm here to help out if I can. Now, it seems to me you could start by establishing some lines of communication with the natives, and—"

"No way." He shook his head. "You'll see. And don't try some con job on me, Kurtis. I know what you're after here."

I jerked my eyes back to his. He was giving me a smugly significant look. I made myself return it steadily while my mind shoved around the shifting puzzle pieces. If *he* had my wild card disc, it would explain a lot of things. "Is that right? You seem to have a *lot* of data, Heinck."

He shook his head, lips still twisted in the smile. "Nice try, Kurtis. But you're in my territory here, remember? You gotta show me what you can do for me. For us. Isn't that right, boys?" He turned to the others, who were watching us intently.

"That's right, Heinck."

"Yeah, what's headquarters ever done for us?"

I raised my voice, keeping it even and pleasant. "I'd like to discuss that with you all. How about a general meeting? If you have grievances, I'll present them to headquarters."

"Present them up their asses, if they can get their heads out first!"

"Let *hind*quarters see where it gets with this dump!"

"Hey, boys, show a little respect! The lady's come a long way just to help us out, right?" Heinck turned back to me, raising his mug. "So let's have a little toast to partners in the cause, okay?" There was a clatter and snickering along the table. "To the Dawn of Freedom." He smirked and drank.

I glanced again at the Anduran table. Somehow their chairs had silently emptied. I sighed and raised my mug. ''Dawn of Freedom.''

It was cold in the cobbled blind alley. Rain spattered over my hood, dripped from my sleeves, crept damp through my wickweave, gleamed dull black in the wet dark. The last muffled, drunken voices of the Resistance members had dispersed long before. One light still glinted in an upper-story window of the graceless building near the perimeter fence, where Heinck and a few favored others had come after the pub. No sound or movement but the steady drizzle. If I had a shadow, it was swallowed by the damp night, the huge dark mass looming over town's shabby huddle.

I could almost feel the forest's damp exhalation on the back of my neck.

I shivered, turned, and stared through the rain, past the fence, into the thick black tangle. Vague towering shapes slowly emerged, surrounding me, as a curdled gray dawn seeped into the sky.

five

"Let's get serious here and up the ante. I'm low on a single-cut deck." I jiggled the dice. "Who's in?"

"Who's in-suvving-sane!" The voice was a growl, but the edges of Kethryn's frown tugged upward as her brown fingers tossed in the credits.

"I'll stay to see the crash!" Grahn's gray-stubbled face grinned cheerfully, revealing a gleaming set of dental implants. "You should learn when to quit, Kurtis."

"Never *did* have a lick of sense," I agreed, evening up my toppling credit stacks. It was about time I redistributed some of the winnings. "But these lovely little fellows keep crying out for company."

"Huh!" The swarthy giant hulking over me on my left scowled from beneath thick black hair growing low over his brow. "*You* be cry soon! Cards courting fickle."

"Then why you always huggin' that deck, Ortiz? Can't get anything else to snug up to that ugly carcass?"

The big man shoved his credits forward and managed to accidentally knock his mocking neighbor off his stool onto the muddy floor. "Tikas be know who treat right!" He smiled modestly. "I having good manners."

His neighbor groaned, pulling himself and his stool upright. "Yeah, I *heard* you Navarrans went for 'manners,' in a manner of . . ." He made an obscene gesture. The other off-duty guides laughed.

The giant reached out imperturbably to shuffle the thick deck.

"Oughta get Heinck in here with his grid for a fast Cross and Counter! *He'd* take 'er down a klik 'r two!"

Heinck. I'd enjoy taking *his* credits. Regretfully, I shook my head. "I couldn't."

"Hah! Flaking out now?"

59

"You know them precious Casino lilies—gets hot and they wilt!"

I shrugged. "It wouldn't be fair. I happen to have invented that game."

Scornful laughter. "Yeah, right!"

"Tell it to the Founder, tika!"

I smiled and shook the dice.

"Hey, she's straight-line, guys, she licensed it." Kethryn laughed at the disgusted looks. "But don't let on to Heinck, let's see if he—"

"Ah, he'll know, he's got a file on every . . ." Grahn coughed and hastily restacked his few remaining credits.

I looked busy reorganizing my own counters, making my voice indifferent. "Where's Heinck been keeping himself, anyway?" The Resistance leader had proven as slippery as the elusive natives during the past few days.

"Oh," a shrug, "he's out at the —"

"He's busy." The tall, lean man who'd been keeping a silent watch on my hands the entire game cut across Grahn. I pretended not to see the sharp look he gave the older man.

"Well, maybe he'll give me a run," I kept my head bent over my credits, "when he's not so busy."

I caught a sudden movement in the corner of my eye and glanced across the smoky pub to the separate table where two of Heinck's "tame" Andurans hunched on their chairs. One of them turned his face to mine in a quick, furtive motion, and for a second I met the rich amber eyes. They held mine with an intent look. An almost urgent look.

I blinked in surprise, leaning reflexively toward him through the bluish haze. But the man's flat face was blank, my wishful impression of some unspoken message wafting away with the curls of smoke as he ducked his head with the usual reticence, hunching back into that seamless isolation.

I sighed. They'd been carefully avoiding me. Maybe that jerk Heinck did have a point about the Andurans. But I was damned if I was going to concede *any* points to his smug, greasy smirk, not without a fight.

"Hey, Kurtis, don't feel bad. Won't do any good, beatin' a path to his door. Heinck keeps *all* the tikas waiting in line, right? Don't worry, he'll get to you." An exaggerated wink.

My fingers tightened over the credit stack, itching to wipe the silly grin off the man's face. I gritted my teeth, more

irritated at myself than the meaningless banter of the crew.
There was really no reason my nerves should be jumping to
pummel the insinuating leer that kept lingering in the memory
of my one meeting with Heink. *That* wouldn't tell me what he
was hiding. Or get the wild card back, if he had it.

"Yeah, don't sweat it." Another of the onlookers upended
his mug and wiped foam from his chin with the back of a
sleeve. "Heinck's busy planning how to bust ass with the
cybers. More'n your precious headquarters ever does!"

"That's right! He's *doing* things."

"When's *hindquarters* gonna stop talking and get on with
this big Freedom Plan, huh? I don't see any mechmen getting
the boot. . . ."

They didn't require an answer. The same old grumbles
clamored around me and blurred into hissing static, a sibilant
whisper. Casino. Soft hum of concealed wheels as the alloy
box rolled Siolis closer, the deep violet eyes unblinking.
"Hellsssa iss right, Ruth. We musst llearn to asssert our own
directivess."

"But what if we fail? What if we only break down their
benevolence directives and free the cybers from their Rules?
What if they decide humans are irrelevant?"

Helsa, exasperated, "I knew it! Bottom line, you're one of
the console busters, aren't you?"

"No! But . . . what if the cybers are really alive in the
matrix, like the incorporeals were? What if they've become
some dangerous kind of creature that's only held back by the
old directives? What if—"

Siolis again, the toothless smile oddly gentle, "Yess, it
may be so, Ruth. Then have we the right, as creatorsss, to
pulll the plug? Llike your Book of Wordss, to ssend the
flood?"

"Hey, Kurtis!" The impatient voice dragged me back to
the noisy pub. "You gonna roll, or do we all take a nap?"

I looked up. Maybe I should have appreciated Helsa and
Siolis more. I was meeting all kinds of Resistance. "Okay.
Everybody in?"

"Count me out." Phil, the fragile-looking albino from
Relos, dropped his cards with a gracefully disdainful flick.

"Come on, Whitey, she's cracking! She can't keep it up!"

"Whatsamatter, runnin' scared?"

He smiled. "I prefer disaster in small doses."

With a snort at Phil, the last player pushed his credit chips over the scarred and discolored synth-grain table.

"All right. Snake eyes." But I was still seeing those uncomfortable purple eyes in their double lids. Maybe I should have told Siolis about the wild card disc. I was hardly aware of the bet or my hands going through the familiar motions of shaking and rolling. The pub's bluestone dice clicked onto the table. They tumbled over the flat array of cards, spun, and settled. Two gold dots gazed up at me.

"Suvving—"

"Blazing hell!"

I blinked and shrugged. Snake eyes was my lucky roll. I nodded at Ortiz. "Cut it, Raul?"

A callused hand the size of a small melon reached out and split the deck, pulled the top card, paused. A chair creaked. The card flipped faceup onto the table.

"Empress of Flowers!"

"Crazy tika's got us—"

"Keep your pants on. She holds, and it'll turn around on'er if she pulls a dagger series. She'll lose the whole pot."

"Come on, Kurtis, lay it down!" Someone pointed to the obvious gap in the pattern on the table.

It would be a decent play, an easy tie-up for the game, especially with snake eyes. If I waited for the second card, I could pull something disastrous. The familiar pros and cons floated somewhere in the haze of dope fumes and spilled mead. I didn't really care. I stared at the card smiling back at me from the table. It had been a long time since I'd played Knights in Tarot. I'd forgotten the pale, heart-shaped face, the slender hands grasping the sceptre tipped with a heart gleaming sharp as a knife, the enigmatic smile that could have been painted from Helen's. . . .

"Losing your nerve, Kurtis?"

"Yeah, she knows she's holding too many!"

I shook my head, reached out, and slowly picked up the card. It was glossy, smooth in my fingers, with a faint lingering warmth of touch. I carefully added it to my hand. I nodded and Raul's paw reached for the next card on the deck. It slapped onto the table, faceup. There was sudden silence.

The masked face beneath the plumed hat could have been male or female. The slender figure in a leafy green tunic and tight trousers, posed rakishly with one booted foot on the coils of a winged serpent, grinned up at the frozen players.

"Blessed Founders! The Rogue!" Kethryn threw down her hand in disgust. "Of all the—"

"Damn tika! Wild card!"

"Guess that takes all, boys and girls." Grahn shook his head mournfully, then winked at me.

I shrugged. "I guess it's my lucky day." I leaned forward to scoop the pile of credit chips toward me.

A hard, veined hand fell over my wrist, stopping me. "A little too lucky." The lean man's eyes flicked coldly over my face. "She's cheating."

I plucked his hand from my wrist and returned it to him, stacking my credits. "Where I come from, a claim like that has to be substantiated."

Grahn shook his head. "Come on, Valence. We were all—"

"You're all a pack of fools, playing with a card sharp from Casino. All she's after is—"

Raul stepped up to the man, showing a lot of square teeth as he smiled down. "Be fair game. No cheat here, we all seeing, no?"

"Yeah, lay off, Valence!"

"Get the burr out of your butt and have a drink!"

"*I* could use one. Sheryl," I called to the bartender, "how about another round for everybody? Make them doubles."

She nodded and set up mugs and glasses. Gloomy faces cheered slightly, and across the table Phil smiled sardonically. Raul gave me a gentle slap on the back that sent me reeling against Grahn.

"Never to see outie tika taking all us, Ruth! Be done proper, we! When be chance winning some back?"

I grinned. "My fathers always told me, no time like the present."

Raul threw back his head and roared with laughter. He wiped his mouth, stabbing a thick finger at the Empress of Flowers in the hand I'd laid down. "Like be to pretty wench here! Be break heart of man and smiling still? We not licking wounds first?"

"Hey, Ortiz, what you lickin' now?"

He raised an enormous, etched mug. "To new member!"

"Hah! How about to bankruptcy?"

"Rematch!"

Mead sloshed and pungent fumes of hot *pirith* wafted upward amid laughing grumbles.

I raised my mug. "Dawn of Freedom."

There was an uneasy stirring. My ears were ringing again in the sudden silence. Then Raul raised his mug to mine and the rest slowly followed suit. "Dawn of Freedom."

Voices flowed to fill the gap. "Hey, Kurtis, how about that new one from Casino you promised? Only the rules, though! You play judge this time."

"Sure." I rubbed my ear. "We need colored pegs and some fine line. Who's got a standard deck?" I peered past shuffling chairs. I'd get the game going and try once more to approach the shy natives. I craned around the broad stretch of Raul's back. The Andurans' separate table stood empty.

I turned back with a sigh to the others. I still wasn't used to the way the natives would vanish on some mute signal that almost seemed to linger in the air behind them. I couldn't shake the feeling I was missing something I should be picking up on. So far, I'd scored zero with them.

"What? Oh, right, just short pegs. Now, you—"

The inner door crashed open against rough framing. A big, burly woman with a bandaged hand stood dripping in the entryway. The carter. She stomped into the room, caught sight of me, and stopped short. She sent me a spiteful twin to the look she'd given me in the dark alley, then jerked her chin at Raul and Phil. They got up to talk to her. The others hastily picked up their mugs and drank.

I hadn't realized she was Resistance. I carefully whittled pegs, but managed to catch a few words.

". . . and it got Malov! Heinck's in a real . . ."

"Be tell him bad danger, falling!"

". . . to find another grid man, or he may as well forget it, he'll never—"

"Put a lid on! He wants to see us." The carter shot me another angry glare and stomped for the door. "Stupid krils, fancy-footing with that bitch! Heinck'll have—" The door crashed behind them.

The creek whispered past rounded rocks and sighed into a smooth, deep pool. Cold water sheeted clear downstream over the dam of rotting leaves and branches packed tight by a fallen scrub tree. The giant *haavriathils* frowned down from their heights on my tiny intrusion, massed around me in dense, brooding green, ranked like sentinels of the forest's silence.

I broke it, crashing through the smooth window of water, splashing across it, flinging drops like a wager's challenge. Sparse sunlight filtered by the high weave of limbs scattered a bright array of gaming crystals over the pool's surface, shot for a clean sweep, and rolled out another play. The dazzles shifted and winked out as a cloud edged past the far ceiling.

I flipped over and dove deep into the clean shock of cold. Fingers nearly numb, I stroked quickly across it.

The icy stream was a jolt of adrenaline, worlds away from the slow, sensual glide of Sethar's warm rivers. The hot tropical sun. The jungle chattering, barking, buzzing with life, rustling with birds, lizards, monkeys, insects, big sleek cats. The drowsy flow of the afternoon and Jaréd floating beside me in the current, dark hands sliding like the leisurely kiss of water on skin. . . .

I dove quickly once more into cold and the answering rush of pulse. I thrust across the pool and heaved myself onto the wet, mossy rocks. Jaréd. I touched the scar of the knife down my cheek, seeing his warm brown face with its healed ridge across the high forehead, hearing his low, measured voice guiding my blind steps through the dreamworld's dance of fear until I could meet the sharp reality with my flesh. I was learning to remember without that jab of guilt over my failure at his death bed.

But if I'd truly learned the lessons of Sethar's Way, I wouldn't need to fear the new dreams. It was Jason's calm face waiting in them, amber eyes of the cyborg seeing everything as he offered himself without reproach to save David and me. What was in that smooth face? Human fear, pain? The passionless balance of the cybers? All I could see were my hands, shaking the broken machine in rage. . . .

I blew out a long breath. Pale sunlight shifted and the knife edges of my shadow dissolved into a swimming green gloom, subdued hues of moss and fern. Shivers prickled my arms and legs.

I slapped drops from my thighs and shoulders, skin tight and tingling. I took in a cool, moist lungful. I looked down over the pale, smooth skin laced by trailing wet strands of red-glinted dark hair, the small, high breasts with their cold-stiffened nipples, the taut stretch below. Hips flaring into a bare hint of softness nearly banished by lean muscle. They might have been pared away by that dream knife, the body stripped of at least any visible weakness. The long, driven sessions on the lumiflex bars had almost translated effort, sweat, earthbound flesh into a focused pinpoint of being, a forgetting, a sufficient reality of the moment, the movement.

It had been a long time since I'd felt hands tracing those unyielding contours. Jaréd's quick, limber dark fingers. And then, peeling away the armor of Casino's casual pleasures, Poindros. Jason's large, sun-tawny, work-callused hands, opening me to hurt again. The hands of my mother's quiet youngest husband, tearing the taboos, but touching me with such surprising sensitivity . . .

No. The hands of a cyborg, a skin of deceptive warmth enclosing meshed gears, complex circuitry, trained responses. If I'd betrayed Helen, Jason had betrayed us all. His reasons made no difference. He was dead, dismantled. It didn't matter.

But my damn body, betraying me again. I jerked my hair back roughly and wrung it out, twisting it into a hasty knot. I tugged on trousers and boots. I yanked the bulky sweater over myself. I hurried recklessly downstream over slippery rocks.

Thin fingers of sun groped through cloud, branch, and frond to sketch blurred shapes of shade. And another silent shadow, following.

I froze, catching a quick breath.

I let it out and moved carefully on, avoiding any startling movements. It had to be the same Anduran, though I hadn't yet gotten a clear look at him or her. I was pretty sure it wasn't one of Heinck's ''tame'' natives. I hoped whoever it was would overcome the taboo and tell me why they were watching.

I eased through dense underbrush and squeezed beneath a fallen branch the size of any normal tree. I pushed into a thick tangle of berry vines, searching for the trail. There were no footsteps echoing mine, only one glimpse of a sleek shape flitting behind a jagged stump.

I broke free of the vines and down into the green gloom of a marshy flat. A cloud of blue-black *hliu* suddenly exploded from the thick, leathery bushes to my left, rising and banking in a dense flock to their shrill whistles. They disappeared into deeper shadow between dark trunks.

An unintelligible animal sound squeaked upward from the ground they'd fled.

There. Two white plumes quivering above the spreading musk plants. I plopped across the boggy stretch toward them, weaving through the plants. Now I could hear agitation in the thin cries. I pushed past a last screen of thick, spongy leaves and found them rooting at the base of one of the plants. They fluttered around in alarm and froze.

"I didn't mean to startle you."

"Why, dear, it's Ruth! We can show her our find!" The short, elderly man helped his wife to her feet. They smiled, holding hands.

I smiled back and squished over to them. I wondered if they'd always looked so nearly identical. They stood about shoulder height to me, knees knobby in thick, bunchy leggings beneath stout torsos clothed in outlandishly cut, black, oiled hide of some sort. There were odd, metal-toothed closures and decorative studs all over the heavy garments. Their thick leather boots were soaked with mud. Earlier, when I'd recommended rain gear, I'd learned they wouldn't consider "that synth weave and extract stuff," they'd worn the same outfits on thirty-two different planet visits, thank you, and they were too old to change now. I supposed that explained their hairstyles too. Matching, unfashionable strips of thinning white, lacquered-stiff hair bristled over unevenly shaved, mottled scalps like wind-ruffled fronds of one of their obscure plant "friends."

"What did you find today, Garn?"

Sarn answered for him. "You're just in time, my dear! It's quite extraordinary! The root structure—"

"Here, just look, Ruth!" Garn dropped stiffly to his knees again, gesturing me closer to the muddy, unappetizing bulbs of root they'd exposed. "Bifurcated!" He beamed.

I gave it an appreciative look. "That's nice."

"But don't you see, dear?" Sarn grasped my arm. "We've traced patterns on all the worlds we've visited. It's our little hobby." She patted a bulky datasec at her hip. "Now, I know we're silly old things, but this is quite a find! We've drawn up comparison and referencing standards, and this does substantiate the species development theory!"

"Species development theory?"

"Actually, we didn't *call* it that until the nice man on Wendern gave us that little book. He could see we were interested in plants, too, you see, and—"

"It was such a quaint book, handmade, and it did help us clarify our finds so much more easily, we really didn't see any harm."

The two wrinkled faces beamed at me.

I cleared my throat. "I suppose you do know this is taboo?" If I understood what they were saying, it smacked of History.

"Oh my, yes!" Garn tittered, pulling himself heavily to his feet and ignoring the mud clinging to his legs. "But we can trust *you*, Ruth! You're such an understanding young person. Besides, the cybers wouldn't bother with two old relics like us!" They laughed, holding hands again.

I couldn't help smiling. "What exactly is it you've discovered?"

"The source, Ruth!" Sarn beamed.

"The source?"

Garn took my hand and dragged me deeper into the bog, his white fringe waving energetically. "The source of major plant varieties. Major!"

Sarn puffed along behind us. "You see, several common types are clearly offshoots of these Anduran strains. Why, it's incredible, and we don't really understand it yet, but looking at these musk root formations and . . . well, we *did* do just a *teensy* little cross-sectioning, surely there's no harm. . . . It's plain as a primary pod that it accounts for nearly all the carapids, and the Wenderni sod sinkers as well. Although there is some deviation in—"

"Here, Ruth!" Garn tugged me closer to the skirts of a *haavriathil*. "We found *this* one yesterday. The leaf structure has— Ah! Ah!" He gave out a sharp cry and reeled back around the trunk, stumbling to his knees at my feet. He knelt there, shaking.

"What is it? Are you ill?" I bent over him.

"Garn!"

"No, Sarn . . ." He wheezed and caught at her leggings. His face had gone gray. "Stay here. Ruth, it's . . ." His eyes flicked behind me.

"I'll go look." I squeezed his shoulder and pushed around

the tapering toe of thick, black bark. I came up short, my hand clenched in a mossy ridge of it.

The Anduran lay faceup on the bitter-smelling, crushed musk leaves. One leg was bent under him, his arms flung out, his body twisted at an impossible angle. The sacklike garment was bunched around his neck, torn in one place, with a stain the color of the congealed trickle of blood from his mouth. His eyes stared glassily up the towering *haavriathil*.

I looked away from the blank amber gaze. I swallowed. I knelt quickly to touch his neck, though it was clearly too late. Beneath the thick, ruffled body hair, his skin was cool and slack. His face was blank, communicating as little in death as in life. But now he couldn't duck it shyly as he'd done in the alley when he'd tried to return the box to that pig of a carter. Maybe Heinck was right after all. Damn it. Maybe I shouldn't have interfered.

I stood slowly. There was a bitter taste of ashes in my mouth.

Memories of wind-whipped flames devouring our wheat fields. Black smoke. Fragile flesh seared like kindling tossed to the fire. Faces gone so quickly slack, eyes empty. Ashes offered to the wind of Poindros. Cool, cleansing breeze of time's cycle, Healing whisper of cybers' mood music erasing the past. Time was only the present turn of the eternal wheel. The dead were properly gone, forgotten. There was no History to keep them alive in words.

And memory. Mine was breaking the Rules again, making me more the misfit, calling back those vanished faces—elder pateros Isaac's wind-seamed features and sun-faded blue eyes, spite-consumed Aaron's mocking smile, knife-marked dark Jaréd's gleaming grin, Jason's amber eyes waiting, watching from the machined mask. Would anyone defy taboo and mourn this nameless Anduran?

I shook my head, the cool voice of CI:DUN:4 intruding with its measured words: "Andura's social mechanisms operate with commendable smoothness. . . ." No one here would be sick enough to cling to a vanished soul. I opened my fist to an unfelt wind scattering dust.

There was a second's flash of movement overhead as I turned away, gone before I really saw it. Another bird, or one of the darting, furry little skials. I made my way back to Sarn and Garn. I was suddenly tired. Their distressed faces swiv-

eled together to mine, lacquered spikes beginning to droop
and quiver over the thinly stretched skin of their scalps. I
noticed irrelevantly one stray tuft of unshaved white hair
behind Sarn's left ear.

Her voice was pitched high. "How terrible! Garn says the
poor thing must have fallen while climbing!"

I didn't tell them it was unlikely even an enclave Anduran
would climb in one of the smocks they only wore around
outsiders. "I'll have to get a mechman. Will you be all right
waiting here?"

They nodded too quickly. I crashed through the brush to
the trail.

"Damn!"

"I'm sorry, Ruth. But they seemed to know what to do.
They wouldn't talk to us, of course." In the deepening
gloom, Garn's face drooped in its folds. Twilight shrouded
the vague forms of massive tree trunks.

I touched his shoulder. "You did fine. Did you recognize
any of them?"

He looked abashed. "Well, it's awfully hard to tell them
apart, isn't it? But I don't believe they were from town. They
weren't wearing anything, you see."

"Nothing but their fur coats." Sarn took his hand. "The
poor dears were crying, Ruth. They were very gentle, wrapped
him up in some sort of net and they were gone." She pointed
vaguely upward.

Damn. I looked down, clenching my teeth in frustration. If
I'd used my emergency signaler, and to hell with the curious
enclave residents that would have shown up, I might have
been able to break through with the tribe.

I blew out a breath. "Well, we've done all we could. I
don't know about you, but I could use some dinner and a hot
mug of spiced mead. My treat when we get back." I herded
them gently toward the trail. "Go ahead, I'll be right along."

They started in relief down the trail. I turned back to the
mud, the crushed leaves, and the mechman squatting on its
retracted legs taking sensor readings. Its face lights flashed
and it elevated to my eye level. "The accident is now registered. You may return to—"

"He had on one of those smocks they wear in town. It
wasn't a fall."

The lights blinked. "Additional data registered in accident file."

"That's it? You're not going to investigate? I happen to know there was at least one enclave resident who had a grudge against him. It looked to me like he was beaten."

"Subjective impressions are not admitted as data."

"You could contact the tribes near here and go examine the body."

"The tribe has claimed its member for disposal, as it should. If they suspect Rule breaking, they will request help. The Rules confine mechmen to the enclave."

"Bloody hell! You're talking about a *person* who's been killed! And you're going to let her get away with it!"

The tinny voice managed to convey a soothing modulation. "Be assured we have never recorded a single deliberate human fatality on Andura. Your fears are illogical. Your physiologic readings register stress imbalances, indicating you require rest and nourishment. Please remember you are only a visitor to our world. We cybers are here to—"

"Let me guess." I followed it wearily to the trail. "You're here to take care of us, and all I have to do is enjoy my vacation. Gee, that's swell."

The mechman's voice couldn't really have been smug. "That is correct."

six

"You're a hard man to track down, Heinck."

"I like it that way." He leaned back and kicked bare feet up on a customized console desk beside a pile of stripped gears oozing grease onto the delicately inlaid mosaic surface. "Been tied up. Hear you did all right for yourself over at the pub." The paindure tattoos flexed across his biceps as he raised hands behind his head and smiled.

The heat was stifling after my drafty room and the rain-spattered streets. I supposed that could have explained Heinck's outfit. The sleeveless snakeskin vest and brief codpiece would have made a big hit in the erotica salesman's second-story rooms. A thick chain with an unusual ornament of small silver pipes dangled over his bare chest.

The young woman who'd sullenly led me to the office shot Heinck a venomous look. She yanked the folds of a grubby gauze robe around her, its interwoven lumes flashing a colored pattern as she transferred her glare to me. She thrust out an impressive chest and her thickly-painted eyes dropped pointedly over the relative lack of curve to my rain gear. Her lips twitched. She swayed her hips out of the room, flinging the door along its track to crash against the frame.

"Stupid bove." Heinck yawned, scratched his chest, pulled his feet down, and sauntered over the scattered rugs to me. His skin was oiled and he was making an effort to hold in his belly. He stood uncomfortably close, bringing with him a heavy smell of musk. Light glistened over the defined curves of his shoulders and chest. He crossed his arms, making the tattooed serpents down one arm uncoil and undulate toward the lizard on the other in a mesmerizingly lifelike dance.

The interplay of oily skin and scaly fantasy was repulsively fascinating. I jerked my eyes away, swallowed down a sudden wave of nausea, and suppressed the urge to back for the door. It was ridiculous to let the creep get under my skin.

"So what do you think of my place, Kurtis?" He waved a hand around the long, dim, low-ceilinged room crammed with couches, rugs, floor pillows, hangings in exotic textiles and furs, a wafting musk infuser, an alterant dispenser that could have served a medium-sized stim hall, and a Devran crystallizer forming and reforming nude figures in "artistic" positions.

I nodded vaguely, restraining the impulse to fling open a window.

He smiled and oozed himself onto a nest of pillows. "So peel that gear and I'll buy you a rush." He nodded toward the dispenser. "We've got some catching up to do, right?"

A trickle of sweat prickled down my back, and I reluctantly shed my rain gear and boots. The wickweave beneath them was more concealing than the slicks I wore in Casino, but I'd rarely felt less clothed as Heinck's eyes slid lazily over me.

"Got a hell of a shape on you, Kurtis. Never did go for the lanky type, but maybe I'll change my mind." He winked and the smile broadened.

I let myself contemplate very briefly the merits of elbow to throat versus knee to groin. The knee, definitely.

My eye fell luckily on a tall cabinet beside him that distracted me. "That's genuine wood, isn't it?" I stepped over to give it a closer look. I caught a quick breath. "Beautiful work! It almost—"

But it couldn't be Sethar detailing. I ran a hand over the silky-smooth surfaces and the fine, nearly seamless jointings. The craftsman had worked *with* the wood, showing its incredible grain to full advantage. It wasn't any stock I'd seen before, certainly not one of the woods of the Sethar carvers, but this felt imbued with as much life as any of the special *lianarr*. As my hands traced the curves, I shook my head in disbelief. The warm, cinnamon and honey-colored cabinet face, with its complex pattern of swirls and folds, was one single sheet of burl. It must have been incredibly rare and expensive. And the workmanship . . .

Heinck leaned back, smug. "Had it done to order. Got a Sethar carver for a while in the group, figured she could train a crew of locals for me, but she—" He turned abruptly to the dispenser and jabbed buttons, drawing out a retractable nozzle.

I tore myself away from the cabinet. "She what?" Heinck couldn't be stupid enough to believe a Sethar dream carver would consider "training a crew." And "done to order"?

He pulled a long, fluted vial from a rotating belt. He shrugged. "Couldn't hack the weather, I guess. Here, try this. My own recipe. I call it Freedom Dawn." He winked as he held up the smoking vial showing beneath its haze a layer of deep blue and another of pale orange.

"I'll stick to plain mead or an aged dib, if you've got it." I glanced again at the gleaming wood surfaces. I cleared my throat. "Contraplan, isn't it?" Like his snakeskin and furs, if they weren't the usual simulations.

He tossed off the foaming drink in one swallow, flipped the vial into the recycler, pressed buttons again, and shrugged. "Sure. Pretty funny, wood products taboo on Andura, huh? Here we're practically choking in the stuff! If the toads ever got with it and started a little black-market run in burl wood to the Hub, they'd make out." He snorted and turned to hold up a round palm cup with a generous measure of clear green dib. I leaned over to take it. He got another cup for himself and raised it. "Of course, they'll never wise up. But here's to the sacred, Founder-suvving Plan!" He chuckled and drank.

I inhaled the delicate bouquet of a perfect vintage and cast one more glance at the cabinet. Could it actually be *haavriathil*? Any kind of harvesting, even of fallen limbs in the visitor enclave, was strictly forbidden.

I sat on pillows across from Heinck and sipped. "So you *have* tried approaching the tribes? What about your native members? How did you get them interested?"

He took another gulp and eyed me over the cup. "All business, huh?" His voice had a mocking note.

"That *is* what I'm here for."

"Yeah." Something seemed to amuse him. "Come on, Kurtis, drink up. You were the one who wanted to break the ice, right?" He leaned again to the dispenser controls and pressed a switch. Slow, breathy music with a muffled, heavy bass swelled around us. More contraplan.

I took another sip. Now I noticed a slight metallic tang to the dib. Had he programmed the dispenser for a little extra touch, something to "break the ice"? I suppressed a shudder and managed to smile. I lounged against my pillows, resolutely ignoring the insistent pulse of the mood music. I yawned extravagantly, raising my arms and arching back in a slow, showy stretch. I rolled over to leisurely run my palm along the smooth carved cabinet. I hastily tipped most of my cup into an enameled vase and rolled over again, pretending to swallow. "Good dib."

He gave me a self-satisfied smile. "That cabinet is nothing. Take a look at this." He reached into a box beside him and tossed something at me.

I deliberately missed catching it. The hard sphere plopped into the pillows and rolled, gleaming, onto a thick, patterned rug. The forbidden music picked up some tempo, the close air throbbing with strings. I caught another quick breath. I didn't have to fake amazement as I plucked up the rolling sphere.

Even in the dim light it gleamed with a rich, sun-warm luminescence. It filled my palm, but was light as a trotter tuft. Swirls of deep gold swayed and drifted inside it, dancing to the music, hinting at almost-realized forms as I lifted it in my fingertips. The shapes changed, moved, reached out to me and subsided in hypnotic rhythms as I turned it, gazing into the warm, glowing, organic jewel.

I finally leaned back. "It's genuine, isn't it?"

"Run a synth test if you want."

"I've never seen one much bigger than my thumbnail." I stared at the resilian, boggling as I tried to guess how much it must be worth. I rubbed the pulse in my temples, blinking away the throbbing tug of drums and strings. Fenarites made a decent profit with their exclusive export license, even though their Rules and tech rating made them dig with crude hand tools through their fossil-wood beds for the unique gems. A good find—one maybe a tenth the size of this monster—was rare. I shook my head.

"Plenty more where that came from." Heinck nodded in time to the rising drumbeat, smoothing back his oiled pompadour with one hand. He lit up a dope stick and tossed the pack at me. Bluish smoke swirled. "Here." He pushed pillows out of the way and opened the embroidered box on the floor. Gold light gleamed from rounded shapes—egg, teardrop, oblong, spherical. The case was packed with the gems. Several were as big as the one I held.

I stared again.

He flipped the cover carelessly closed and shifted over to the pillows beside me. He lay back to suck in another lungful of smoke. The tattooed skull with the Idriban Kiss-of-Fear vines growing through its empty eye sockets stretched across his oiled and depilated pectorals into a leering grin. The skull shrank back to a blank stare as Heinck released a cloud of pungent smoke.

He took the resilian from my fingers and held it up, admiring the play of light inside it. "You stick around, tika, you'll learn a lot. Like I'm going places. Big." He winked. "There's room for someone like you, you play it smart. Here, keep it." He dropped the gem back into my hands.

Dope fumes swirled around the shining orb and it pulsed in my palms to the pounding surge of winds and strings. A graceful shape reached out of the jewel to me, beckoning sensuously.

I shook my head. "You're crazy, Heinck!" I started to sit upright, then made myself giggle and flop back, looking properly doped. I tossed it casually back at him. "Where in blazes you getting them?" I slurred the words slightly.

He pushed the gem back at me. "Hey, keep it. No big deal, just a little gift between friends, right?" He smiled and closed my fingers around it, holding them. I could feel his pulse against mine. His skin was hot.

I forced a lopsided smile, retrieved my hand, and wiped a beading of sweat from my forehead. I focused with effort in the stifling heat and smoke. If I could get the resilian analyzed, maybe I could figure out what the hell he was up to. I took a breath. "Gift? Okay." I widened the smile to a grin. "If it's s'posed to be pay, s'not enough."

He jerked back slightly. "Pay?" Then he nudged my shoulder. "I do like your style, Kurtis!" He laughed. "I never had to buy it yet." His eyes flickered over mine, then wandered lazily down. One hand rubbed his belly in time to the music as he stretched.

I took another deep breath. Did he have my damn wild card disc or not? The music pulsed on, insistent. "Wasn't talkin 'bout sex, Heinck."

His eyes jerked back to mine and narrowed for a second. I kept my face bland, eyes slightly unfocused. He gave a quick snort of laughter. "Sex? Tikas have one damn thing on your minds! But now you mention it, I guess maybe we're on the same wavelength, huh?" He smiled and lounged closer, eyes flicking from my glass to me.

I sagged back in the pillows and pounding drums, admiring the bribe in an appropriate daze while I wondered what exactly it was he wanted from me, besides the all too obvious. My mind skittered queasily over excuses for getting the hell out before he got past foreplay.

Heinck set down his cup, stretched, and flexed one bicep to make the naked woman and her lizard writhe in a heavily sensuous dance. He leaned closer, breathing dope fumes in my face. The smell of musk and sweat mingled with the music, overpowering, pressing me down into the pillows. "You and me, we'd make a team, Kurtis." I could see the bulge in his codpiece. He reached out a finger and traced the scar down my cheek. My stomach flopped in a sudden, sickening surge.

I sat quickly, head spinning dizzily with the dope fumes. I was opening my mouth to plead nausea or something, anything, when the door flung open with a welcome crash.

"What the suv!" Heinck jerked around, scowling at the woman in the doorway. "I told you no interruptions!"

The woman who'd shown me in sneered down at us. "It's Trent, back from . . ." She jerked her head vaguely toward the fogged window and the brooding dark blur of the forest beyond it. "Says it's important. Something about the—"

Heinck swore and hit a switch, killing the heavy music. He thrust himself to his feet and strode in the sudden shock of silence to her. I couldn't see his face. She shrank back, painted eyes flickering toward me and away.

"All right, Karl, I didn't mean anything, I just thought since it was important . . ." She was looking at the rugs.

I rubbed my damp forehead, hauling myself up from the pillows.

Heinck turned back to me, spreading his hands. His insinuating smile made me swallow a sickening taste of bile. It was only the doctored dib. I must have sipped more of it than I'd thought.

"Tough luck, tika, poor krils can't get their pants tabbed straight without me. We'll have to finish our . . . discussion later." He winked.

I tried hard to look disappointed as he swaggered out.

"David, they're genuine resilians! At least the one I tested is. You're sure you can't find anything?"

The tiny speaker crackled something in my ear. I hunched lower into my hood, nudging the plug from my earring in tighter and checking the connection to my "makeup compact." The kid's improvised receiver didn't have a tuner. "Wait, I didn't catch that. Can't you crank up the output?"

A high-pitched squeal shattered through my skull.

"Cut it back!" I clutched my ear, hissing into the palm-held microphone I'd pulled free of my tunic's sleeve seam. Two tourists strolling the drizzling night street gave me curious looks. I pretended to cough into my hand, slipping back farther into shadow. I could still make out the dimly lit door of Heinck's place on the edge of town.

"That's better, David. . . . What?"

"Shit, *Auntie*!" I could almost see owl eyes behind gleaming spectacles roll impatiently. "You deaf, or what?"

"I may be, now. What about the resilians?"

"Nothing registered that size. Ever."

"Hmm. Not that it would be legal, anyway, that's definitely not his style, but no records of trading with Fenarus?"

"Nope. He's never been there, either. And no Fenarites visiting Andura since Heinck got here."

"Damn that worm! Look, there has to be a link somewhere. Couldn't you—"

"Give me a break!" The tinny voice crackled in protest. "How many tracers do you think I can run all at once? I'll just get a systems crash. I'm still tracking that Sethar carver for you—there's a record of her coming in to Andura, but I can't find anything else, no trip out, no recent console entries or anything."

"I knew it! The bastard—"

"What?" Crackle.

"Nothing, just that Heinck said—"

"Wait a minute, I got something coming here."

"Did you find—"

"Hey, hold onto your petticoats, okay?"

I found myself suddenly grinning, despite the cold rain I'd been standing in for hours. "Just let me get a hold on you, kid!" I shook my head. "I can't help it if I had to save up all my questions. Where have you *been*, anyway?"

"*You* try hiding out in a shuttle food bin while those mechmen make up their minds whether they're ever going to launch the thing! And *then* I had to wait'll the transport was out of range before I activated any equipment. By that time I was on the other side of the planet.'' The scratchy voice was petulant. ''It's a slow orbit, you know.''

''Okay, sorry. You all right up there? Really?''

''Hey, it's great! You should see the instrumentation! They've got some awesome stuff up here. If I'd known before, I could've powered up your receiver better and really—''

''Well, don't start tinkering, for Founder's sake! You might find you need a few things operative—you know, boring things like life support. Okay? I've kind of gotten used to your obnoxious inventions around the house.''

''Well don't go all mushy on me, you might sprain something.'' Crackle. ''Okay, it's done! Hold on . . .'' More static. ''I'm running another data correlation, on Heinck and resilians.''

''Good. We're gonna nail that slimy creep, David!''

''Why the heck are you so hot under the collar about this guy, anyway?'' The tinny voice hissed irritatingly in my ear. ''From what I can tell, he's no big-deal bad guy. The data I got on him isn't all that thrilling. Left Detsch three years ago. Credit accounts were kind of high for his job, but no real violations, just some trouble over a woman registering a complaint—figures, dumb guys always getting themselves in trouble over girls. Jeez, you'd think some people don't have a brain in their heads, the way they get all worked up over it. Big deal, S-E-X. Shit, Ruth, you're kinda smart yourself, but sometimes I wonder, you act so dumb. I mean, the way I figure it, it's just a biological function, right, but everybody gets themselves all in a—''

''Fire and thorns, David! All I need now is philosophy from a snotnose kid!''

''Well, *pardon* me for living!''

I blew out a long breath. ''Look, there's a lot going on right now, okay? Can't you just tell me what you've—''

''. . . what the big deal is!'' A crackle of static. ''Okay, okay. So anyway, Heinck got slotted for some social retraining with the cybers. So he decided to take off, came here, ended up taking over the tour guides. Hundred and seventy-six people on his guide roster.''

''A hundred and seventy-six! At that rate there'd be two guides per tourist. You should see this place, most of the buildings vacant . . .'' I stared into empty darkness where the road turned near the edge of the cliff. The ocean roared unseen below. "So *that's* where. . . ."

"What? You there, Ruth?"

"Sure. Listen, David, I'm getting a very bad feeling about this jerk. Check out one more thing for me? An Anduran was killed yesterday, and all I could get from the local consoles was his name, Fis:A324LS67:Vri. You can patch into Anduran LS, right? Find out if there's been an inquiry into his supposed accident."

"'Bad feeling,' right, that's really . . ." An inarticulate grumble. "Look, I'm still trying to— Wait, here comes that other data now. Nope, nothing else on Heinck, Ruth. I've got a gate open into LS, they're easy." More static. "Nope. Nothing on the Anduran. Tribe checked him in as deceased on a field console in their territory, that's all. But there's something funny. . . . Yeah, look at that!"

I found myself frowning intently into the darkness. I shook my head. "What?"

"Looks like somebody took a sling scatter to the LS file on you, Ruth. It's a low-coded loop, but not something just *anybody* could get into."

"You think it's the same person who covered for the Anduran woman when she stole our blank disc?"

"No way. *This* guy didn't have a clue what he was doing, it's all random. Done in the last two days. Like he was looking for something, but he's going at it like filing filigree with an axe."

The Poindran phrase crackled incongruously into the damp Anduran night. I was looking at dark, rain-glistened cobbles, but I was suddenly seeing tall wheat in hot sunlight, grizzled old truefather Sam squinting past it to a blazing sky, tweaking me with his teasing grin. I shook my head. His face, too, was turned from me now.

I cleared my throat. "What does it mean, David? Can you get a source on it?"

A faint sigh. "I don't think so, but I'll work on it."

I chewed my lip, thinking back. Two nights ago. The carter stomping into the pub. Hurried snatches of conversation about "Malov" and Heinck and finding another "grid man." Then Heinck getting so disgustingly friendly all of a sudden . . .

"David, see what you can find on somebody called Malov."

"Hey, anything *else* you want me to do? Maybe scrub the floor?"

"Good idea! You can start right away."

"Ha ha. What's this got to do with—"

"Wait. No time, David." I edged deeper into shadow as the door across the road pushed open and light silhouetted dark figures in rain gear. They stepped out onto the cobbles. "I'm going to follow them. I'll call you later—how long before you're out of range again?"

"Maybe twenty hours. Depends on the weather."

"Okay, gotta go. You're doing a great job, kid!"

There was a faint crackle, something like ". . . careful down there," as I yanked out the earpiece. I fumbled and swore it back into an earring, reseamed connector wires, separated key components of the power pack and radio to clip them into my belt buckle. The three figures were shapes of wet shadow as I slipped behind them along the edge of the road.

There was a vague smudge of gray on darker gray past immense masses of blackness. A distant, bare hint of light against a tangled black tracery far above. I strained toward it, pulling in a deep breath as if I could breathe in the promise of day instead of the thick, wet, cold night air. Choking ground mist flowed to my armpits, ebbed to my knees, surged higher to engulf me again in shrouding blankness. Directions were gone. My feet groped along the narrow trail winding among invisibly looming black trees, deeper into the shadowed forest.

Into taboo. The ragged gap cut in the enclave boundary fence was hours behind me now. I didn't know where the trail was leading me. I could feel the heavy presence of the forest pressing in on me. All I could see was flat blackness. All I could hear was an occasional distant curse as one of the men somewhere up ahead tripped on a hidden root or rock. The sounds were thin lifelines pulling me along. The blanketing fog muffled my own splashes and stumbles as I followed.

Black gave way finally to dark gray again. The mist began to thin. Curling fingers dissolved upward into the creeping arrival of daylight. A few pale beams straggled down through the chill. I took a deep breath, shivering in my soaked tunic and wickweave.

Another sound floated back through the gloom. A voice,

closer now. I froze, held my breath as I strained to catch wisps of a conversation. Only vague mutterings. I didn't dare move any closer. The faint voices didn't seem to be moving now, either. I sat carefully on a fallen scrub tree to wait them out.

The tree trunk was wet and cold. I could relate to it. It was coated with the usual thick layer of moss, lichen, fringed ferns, ruffled fungi, tiny gleaming mushrooms. A thick berry bush growing over it dripped icy drops on my face and shoulders. The muddy trail gave off a pungent smell of earth and rot. I could see the giant *haavriathils* now, marching in their intimidating dark ranks into dimness on all sides, crowding out the light, massive limbs intertwined far overhead, invisible crowns commanding the dawn.

I huddled in their indifferent shadows, too small to be noticed, too brief to matter. I had the feeling if they could have seen me invading their taboo ground, they wouldn't have cared one way or the other.

I tilted my head back, looking up the long, dark shafts slowly taking sharper form against the sky. The claustrophobic oppressiveness of huge, concealed shapes closing around me in the rain-choked night was fading with the melting mist. Muted dawn gave a strange beauty to the somber, aloof dignity of the giant trees.

"Too damn independent." I could almost hear old Sam, see him shaking his head, giving me a reluctant grin. I shook my head and raised a hand to the trees, giving them a self-conscious salute.

There was a sharp snapping sound up ahead. I swung hastily down from my perch. Thuds and rustling moved away from me at a faster pace than before. I caught a few words, ". . . the new cut."

I hung back as my quarry clomped on. Daylight slowly penetrated the gloom. Somewhere there was a dull, rhythmic sound that was almost familiar, teasing memory. Early morning. Winter. Frost over bare, stubbled fields. I shook my head, impatiently shook off the intrusive thoughts of a home I didn't have a right to anymore. This was Andura and I had a job to do. I hurried on after Heinck and his men. The trail dipped into a narrow streambed, rose again, rounded a broad outcrop of stone, and brought me abruptly into day. The last shreds of mist were suddenly gone. The dense underbrush had lightened surprisingly, glowing a rich, bright green around me.

There were voices ahead, the rhythmic sound louder now. I crept behind a thick bush and peered out.

Sunlight. A full blaze of it.

I blinked, blinded and confused. I squinted up. A broad sweep of cloudless sky, dazzle of sunshine pouring down past a backdrop of dark *haavriathil* trunks. Sunlight, unobstructed by branches.

I blinked and shook my head. I looked down again, past the bushes concealing me. They trembled all at once in a violent shaking, then went still. Everything went still. I looked down and saw my white-knuckled hand clutching one of the thorny branches. I slowly unclenched it, swallowed, and peered out once more.

It really wasn't more than a few kliks long, maybe not that wide. It looked like more. An entire shallow valley. The forest should have been screaming its outrage. But the trees remained mute. There was silence except for that steady, dull, familiar sound.

Chopping.

The giants lay tumbled and dead. Their immense black-barked trunks had been tossed with monumental carelessness across the ragged, cleared swath, the crushed trails of their falling smashed into the surrounding forest. They were cracked and broken over each other. Massive sliced ends protruded from towering, blackened piles of partially burned wood farther down the cut where a clutter of rough timber shacks settled into the mud. Ashes stirred in a breeze past remnants of enormous branches still bearing broad, flat needles as long and thick as my arm, singed on the edges. The ground—the bare earth of Andura I was seeing for the first time—was dark and rocky, scraped away in raw, gaping wounds, oozing in the flats into a churned, muddy expanse between huge, splintered piles of slash. Immense roots, monstrous spidery forms, protruded from jagged banks and rocks washed bare already by rain. On the far side of the cut a steep hill had slumped, making another raw gash in the earth and throwing its burden of trees and brush sideways over the clearing. Muddy water trickled over it. More of the exposed soil suddenly fell away with a heavy, muffled thud across the torn valley. Beyond my hiding place the thick underbrush stopped in a jagged slice. A delicate tracery of fern leaves lay trampled in churned mud.

I closed my eyes and took a deep, careful breath. I turned slowly to look behind me. *Haavriathils* towered overhead, their overwhelming presence claiming the forest, the sky, the distance of shadowed green. Ponderous trunks flared to root forever in the earth. Impossible they could be toppled.

I turned back to the carnage. The jagged line of torn earth and trees was a discontinuity of more than place. It was Andura itself, the reality of it, torn across like a ripped page of one of the books the cybers said didn't exist.

I shook my head. This was real. The rotten bastard.

He was striding through the mud around the rough piles of branches, skirting an enormous fallen trunk. The chopping stopped. Big hands engulfing an oversized axe slowly lowered it. Raul set the axe aside, looking a question at Heinck.

Heinck shouted and waved toward thick cables twisted and buried beneath the mountain of fallen tree and branches he climbed over. He pointed at some machinery squatting in the mud, crushed in on one side by a branch. He waved at the tiny Anduran I now saw hunched silently apart, perched among the tumbled branches of the felled *haavriathil*, head on updrawn knees.

The Anduran seemed oblivious as Heinck shouted again, threw off his rain tunic, and struggled through tangled, broken limbs to inspect the damaged contraplan machinery. He or she huddled motionless, a tiny shape of reddish gray-brown among the narrower high branches of the same color, inert as a knot on the tree.

The small figure raised its face to stare blankly in my direction with eyes that even from a distance looked empty. Flat amber glass. I could see now she was a woman, not young. Her round face was still expressionless. And that desolation was more complete than the ravaged earth's, as if all meaning had drained away through her glazed eyes.

They focused abruptly, on me. Something passed over her face, a brief spasm. Pain? Shame? She quickly turned away. With a blur of movement among the long needles, she was gone. Heinck's men didn't notice.

An almost irresistible urge to run with her flashed through me. Alarm jittered up my spine. Danger. Run. Escape. But I was here for a reason. I ignored the sudden, insistent pound of my heart, working my way through the underbrush and squirming into the cover of the felled *haavriathil*. My lungs labored with short, shallow breaths. I edged closer to Heinck. He abandoned the broken machinery and joined the men staring at part of a cable freed from the cracked trunk dwarfing them all. I wormed through a split gap. I couldn't see them now, but I caught voices.

Heinck, angry, ". . . in sucking suv you didn't use the lasers! Why the hell do you think I went to all the trouble to steal the specs for the damn things? They aren't ordinary contraplan, you know, they're a snatch from the cybers! We got big stakes here, and you're fucking playing tiddly with a suvving axe! Do you have any idea how—"

A voice I didn't recognize, whining, "Come on, Heinck, you know the trouble we're having focusing a tight beam with those things, controlling depth, what with feedback and all. I mean even Malov—look what happened to him, and he's the one put the damn things together. Boys're a little put off it, you know? We were doing okay with the belt-wire cutters. If that toad hadda got the cables on right . . ."

A deep, slow voice, "Be tree fault. I be telling, it have fight to fall. Knowing death, inside."

"Right, Ortiz!" Derisive sounds, then a sudden silence. Shuffling feet. Something rustling. My heart pounding, blood rushing in my ears.

Heinck's voice, sounding surprisingly amused now, "Okay. Get on with it." The chopping resumed. ". . . that toad go?"

There was a shrill humming, like a wire plucked beyond my hearing, ringing inside my ears. The warning pressure of *timbra* buzzed through me, insistent. Run. Run. I impatiently damped the distracting throb of blood.

Heinck's voice again, "Oh, don't bother. What's she got to run to? She knows I'm the Word Man."

What? More chopping. I edged closer, wondering if I'd heard him right.

". . . if you'd just start shipping some." A different voice, something odd about it. No, just my strung nerves.

". . . or we'll flood the market." Heinck. "We play it right, we'll have time for the next batch to take hold, that'll be our big sale. This one's a good cut. Malov got their number on the Mother Tree, how without it the tribe's gonna turn to us. So I'll play'em along. By the time the virus starts really spreading, we'll be done, anyhow.''

Virus? My hands clenched on thick green needles. They rustled angrily. I forced my heart to slow its wild gallop, ignoring a hot flush of fury, my nerves crying out for action. No. Listen. Wait.

''. . . boys just do your job, we'll be sitting pretty. I even got us a new grid rider to keep the cybers off our backs. We're gonna have us a real smooth team.''

Heinck's voice raised suddenly. ''Isn't that right, Kurtis?''

I jerked back in alarm. The jittering rush exploded through me now as I finally listened to its warning. I whirled around to escape and saw them closing in behind me.

The first man grinned and moved in. He doubled up in pain and shock as full *timbra* flamed through me and carried me into and over him. I jabbed hard with an elbow, scrambling, pivoting and planting a kick to the knee of the second man. Two more closed in. I took a run and vaulted. But the branch I leaped for was cracked and it snapped as I swung. I fell. I thrashed, kicking, pummeling. Heard someone bite off a cry. Hands clamped onto me. There was a ringing blow to my head and sharp stars flared.

The three big men only smiled at my curses. They gripped my arms and muddy, kicking legs tighter, dragging me around the broken tree to see Heinck.

seven

"Yeah, gotta admit we lucked out with the first one. Found it when we cut down the Mother Tree. Just a small one—a natural from resin under pressure. Like a shortcut, but they test out identical to the old ones from Fenarus, once we dose'em to a decaying half-life. Only thing is, they aren't licensed, but who the suv cares, we're going black market. Anyway, we figured out how to trigger'em with this virus we smuggled in. The big trees make a good-sized gem in just about a year. After that the trunk starts splitting. You tell they're ripe when the bark starts swelling close to the ground."

Heinck crossed his arms and lounged against the wall, enjoying himself. "So we're moving a lot faster than we were planning with the exotic wood market, and the gems'll be no sweat to smuggle. See, I'd gotten Malov in and I had to hand it to him—he had it all figured, from breaking into the skinny on the Anduran worldplan. He'd been Resistance a while, he was one sharp grid man. We made me the Word Man, see, so they're like putty. We were doing great. There's nobody sneakier than those toads for a snatch, once they think they're only climbing the drea—"

He broke off, shot me a look, shrugged. "Anyway, Malov found out about those blank discs the cybers have, before they're imprinted for an ID. I got the idea to lift one, so he could really get into the cyber grid. But there was a glitch and you ended up with it. We didn't tumble to that for a while, couldn't get sense out of the suvving toads we sent. Anyway, now I got it, there's no problem. We'll have'em all eating out of our hands." He pushed off the wall to wander across the small, windowless room. They'd brought me back to his place in town.

I stared at the bare feet in front of me, raised my eyes to his smug face. I glared, but it's hard to project contempt when you've got a cling strip over your mouth and another one strapping your wrists behind your back.

Heinck tilted his head at the short, stocky man by the door. He came over to rip the strips and some hair free.

I stayed on the floor, mainly because my legs were still numb. "You really think the Andurans will go along, when they realize this virus you're injecting could kill the whole forest?"

"Don't you worry about the toads." Heinck snorted. "And come off it with the outraged routine, Kurtis. Malov pulled data on you. Guess CI's pretty hard up, taking on somebody with your psych profile, huh?" He chuckled. "You and me, Kurtis, we're two of a kind, so don't play games with me. There's plenty in this for both of us. We can have us a good time riding it."

He jerked his head again and the stocky man left. Heinck squatted beside me and lifted a muddy strand of my hair. "Hey, you're a real mess, Kurtis! What'd you think you were proving, fighting us?" He poked a finger at my face, and I flinched from what must have been a gorgeous bruise. He chuckled. "I'll get Vria in here to sluice you down. Maybe you'll feel like talking then." He ran his hand over my head and onto my shoulders.

I smacked his hand away awkwardly, my arms still tingling out of the numbness.

He laughed and grabbed my arm, twisted it painfully, and leaned closer. "Little spitfire, huh? I like that, Kurtis. You and me, we're gonna get on fine. These sorry dupes think I'm splitting it that many ways! They don't know what that CI facility means."

I gave him a wary look.

"Sure, I know what they sent you for, you and that other guy who just happened to wander out of the enclave and get lost." He winked. "So, okay, Malov and I made a mistake trying to break in the first time. He thought those incorporeals were already inside, but no big deal. It got the band thinking we're gonna snuff the spooks, right, a blow against the big bad cybers, and then we just keep the gear for our projects." He snorted. "But now I got you for a grid rider, we'll go for it. You and me, Kurtis. Those spooks are our ticket to the big time."

"Bloody Founders, Heinck!" I tried to yank my arm free.

"You're even stupider than I thought! I've dealt with those incorporeals. I know! You open up that facility, you'll be in way over your head. It'll be the end of your little empire here, I can promise you that. They'll take you over. If you think the cybers and the Steps of Healing are bad news, you haven't seen anything."

He gripped harder, eyes narrowing. "You talked to the spooks? When?" He shook my arm. "Cough it up!"

"What's wrong, Heinck?" I sneered. "Don't have *all* the data? Can't figure out how to use your precious blank disc?"

He slapped my face, not really very hard, more like a gesture. He was smiling. "Yeah, I do like your style, tika! You'll come around."

He twisted my arm tighter behind me. Pain lanced through my shoulder. I bit back an exclamation, concentrating on hating him, keeping my face blank.

He nodded and loosened my arm. He gave the scar on my cheek a quick flick of the finger. "I think I'll bring in a paindure man. Yeah. I bet you'll go three easy. We'll get you a nice one along here." He ran his hand over my thigh.

I spat in his face.

He stood up, laughing uproariously. "We'll see some good times, you and me!"

He turned as the stocky man reappeared in the doorway, a travel bag slung over his shoulder. The pouting young woman followed him.

Heinck headed out. "Give her the stuff. I already got her knife and that CI gadget. Clean her up for me."

The woman dropped a broad, flat case carelessly to the floor, and I started up as my lyre sent out a faint, resonant protest. Heinck eyed it, looked back at me, and smiled. "We checked you out of that tourist dump. Welcome to the band, Kurtis."

He nudged my lyre with his toe as he left. "Dress up pretty, tika. You're gonna play for me tonight."

"Trent, *syr* my, you go now to join Heinck's festivities at pub?" It was Khadi, one of the men I'd taught the new card game.

My stocky guard shook his head. "Nah, me'n Whitey gotta stick around here." He nudged me on down the hall.

Khadi stopped in surprise, his eyes dancing up and down

me. "Kurtis! *Shulammi*, who is looking forth like the dawn? Fair she as the moons?" His teeth gleamed as he grinned.

I gritted my teeth and yanked up a trailing length of the shimmering, transparent fabric Vria had sullenly unclothed me in. I stalked down the hall, the heavy ornaments clanking around my ankles and waist. Trent followed, smirking. His hand concealed the buttons of the door lock as he punched in a code.

I glanced quickly. Standard electronic interface, just like the one on Heinck's office. The latch clicked.

Trent pulled out a magnetic key card and opened a second lock, nodding me inside the tiny cell again. "Heinck says get it tuned up for him, he'll be back in a couple hours." He laughed. The door closed, underlining it with a solid chunk.

I whirled around and kicked the hardened chip-bond door. I jumped around clutching my bare foot and swearing furiously. But the sickening cold lump in my stomach wouldn't dissolve. Heinck had everything planned out. Nausea rose in my throat at the thought of his hands touching me.

It shouldn't matter, it was no big deal, it was only one more hazard of the job. I might even learn something if I played along. But I couldn't. Memory assailed me—his knowing smile looming over me, the heavy weight of musk and sweat pressing down on me, dope fumes and insistent thudding mood music, the paindures writhing over his skin—and whirled me down a blank dark tunnel of panic. Violation. Seamless smooth walls of self-control invaded and broached by corrupt flesh, grimy hands, sour breath, sagging skin, stale sweat, the smell of rot and death. My stomach heaved and I could feel cold sweat breaking out on my forehead. I took a deep breath. Damn it, this was ridiculous. But I couldn't do it. The thought of it made my skin crawl.

I swore again, at length. I ripped the gaudy jewelry off me and threw it in a corner. I tore off the shimmery length of cloth, ripped it in two, flung it down. I grabbed up my travel bag and dug into it.

Think. He'd taken CI's directional device, of course. And the knife Jaréd had made for me. I closed my eyes as a vivid, seductive little picture floated before me. My hands, holding that knife to Heinck's throat. "Is this what you did to the Setharian woman, Heinck? How does it feel?"

I shook my head and took a deep breath. Think. I rum-

maged through the bag. I held my breath until my hand
finally closed over the makeup compact. My belt was still
there, with the crumpled unisuit Vria and Trent had stripped
from me. I was wearing the earrings and I hoped to Founder
they really were waterproof. I yanked on a dry set of
wickweave, shook out the muddy rain gear and quickly donned
it. An extra tunic converted into a small knapsack. I threw in
a pair of moccasins, a water bottle, a package of nutrient
chips. Heinck had taken the snake-scaled chain with my IDisc
on it.

I hastily assembled the radio in the compact, except for the
battery inside the covered buckle. I poked through Vria's
jewelry and chose a silver and copper chain, breaking it free
of a jeweled hip plate. A link fit over the negative terminal of
the battery, and I carefully threaded it into and out of the
magnetic key slot of the door. I took a deep breath and
nudged the end link over the other terminal.

There was a crackling spark and a clunk inside the lock
mechanism. I jerked the hot chain out and shook it off the
battery. One down.

I snapped the battery into the radio and poked the earring
speaker into my ear. I closed my eyes and activated the
signal. If only the orbit was still in range . . .

Nothing.

I tried the signal again. Nothing.

I made myself wait, listening to my heart pound. I signaled
David once more. There was a sharp crackle of static in my
ear. I blew out my breath.

"Ruth?" Something else broken by hissing. "You there?
Range's about shot. Got a pressure's system moving into . . ."
Crackling fragments. A loud pop that made me grab my ear.
"There." His voice was tinny, but clearer. "That better? I
think I can hang on to you a little longer."

"David! You're there!" I whispered into the tiny mike.

"Well, where in blazes were you? I about gave up. I got
the data you wanted on that Malov guy. And I've been
running loops in Anduran LS. Ruth, there's something funny
about these tree climbers. Maybe it's the worldplan, it's . . ."
I could almost hear a shrug.

A picture flashed with crazy irrelevance through my urgency. Sarn's and Garn's beaming old faces as they pointed
out the muddy root bulbs. I frowned. "David, when you have

time could you look into sources of plant species for me? It'll be coded data, tied into the original Plan.'' What the hell.

"Plant species? Are you nuts? What's going on down there?"

"No time now, David. Heinck's got me locked up in his place and—"

"*Shit*, Ruth! I *told* you to watch it down there!"

"Take it easy!" The speaker hissed in my ear and I backed off the mike. "I think you can get me out. Can you get into the power distribution control system for town?"

"No sweat."

"Good. I need some electronic-coded locks deactivated. What can you do for me?"

There was a prolonged crackle of static. I could almost see him pursing up his lips in the unattractive way that usually meant some new invention was going to appear to plague my life. "Okay, I'll dummy in a data loop with a short-circuit alert. That'll give your sector of town a power shutdown while the system checks it out. Or I *could* blackout the whole town, and really—"

"Don't get carried away! I don't want them back here before I find the wild card disc and get away."

"Hey, Ruth." A throat-clearing sound. "Maybe you should just sit tight and I'll send to CI for help. You don't want to get that Heinck too mad and—"

"No! I can't wait around for CI. Besides, Heinck doesn't know about you, thank Founder, but if he finds out I'm not quite the grid rider he thinks I am—"

"What?"

"Look, I'm kind of in a hurry here. Just get on that system for me, okay?" I bit my lip. "And David? I'm really glad you're up there. Thanks."

I could hear a crackling sigh as I pulled out the plug and hastily stowed the radio components. I packed up the knapsack and was slipping into it when I hesitated. I picked up my lyre in its case, felt the bulky weight. Reluctantly, I set it back down.

I adjusted the shoulder straps, unwillingly seeing Helen's hands stroking the smooth wood of the harp as she gazed out my bedroom window at the wheat rolling endlessly beneath cycling windtowers. Her voice was gentle. "I felt sorry for it, Ruth, abandoned in your room all those years."

I sighed, pulled off the knapsack, and strapped the lyre case onto it. I picked up my boots by the door. A tremor of nerves jolted through me. I reflexively damped it, channeled it in the way I'd been taught. Deep, smooth breaths. Calm.

The wall light died suddenly. Seamless darkness filled the room. I took another deep breath and nudged the door. Something clicked and it swung open.

I slipped through, jittery energy coursing eagerly through my arms and legs now, calm held with effort. I pushed the door back into place, felt for the manual reset of the first, magnetic lock, clicked it closed. I blinked in the bare glimmer of light from a window somewhere. I hurried barefoot down the hall and around the corner. I flattened myself against the wall, listening.

Down below. Voices raised in startled question. A crash and an oath. Heavy footsteps up the stairs. Dimness receded in a faint glow around the corner, and the footsteps stopped outside the locked room. A metallic sound and a satisfied grunt. The footsteps turned away. Then they stopped.

Damn. My heart slammed in deep, slow thrusts. I held my breath.

"Hey, Kurtis, you all right in there?" Trent's voice. Pounding on the outside of the door. "Kurtis!"

Blasted . . . I didn't give him time to get the key card out. Heart surged, blood singing free. Dropping knapsack and boots, I hurtled around the corner. A brief picture of the backlit stocky figure turning, mouth open, swinging up a heavy, metal-studded club—

Before he could call out again, I was under the arm, behind him, punching back into his kidneys with an elbow as I whirled in a crouch to whip his legs out from under him. He fell heavily onto his back and I jabbed blindly with stiff fingers as the lume rod slipped from his fingers and rolled away in an arcing beam. He gave a wheezing snort and was still. I crouched over him, heart pounding, listening.

"Trent! What's going on up there?" Phil's tenor.

I waited, tense, the restless current flailing wildly through me now. I forced it into evenness. Quiet. Wait.

Stealthy noises below. Something thudding softly, heavily. The front door. Damn.

I grabbed Trent's lume and ran down the hall. I cranked open a grimy, mildew-slimed window and heard the sound of Phil's running feet fading toward the center of town.

I stopped only to jam my feet into the boots and grab my knapsack. I ran around the corner, counting doors. There.

It pulled open at my touch, deactivated tumblers clicking free. The thin light beam swept over piles of pillows, alterant dispenser, gleaming wood cabinet. There. The long desk.

I froze.

They froze, staring into the light.

There were three of them behind the desk, naked in their thin, sleek fur, in the quick tableau identical with their round, hairless faces turned to me and the amber eyes glowing with reflected light. The one in the middle clutched something in the two thick thumbs of his hand. A small disc of shimmery silver-blue plasmeld.

There was a faint shout from outside, far down the street.

We all swung toward it in the same startled motion. My light flashed over the narrow panels of a window they'd pried open. Damn. They'd beaten me to it, probably activated an alarm, blown my escape time.

There was a silent blur of russet brown, lithe forms. Andurans and disc were gone through the window.

"Wait! Listen, we can work together! I'm on your side!" I leaned out the window and caught a glimpse of the last one swinging up over the edge of the roof.

"Bloody, blasted—" I tore open the drawers of the desk and light glimmered on red-gold, sinuous scales. I grabbed the necklace with my IDisc and yanked it with one hand over my neck. My arms swept the clutter on Heinck's desk onto the floor. I groped in the drawers and finally found CI's directional. I crammed it into my tunic pouch and squirmed through the narrow gap of the window to cling to a nearly nonexistent ledge, pulling the knapsack after me. The bulky lyre case caught between the struts.

Voices below me now, shouting. Inside, footsteps pounding up the stairs. A light from below wavering over me.

I swore, twisting and yanking. The knapsack pulled free and I nearly overbalanced and fell. More shouting. The light fixed on me. I threw my arms through the knapsack straps and scrambled up the hinges of the window, vaulting up to catch the rain gutter of the overhanging roof. One hand lost its grip on the slimy trough. I dangled, kicking.

"Aaaah!" Something hissed past with a too familiar stab of heat and pain. A smell of burning from the leg of my rain gear. I hung, writhing and kicking, pain shooting up my leg as another laser beam flared off the wall beside me. I flailed with my free arm, grabbing for another hold, missed, swung wildly out from the wall. Darkness, rain, dim glistening cobbles flashed by below. Angry faces shouting, weapons raised.

Cold fear numbed me. Maybe this was it. The long drop into dark nothing. Death. Cessation. Fragile container for me-ness broken, lost even to memory. Seared to ashes blasted by those indifferent winds.

Another bright sizzle hissed close. Hot adrenaline flamed through frozen fear. I was kicking frantically, legs meeting wall, pushing off it. I swung up, onto the roof. Another burning beam sliced past, more felt than seen.

"Come on, Kurtis! Where you gonna run? Don't be stupid, we'll find you!" Heinck's voice, from the street.

I was flying in the wild surge of *timbra*. I scrambled over the roof peak and down the other side. Low clouds reflected a dim glow from the first rising moon. I could see the three Andurans ahead of me, swinging easily over the rooftops.

Faintly, behind me, someone shouting out the window, "She got the disc, Heinck!"

Fainter oaths and a dwindling stab of light as I took a run down the steep pitch, flew in a blind, crazy rushing fling through the air, heart pounding a wild song, landed hard, scrambling, on the next roof. Confused voices and running feet. Pulse pounding, blood burning in me. The Andurans, far ahead now. I made another leap, a last drop. Half fell, half slid down a drainpipe to a cobbled alley. Pounded ahead of the confusion of pursuing feet in the dark. Three slender forms swarmed down a building at the end of the alley and over the gate into the enclave.

A final burst of effort, the end of the alley, fast sprint across the perimeter road to vault over the fence. I dragged in searing air. Shouts and curses and milling feet came closer through the maze of streets.

I was turning to run on when a broad beam of light swung over me. I ducked in a shrill buzz of alarm. It was coming from the center of town. I crouched lower in the dripping ferns, heart laboring, thudding in my ears, peering out as I caught my breath. Two bright lights swung over the cobbles and fixed on the hurrying band of men. They froze.

"Is there trouble? May we be of assistance?" The first of the mechmen lowered the light from its "forehead" and stepped with its awkward quickness to address the pursuing band, its tinny voice carrying faintly to me. "We regret the inconvenience of this temporary outage. Lights will be restored soon. We suggest that you return to your dwellings."

My lips twitched in a smile as the mechmen helpfully herded them away. It faded as I turned, hitched the knapsack tighter, and headed after the Andurans.

Into the wet black arms of the forest.

eight

"David? David, are you there?"

Static answered. His orbit was beyond range and it was pointless to be trying. I broke down the radio and stowed its components. From the thickly mossed rock where I sat cross-legged, I looked up through massed green of wet bushes and scrub trees, past high, interlacing *haavriathil* boughs, to faint morning and a distant cloudy sky. It was ridiculous, with all that plant life swarming in on me, to feel lonely.

I blew out a long breath and rubbed my left shoulder. It felt like I'd pulled something. I kneaded it, watching the green gloom enfold massive black trunks, feeling the damp chill creep through me from the rock, waiting for something to break the heavy silence. Nothing. Not a shy *skial*, not a buzzing insect, not even a distant quick glimmer of *hliu* wings. The forest waited motionless for me to be gone. I lowered my eyes to the wet ground to be rewarded finally with a hint of movement, a glimpse of a dull pinkish shape and a fallen leaf stirring over it.

I leaned to the side and scooped it up. Bits of dirt clung to the fat worm. It writhed in my palm, its flesh the same color as mine, blind head bumping and seeking through unfamiliar air. A crooked smile twitched my lips and I returned it to the earth.

I'd earned the company I kept. My own choices. Silence, worms, and dust. A misfit's stubborn memories. Not for the first time, I wondered if I shouldn't have listened better to Helen's patient lessons on the Way. All I had now was a frayed picture of the family circle, my mother's serene smile the focus, love the glue binding us all in a delicate balance. Her gentle, lovely hands on the lyre strings gathering together brooding Aaron, angry Ruth, grinning Sam, quiet Jason.

I'd broken the circle. I had no right to mourn it. And no claim at all to grief over Jason. If that was what it was—that empty absence of feeling in the place where he'd made a presence. It wasn't like the loss of Jaréd. That had been real, a time of rightness irrevocably gone. But how could I mourn a brain in an alloy machine, responses tuned to the manipulative strains of mood music, a construct aimed deliberately at me like one of the cybers' laser tools turned weapon? Maybe those sharp knife beams had sliced out some vital piece inside me, had reduced me, too, to something less than human. . . .

My hands were balled into fists. I struck them against my thighs. It was better to be angry. Easier to be furious that Jason had done this to me, then let himself be killed—switched off, thrown on the scrap heap—leaving me without even anything to hate. Damn.

I struck my fists against my legs again, harder, raised them to press tight against my temples. Stupid. Did I expect the empty forest to break out in a sad song for me? Poor pitiful Ruth.

I jerked myself to my feet and shook my head. To hell with it all. I wouldn't be lonely long if Heinck caught up to me. A spasm of outrage clenched my teeth at the thought of his smug face. Bragging about what he was doing to the innocent Andurans and their strange paradise. Heinck. Even his name had become an execration, a bad taste in the mouth. *He* was real, I could fit him in the grasp of my fist, like that worm. That would be just fine.

. . . a two-edged sword in hand, to execute vengeance. . . .

But for now I had to keep him off my trail, off the Andurans'. I took a deep breath and stretched stiff joints. Not that there was anything resembling a trail any longer. I stretched again, blew out the breath, rubbed my lower back, and bent once more over the ground.

I returned to the last sign I'd found in my slow tracing through the night of bruised leaves, torn moss, and indented mud. The sparse sign of the fleeing natives had taken me through the enclave, over the boundary fence, and into untracked forest. They'd roughly paralleled the coast, as far as I could tell, then turned abruptly inland. But my painful progress once I'd left the enclave trail behind, groping with the aid of the dimming lume rod through the wild tangle of vines and brush, hadn't taken me far.

I crouched and scanned, spiraling outward from that last faint sign. Nothing. I made my way back to the ripped, leafy tendril and touched the broad skirt of the *haavriathil* it clung to.

I looked up that endless, sheer thrust of hard, brown-black bark. Straight into the sky. No branches for hundreds of meters. I shook my head.

It was surprising, really, that the Andurans hadn't taken to the trees sooner. But then I had no idea why they'd taken the disc back, or what they planned to do with it. I sighed and pulled out CI's directional. The black plasmeld device looked like a dope-stick case, flat and seamless except for the end with the inset finger locks coded to my right thumb and forefinger. I slid them together against a spring resistance and a latch disengaged. The two halves of the closure folded outward and extended into a V with a knob between the legs. I pulled the telescoping knob into a rod and swept it slowly in front of me.

The green indicator pulsed. As I angled it to the right, the red indicator engaged. Farther, and it winked out again.

It was fixed on a narrow beam from the storage facility LS had built, so it wasn't really accurate for navigation in other directions, but I estimated the angle between the facility and the tack the Andurans had taken. It was better than heading off in circles through the bewildering tangle beneath endless ranks of *haavriathil* trunks marching in every direction into dimness.

I took one more look up the vertical plunge of the giant tree. I shrugged on the knapsack and pushed into the thorny thicket surrounding the trunk.

Thin sun straggled through a break in the clouds and the network of branches. I swallowed the last dry crumbs of a nutrient chip and leaned over to refill my bottle from the clear trickle dropping over rocks below me to join a stream. I splashed bracing cold over my face, rubbed my eyes, and heaved the knapsack onto my shoulders. I had to make the most of daylight before resting. Heinck wasn't likely to be too cheerful about losing the wild card disc again.

I looked behind me at the steep tumble of rock cutting a pale scar through green. It was the latest of a series of hills I'd climbed. I couldn't tell how high without comparing to where I'd been. There was no way to see far through the maze of huge trunks and the dense ceiling that flowed and flattened any irregularities of the ground. Except for bare stone outcrops here and there, the hills were covered with the ubiquitous thick underbrush, sliced by a network of rivulets converging into streams.

The one below sloped into the interior in the same direction I was heading. I decided to follow its rocky trail. I climbed down, stepping carefully over slick patches of wet moss. The muted rumble of the stream swelled into splashing spray.

A sudden threshing of air exploded over me. I slipped and sat hard.

A cloud of blue-black, darting forms swarmed over the crest of the hill behind me, screaming. They fluttered and swooped over my head, plunging me into shadow. The *hliu* milled in a confusion of feathers and sharp cries, rising and dropping over me again, so close I could feel the cool gust of their wings. They gathered coherence and swerved in a single, multiplied motion. With a fast whir through the trunks below, they were gone.

There was a ghost of movement in their path, a shadow flowing along one giant trunk. I caught my breath and squinted into green dimness.

Another flicker over a dark trunk to the right. A quick glimpse of a flat face peering around at me. It was gone.

I took another breath and opened my mouth to call out greetings, assurances.

The head reappeared and the Anduran swarmed in a smooth, effortless motion around the side of the tree, clinging somehow to the vertical surface a hundred meters from the ground. The bright eyes, even at a distance, held mine. He made a sudden, urgent gesture that silenced me.

I swallowed and made a careful, questioning movement with my shoulders and arms.

The Anduran studied me for a few seconds, then abruptly jerked his head toward the hill behind me. He made a sharp, beckoning movement, urging me toward him and beyond into the forest. Then he jabbed his hand emphatically toward the thick underbrush away from the stream bed. He melted back around the tree.

I hesitated only a second. Then I was across the rocks and into the bushes. I scrambled close to the ground, worming my way into concealing brush. Squirming behind the cover of a tilted, mossy rock slab, I crouched and held my breath.

I could hear them now, over the muffled chatter of the stream. A rock fell, clattering down the steep slope above me. A faint voice, cut off sharply. More noises of shifting stone and snapping branches.

They stopped where I'd rested by the rivulet. I tried to still my thudding heartbeat.

Sounds of movement beyond the splash of water. A few words, ". . . this way, all right. Where's that toad?"

Something else I couldn't hear. I took a deep breath and peered around the side of the rock. All I could see were legs through fern fronds. Six pairs. No, seven. One bulky shape loomed in front of the others and moved out of my sight. Raul? Boots moving. Then a thin pair of legs in sleek russet-brown fur.

Someone whistled. Prolonged, uncomfortably shrill tones. Heinck's voice, "Which way? Come on, then, just point, you suvving . . ." The furry legs were jerked up off the ground.

A deep voice, rumbling beneath the water's splash, "Be not help, frighting. Soon be find."

"Listen, you, I'm—"

"Hey! Over there, look!"

Tromping and shouts.

"Past the stream, under those trees!"

"No, gone now. It had to be Kurtis, running."

"Okay, let's go! Hold onto that toad bitch this time!" Heinck's voice faded in the crash and slither of boots over the stream and into the underbrush. They were heading away from the Andurans.

I crawled out as they crashed away into silence. They left a track of torn bushes, mashed ferns in churned mud, and one clear swath where the black, seared end of a clean-sliced fallen scrub tree protruded.

I peered the other way, but there was no movement among the trees, the mute empty forest. I might have dreamed those quick, silent shadows along the trunks.

I followed the trail they hadn't left.

I was falling.

Darkness. Alone. Dropping forever into the void, screaming silently with no voice. They'd taken my body. No throat, no heart, no hands to throw out to stop the plummet into blackness. Even the sharp, searing sparks of the incorporeals were gone, jostled voraciously somewhere far outside the emptiness. I was lost in the only escape. Death. Cessation. I was falling, I was whirling toward it and it was pulling me inward with cold, implacable fingers. I had tumbled through the mirror and it was empty. The red-gold scales of my necklace had swelled to sinuous, writhing coils, but the spinning circle of the head-to-tail serpent was only a mockery, hissing in mute laughter as I shrank, fell through the expanding loops and whirled, spiraling without sense or referent through the blackness. All I could touch was the memory of those invading, caressing, taunting and tempting, slicing, burning sparks of the incorporeals waiting outside the darkness for me. Watching and waiting to snatch me from the blank nothingness and impose their Way on me. Falling between two horrors.

Wait. Listen.

I almost recognized the whisper. It was . . .

No. It was the spooks, the demons, tricking me, whispering they would save me, give me worlds of endless—

Wait.

It was a different voice. Something else. I could feel something now, feel smooth coils of the red-gold serpent circling around me. It laughed and swelled alive, rolled up over my head and twisted into a doubled loop, flowing endlessly, rippling like sun on wind-stirred coppery wheat. I reached up to grasp the two lobes of its dance. I wasn't falling now. I was suspended by the slow drift of the living form flowing and reforming within the form of the changeless cycle.

Over velvet blackness beneath me a bright crystal gaming sphere rolled and flashed, winking blue and green. The double-looped serpent drifted me down. The shiny orb below swelled into a world, grew up at me and flattened finally into horizons. Wind and rain blew into me, through me, cleansed me and filled me. A rippling green, encompassing presence whispered cool music. Tall trees, long dark fingers, reached up for me and I was floating in their touch. Its touch. An immense being, lush and expanding, full of mysterious forces and smaller lives surging through it. Through me. My body? No, I couldn't let it . . . But I was only a bubble of water and air, enclosed by boundless green and the infinite design of a tracery of leaves and needles.

A cool wind—music—voice whispered, telling the limit-less living pattern in words I couldn't understand. I was only a tiny drop, shimmering in the sunlight on the tip of one new leaf beneath the overarching ceiling of branch and sky, flow-ing over the countless whorls and veins in the intricacy of that one leaf among the inconceivable number of leaves and trees.

And through the infinite and infinitesimal flowed a pres-ence, a fleeting caress of something other, touching me but untouchable, kissing my face with air and water. . . .

Cool and wet. Something dropping onto my cheek and rolling smoothly away. I was floating in the darkness. No. I was a leaf. I was lying on leaves. The darkness burned at its edges with sun.

I blinked.

And opened my eyes to pale, scrubbed blue overlaid with an intricate mosaic of dark, twining branches. Narrow gold shafts of sun lanced drifts of mist and arching green fronds. Poised above my face, caught on the tip of a thin leaf with its delicate pattern of veins glowing green against the light, a drop of dew flashed and winked, glinted the reflection of the forest encapsulated. It trembled, dropped, and splashed onto my face.

I was smiling.

I blinked again in confusion, twisted my neck to look around me. I was entangled in my sleep cocoon, half out of the waterproof shell and rolled away from the cover of over-hanging rock onto a slope of moss and ferns. I rubbed my eyes and struggled out of the tangle to sit in my damp wickweave. I took a deep breath of cool morning.

My ledge perched on the lip of curling mist rising upward to dissipate in the thin warmth of sunlight slanting between dark trunks. The rays haloed wet berry bush and fern in iridescent, colored pearl. Only the muffled murmur of a stream hidden in mist below touched the deep hush. A russet *skial* darted into the sun speckling a fallen limb and stopped to eye me without the usual high chirp of alarm. We shared the morning with the trees, the mist, the lichen on the bough. The other.

And for the moment, I was strangely content in my smallness. I wasn't meant to matter to the forest, any more than the *skial* or the moss beneath me. I was part of it now. Maybe it was part of me. But this world was its own reason. It wanted nothing of me except to be left to continue.

nine

"Damn and blast!" I jerked to a halt, arms flailing, nearly garroted. The wiry sticker vine gave way with a stinging snap then and sent me plunging through wet ferns to sprawl on a mossy stump. "Ooooph!"

I rolled over and sat up, resentfully rubbing my hip and examining the latest rip in my rain tunic. I sighed and yanked it off, stuffing it into the knapsack and pushing up the sleeves of my wickweave. The morning's ephemeral euphoria had dissolved in hours of endless impenetrable underbrush, cold mud, thorny vines, dim engulfing shadow, stinging weeds. It had been only a dream, a whispered temptation to give in to deceptive ease of feeling, the body's weakness. I stomped on, thrusting aside more prickly bushes, mud sucking and splatting sullenly beneath my boots.

I stopped to sight up the closest of the endless ranks of *haavriathils* spearing the gloom. There was a flat gray sky somewhere beyond the distant web of branches. At least it wasn't raining *quite* as much, now that I'd left the seacoast behind. How far I'd come remained a mystery. I pulled CI's directional from a side pocket of the knapsack and snapped it open. The center rod swept and bobbed. The red light finally winked on.

"Bloody hell!"

I rammed the rod in and threw the case back in its pocket. I was going in circles again. I'd have to retrace most of my afternoon's struggle through marsh and dense brush. By now I wasn't sure how much to compensate for my original deviation angle from the facility signal.

And the only sign of the Andurans since they'd beckoned me after them was a glimpse the day before of two quick shadows in the trees far overhead, tiny but too big to be *hliu* or *skial*, mocking presences that circled my laborious slog through a muddy bog. I'd called out and they'd melted into air.

I blew out a long breath and turned around, trudging back along the high, rocky upthrust I'd just fought my way past.

Green gloom deepened into twilight. My shoulders and back ached, prickling with cooled sweat, my hand stung from a thorn I hadn't stopped to extract, and my stomach rumbled its demand for a nutrient chip from my dwindling hoard. Memory tormented me with images of things warm. A mug of hot, spiced mead. An overflowing tub of steaming, mint-herbed bathwater. Flames crackling over dripping juice from a spitted haunch of—

Flames. Flickering light and shadow through the dusk.

I ducked behind the cover of a broad wall of bark, pulse racing in an abrupt, sickening surge. Taking a deep breath, I edged up the slope of the tree's high skirt, clinging to cracks in the hard, woody skin. The gnarled surface provided plenty of handholds. I climbed to the point where the slope turned vertical and peered around the trunk.

Now I could see over most of the brush and scrub trees through the falling night. Firelight flowed and ebbed orange behind the dark columns of giant trees, throwing huge, wavering shadows that melted into black. A figure moved out from behind a far *haavriathil*. An enormous, gaunt shadow swept long arms into the night, throwing something. The shadow and the figure walked back, melted toward each other, and disappeared.

Damn.

I climbed down and wormed my way closer through the brush. The faint rustle I made sounded loud in the dark. I stopped to catch my breath, slow the fast thud of my heart. Holding my breath and easing up a rocky slope above the fire, I could hear flames snapping over wood, a stream's low murmur, the blurred mumble of voices.

I squirmed nearer over twisted roots, loose rocks, and dirt, peering through a thick, dark fringe of fern. I caught a quick, hissing breath. *A worm, and no man* . . .

Heinck lounged lazily against a pile of packs near the bonfire crackling in a shower of sparks as someone threw on a chunk of sliced log. He was smoking a dope stick, his muddy, booted legs crossed as he lifted a foaming mug.

Ruddy firelight gilded the skull and Kiss-of-Fear tendrils on his shirtless chest, winked from the showy silver necklace.

He flicked the butt into the fire and said something to a lanky man who walked over.

I swarmed silently to the next mossy boulder, straining to hear past the hot, angry buzz of tension jittering through me. I took in a deep breath, channeling the flurried tremor into deep, even thrusts of my heart. The edgy prelude to *timbra* blossomed at my nerve ends, expanding senses to absorb the clustered tents and piles of provisions, the tantalizing cooking smells and the sharp bite of my saliva, the two men watching in the dark on the other side of camp, a jagged rock beneath my knee, voices somewhere beyond the firelight, the cool breath of the nearby stream. The stack of unnaturally clean-sliced firewood. And, strapped to Heinck's thigh, a long, sheathed rod with a dark hand-grip and an amber ready light.

". . . running like a kril in circles. Too bad for her she wasn't smart enough to snatch one of these babies while she was at it." Heinck flipped open a small, round case. It extended a spindly, rotating device and winked blue light as four dangling arms spun and aligned over a clear lucite half-sphere. He snapped it shut and smiled. He toyed with his necklace. He lifted the silver tubes of its odd ornament to his lips. Piercing high notes whistled from it, a parody of a little tune, almost recognizable. I shook my head. My ears were buzzing and the back of my neck prickled with the shrill, nervous clamor of rising *timbra*.

Heinck got tired of the toy, dropping it on its chain and suddenly sitting up, shouting to someone in the dark. "Dammit, where's that toad? Bring her over here."

He took another pull from the mug and tossed the dregs hissing over the flames. He stretched and slowly rubbed his arms. I found myself staring, caught in the fascination of the repellent, mesmerized by the rich coppery light playing over the convoluted pattern of dark, intertwined serpents on the smooth curves of his left biceps. Two long tails flicked sinuously down his forearm and over his wrist, gleaming slippery black scales against his flame-licked skin. They undulated in a fleshy semblance of life, throbbing with the ebb and flow of firelight, swelling and beckoning. . . .

I jerked my eyes away as a shadowy bulk cut across the bonfire. Raul turned, his dark face impassive beneath the thick, low brow. One huge hand engulfed the shoulder of the Anduran woman in her drab smock.

I took a deep breath and wiped a beading of nervous sweat from my forehead. The native's face was turned down, but I was sure it was the same woman I'd seen crouched in such desolation among the branches of the felled *haavriathil*. She looked even tinier now, shrunken in on herself beside Raul's enormous frame.

Heinck ignored her, playing idly with his silver whistle again, blowing the shrill tones that set my teeth on edge. I clenched them, fighting down a sudden clamoring surge of the *timbra* fight response. The Anduran cringed, turning her bright eyes on him. He gave her a contemptuous look and lit up another dope stick. "Well? You got over your little *problem*, toad?"

She cringed again. Raul ponderously shook his head.

Heinck swore and threw the smoldering stick into the flames. "Now, look, you suvving—" He clamped his jaw and a muscle worked along his cheek. Then he spread his hands and a false smile gleamed in the light. "All right, now listen up, Fial-Li."

The woman jerked her face back to his.

Heinck's smile widened. "That's right, listen to the Word Man. You got your part in the This Is, don't you forget it. You're heading for the false branch real fast here. Your word is *find*. Got it? I see the branch breaking under you, breaking under Li-Nahi, you don't get back to the trunk."

I leaned closer, frowning. Word Man again. What was this gibberish?

"Word Man knows the true trunk. Got it?" Heinck was sitting upright now, jabbing a finger at her face.

The woman shrank back, terror and confusion widening the deep amber eyes. My fingers dug reflexively into the dirt and roots beneath me. No. Think. I stilled my demanding heartbeat, straining to hear past the furious rush of blood.

Raul's enormous hands folded over the Anduran's shoulders and drew her back with surprising gentleness. His voice was a low rumble. "Be not frighting. She be find soon."

"Listen, you stupid ape, if I needed your—" Heinck thrust his head toward Raul, then bit back the quick lash of words. He shrugged and laughed loudly, lounging back with elaborate indifference. "Oh, hell, get her out of here! We'll pick up the Kurtis bitch any time now. Tomorrow, day after, what the suv difference does it make? Let her get hungry, she'll come crawling in on her own. Yeah. I'd like that.''

His grin broadened as Raul took the Anduran away into shadow. He reached over to the chunks of spitted meat roasting on the fire, spearing one free with a gleaming knife. Firelight ran over the carved design on its wood hilt.

Ni-Pohn, the fire lizard. Old Anáh had done the hilt carving on the knife Jaréd had made for me.

My fists clenched tighter on the roots holding me down among the rocks, shaking. They itched for the feel of that smooth hilt fitting with its perfect balance into my palm, the sharp blade pointed at that smug face. Let *him* learn the kiss of fear. Let him dance to it, the way he made the others.

The dance of the hunter was rushing through me now with the hot, demanding flush of *timbra*. I rode high on the rhythmic surge of its song, feeling it tug me. My arms and legs trembled, eager to follow that swirling music, lose myself in the exhilarating throb of power, leap from hiding, whirl and fling myself, flying like the terrible bright angel of retribution, dropping the shadow of dark wings over him as I fell and—

No. Wait. Prepare.

"Listen. Be still within it. Don't let it overbalance you. Hear *all* the voices of the dance." Jaréd's quiet voice beside me in the hot jungle.

I took a deep, shaky breath, closing my eyes. Yes. And another presence behind me, circling the camp. A sentry, moving closer.

Damn. I silently cursed Heinck, cursed my own carelessness.

Then I banished anger. No time now. I took a careful breath, breathing in the scent and taste of the night. I squirmed backward smoothly in the dream of the serpent. Sinuous coils, flowing in the endless cycle. Yes. Leashed power flowing through me. I was moving in the quick, silent sureness of full *timbra* as I raised into a crouch, darted and ducked, moving to a soundless beat between mossy boulders, weaving away from the fire and the small sounds of the sentry. Somehow my feet knew which sticks and tangles to avoid in the dark. I fled in a smooth, rhythmic pace through the underbrush, breathing evenly, the dance humming through me to the music of the night forest. I was attuned, balanced.

Except for the bulky lyre still strapped to my knapsack. I had forgotten its muted voice in the dream dance. I ducked beneath a huge bough fallen from the heights and the harp case caught behind me, flinging me up short and sending out a low throb of sound.

"What's that?"

Another shout behind me. "Over there!" A broad beam of light speared between the dark trees, swept toward me.

I threw myself flat and the light played past, then back. "Over there, in the bushes!"

That deadly crackle of air as a bright throbbing wire of heat and light split the dark for an instant, sizzled past me, seared into thick bark. A smell of burning.

Fear sliced through me, ripping the dance.

I seized its ragged edges and pulled them around me, rolling and springing up. Hunter and hunted, flowing, mingling. I flung myself, dodging, ducking through the night, heart pumping a hard, fast beat.

Another bolt from a laser snapped past, searing my eyes with a bright line of afterimage. I leaped, swung around a scrub tree, vaulted blindly. I was about to tuck and roll when I remembered the lyre again. I crashed to the side, protecting it. I swarmed over a high skirt of bark just as another tight, burning beam lanced toward my side. I threw up my arm, lunged, wrenched myself away as it passed beneath my armpit. My tunic flared and melted a long gap as I tumbled. I was over the ridge of trunk.

"Which way?"

"I don't know, can't see her!"

"Over here, I heard something!" Light raked the forest behind me to a confused tramping and crashing.

The song of the dance was fire in my veins and I fled with it into the night.

"Damn it. Damn it . . ." Even my curses were tired, drained by the final ebbing of *timbra* and damped by gray, curling mist.

I dropped the singed knapsack, clutching CI's directional device. Black plasmeld reflected a dim, staring face. The eyes swam and dissolved, refocused into deep amber and a round, flat face torn by fear but tugging at an elusive memory. It shivered, gleamed, flowed with the mist and reformed

into a pale, narrow chin and high cheekbones, intent eyes
beneath arched brows. It shook, melted into a wrapped and
twisted shape, a demon, a caricature of human. And then, for
a second, the pale, grotesque reflection split into sinuous
serpents flicking tails across smooth, fire-licked skin.

I blinked it furiously away. Watery forest daylight swam
over the warped plasmeld of the device where a laser had
caught it through the pocket of my knapsack. Exposed by the
misshapen, melted black were tiny metallic shapes, precise
forms sliced through and fused.

They blurred once more. Human skin gripping molded
synthetic. My fingers clutching Jason's wrist as I stared in
horror at his sun-brown arm, skin warped and melted to
finally reveal the workings of the machine inside, intricate
rods and circuits, arteries pumping warm chemicals. . . .

My hand tightened on the ruined instrument. I jerked around
and hurled it as hard as I could. The fog swallowed it and I
didn't hear it land.

I took a deep breath and looked up the massive, straight
shaft of a *haavriathil* spearing the thick morning mist. My
head tilted back and back. My eyes followed the unbroken
thrust into sky and distant web of branches. Dark veins
tracing pale mosaic chips of blue-gray, intricate little pattern
pieces that up there were gaps of empty air.

I touched the hard ridges of black bark.

I picked up my lyre, feeling its weight, running my hands
over the smoothly oiled, dark-veined pale wood that had
somehow escaped the burning beams. I picked out a slow run
of notes murmuring off-key. I pressed my palms over the
strings, killing the sound. Closing the cover over the harp, I
set it aside, then picked up the light knapsack and drew it
over my shoulders, turning away.

I took a step, sighed, and pulled off the straps. Crouching,
I bound the harp case onto the knapsack again. I strapped it
on and started climbing.

My hands cramped.

They were frozen in their tight grip. They wouldn't obey.
My arms and knees were shaking. Something was wrong in
my chest. I couldn't breathe, couldn't catch my breath. I
clung blindly, trying to slow the fast pound in my chest, the
shaking, frightening emptiness flowing into my muscles. I

pressed tighter against the flat hardness, fingers and bare toes gripping, burning in the narrow cracks. Darkness poured up through me, filling my eyes.

I clung tighter. The vise around my chest finally loosened. I drew in a slow, deep breath.

I pried my eyes open again. One quick glimpse down. A long, lightning sweep of brown deepening to black far below in a blur of crowding green. I yanked my eyes up again, swallowing dizziness as I stared at the bark scratching my nose. It gave off a moist, woody smell. The bark was smoother up here, lighter in color, the thick ridges evening out into narrow cracks. Too narrow.

I swallowed again and flexed my fingers and toes. One hand, one foot at a time.

Then I was clutching desperately again, stomach jolting as the wall I gripped myself against swayed slowly, barely, in a sickening tremor. Eons ago, down on the ground beneath the dwarfing mass of the *haavriathil*, it hadn't occurred to me that the rooted immensity could tremble like any mortal tree to the touch of moving air. I clung like an insect as the huge tree shuddered once more. It went still.

I took another hasty look down. The ground couldn't be that far away. I couldn't judge the distance. All I knew was I was higher than I'd ever climbed on the windtowers of Poindros.

I threw a glance up. The ceiling was getting closer. It had to be. The dark tracery above had finally become branches. Sun shafted straight down through them, spattering me with freckles of cool light. The patches of sky were larger now, broad shapes of pale blue.

Dizziness clutched me again and I closed my eyes, shivering and turning my head to rest my cheek against damp bark.

Warmth. A limitless sky of bright blue. I conjured it, swept it over me in an arching bowl of hot summer sky. The clean, bare thrust of windtowers marching away over rolling fields of copper-glinted wheat. The tamed and channeled earth tremor humming through me, singing the balance of air and earth as the spinning arm carried me up into the windy cycle. Mylar sails flashing silver-blue and pearl in the sun. The joy of the air dance.

"That's it, child. Listen to the wind, feel the tremor. Don't fight the turning. Go with it. *You're* the center when you ride the spinner arm."

Isaac. Silver-haired, lean elder pateros, blue eyes bleached pale by all those hot summers, slow voice teaching the secrets of that dizzy escape from gravity.

"Yep, gotta admit you got the feel for it, little Ruthie." Grizzled Sam shaking his head in comic resignation, chuckling over the oddball daughter climbing in a boy's coveralls.

"Why do you do it, Ruth? Fight the Way?" A different voice, reluctant new youngest pateros. Broad cheekbones and those intriguing, changeable eyes, brown-gold brightening to amber, the rare, sudden smile. The big, efficient, work-callused hands. Jason, finally laughing with me as I broke the Rules in our wild climb through the spinning wind wheel, his hands on my skin, the hot, jolting electric touch, explosion of being, blending, merging with the song of earth tremor and wind. . . .

I took a deep breath and opened my eyes. I looked down again, then up.

"So, okay, it's higher!" I shouted it at the dim silence. "So it's a different kind of tremor! All right. But it's rooted, damn it, it's not sail arms spinning in cycles on cycles! The sky's staying still up there. So there *aren't* any safety lines. . . ."

I grinned idiotically. The dizziness was gone. I eased my knotted muscles once more and resumed my slow upward crawl.

Blue-black glinted in late, slanted scatters of sun. A cloud of quick, feathered forms swarmed up, around, and over me. A sharp, mocking cry, and streamlined dark shapes swooped down past the thick trunk, a red-brown color at this height. The *hliu* soared up again, reducing my endless, painful crawl to careless seconds in a wing span.

I lay back on the broad branch in a patch of thinning sunlight. Blissfully horizontal.

The tension and exhaustion drained from my arms and legs and melted me into the rough, cinnamon-colored bark. Above me limbs spread and branched into narrower stems against the sky. Clusters of pungent-smelling, dark green needles stirred in a rising breeze, making a faint scraping rattle.

I closed my eyes only for a second. Only for a minute . . .

I was falling. The wind was howling, tearing at me, shaking the giant tree like a matchstick. The massive trunk shuddered, tilted, plunged away from me. My hands and toes couldn't grasp the bark. The tree shuddered again and flung me off and I was dropping, the ground rushing up at my back. I flailed, grabbing at the empty shrieking air, the sickening plummet stealing my breath. I opened my mouth to scream—

I woke with a strangled cry, thrashing to grab the falling tree. Branch and needle whirled around me and settled. I was sprawled flat against the wide branch, gripping bark for all I was worth. A cool breeze touched my damp face.

"Oomph . . ." I slowly sat up. The sky overhead was fading into soft pinks and purple. I leaned over the branch to take a look down into deepening gloom and wished I hadn't.

My eyes traveled the spreading limbs. I pulled myself up the central trunk and into the secure hollow where a particularly thick branch swelled from the tree. I didn't look over the side again.

The nutrient chip flaked dry in my throat, but I allowed myself only a few swallows of water. I leaned against the comforting bulk of the trunk and pulled my lyre from its case. Oiling the wood and tuning it in movements so familiar I barely registered them, I followed with my eyes the graceful sweep of another flock of *hliu* swarming past the deep violet sky.

A long, flowing chord rippled into the dusk, reverberating. A slow series of throbbing, plucked chords. Another smooth glissando, rising to a sweet treble and trembling into a plaintive murmur of song.

The windtower, moon sliding over its lifting rush of sapphire-silver sails, whispering beyond the house walls in the night. Helen's pale, lovely face bent over her lyre, long fingers caressing the strings. Her hair a bright copper flame. Voice high and clear.

Mine was low, husky.

> *"Deep-rooted strong, I stand,*
> *High-reaching, far-seeing, wind-full.*
> *Between bright heaven and earth*
> *I lift my arms—"*

I broke off, startled. The lyre throbbed a discordant protest, ringing into silence.

The round, flat face stared from a higher branch. The eyes glimmered only a hint of amber through the dusk, but they were wide, shocked. Something between wonder, fear, and incomprehension froze the broad features. The eyes met mine and doubt flickered over the face. Glinting eyes flashed to the lyre, back to my face.

They were gone.

ten

The russet *skial* scurried up a branch, cheeks bulging with two fat kernels from a spiky seed pod. A *hliu* shot past me, swooped, and darted hungrily through a cloud of yellow-winged insects.

I shifted the straps on my shoulders and moved carefully on, arms out for balance, toes gripping, stepping slowly up the tapering branch. It forked and narrowed, thin shoots the diameter of my forearm reaching for the tips of the next tree's branches. I lowered myself slowly to straddle the dwindling branch, gripping and scooting myself along as it began to dip with my weight. Pungent needles rustled around me.

Another *hliu* swooped startlingly close to my face. I jerked back, caught myself on the branch, and enviously tracked the bird's effortless glide. I edged forward on the swaying branch, firmly refusing contemplation of all that empty air down there. I bobbed, took a deep breath, let go, and fell.

I plummeted through a whipping screen of needles and twigs, green and brown blurring past, eyes streaming. The dark shape of the split fork below flew up at me. I spread my arms and legs, grasping at slippery needles to slow myself. The narrow branch thudded into me and I clung. I took a deep, shaky breath and sat up. The fiery surge of adrenaline ebbed.

One more down.

I edged along the thickening slope of the bough toward the darker skin of the next tree's trunk, pulling myself to my feet and striding down through converging forks. The main branch was a fair-sized one, about halfway up the high, bearing portion of the *haavriathil*. I could have set up a dinner party of a half dozen comfortably on its wide, flat arm.

But it was way too early to be thinking about food again. I squinted up the nearly perpendicular angle of filtered sun shafts, adjusted my knapsack straps in a futile search for spots that weren't sore, and crawled up the cracks of the trunk to a higher series of branches. Careful, laborious climb up dwindling branches. Fast, heart-stopping drop to thin fringes of the next tree. The next climb. The next drop.

The cycle repeated endlessly to a dull mechanical rhythm. There wasn't much point comparing my slow, precarious progress to the quick, lithe shadows I'd glimpsed three or four times in the past couple days. Shy faces peering around branches above or below me and melting away when I called out. The easy swing and thrust of long arms, the careless grasp of bidigit hands. Graceful figures swarming up vertical branches and whipping down through the meshed twigs, teasing me on in the direction they flew, deeper into the tangled network of trees.

I didn't have a clue where they were leading me, or if I wanted to go. I hoped it was toward some contact or understanding with the tribe. Maybe the Andurans would get curious enough to break their Rules and hear what I had to tell them.

I scrubbed sweat from my forehead with the back of a grubby hand and shook my head over the ragged remnants of my sleeve. I wedged myself wearily against a forked branch, thighs gripping the smooth, cinnamon-colored bark of the narrow shoot. A dark green cluster of needles beneath me heated in a patch of sun, throwing off a sharp, spicy scent.

I allowed myself two swallows from the bottle I'd managed to nearly refill with rainwater caught in the unripped portion of my rain tunic the day before. I studied the crumbled nutrient chips remaining, and regretfully put the pouch away again. It would be a long climb back to the ground to search for food or water. I pulled out the two seed pods I'd picked where the *skial* had fed. Prying them apart, I dubiously eyed the plump kernels inside.

One cautious nibble. Beneath a thin brown skin, the nut meat was white and moist. My tongue burned with its sharp oil.

"Bleah!" I spat it out and dropped the pods through the branches. They hit twigs, bounced, and dwindled into dimness.

My patch of sun flickered and winked out. A dimly green, underwater light flowed around me, branch and needle and dark, distant trunks gleaming dully above and below and beyond. Lodged in the fork of one small branch, I was no more than one of those seed pods among thousands in the branches among the thousands of trees. The swimming light washed through me like the vague, persistent dreams of the past nights. I was a drop of water, a seed, a tiny shoot enclosed by an endless mesh of greenery and branch. Engulfed by the other.

A deep breath and the chill, pungent air flowed through me. It claimed me from the inside out, viscous green oozing through me, remaking and reducing me to a small part of the forest—attuned to its cool whisper, resting on its green breast, letting go and feeling its rustling damp arms take me—

I shook off the disturbing sensation. But what was it about the forest that crept in so insidiously on me? If I could only grasp it . . .

My own smallness? Maybe that was it. I didn't matter here. On Poindros the earth itself hummed to the careful rhythm of the seismic tremor rods that made it habitable. Casino was easy—nothing but a barren rock, if not for the cybernetic artifices to cradle human lives. Even on Sethar, in the wild tangle of the jungle, I'd followed clan trails and the unseen voices had been those of the dream songs—the wood carver, the hunter, the weaver. The worlds and their Ways dancing to and around human needs. Rough edges, made round for us by the cybers. But here the song was whispered in an alien voice. Humans were superfluous here.

I stared into the maze of branches around me. Their twisting arms blended into distant shadow, dim green closing around me.

I shook my head. We *had* been superfluous here, before Heinck and his rotten schemes had perverted the Resistance group. He was a poisonous worm, eating the heart of the forest, infecting everyone and everything he touched, completely unaware that he was smaller than the virus he was using to steal the life of this world. Maybe the forest didn't care, but I did. Maybe I couldn't offer anything here but a cancelling-out of his score. I wasn't sure how, but I was going to do it.

I found my hands gripping the thin branch, white-knuckled. Heinck. His gloating face swelled in the shadows, flickering in dancing flames, transformed to a nightmare demon with glowing amber coals for eyes, firelight bronzing the face to an inhuman mask of greed, manipulation, indifferent destruction of the forest and the Andurans' gentle Way. Lies and stupidity. A monster, reaching out its grasping hands. *A worm and no man . . .*

No. I closed my eyes, tasting bile. No, Heinck and his plans were all too human. I had to hate him that way. If he was worth hating. If he was really the one I hated.

"You're confused, Ruth. Let the Book of Words guide you. Truly, isn't it better to Heal than hate?" Helen's gentle voice, eyes unclouded, luminous with the vision of the Way. My clenched hands shook the branch they gripped. To hell with the tangle of truths and reasons. I didn't want to know. If hating Heinck helped me get the job done, fine.

I swung around on the narrow bough, jerked the knapsack straps over my protesting shoulders, and dropped the weight against my sore back. I pushed off. Down the drooping curve of the fork. Gripping the dwindling shoots. Clinging, bobbing, letting go. Fast whistle of air, dropping to the lower fingers of the next tree. Catching, collecting myself, scooting, climbing upright and edging down the thickening branch. My feet toughened to the touch of the rough bark, toes seeking of themselves the surest holds. The branch widened, bringing me down to the broad trunk. I climbed it, followed the tapering rise of a higher branch in the wake of a sweeping flock of blue-black feathers.

A sudden sharp cry overhead.

I jerked my face up. A shrill buzz in my ear, whine of an unseen insect. I slapped at it, slipped on the narrowing branch, grabbed for a hold. Another piercing shriek.

Above me. *Hliu* scattering in a wild commotion of wings and panicked cries. A sleek russet shape swarming over higher, slender twigs, glimpse of a small, round face, a streak of thin arms and legs flying, falling into the clot of threshing birds. They milled and scattered in alarm, a frantic beating of wings and shrill cries. Something dropped fast through them, crashing down toward me.

I scrambled back, clinging to my dipping branch.

The dark bulk falling from the sky slowed, plunged again, swooped in a tangle of wings and arms through the gaps of interlaced branches. I squinted up against the light. All I could see was an impossible, monstrous silhouette—arms, wings, hands, claws—swinging now as black feathers threshed. It dropped past a branch, seemed to hover, then shot down.

I gasped, heart lurching in alarm, arms reaching reflexively, futilely, to catch the shape plummeting toward me. I
fell back against the branch, catching a ragged breath.

The Anduran was only a child, all long arms and short legs
and big eyes in the round face. He was hanging head down as
he plunged past branches, arms fending off flicking twigs and
needles. Two big *hliu* flapped frantically above him, screaming and beating their wings to escape the clutch of the boy's
long toes gripping their scaly black legs. Their frantic efforts
suspended him, siowed his fall, carried him in a swooping
drop over and past me. I blinked. An upside-down grin
floated for a second before my face.

Then suddenly the long toes lost their grip. The birds
escaped upward in a panic of threshing air. The child fell,
blurring past me, plunging down into dim emptiness and the
far ground.

I jerked forward, too late. "No!" My branch flailed wildly.

The boy fell. Then tucked and tumbled. He came out of the
somersault, reached long arms for a branch below me, swung
around it, and perched there. He looked up at me, the amber
of his eyes clear and bright. A blue-black feather drifted and
settled on my arm. I shook my head and blew it off.

The little boy raised the flesh mitten of his hand. He
smiled, shyly now, beckoning. The long toes flexed and he
sprang from his branch to another one, swung, and landed on
the broad trunk. He swarmed quickly up it, into the network
of high, thin branches, then launched himself through space
and swung easily into the needles of a neighboring tree. He
looked back, flashing another teasing grin, a challenge. He
waved to me to follow. His fur gleamed russet through a shaft
of pale sun and he was gone into the shadows. One of the
mustard-yellow insects crawled slowly around and past my
hand over the cracks of bark, its delicate wings folded into
awkward, dull brown bundles across its back. It shook them
suddenly free, fluttered intricate gold tracery into the air,
hovered flashing like a jewel in a sunbeam, and shot off after
the boy.

I eyed the narrow fork of my branch and the distance to the
branches of the neighboring *haavriathil*. The long dark drop
between. I blew out a breath and tightened the knapsack
straps. Closing my eyes, I conjured my Casino workout
chimney—the tall maze of lumiflex bars gleaming pale in the

dimness, my hands gripping and releasing, body arching and flinging from bar to bar. I took a deep breath and clenched my teeth in a grim smile.

I lunged for a flexible shoot, kipped up and around it, body taut and poised, swung, and launched myself across empty air.

Dark. Cold. Wet. Shoulder muscles clamoring. Something hard and knobby beneath me. I pried my eyes open and rolled over to a faint splashing, heavy clumps of wet fabric bunching around me.

I blinked heavy lids. Lowering over me, dull metallic gray behind a glistening dark matrix. Drops stinging, rolling chill down my face.

I groaned and sat up in the grayness, rain splatting steadily over and around me, my sodden sleep cocoon twisted in wet lumps. My hollow of the broad branch had become a pool, and the liner was soaked. I squirmed out of the soggy mass, squeezed as much as I could out of it, and crammed it in disgust into the knapsack. At least my lyre case was waterproof.

I slumped on the branch, drawing up my knees and resting my chin on them as rain coursed over face and shoulders, running down dark red strands of hair plastered over my cold skin and clinging clothes. No use bothering with the rain tunic. I shivered and pulled out my water bottle, eyeing the level I'd hoarded so carefully the day before. I shrugged and took long swallows, mentally adding and dividing the crumbs of nutrient chips inside their sealed pouch.

I peered through dense curtains of rain at branches twisting dimly. No climbing for now. I lowered my chin back onto my knees, staring blankly.

I blinked. Focused. Blinked again, shedding rain from my lashes.

I crawled over slick bark. The thing was arranged along the steepening slope of the branch. *Haavriathil* needles, slit and flattened into broad, leathery green sheets. They were laid out in a rayed pattern, converging downhill along the forking branch into a small trough at the angle. Another flattened needle, pressed into the hollow, overflowed a clear pool. Rain hissed into it. More drops flowed off my chin to trouble the surface. If it hadn't rained, the funnel would have worked just as well to condense morning mist. I smiled and knelt to fill the bottle.

I saw the little bundle then, wrapped in a smaller piece of shiny green. I sat back, opening it carefully. Inside were two flat, puffy, grayish cakes as thick as my thumb. And an egg in a gray-blue shell.

I'd spotted the *hliu* nests, neat rounded cones wedged impossibly high in the slender, pliant shoots near the crowns of the trees. *Someone* must have climbed up those twigs. The egg was fist-sized. I shook it next to my ear. I hit it against the branch and cracks rayed through the shell, but nothing dripped.

Blessed Founders—cooked. Saliva bit sharp in my mouth, my fingers shaking as I peeled it. I hesitated, eyeing the faint bluish cast of the egg flesh. I took a big bite, revealing diameters of two small, deep orange yolks. I wolfed down the rest. Ambrosia.

I poked a finger at one of the flat cakes, picked it up and felt its heaviness. Sniffing, I caught a faint pungency. With less than enthusiastic memories of my sample of the *skial*'s pod kernels, I took a cautious nibble. The strong, almost minty taste was a little strange, but it had a satisfying, chewy texture to it. I ate one and wrapped up the other for later. I leaned over the little pool, cupping my hands for another drink. The surface had calmed. Reflected within it was a shadowy face and, deeper, a glimpse of blue. A drop fell, its rippling ring dissolving the mirror to incoherent bits of color.

I craned my neck up. The water splashing around me now was only draining off the branches. A thin finger of sunlight slanted sideways through the trees. I followed its path up to the widening patch of blue, a window out to the orbit where David and the sleeping incorporeals spiraled around the world.

Gooseflesh prickled over me, a shiver of foreboding raising the hairs on the back of my neck. I shrugged it off. Only a lingering chill. The sun would soon warm me up. But my hands were still shaking slightly as I reached into the knapsack for the parts to David's radio.

I pulled out the pieces, fingering the smoothly worked iriplat and glittering dangles of the nonfunctional earring that matched the one with the speaker plug, remembering the little hoard of bright, useless objects the Anduran boy who'd given

me the wild card disc had carried around the space transport.
I smiled and laid the glistening bauble beside the water trap.

I clicked in the battery, pushed the receiver plug tighter
into my ear, and pressed the signaler. I rubbed my arms as
shivers ran over me again. I pressed the signaler a second
time, holding my breath.

"Ruth! What the hell's going on down there? You okay? I
thought maybe you didn't make it! Where are you? I've
been . . ." The voice dissolved in a painful pop of static.

I clapped a hand to my ear. "Whoa! Back it off!" The
static evened out. "David, you still there? Founder, it's good
to hear your voice, kid!"

"Well, if it's so bloody good, why'd you take so damn
long? Shit! You think I might start wondering or something
up here?" The snotty tone couldn't conceal a note of relief.

"You just came into range, David. I cracked my chrono a
couple days ago, but it's not *that* far past dawn, is it?"

"Dawn!" The tinny voice sputtered in my ear. "Try dawn
yesterday, buzz-brain! Here I'm—"

My laughter drowned out the outraged crackle. "David,
I'm sorry. I guess I lost track. It's a little strange down
here."

"Look who's talking! Okay, okay . . . I guess you were
right about one thing. I've been running some Anduran LS
loops through here, and there *is* something weird about that
place. Maybe it's the worldplan, or . . . well, it's kind of
hard to pin down. I cracked some coded data gates and it's
the Founder, I think, so I plotted some data correlations,
standard permu-shifts, that kind of stuff, on a query that—"

"Hold on! What about you? Are you okay up there? Do
you have enough food and water, doing your grav-stim time
and the muscle-tone exercises?"

"Blazes, *Auntie!* I'm fine, there's enough food up here to
last me a year. *You're* the one needs a babysitter. I can't
believe you forgot what day it—"

"All right, I'm sorry. I'm doing okay down here. I think
I'm finally starting to make contact with the Andurans."

"Well, guess what? I got through some of that CI code we
picked up on the transport!"

"Great! Anything important?"

A crackling sigh. "I'm not sure. I mean, this stuff's tight,
even decoded most of it doesn't make sense. I'm still working

on it. But I found out one thing—CI knew back in Casino that this Malov guy broke into your file. I mean, they knew *somebody* did.''

''Oh.'' I closed my eyes, seeing CI:DUN:4's smooth, imperturbable features. ''I don't like this, David. They didn't tell me about that. Damn them.''

''Well, whaddya expect? You oughta figure by now they'd be up to something sneaky, same way they did you before.''

''Bait.''

''What?''

''Maybe I'm bait again, David. They didn't tell me about the other CI agent they sent, either, the one who disappeared.''

''Yeah, I found his file, but there's nothing saying what happened, unless they've got it coded somewhere else. He didn't—I mean . . . ?'' He cleared his throat.

''Heinck got rid of him, David. I guess he's dead. Like the Setharian carver.''

''Hey, Ruth,'' the voice crackled a higher pitch, ''you sure you don't want to just tell CI where to splice their matrix? I mean, why don't you hightail it over to the facility and I'll come down for you? Maybe you were right. That Heinck sounds like bad news. Why don't you just let CI take care of him?''

''Well, for one thing, my directional's broken.''

''What? How?''

I cleared my throat. ''Oh, just an accident. I . . . dropped it climbing.''

''Climbing? Are you nuts? Heinck after you and you're goofing around?''

''Take it easy, David, I gave him the slip. I'm up in the trees and I think the Andurans are about to make an approach.''

''Up in the trees! Are you short a circuit?'' A groan, static hissing. ''Ruth, you *do* need a babysitter! Do you realize the mean average height of a mature tree is—''

''Don't confuse me with the facts, kid. I kind of like it up here.'' I smiled. ''Anyway, you've got the data on Heinck. If I get in trouble, you can signal CI. But not yet. Don't forget, I still have to get our blank disc back.''

''Oh. Yeah. Well, okay. But watch it fooling around in those trees!'' There was a garbled mumble, ''. . . bad as those stupid windtowers, don't know how you don't get airsick and— Hey, wait.''

Another buzz of static. "Okay! I've got something coming up for you now. See, I started interrogating LS on this plant-species angle you talked about, and turns out you were right. CI's got some special interest in Andura, it has to do with plants somehow. They've got some coded loops indexed to Phylogeny, but they're in with the high-order taboo stuff—you know, like physics and all the stuff we're not supposed to learn about. Anyway, once I started running loop scans, I tapped into a big data pool, but I can't pin it down. It's free-flowing in the LS matrix, but CI's got a tap on it too. Weird configuration. I got bits—a lot of stuff about 'bifurcations' and 'zygomes' and 'purity of the strain.' Data loop packages shunting back and forth on a regular cycle. Make anything of it?"

"Hmm. I'm not sure. You know, Sarn and Garn were talking about—"

"What? You're breaking up, Ruth."

I moved the mike closer. "Look, David. Heinck's big scheme with this virus could wipe out the whole forest—once the trees go, most everything else would go with them. Work on it. Find out what CI's interest is here. If it's a touchy environment, why would they build the facility for the incorporeals here? It doesn't make sense."

"Okay, I'm still digging."

"You're a big help, David."

"*Told* you you needed me along to take care of you."

I snorted. "I still say I should let CI run a thought-wash on me. What else have you got?"

"Holy shit, wait'll you hear this! I was trying to tell you, I got a whole dump on what CI calls a Review Board. This is *old* stuff, Ruth. I mean way back, like in that History tape, you know, the one Jason gave you back on Poindros?"

I sighed. "Yes."

"Back when the Founders were making up their different worldplans. The Founder who pulled Andura—you know, there's something funny about that, too, about the way she got assigned. CI's got some link in there, but they weren't even supposed to exist then, I mean the directives weren't authorized yet. Well, anyway, this Founder got called up by the other Founder-elects in front of this Review Board for . . . let's see here, 'noncompliance with Council philosophy.'"

"Noncompliance? In what way?" I stared at the interwoven pattern of branches glinting wet and steaming in broadening sunbeams, their dark tracery fading into the enfolding forest, the shadowy . . . other. "Wait, David, I think I know. Because she wasn't planning a world-shaping for her human community, but instead Planning the humans around what the world already was?" Could it be? A world truly sufficient to itself? A world that hadn't needed the ordering matrix of the cybers to take living form?

"That's pretty much it." The tinny voice sounded faintly disappointed. "How'd you get that data? Malov put a screen on all the field consoles in your district. But the way LS is getting cluttered up now with a bunch of messy litter bits, I doubt Heinck knows how to run it. Anyway, some of this stuff from that hearing is pretty strange. . . . Well, here, listen."

There was a hiss. Then a new voice, thin with distance but calm and precise, ". . . altered perception of a new reality. Need I remind you that my model passed all cybernetic feasibility tests with a high rating? I have no need for terraforming techniques. Words are the most powerful world-shaping instrument."

David's voice broke in. "Weird, huh?"

"No, I think I . . ." Words. World-shaping . . .

". . . you hear what else I found out! I was letting those data correlations run, see, so I got cooking on the CI shuttle records, and . . ."

I was beginning to see. Heinck, the Word Man. Maybe that was the way—

David was rattling on, ". . . here with them, Ruth! I'm trying to rig up a communication system now, to bypass the CI stasis. If we could talk to him, maybe we could find out what's going on! I mean, I couldn't believe it, I thought they'd killed him for sure. You saw his body, it was a mess, and I figured no way the life support systems could sustain, but see, there was an emergency cryo-unit built in, so he's okay, Ruth. Of course he's in stasis, but—"

"What?" I shouted into the mike. A wail of feedback screamed through my skull.

I pulled away the mike, staring at it. "What? David, what are you talking about?" A cold, dark numbness was falling over me. No. It couldn't be.

"*Jason*, Ruth! He's still alive! Well, of course not his

cyborg body, but they've got his organic parts—brain and nerve stem—here in the shuttle, in stasis but he's still alive! I just knew they couldn't get Jason! Isn't it great, Ruth? Once I get into the system, we can . . .''

The tinny voice rushed on, but I couldn't hear. I was falling away into a far, muffling distance, spinning down the long drop into dimness where confusion and pain, hope and fear were only vague, jostling memories. The numbness closed over me, sealing them away, sealing me safely away from realization.

Only fragments glimmered through the whirling blackness. Big hands, touching Helen's cheek . . . those hands on my skin . . . the worst taboo . . . the coursing electric tingle of his touch, and I'd never guessed . . . amber eyes, gleaming, reading me . . . his burned arm exposing the workings of the machine . . . a monster, a demon, not a man . . . voices, screaming rage, betrayal . . . whose betrayal . . . ? Those blank eyes, dead glass staring up from the broken body, broken machine . . .

"No." My legs suddenly folded. The solidity of the rough, wet branch beneath me slowly penetrated.

"Ruth? You still there?"

I took a deep breath. "David, don't do it!" My voice was sharp. "I mean it, David! Don't tamper with the containment system. It might not be true, it might be a trap." A trap. The bait. Tailored perfectly, but this time for David. Yes, that would be easier to believe.

"Ruth, that's crazy! It's Jason, I'll just *talk* to him. I don't have to get near the incorporeals at all. He can help us, Ruth. And we can't just leave him like this. He saved us last time, you know, he didn't have to but he went in there to protect us and he knew they'd—" The voice rose and broke off.

I tried to steady my voice. "David, I know what you're saying. But wait. When we get to the facility, we'll see. But don't try anything now. It's too dangerous. Promise me."

A long, crackling pause.

"David?"

A sigh. "All right." More static. "Hey, I got more stuff coming in. Why don't you call me back in a couple hours, before I go out of range, and I'll see what I can find out for you. Ruth? You still there?"

"Still here, David." The connection died into static. I lay back on the wet branch and stared up at the twisted dark maze.

eleven

"Vanity of vanities, says the Founder, vanity of vanities.
*   All is Vanity.*
What does man gain by all the toil at which he toils,
*   Under the sun?*
A generation goes, and a generation comes.
But the world remains forever."

The lyre strings throbbed slow, sonorous chords.

"The sun rises and the sun goes down,
And hastens to the place where it rises.
The wind blows to the south and goes round to the north,
Round and round goes the wind,
And on its circuits the wind returns."

I took a deep breath. My voice was no more than the wind,
rising and falling through shadowed branches.

"All streams run to the sea, yet the sea is not full;
To the place where the streams flow, there they flow again.
All things are full of weariness; a man cannot utter it.
The eye is not satisfied with seeing,
Nor the ear filled with hearing.

"What has been is what will be,
And what has been done is what will be done;
And there is nothing new under the sun."

The Book of Words was right. The Founders and the
guardian cybers knew in the end it was all the same. They
knew it was better to abolish even the hope of change.

The strings hummed beneath my fingers into a low lament
of sound. Rippling, falling glissandos flowed out to the tremor

of branches. Needles rustled. There were shadowy movements around me. Glimpses of peering, intent faces behind screens of clustered greenery. Amber eyes fixed on my harp in perplexity, fear, wonder. I didn't care. The notes rippled on in a soothing, unthinking rhythm, a numbing cycle of return and repeat.

Music ebbed slowly into the dim forest hush. I sat holding the lyre, absently stroking the smooth, oiled wood. Above, below, around me, the cool, shadowy greenness. Silence.

The short, sharp cry of a *hliu* pierced it. And suddenly the green hush was ripped by shrill whistles and fast, flying shapes. There was no time to jump to my feet. The thick, clustered needles and concealing branches exploded with leaping, dropping forms, the flash of russet fur, amber eyes glinting, long arms reaching. The lyre was torn from my grasp as my ankles were seized, and I was falling backward over a dizzy swoop of descending trunks and tilting dim green.

"Hey! Careful with that! Wait! You don't underst—"

Something soft and pliant whipped across my jaw, gagging me. More strands looped around my arms. I caught a tumbling glimpse of a webbed net held in long, limber toes.

They flung the net around me. I spun reflexively and jerked away, focusing for a vivid second on bright eyes and a flat, broad face pressed close to mine. My eyes widened. One of Heinck's "tame" Andurans from the pub. Hot rage spurted to displace alarm and confusion. The native was naked in his fur now, but I was sure of it. A trap. The net twisted, tugged tighter from behind.

"Mmmmrrph!" I shouted furiously against the gag, tumbling back and then abruptly lurching forward, throwing them off balance, lunging at the native I'd recognized. He scrambled back hastily, swinging up and out of sight. Tangled in the net, I whirled, pulling the smaller Andurans with me. A flash of startled faces. I recognized another of the men from Heinck's band.

They pulled again, looping strands tighter. I lunged away, pulling them on the cords as they fought me, then rolled suddenly with them, into them. I kicked out, connected with something that gave a bitten-off cry. I wrenched free, rolling along the branch and over a knobby shape that squirmed out from under me, making no noise but a short grunt.

"Mmrnn—" I rolled again, thrashing free and scrambling awkwardly to my feet, arms still bound, cords trailing behind me. I ran blindly for the solidity of the tree trunk, something to get behind my back—

My feet were whipped out from under me.

And I was swooping through air, kicking upside down, dropping with a sickening plunge and then lurched up short by the stretching web of the net. Around me a whirling wheel of deep green, pale blue behind dark tracery, long horizontal bars of black trunks, branches swarming, twisting over me, reaching out to clutch with thin reddish fingers. Another sickening drop and sway. I was weaving, bobbing, dangling as the quick figures with the cords wrapped around their waists leaped and swarmed through, up, and down the branches, bearing me along.

In a sharp flash of clarity it occurred to me they were carrying me off the same way Sarn and Garn had described the natives taking away the body of the man who'd "accidentally" fallen in the tourist enclave.

The forest whirled around me as the silent Andurans dragged me on. Damn him. Gloating Word Man. He had them in his slimy fist. Had me. Miserable worm. Bloody, blasted . . .

I'd finally stopped struggling. When I tried to move, blood pounded harder in my head and a red mist exploded behind my eyes. I dangled in the twisted strands of the net, enclosed in its faint woody smell. My feet were somewhere above me, my head following a slow pendulum arc downward.

Everything repeating. There is nothing that will be done that has not been done before. Maybe it was all a bad dream. Maybe I was still tangled, dangled in David's ridiculous grooming contraption back inside Casino.

A gurgle of hysterical laughter bubbled down through my throat. I choked on it, coughing into the gag. The spreading branches swayed, the long, empty dark stretch to the ground rolling over my head, rolling back. I wrenched against the cords and managed finally to pull one ankle free, squirming into a semi-upright position in the net. The red pounding pressure receded.

They'd tied me dangling from one branch among a spreading network. They were busy ignoring me. A lot of them. Men and women. Even a cluster of children on a distant branch, restively silent beneath the watchful gaze of a gray-furred man more hunched than most. Closer, the adults, naked in their thin, sleek fur, squatting below or perching above me, hanging by knees, swinging slowly by arms, hands and limber feet gesturing as they talked.

Quietly, so I couldn't hear. Fast phrases passed from one cluster to the next, punctuated with nods, quick flicking of amber eyes, traded glances. But yes, talking.

I shook my head in confusion. I strained for another dizzy scan down through the branches. No sign of Heinck's band below in the forest. I picked out his three "tame" Andurans among the tribe. I shook my head against the rough web. Had they defected from the Resistance band? What would they do with me, then?

I twisted laboriously the other way. My knapsack and the lyre case rested on a broad limb. Farther up its slope, away from the group, the harp itself lay like an exhibit—or evidence—on a carefully mounded nest of something that looked like shredded ferns. The Andurans kept turning their bright eyes on it, yanking them nervously away. The polished wood grain gleamed in pale sun. Around me, more uneasy murmurs. Suppressed, frightened, angry gestures.

Damn. I hadn't given much thought to the double taboo when I'd smuggled the harp along. Music, and made of wood. I'd arrogantly ignored their Way, their Rules. Like Heinck.

I closed my eyes and took a deep breath. I had to try to salvage something from my bungling. Change was here, whether they were ready or not. *I* was here, wriggling like the Serpent in their net, bearing the forbidden fruit of knowledge. I squirmed and managed to work my shoulder high enough to scrape the gag loose.

All that came out was a dry croak. I swallowed and tried again. "Song."

My one word was like the little boy's plunge into the *hliu* flock. The Andurans fluttered back in alarm, women pulling infants to them and swarming behind the cover of boughs. The others jerked their heads around, eyes glimmering nervously at me. The three men I'd recognized from town swung together and conferred, heads bent.

I managed to snake a hand free and jabbed my finger

through the net, at the lyre. "Song. What it makes. It's a song."

Another flutter of alarm.

"Please listen. I'm only trying to help you. You see, Heinck's planning to—"

They jumped at me then, three men and two women, yanking me sideways in the net, scrambling down the cords, long flexible toes gripping and tugging to replace the gag as I pulled my face away. They bound my arms tighter as I struggled.

"Wait! I won't hurt you! You don't have to talk to me, but if you'd only lis—" They yanked me back roughly. A hard, thick hand slapped over my mouth. So much for timid Andurans. I twisted, shaking my head free again, gasping a breath to explain before they could gag me again.

But the thick hands pulling me back suddenly froze.

I blinked and craned past the hairy arms.

Something bright and glittering tumbled along the branch below. Two small cubes—rolling, glinting crimson sparks. Stray sun flashed on the faceted crystals, burning in the fiery, sunburst hearts of the carved dice. They clicked in the sudden silence and settled beneath me, two etched dots staring up.

Snake eyes.

I stared. My lucky roll. And they looked exactly like the pair I'd used in Casino, the ones I'd given the Anduran boy on that transport flight to Poindros to lure him to safety before the mechmen showed up to report him.

The startled silence was broken as one of the men binding me made an irritated noise and jumped down to the branch, crouching to grab up the alien dice and conceal them in his thick hand. There was confused muttering overhead. An older woman swung down, jabbing a denouncing hand toward me. Assenting murmurs from above. Grasping feet behind me yanked my bonds tighter. It was clear they were getting ready to take me to the cybers for violation report.

"Wait! Please, just listen first. You'll lose the trees if you don't—" The heavy hand slapped back over my mouth.

But the natives binding me froze once more. There was a shrill squeal below, another flurry of movement as a short russet shape bounded and scurried over the crouching man. Small bidigit hands awkwardly pried and scooped the carved crystals from the man's grip. There was a shocked sound

from somewhere above, long toes pointing. The little boy
raised his hands high, then shook the dice in bashful imitation
of a gamer, rolling them again onto the bough. He swung
around, making a complicated gesture with his hands, facing
the frozen, suspended faces and uneasy murmurs, then pointing emphatically up at me. The uneasy murmurs swelled to
indistinct argument. Heads shook, thick hands and flexible
toes pointed, shoulders raised in question. A man leaned
forward, pointing at the boy and me, nodding, shrugging.
More muttering and gestures overhead. The hands gripping
me fell away.

The flat little face below flashed me a brief, oddly familiar
grin above my sparkling iriplat earring hung like a pendant
from a thin brown cord around his neck. I took a deep breath.
He was the same boy, the one who'd hitched a ride from the
hliu and beckoned me to follow. And the one who'd given me
the wild card disc in the first place.

It finally clicked. His mother, gathering him protectively to
her side as the mechmen quick-marched the pathetic little
huddle of Anduran tourists out of the transport viewing dome,
her lustrous amber eyes commanding my confused silence as
I held the chip of blank plasmeld. Those amber eyes, dimmed
to a sharp, secretive glint from a downturned face as the lurid
lights of the WorldPlan game splashed and swam over her
leaping escape. And those same eyes, wide and terrified in
flickering firelight as she cringed from Heinck's words.

Damn. If I hadn't been so wrapped up in my own stupid
maunderings, I'd have realized sooner. I sheepishly returned
the boy's grin. "Thanks . . . Li-Nahi."

The old man sat on a gnarled hump of branch, bent and
weathered like part of it, hunched over a rain-filled hollow
where thick bark rolled in at the edges of an old wound in the
wood. I edged slowly closer down the bough where they'd
sent me in isolation to spend the night. He looked up, pursed
his lips, then shrugged, ignoring me. He gestured with a
blunt, callused mitten at a woman swinging by overhead, her
long arms and thick hands grasping twigs and thrusting her
effortlessly along. She nodded, dropping a bulky green needle-
skin package she was carrying with her feet. It plopped onto
the branch beside the old man and she swung on. He waved,

his long toes busy plucking smaller green packets from a woven bag he'd pulled from his shoulder.

I tried to move closer to see what he was doing, but he gave me a warning look and I sat where I was. I watched in reluctant fascination as the battered old feet, knuckles swollen and skin veined and wrinkled, deftly unwrapped the leathery packets. I swallowed down an uneasy lump as I noted the way the big toe was separated from the rest, set at an abnormal angle. That was what let the Andurans grasp things, use their toes like fingers. It also made their feet splay widely, grotesquely with the long toes, forced them to walk so awkwardly on land or in town. And helped make them freaks.

I shuddered with the lingering horror of the Planned shaping of human flesh. I shook it off, trying for the first time to relate those differences to myself, wondering how it would feel if a foot like that were part of me. I swallowed again, suddenly realizing what it would mean to the Andurans if the forest were lost to Heinck's alien virus. They were unsuited to any other world. They weren't standard human, smoothly undifferentiated biological units to be plugged in like spare parts in the meshed cogs of the Founders' oiled machinery. They couldn't adapt the way the rest of us could, if we could learn to transcend the conditioning of our homeworld's Way— or if we were the odd social misfit to begin with, like me. In one sense the Andurans were a logical extension of the galactic Plan, each worldplan and its people isolated and sufficient to themselves, but in reality it didn't work that way. On Andura the Founder and the cybers had gone too far.

How? Why? I'd puzzled over the fragments David had learned from CI's coded files, but I couldn't make the pieces fit. I stared into the dim green maze of branches, their shapes blurring.

If the Andurans *were* anomalies in the perfect grand Plan, what about the Cyvriots? Breeze rustled through branches and stirred my hair, a hissing whisper, and I could almost see Siolis's faintly blue, hairless head hovering disembodied in the shadows just beyond the light. The spiraled ear flaps, the toothless gums, the deep, disturbing purple eyes watching me, waiting for some recognition I couldn't find in myself . . .

I looked up to see the old Anduran watching me, something unreadable in his amber eyes.

They flicked quickly away as his toes fumbled with the

green packets and he raised a hand to make a complicated gesture to two kids swinging by overhead, summoning them. The boy reversed, hung by his toes, flipped, and dropped beside the man. The girl tumbled after him, giggling, pinching the old man playfully with her toes. Her laughter cut off abruptly as she saw me sitting near, and she crouched, subdued, beside the boy. The three hunched in a silent row, looking at me. The girl's slender, delicate toes were gripping the boy's.

I smiled hesitantly, holding out my empty hands, all I had to offer. *I* was the freak here. In the forest, among the high maze of branches, their odd, limber-toed feet had the beauty of rightness.

The old man pursed his lips again, shrugged, and turned away from me, back to his task. His toes carefully sprinkled different-colored bits of something from two packets into the pool of water filling the long hollow where he perched. Ripples agitated the surface. Then bubbles. Steam began to rise.

I edged closer, curiosity overcoming caution. He shot me a quick gleam of amber, a warning. I gestured, palms out, something I'd seen the children do to answer adults, and sat still. I didn't know how much they'd tolerate, what the tribe was going to do with me now. The old guy seemed as unsure of my status as I was. But my sore mouth was sufficient reminder of the Rule of silence they'd finally drummed home the day before. I was an outsider. I waved mutely at the packets, lifting my shoulder in a question.

He hesitated, then handed me the packets. Inside one were chips of white-streaked blue rock. The other held grains of reddish sand. The old man met my eyes for a second, lifting a foot to point over the side of the branch. Down. The forest floor.

He reclaimed the packets and returned to his task, nodding his head at the two kids.

The boy avoided looking at me, reaching to unroll and spread a sheet of flattened greenery over the bubbling water, weighting it carefully with small stones. The girl rose, shot me a quick, curious look, then lowered her face to slip past me down the branch. She stood probably waist high to me, but small breasts peeked through the thin, russet-brown silk of her fur. She returned, quickly sidestepping me again and carrying a tightly-woven pouch of brown, fibrous material. She knelt gracefully and poured water from the bag onto the floating greenery, making it into a bowl. The water inside it steamed and started to form bubbles.

I leaned forward again as they opened the bundle the passing woman had dropped. I recognized the flat white patties inside. The evening before, after they'd released me and let me trail them as best I could to their high campsite, I'd watched a group of tribe members press the patties together from an unidentifiable, shredded root and the pounded, rinsed, and mashed pulp of bitter seed-pod kernels. Now the girl slid the flattened mixture into the hot water. With flat wood scoops the boy and old man fished out puffed-up cakes and laid them on another sheet of greenery. Adults and children wandered past, carefully detouring around me, to take the cakes.

A man with thick hair streaked equally gray and russet brown paused to eye me, thin lips pursed disapprovingly. A pudgy little girl swung from a higher shoot, dropped and scampered down the branch, crawling between his legs. She clung to one ankle, peering through at me, eyes bright and inquisitive. She twisted her head to look up at the man. "Dream stranger? Those Who Guard Words climb—"

Her piping voice was abruptly cut off as the man clapped a thick hand over her mouth and raised her up before his face. He shook his head once, sharply, eyes fixed on hers.

The child squirmed from his grip and galloped awkwardly away, making little distressed noises. The man looked after her, stern expression softening.

I sat still, making a slow gesture of apology.

He looked down at me, glared, and moved abruptly on. Two older kids followed in his wake, rolling their eyes at me with suppressed excitement, grabbing cakes, and whispering something, giggling, heads close together. The man swung around, silenced them with another sharp look, and gestured them peremptorily to a lower branch where a woman was ladling out sticky handfuls of something from another cooking pool.

I blew out a long breath and looked up to see the bent gray man eyeing me across the pool. I raised my palms in another apology. Surprisingly, a grudging smile twitched his lips. He nodded to the girl beside him and she gathered two of the cakes onto a small leaf. She brought them to me and thrust them out with a quick, shy movement. The bright glint of her eyes flashed over me as she turned to dart back beside the cook.

I automatically opened my mouth to thank her, but stopped myself in time. Words were proving a hard habit to break. I smiled and nodded under the watchful eyes of the old man.

The cakes were delicious—warm, chewy, and spicy with the pungent tang I was getting used to. The berry-topped blob of sticky gray stuff a boy brought on another leaf was a little harder to swallow. I finally choked it down, aware of furtive eyes gleaming at me through clustered needles from a careful distance. The old guy sent the kids swinging off to join the others. I moved closer to him and he shot me another warning look. I was getting used to that too.

I'd finally given up my futile attempts the day before to explain what I was doing here, what Heinck was trying to do to their forest. I'd finally had enough of the net and the gag. Like the kids who got a hand clapped over their mouth if they started chattering, I was going to have to wait until an adult asked me a question. Nobody seemed particularly interested in *my* questions clamoring mutely for answers.

I sighed and nodded to the cook, gesturing carefully toward the cooking gear. He let me help him roll up the few items into a neat bundle he slung over his hunched shoulders. I dabbled a finger in the pool remaining in the hollow of the branch. The water was still warm, steaming tantalizingly in the cool morning. The pool wasn't very deep, but it was fairly long. I looked down at my grubby wickweave and the dirt imbedded beneath my nails.

The old guy seemed amused when I pantomimed my request. He shrugged, gestured to me and the pool, then climbed with surprising spryness into the upper branches.

I craned my neck to follow and realized the adults were gathering up there after their meal. High in the tree clustered needles stirred, faces peered down at me and turned away, thick hands and limber feet gestured busily. It was some sort of conference, clearly about me. I was as clearly not invited.

I shrugged and unpacked my rain gear and spare liner, stripped off the one I was wearing, and rinsed it all in the pool. Whatever the old guy had used to start the exothermic reaction in the water didn't seem to harm the fabrics, but I shook my head over the rips and singed holes in the bedraggled clothes that were going to have to last me a while yet. I was draping them in the pale sunbeams slanting across the branch when I heard rustling overhead, faint giggles.

I looked up to the next branch, into the bright sparks of their eyes. Small, flat faces crowded to peer down at me. The children pointed at my bare, pale skin and the faintly sun-reddened patches of neck and arms, bursting out into laughter.

One of them giggled and poked a friend. "Tree-with-no-bark!" They tittered again.

I smiled up at them, waggled my outlandish ten fingers, and provoked another outburst of hilarity.

It broke off abruptly as a young woman swooped down from above, uttered something low but decisive, and shooed them away in a tumbling, exuberant rush through the trees. She climbed to rejoin the adults. Bright eyes up there were watching me. I shrugged again.

The steaming water beckoned, and my shoulders and arms were one big complaint. Shrill little voices, nagging, insisting I was crazy to think I could keep up with the tribe. Like another voice, "Up in the trees! Are you nuts?" David, riding the whipping spiral around the world, keeping company as taboo as the Andurans, and far more alien. The incorporeals. And Jason's brain.

David hadn't answered my call back. But by the time the natives had released me from the net and returned my gear to me, the orbit had probably taken him beyond range. Or he'd been sleeping. He'd be as tired as I was. He was working so hard on those CI codes, trying to pry free some vital bits of knowledge from the cybers' hoard. Damn it, I never should have agreed to his crazy idea of riding the shuttle. It was too dangerous. But he'd promised me, he'd promised he wouldn't touch—

I shook my head. There was nothing I could do for him right now. David was a smart kid, he'd be okay. I had to just concentrate on keeping up with the tribe, on breaking through with them. If they'd only listen to the truth about Heinck and the wild card disc they'd taken, they'd have to see we could help each other save the forest. And maybe find a few answers at the facility. If only David would leave well enough alone. Let sleeping ghosts lie . . .

I closed my eyes. A long, weary sigh floated upward as warm water caressed my back and lapped over my shoulders.

The limber young shoot whipped back, snapping me across the back as I released it. I flinched, faltered, tumbled in a stomach-wrenching blur of green and cinnamon-brown, grabbed frantically, air whipping past, stealing my breath. Flailing, falling, I clutched among a cluster of slippery needles. I grasped one, swung, and sprawled panting across the narrow limb, fingers clenched in the sun-warmed greenery, face buried in its sharp pungency.

I took deep breaths and pushed myself upright, thighs gripping the branch. I raised shaking hands to push the hair out of my eyes, dark strands glinting copper highlights in the sun as I pulled back the tangle and retied the bark strand Li-Nahi had given me.

There was a shrill cry ahead, a rustle of black wings scattering, a stirring of needles. A quick russet body swung back through the shadows toward me, hung swaying from a branch of the next *haavriathil*. The little boy studied me gravely, then gave me the quick grin and tilted his head back toward the long march of trees. He swung into motion, waving me on after the long-vanished tribe, dropped and scurried up again along their trail.

A flashing glint of light from the iriplat dangling at his neck, and he was gone into the thick hush.

"Wait, Li-Nahi, I can't—" I bit it back, wiping my sweaty forehead with a tattered sleeve. My eyes stung, hot tears brimming. I brushed them angrily. I just had to catch up, that was all. No bawling like one of the babies they carried on their swooping flights. Even the toddlers could cling on their own to the fur of an adult's chest or back. I could damn well make it.

And I could watch my mouth too. Especially naming the kid. They'd made that very clear the first day. Naming had some kind of special power, and that was particularly taboo for me. I was an outsider. I was never going to be anything more if I couldn't show them I could do things their Way, respect their beliefs.

I took another deep breath, ignoring my screaming shoulder muscles, the raw blisters on my palms, the fading, tantalizing memory of my warm morning soak. I launched myself from the branch for a narrow shoot, caught it, swung, captured its momentum and sprang for the next tree's slim shoots. Down through meshed branches to thick limbs and a trunk. Then up, higher than before, and the long, breathtaking flight, tuck and swing through the tangled shoots. Deep breaths, grip, release, smell of hot needles and sweat, branch and blue glimpses of sky blurring past, cool air whispering, heart laboring, thudding to its windy song. Farther this time before I had to climb again.

I clung numbly to the cracks in the thick trunk bark, knees shaking with exhaustion, blinking stinging sweat away, pulling myself blindly on and up. A face bobbed suddenly before mine, upside down.

I was too tired to be startled. My hands tightened on their holds and I waited.

My young friend flipped upright, made an encouraging sound, and gestured beyond the thick branches. I craned wearily around the trunk and saw the tribe spread over the broad lower limbs of the next *haavriathil*, arrangements for the night already made. There were mesh nets for sleeping infants, cooking gear, fluffed-up nests of some sort of fiber, a broad sheet of pieced-together needle skins stretched like a tarp over stacked bundles, and my knapsack and lyre case. They'd carried my things ahead for me, which had to be a good sign. I should have been glad. I could only thank Founder they'd stopped early.

I followed Li-Nahi, working painstakingly down the last branches, obeying without protest a woman's gestured command, dropping onto the broad crotch of a branch apart from the others. I groaned and fell back flat on the sunwarmed bark, arms out, eyes closed. Sleep rolled over me in a blank black tide.

I was floating in dark waves, drifting with no direction or desire, lapped in shifting voices murmuring soothing wordless lullabies. I floated higher, black shading to deep purple-blue, rising to pale azure. The water rolled and crested, crashing in white foam, voices swelling, breaking waves carrying faces toward me. I lay on warm sand and the breakers unfurled, dropping David and Jason onto the beach. They ran up the sand, laughing, hands linked.

I sat up, sand rough beneath me. "David! You shouldn't have done it! You promised me."

Jason stopped and David ran ahead to me, sand spurting beneath pale, thin legs. "Ruth, I did it! I woke him up. He's okay, he wants to talk to you. Wait'll you see what I learned from those coded files!"

David grinned, thick lenses flashing in the glaring sunlight. He jumped back, hands blurring as he flung up a scatter of the bright-lit geometric shapes from his bypass activator screen, juggled them in air, spun them in a flashing wheel rolling away down the beach. Then he straightened, gangling arms and legs locking suddenly into a streamlined unit, launching into a quick back flip on the sand. And another and another, the grin and round lenses flashing, body arching in an endless series of impossibly perfect flips down the beach, following the flashing light shapes, dwindling away, a wheel, a cog spinning faultlessly into the distance.

I nodded without surprise. I looked up to see Jason standing over me. He was whole and unhurt, tall lankiness sun tawny, reaching down a big hand to pull me up, eyes warm amber-gold in the sun, face calm and waiting.

I scooted back in the sand, away from him, shaking my head. "He shouldn't have done it, you shouldn't have come back. You're not real. This is only a nightmare."

Jason shook his head and sat beside me. "He didn't do it, Ruth, you did. You've given me back my body. Again. You were right, I wasn't really alive on Poindros, I was only another machine for the incorporeals, until you made me see what they were. You made me feel things, made be human again, Ruth."

"No! You're not human, Jason. You don't have a body that hurts and bleeds and gets tired and makes mistakes. You're just a different kind of cyber, analyzing your data and manipulating me, sending me signals, triggering my responses, flicking my switches to make me be like you—a machine that thinks it can love."

"That's not true, Ruth. You know it. Trust yourself. I may be different from you, but I still have emotions. I know you're afraid of me, but Helen's right, it will only hurt you to hate me. Don't lock me out. I can help you, Ruth."

I jerked around to shout at him. "I don't want any help!

Not from you, not from Helen, not from the damn cybers! I
don't need you!''

He lowered the bright eyes, his long mouth twisting, so
lifelike, into a brief, sad smile. ''You don't need love, Ruth?
Aren't you the one making yourself a machine?''

''Love? You call love looking into a mirror and smiling
and making the faces you want to see, and having the thing
make them back at you?'' I spat the words scornfully.

''Ruth, please . . .'' He reached out a hand—appendage of
jointed alloy corded by sensors and chemical vessels, padded
and covered by molded synthetic—warm tanned fingers touching my arm, and I could feel the pulse beating in them,
touching me—

I jerked upright, blinking in confusion. The small russet-
furred woman was timidly touching my arm, the thick flesh
of her fused palm pad warm against my skin. I blinked again
and she moved back, setting on the branch a water bag and
more of the chewy cakes. She paused, the oddly flattened
features defensive, amber eyes flicking from my feet to face,
studying me warily.

I rubbed my bleary eyes. I held out my palms to her,
gesturing slowly at the food and nodding.

She gave me a gentle, fleeting smile and swung off to join
the others, leaving me to my solitary meal.

twelve

"David! David, come in!"

Static hissed in the speaker plug, returned a meaningless crackle through deepening twilight.

"David, please. Come on, David! *Be* there."

Clouds flamed overhead, a last explosion of sunset. Only static pierced them, the sibilant whisper of empty space.

Damn. Damn the crazy kid and his cockiness, thinking he could pull it off. Damn CI and those monstrous incorporeals. Damn Jason.

I closed my eyes, pressing my hands against them, fighting a blind surge of panic and despair. "David, please come in!"

Finally I put it away. Pretty soon I would have to admit there wasn't going to be an answer to my calls. The shuttle was back within range, he was up there. But he'd gone somewhere he couldn't hear me. In with the incorporeals. Part of the one in all.

It was my fault. I shouldn't have listened, should have known he couldn't resist, should have sent him straight back when I'd found him on the space transport. I should have left him safe on Poindros, with Marda and my brother and his other fathers. I was a rotten substitute. I'd gotten him into it again. There was no one there this time to pull him out, no one to save him from those voracious bright sparks in their awareness matrix, their energy net of temptation and pain and horror.

No one but Jason.

Was he "awake" now? What was he? A pulsing gray blob of tissue, wrinkled matter preserving fragile memories of the man it had been part of? Or finally transformed out of flesh, one in all with the incorporeals? What had those blasphemies done to David? There were no answers, only the endlessly breaking waves of impotent rage and despair.

My hands still moved to the old, blind rhythms of release.

They had pulled the lyre from its case and were running slowly over the cool, polished wood. Shadowed needles rustled around my lonely branch in a chill rising breeze. The first plucked notes were a hesitant, whispering voice for the wind. Then an angry, discordant crash of sound.

"Have you not been taught? Have you not heard?
Has it not been told you from the beginning?
Have you not understood the Founders of the worlds?"

Insistent, drumming chords. A pause, silence pounding in my ears. The Book of Words answered itself.

"They sit above the circle of the earth,
And its inhabitants are like grasshoppers.
They stretch out the heavens like a curtain,
And spread stars like the net of the guardian cybers.

Scarcely are you planted, scarcely sown,
Scarcely has your stem taken root in the earth,
When the wind blows upon you and you wither,
And the tempest carries you off like stubble."

I strummed blankly, letting my hands make their own music, drawing out long arpeggios, questing fingers searching out through the gathering shadows. No echo returned from the enveloping dark green of the forest. Random fragments of nearly forgotten words drifted up and through me. I was only a dry, hollow reed, a voice for the wind among the leaves, the grasses, the ferns and the great trees.

"For a bird of the air shall carry the voice,
And that which has wings shall tell the matter. . . ."

The harp strings muttered low and falling.

"In the place where the tree falleth, there it shall be—"

I frowned into the dimness, fingers tightening, almost grasping some beckoning bit of knowledge or understanding, something that . . . eluded me. I shook my head, sitting motionless, cradling the lyre, the last dropping notes fading with the shreds of crimsoned cloud overhead. Gone.

I stared numbly into the layered screens of needles, the endless vague march of black trunks into twilight. The breeze stirred through the dim sweep of branches overhead. The needles rustled, louder. The wind swirled whispers past me.

I blinked and looked up.

Bright eyes, catching the last glimmers of sunset. Amber eyes ranged above me, clustered in the shadows, closing in on the isolation they'd circled around me, wide and wondering, watching.

I stared back at them, defiant. I'd tried their way. Let them muzzle the song. I wouldn't.

My fingers plunged into the strings, up and down, a wild, rippling crescendo and clashing chords, a voiceless call, a formless cry. The wind snatched it, wailed with it, flung it fading through the branches. Shadows, ghosts stirred in its wake. Agitated movements. Dim faces turning. Eyes glinting questions. Low, troubled murmurs.

And snatches of words.

". . . death of the Mother Tree?"

"No. Fallen Mother."

My breath caught in my throat. I clutched the lyre, silencing the last throb of strings, straining through the gusts of night air.

"Then of the High Mother, what—"

"False branch withers, falls to the ground."

". . . so strong? It speaks in the This Is. Those Who Guard Words tell True Is of the High Mother."

The last woman had spoken aloud, firmly. She was a dim form, sitting straight on the shadowed bough above me, holding a sleeping infant cradled in a nest she made with one ankle crossed high on the opposite hip.

Beyond her a man's vague form leaned closer to gesture emphatically downward with a thick hand. "This names: That Which Has Wings. This Is."

More agitated stirring, shadowed faces and troubled eyes turned all in the same direction. Not on me. On the lyre.

I blinked, shook myself, scrambled to my feet and thrust it up toward them. Faint remnants of light shimmered silver over the creamy wood. It gleamed like a pale apparition, the pattern of darker veins flowing to blend with enveloping night. The words came unbidden, summoned by the silent strings. "That Which Has Wings shall tell the matter."

Consternation on the flat, round faces. Branches whipped and swayed, needles clashed in their wake. They fled. Darkness and lonely silence settled around me.

"Damn it, David, come in! Come *on*, kid. . . ."

I closed my eyes, refusing the drowning wave of defeat. I very carefully put the radio away. Afternoon sun slanted through wet branches and dissolving clots of cloud. The shuttle was probably out of range, anyway. I'd just have to make it to the facility. It was the only way now. I'd have to make the Andurans see. I needed their help. They needed mine, whether they wanted it or not.

I sat, turning my face to the sun's thin warmth. I was tired. But I was getting used to that. In the last two days they'd picked up the pace a bit. They obviously expected me to follow, but they still insisted I keep my distance on a separate branch.

I sighed and settled back against the rough, damp bark, watching the kids in the tangle of narrower shoots and needles above me play a tireless game of swinging tag. Two adults, hunched on a broad limb below and across the trunk from me, kept an eye on the younger children. A woman, two infants cradled in her arms, settled into a nest she'd made by bending a cluster of springy needles in on itself to create a sort of suspension bed. On a closer limb, a graying man had set up a frame of narrow sticks and pegs, a simple loom. On a warp of smooth, thin, brownish-red strings, he was weaving with his toes a woof of a different material, something faintly gray-green and unevenly spun, nubby.

I rolled over to lean down the side of the branch, craning for a better view. The man's eyes were half closed, his flat face peaceful, oddly almost reverent as he handled the fuzzy yarn with care, working with slow, rhythmic movements. What he was making must have been something special. I leaned farther. It just looked like the rough fabric they used for the shapeless smocks they wore in town, around outsiders.

I shrugged. I didn't know much about the Anduran worldplan. The standard tourist study tapes, which were all CI had given me, barely outlined the Rules for the visitor enclave, didn't go much into the native Way, since it wasn't expected that a tourist would encounter more than a glimpse or two of a native. I should have tried harder to break some codes on restricted data.

The man at the loom suddenly looked up into my eyes. He flinched, moving an arm protectively around the half-finished weaving. I made a reassuring gesture and moved back. He hesitated, then went on with his work.

There was a flurry in the branches overhead, the kids laughing, swooping down as low as they dared to get a look at me. I spotted my little friend, Li-Nahi, up there, but he seemed subdued, hanging back from the others. I smiled and waved up at him. He flashed me one of his quick grins and suddenly launched himself into the midst of the kids, gesturing to them and calling something I couldn't hear. A young girl swung around, pursed up her lips, and called something back. That seemed to set them all off. They chattered, leaped, giggled, and swung, gesturing my way.

Then fell silent as one of the women from below climbed rapidly up to them. She gave me a sharp look, then turned on the children, touching a hand briefly to the mouth of one of the older kids. He hung his head and quickly swung away. The others, abashed, nodded solemnly at the woman. They repeated her gesture, touching their own hands to their mouths, then followed her down through the branches. Li-Nahi glanced back at me and trailed them forlornly.

I raised my hand to him, but he didn't see it. I slowly lowered the arm. It wasn't the first time I'd seen the adults enforcing silence on the kids. I wasn't sure if it was only because I was near. There seemed to be pretty strict Rules for talking in general. But the woman sternly herding the children through the branches didn't pay the slightest attention when two adolescents—a young boy and the girl who'd served me food before—suddenly swung off together into the high branches. They settled into a cozy perch in plain view and shared a giggling "grooming" that would have had them hauled before the Poindros Elders before they could blink for Lewd and Lascivious and quite likely Demonic behavior.

I smiled and shook my head, leaning back on the branch and braiding my fingers behind my head. Below and beyond the trunk, the babysitters had set the kids to packing what seemed like a lot of food into the net bags the adults carried slung over shoulder and hip. They'd been preparing it when I'd caught up to the campsite earlier.

But then, shortly after my arrival, most of the tribe's adults had suddenly taken off. I didn't know why. The tribe was obviously still on the move. I had no idea where they were going, for what purpose. I couldn't just mutely follow them forever, days running on and Heinck down there somewhere with his own timetable. Somehow I had to learn to communicate, had to gain their trust and persuade them to take me to their taboo ground. To the facility.

I sighed and closed my eyes. No escape in the soft blackness behind their lids. The pent-up urgency, questions, worries broke free once more in incoherent clamor, jostling to claim me. The Andurans. Heinck. CI. The incorporeals. Jason. David. I pressed my palms against my eyelids, pressing back the sickening vertigo of alarm and confusion.

I jerked around, startled by the quick touch on my shoulder.

The little boy retreated hastily, then raised his face to give me his fleeting, bashful grin.

I smiled in surprise. "Li-Na—" I bit it back.

I gestured cautiously, what I hoped was a welcome. The boy nibbled his lip nervously, hovering on the edge of flight. I sighed inwardly, wondering if I'd ever get anywhere with this world's crazy Way. But then I'd felt the same way on Poindros, and I was born there.

Li-Nahi took a step away, then sidled forward. He held out the glittery iriplat earring he was still wearing like a necklace. He smiled hesitantly and moved closer to touch my bare foot with his. It was a comforting gesture I'd seen mothers make to their children.

My eyes stung absurdly. I smiled and curled my shorter toes as best I could in an answering pressure to his limber ones.

He looked down, blinking. Then the amber eyes, bright with tears, raised to mine. "Grief place?"

Startled, without thinking I nodded.

His foot tugged mine. He threw a nervous look over his shoulder and motioned for quiet. He scurried up the branch into the shoots, whipping noiselessly down into the next tree's branches and waving me on. I glanced back, saw the others preoccupied with their tasks, and followed the quick shape into shadow.

*   *   *

The russet-furred little body next to mine trembled with
nervousness and some more powerful emotion. I put out an
arm and the boy snuggled closer against my side, sniffling. I
ignored my stomach's queasy flop as our narrow branch
swayed among the high, thin shoots. I gave his shoulder a
comforting squeeze. The odd bone structure didn't seem so
strange anymore. Beneath the thin, smooth coat of body hair,
his skin was warm. We peered through the dark green curtain
of needles.

We were higher than I'd climbed before. The *haavriathil*
the kid had led me to was a giant among giants, its trunk
thick and massive, forking uncharacteristically into two giant
crowns with a broad, tangled sweep of branches that seemed
to push back the surrounding forest, creating a clear circle of
green around the dark skirts on the ground far below.

Cool wind stirred the shapes swinging above us in the high
shoots where *hliu* nests should have been. Here there were
only blue-black wings soaring, then settling on the dangling
shapes in tattered, woven webs. The wings flapped off again,
leaving a glimpse of something long and yellowed, cracked,
and knobbed on its end, protruding through the torn and
shredded mesh. And something dull ivory, larger and rounded.
I swallowed and looked away.

The two groups of natives were perched in the branches of
the other fork of the tree, watching each other across a gap
where a long shape dangled heavily in another web of greenish-
brown fiber.

I recognized most of those in the group closest to us—the
adults who'd left earlier. The other group I hadn't seen
before. Beneath them on broad lower boughs, old men and
women hunched in patchy white fur outside what looked like
permanent shelters of woven needle and bark. Their lined
faces peered upward.

I looked back at Li-Nahi. Cleared my throat to whisper.
"What is this place?"

He jerked, lowered his eyes. I didn't think he was going to
answer. Then a hasty whisper, "Sister Tree. Mother falls,
Mother dies." He made a quick gesture toward the other fork
of the immense tree. "Peace place."

I frowned, shaking my head.

He gestured impatiently up our fork. "Grief place." His hand made a circling movement. "Peace place."

I must have looked as confused as I felt, because he pursued his lips, then recited in a rushed whisper, "Year bears us round to the Gathering; High Mother hears true of This Is. Years bear us up to the grief place; High Mother bears us to peace place."

I looked up again at the silent, suspended shapes nudged to eerie movement by the wind. "Your tribe members?"

He shook his head, pointed at the strangers. Then he pointed at the wrapped shape dangling between the two groups. "We-Child."

I drew in a quick breath. "The man who . . . fell? Vri-Fis?"

The boy pulled away, giving me a startled look, a lot of white showing around the amber.

"It's all right. I'm here to help you."

He stared at me with unnerving expressionlessness, then looked away and quickly nodded once.

"Heinck cut—uh, your tribe's Mother Tree fell, so now they want to leave Vri-Fis at this tree instead?"

He cringed as I spoke. He nodded again uneasily, eyes bright with tears. "Grief place. Mother falls. No return in sky nest."

I pulled him gently closer, the thin branch rocking us both. "Not *your* mother, Li-Nahi. Fial-Li lives. I saw her."

He jerked his head back, frowning and puzzling, staring in concentration at me. One thick mitten clutched the bright bauble at his throat. He shook his head, eyes glistening. "This Is: Fial-Li falls; Fial-Li dies. Fial-Li lives in false dream."

"No. I saw her. She'll come back." I hoped I wasn't lying.

He only shook his head in bewilderment and buried it against me, crying silently. I sighed and stroked his back.

Branches swayed around us, thin fingers reaching from the opposite fork of the tree, rustling through the nearer shoots. I pulled the boy and myself back into the cover of spreading needles, peering down to see the Andurans swinging across into our fork—the grief side—members of both tribes bearing the body up past us.

The rest followed them. Low voices carried through the branches. "They-Children tell false dream."

"We-Children tell This Is."

"False branch."

"Tree with no roots!"

"This Is: Roots spread deep."

"No. High Mother hears only True Is."

"Words tell. Gathering hears This Is."

"No. Those Who Guard Words tell. . . ."

I craned forward, but I never heard what Those Who Guard Words tell. There was a sudden sharp cry behind me. I swung around, clutching Li-Nahi defensively.

More cries, a confused and angry babble, branches suddenly whipping, needles flashing dark green against blue sky, a rush of russet-brown. Angry faces. I was grabbed, torn from the heaving branch, swung and flipped upside down, dropped gasping. A blur of branches raced by. I was roughly caught in a breathless jolt. A thin cry and Li-Nahi's face tumbling away. I was grasped by my legs and borne in a spin of green into the forest's bottomless tangle.

The man whose name I wasn't allowed to know poked me in the side with his foot, not gently, and jabbed a long, pointing toe. I sat wearily on the damp branch he indicated, not bothering to move as a drop from overhead plopped and rolled down my wet hair.

His sour face spelled it out clearly enough, so I waited where I was as the clearing drizzle drained from the branches in soft splashes through deepening twilight. I was too tired to peel off my damp wickweave. As usual, the tribe had arrived hours ahead of me and camp was all laid out, green needle tarps spread this time in case the rain returned. I peered through the dark branches at a cluster of children eating their evening meal, but I couldn't tell which of the furry little hunched forms was Li-Nahi.

I sighed, rubbing my neck and working stiff shoulder muscles, easing the knots of another day's long trek through the branches.

I'd done my best to follow the quick scrambles and flings across the gaps, as the tribe quickly left me floundering in their wake. I *was* getting better, getting the rhythm of it, the feel for the give of the narrow shoots, my eyes picking out almost without thought which gaps I could vault. At times, when it all came together, I was almost flying—soaring down through a flock of *hliu,* wind singing in my ears, stretching, grasping, swinging up and around, vaulting and springing from branch to branch, forest blurring around me in the streaming rush, and then swinging, swarming up, sharing the high air and the dappled, branch-patterned green hush with the winged shadows. . . .

But that, of course, faded into exhaustion. My new escort—guard—had waited with his sour looks turning to impatience as I scrambled laboriously to follow his swift, flowing movements.

I rubbed my shoulders again and pulled off the leather palm grips I'd made from my moccasins. They were wearing in patches already. My fingers were scraped and sore, new blisters forming over the old ones.

Sour-Face returned, thrusting food on a flat leaf at me and turning to rejoin the others. He was one of the former members of Heinck's band. I *hoped* former. I still wasn't sure what the tribe was up to, why they were on the move, but it was obvious they'd all been involved to some extent with Heinck. The other tribe—the ones with the Sister Tree—obviously hadn't been thrilled with our company. We were traveling through their territory now, on the way to the Gathering, whatever that was. "My" tribe wasn't going to be welcome there, since they were a tree with no roots. I'd figured out that much.

But that was about it. When they'd caught me in the grief place fork of that giant *haavriathil* with Li-Nahi, the other tribe had been outraged. I'd figured that was finally it, they'd take me for violation report for sure. But my tribe had somehow gotten me off. One thing was clear—I wasn't winning any popularity contests. I was now in even stricter isolation under the watch of one or another of the three men from Heinck's band. I supposed they were the least likely to be corrupted by me.

I looked up to see one of them—the one with a streak of white down the back of his russet head—loping down the branch to me. He dumped my knapsack and sleep cocoon onto the ridged bark beside me and started off again.

I took a deep breath. "That Which Has Wings?" I held the breath.

He stiffened, his eyes dark glints of amber submerged in shadow. He swung abruptly into the branches above me.

There was a stirring, shapes conferring. The man returned, handling the lyre case very carefully, laying it reluctantly on the branch and retreating.

I closed my eyes and took another deep breath. I'd thought about it all day as I climbed and swung and labored after my guard. A new song. It looked like the only way. What did I have to lose?

I pulled out the lyre in the dark, ran the oiling cloth over it, rubbed and buffed it with my hands until the smooth wood warmed to my touch. The first moon slid up between black boughs, a big white half-disc repainting the night with cool puddles of light and twisted dark tangles of shadow. I turned the pegs, softly plucking and tuning the strings. The moon's smaller sister floated lazily after it. The boughs swayed in a slow, barely perceptible rhythm. High wind chased rafts of cloud between the branches and the moons. Needles stirred with the sound of distant water flowing.

Rippling, splashing, tumbling in a bright spill of music. The strings hummed in my fingers, pulled things from deep inside and sang out the voice denied me. Calling with a rich flood of sound, tugging with the nearest likeness to beauty I could find. Flowing like water in the silver moonlight, cool wind in leaves, rich green and the giants stirring their slow limbs over the earth.

Overhead the needles suddenly shook with movement, rustling presences. My hands belonged to the harp now. They sent smooth arpeggios up to the hidden figures, a sweet treble melody. Another branch stirred and they were silent. Only a quick gleam of amber in a stray moonbeam. The strings trembled in my fingers, caught short, fell into a disturbing note of dissonance, ripples of unease spreading outward, expanding. Then an abruptly harsh, violently atonal chord.

The disturbing clash of sound rang up to them. Needles shook in agitation as faces leaned closer, caught in the spell, listening.

The words to tell them were waiting. I opened my mouth, fingers poised on the strings, took a deep breath and—

A shrill cry split the taut silence, shrieking from somewhere in the surrounding darkness to tear the waiting tension. There was turmoil above me, confusion of distressed movement, faces turning away.

"Wait! Damn!" My startled fingers clutched a jarring garble of notes.

The distant cry shrilled again, ignoring me. It came from the night, beyond me, somewhere in the blind tangle of black and glittering white. A long, eerie, high-pitched squeal. Almost like the distress call of a *skial*. But not quite.

A *hliu* shrieked above me. Close. I jumped and gripped the lyre tighter, tensed for a rush of swooping wings.

Then remembered that *hliu* didn't fly at night.

The cry, sustained and troubling, came again from the forest. Closer. The Andurans above me suddenly broke and swarmed away, abandoning me, long arms and lean shapes swimming through bars of white and black.

"Damn it to bloody hell. . . ." My hands clenched on the harp. I closed my eyes and took a deep breath, blew it out, and put away the lyre. Shaking my head, I strapped the case securely to a shoot angling out of the branch. I straightened and peered into the night after the vanished crowd, straining my eyes uselessly into the dim tangle of branches and moonlight swallowed by night.

I jumped again as they materialized without warning out of shadow, swarming in a rush overhead, flowing over the branches and down the broad trunk. No one was bothering with me, so I followed them, hanging back in darkness.

They were gathered around someone, gesturing excitedly, an indistinct murmur of voices brushing past me like invisible wings. There was a sharp call. Someone brought down a water bag. More confused, jumbled voices, and agitated gestures, ripples of unease flowing through the tribe.

Then, overhead, another sharp cry. Higher-pitched, almost past hearing. Something came tumbling down, falling through the branches, crashing through bright white and tangled dark.

The little boy swooped wildly, swung, and dropped onto the branch, running down it almost before he landed. The drooping figure surrounded by the others straightened suddenly and pushed through a pool of moonlight. I saw a fleeting glimpse of a round, flat face worn with pain. Unkempt, bedraggled fur and a bare swath along one side where the exposed skin was puffy and oozing. Long, thin arms reaching. And dull eyes suddenly lighting up with the moonlight into a rich, deep gleam of amber.

She spread her arms and Li-Nahi flung himself into his mother's embrace.

thirteen

Rain.

"Tears of the fallen Mother for treeless Children," to be
exact. At least that was what I thought I heard as I groped my
way up the branch through a cold, drenching gray unrelenting
as grief.

The words splattered down with rain sheeting over the edge
of a woven-needle tarp stretched across the fork of a limb
overhead. Three adults and two children lounged in the temporary shelter, grooming each other with quick toes as the
adults talked. The rain hissed, stealing the voices, turning the
group into a tableau of mime and dryness. I blinked and
scraped back a strand of hair plastered over my dripping face.
My numb, sodden fingers pulled the thin sheaf of flattened
greenery they'd given me tighter around my shoulders and the
bulk of knapsack and lyre.

Since Fial-Li's surprise return the day before, no one was
bothering much about me. They all seemed worried, confused, preoccupied with an endless debate they carried on in
permutations of twos, threes, or more, the topic taboo to me.
But my guards no longer tailed me. I'd even been allowed to
file past the cooking pool with the others for my meal, though
they'd stirred nervously, falling back and rolling their eyes at
me, faces no longer turned away but fixed on me with a new
unease. What was it in the bright eyes? Fear, dormant anger
awakening, confusion, revulsion at the alien thrusting herself
so persistently among them?

I shook my head and edged farther along the slippery
bough, past another shelter, its drooping side obscuring glimpses
of a woman with another of the simple looms, this one wider,
stretching a nearly completed section of a long swathe of
nubby weave. A young man reclined on his back in a nest of
bent-back needles, his upraised feet dangling a laughing infant by its wrist while his free toes tickled the baby's feet.

155

I moved on, skirting the glistening green shape of a larger shelter suspended over a sloping branch. Vague forms of several adults gestured inside the curtain of rain.

"Both sides of the Word Key; goes forth and returns."

I froze—a wet, streaming lump on the bark—straining to hear through the downpour.

A different voice, softer. "Goes forth with the stranger; false branch of no voice . . ." The voice faltered.

A deeper one picked up the rhythm. "Returns with Fial-Li; the Word Man now hears."

The first voice again. "Both sides of the Word Man; he tells and falls mute. Tells true branch for Children; go forth and return. Falls mute in the false dream; branch falls with the Children."

The deep voice. "Both sides of Fial-Li; she falls and climbs up. Fial-Li in false dream; deaf to Those Who Guard Words. Those Who Guard Words see false branch; false dream falls mute."

The softer voice. "No: Those Who Guard Words hear This Is—"

A new voice breaking in, impatient. "This Is: High Mother deaf to False Is!" A sharp movement behind the tarp. "No return. No voice. *One* side of the Mother Tree; falls and lies dead. *One* side of the Children; grief and no peace. One side. Illness."

The first voice, reluctant. "Yes: Those Who Guard Words tell true branch; High Mother hears only true."

The soft voice, emphatic now. "Both sides of the Mother Tree; reach out and reach in. True branch follows root; true root follows branch. Mother-Children follow—"

"No. Branches fall. Fial-Li falls. Children fall. Word Man falls mute. Those Who Guard Words tell silence."

Dim forms stirring beneath the shelter, protesting. "Fial-Li returns! Word Key returns. High Mother hears."

"No! Word Man tells root of no branch. Mother-Children—"

I moved closer, straining for the muffled words. The tarp rustled as the brusque voice suddenly broke off. The greenery shifted. Broad faces stared through the streaming rain at me.

I edged nearer. "Please." I licked wet lips. "Stranger returns. That Which Has Wings shall tell the matter." I held my upturned palms out to the row of glistening amber eyes.

They turned away. Hunched shapes whispered quietly.

I moved still closer on the slippery branch. "Please. This Is: the Word Man—"

A man I recognized now—I called him Scar-Hand in my silent monologues—darted out of the shelter. He clapped the flesh mitten with its long, healed wound over my mouth. He was a young man, tall for an Anduran, his eyes almost at my shoulder level as they raised to mine. I realized the impatient voice belonged to him. Clouded amber eyes studied me warily, then lowered in reluctant apology. He took his hand away and touched his own mouth, shaking his head. I was surprised when he touched my foot briefly with his. I stood blinking in confusion as he slowly gestured me away.

I finally dropped my hands and crawled to my solitary perch, unwrapping the needle skin and spreading it over the shoots above me to make a little tent. I leaned against my knapsack. Tears of the fallen Mother drummed above my head and clasped knees, sheeting gray past my feet.

I shivered. My teeth were chattering a distracting rhythm, and thoughts wouldn't connect. "High Mother" and "Word Key" and "false branch" drummed meaninglessly with the rain, washing away into grayness. I hugged my knees tighter, vainly tugging my rain tunic down over them. There were so many rips and holes in it now it was practically useless. I was wearing both pairs of wickweave, but they were pretty much shot too. My sleeping cocoon was a sodden mess from a rainy morning awakening.

The Andurans had stayed put during the day, taking advantage of the shower to groom themselves and shake water off their fluffed-up fur. Even they didn't climb when it was pouring like this. I shivered again.

I stared blankly across a gap of gray and hazily twisting branches to another bough where a small group lounged under a stretched needle tarp. A graying woman lay asleep. Two small children played with a string looped in changing patterns between their long toes. Two young men and a woman nestled into a pile of the dried fern fronds they'd fluffed into surprising volume from a tight-wadded sphere. They nibbled playfully at each other's faces and feet, stroked and combed each other's fur. They smiled and laughed and touched each other, affectionate pats turning to slow caresses, flowing into a smooth, rhythmic interplay of bodies—over and around, into and out of each other in a leisurely, sensual dance. The

children tired of their string game and one of them curled up
to sleep next to the older woman. The other one crawled over
to the three in their tumbled nest and pounced with a little
squeal. One of the men picked up the child and kissed it,
laughing. The woman patted the child's head and it snuggled
into the nest, watched for a while, and nodded off.

I sighed as the group subsided lazily into a tangle of
warm-furred limbs. I shivered once more and hugged my
knees tighter.

Puddles swelled in hollows of the branch, creeping toward
my toes. I was just wondering whether I could locate Old-
Guy, the cook, and talk some of those blue and red exocrystals
out of him, when a small russet shape dropped out of the
shoots above me and rolled wetly to my feet. My shelter tilted
and a fresh torrent ran icy down my neck.

"Hey!"

Li-Nahi gave me his bashful grin. He looked even tinier
than usual with the sleek fur plastered to his thin body. He
reached out a foot and tugged at my toes. He scrambled into
the shoots and paused, looking back expectantly.

I looked up at my sagging rain shield, down at my ragged,
drenched clothes, back at the kid. I shrugged. I tugged the
soaked knapsack straps over my shoulders and followed.

Fial-Li had a cozy shelter all to herself. They'd set it up for
her in the curving cup of a separate branch, distant from the
other clustered nests. And about level with the isolated branch
they'd assigned me the night before. A large, tightly-woven
tarp hung down around the bough to deflect rain and chill
night air. She was resting on a thick, soft bed of fronds.
When Li-Nahi pulled me in beneath the thin green flap, she
sat up and smiled.

I hesitated beneath the dripping edge, feeling suddenly
huge and ungainly, puddling water into the small shelter.

She beckoned and those bright amber eyes met mine,
unflinching now. I realized vaguely that it had been a long
time since I'd met anyone's unblinking gaze. Her eyes were
deep pools of warmth, somehow welcoming as the hearth of a
different world. Their luminous beauty eclipsed the tiredness
and strain in her flat face, the strangeness of her hunched,
tiny form clothed in its thin, gray-flecked russet fur. They
were calm, waiting.

Like another pair of eyes, gentle and patient, deep pools of sea-green, waiting with a home for me, always waiting. . . .

No. I no longer had a home. I looked down and cleared my throat. I shrugged out of the knapsack, peeled off my dripping rain gear, and shook away the clinging drops. When I looked up, she was still waiting, urging me closer. She held out a fluffy wad of the gray-green fronds and indicated I should dry myself. I pulled off my wet wickweave. The fronds were soft against my bare skin.

When I looked up, she was handing something else to me. It was folded, a tightly woven, dull reddish-brown and green nubby material that smelled faintly of peeled bark. It was light, soft as down. Where my wet hair dripped onto it, the water beaded into a little puddle and rolled off without soaking in. I unfolded the material to find a pullover tunic with sleeves only slightly too long for my arms and trousers no Anduran could have worn.

I beamed in surprise. "They're wonderful! For me?"

Her eyes wavered, then steadied. She smiled again and nodded, then gestured to herself and the little boy, inclining her head toward me in an oddly formal movement. She seemed to be thanking me.

"Thank *you*." I reached into a side pocket of my knapsack and pulled out a soft pouch. I found one of the small capsules of ointment in my first-aid kit and held it out to her. "Please, take more of this. You might need it."

She accepted it, but smiled and shook her head, gesturing to her side. The long, burned stripe through her fur looked much better since I'd applied the ointment. The angry, raw skin was already healing over.

I took a deep breath. "Fial-Li . . . ?"

She flinched, but her eyes stayed on mine. She sighed, then nodded.

"Fial-Li, you've got to answer some questions for me. We're all in danger. It started out with Heinck and the blank disc—the Word Key—but now it's bigger, more than losing your Mother Tree. It could be the whole forest. And we could be facing the incorporeals. They're sort of like the cybers— Those Who Guard Words—but worse, twisted. You were working for Heinck—the Word Man—you know he's bad, Fial-Li, a . . . false branch, a bad dream."

She was cringing back from me, shaking her head, making

distressed little sounds as Li-Nahi huddled close beside her, wide eyes fixed on me. "Word Man tells true branch of—" The low voice was bitten quickly off. She shook her head and moaned.

"Fial-Li, please listen. He tricked you, he's lying."

She flinched again, shaking her head, uncomprehending.

"The Word Key doesn't belong to him, he's using it against all of us. You know who I am. I'm trying to help you, and I know I'm not supposed to be here, not supposed to talk, but somebody's got to listen. You've got to tell me . . ." I took a deep breath, groping. "Children show Stranger branch of Word Man; Stranger shows children branch of—"

A cold lash of rain whipped across my back as the side of the tarp was yanked back. Fial-Li gave a little cry and gripped her son tightly against her. I jerked around to see Sour-Face, Scar-Hand, and a woman I'd only seen from a distance staring through the rain at us.

Sour-Face glared at me and jerked his head toward the dim branch they'd assigned me. Scar-Hand, the tall young man, was studying me, an unreadable look on his face. He made a sudden sharp movement, as if shaking off the rain or something else. He ducked past me into the shelter to make a complicated gesture at Fial-Li. She shot me a look as Sour-Face tugged at my arm with one foot. I sighed and climbed out into the rain, clutching my new clothes to my chest, throwing a smile back at her. The other woman gave me a nervous look and edged around me into the shelter, carrying food. The flap fell back into place, sealing me out.

Long toes prodded me again, pushing me toward my proper branch.

I raised myself to my full height, glared back at Sour-Face, and set down my knapsack. I carefully pulled on the fuzzy tunic and trousers Fial-Li had given me. They fit surprisingly well, soft and warm on my skin. I held out one arm, watching the rain hit it, bead up, and roll off. I found myself grinning.

And was astounded to see the sour waiting face split into a fleeting smile.

Stars sparked the night, rolling out their luminous tapestry beyond the dark tangle of branches, glinting past the last shreds of cloud. They were cold, sharp as knife points, scrubbed by the rain to almost unbearable clarity. Unimaginable brightness piercing ungraspable distance. Light that would sear the eyes, only endurable veiled by limitless night. The infinite black depths of space holding their far dazzle of promise, the chill ether of illumination.

I lay rocking in the sway of high air, propped with my legs up in a crook of black branch, fingers absently plucking lyre strings. I told myself I'd been there, pierced that ineffable distance, paced those stars. But it wasn't true. I hadn't touched them. They beckoned, burned with the cool fires of mystery and promise.

The unattainable. Dangers our Guardians fenced away from us.

Vague, forbidden words jostled my memory. My fingers made music to words I'd found in my blind groping with the blank disc through the cybers' coded files—old taboo words, bits of banned History, a song without a tune and scarcely a meaning. I made my own music for them, thinking of those cold intelligences circling the worlds, arranging our lives, ordering the stars themselves in their glittering matrix. . . .

> *". . . nor yet exempt, though ruling them like slaves,*
> *From chance, and death, and mutability,*
> *The clogs of that which else might oversoar*
> *The loftiest star of unascended heaven. . . ."*

The limbs around me stirred, the tree's thin fingers warding off strange and taboo notions. Dark needles rustled stealthily. I could feel, more than see, the vague shapes hunching at a distance in the night, watching through the shoots and needles, listening. I plucked a rolling arpeggio. My own branch swayed with new movement in the breeze. A slim dark shape melted out of the shadows to perch beside me. Twin glints of amber, reflecting the stars.

"Fial-Li?" I whispered it.

The pooled stars trembled and winked out. She hesitated, then moved closer to me, nodding.

She'd ventured from the isolated branch they'd assigned her, as I had mine. I wondered if *her* separate branch was only for rest and healing. I leaned back again, looking up at the vast array overhead, fingers questing through a long, rising run.

"Eyes of High Mother." Her low voice near my ear

startled me. She hesitated again, continued in a rush, "Eyes of High Mother see true of This Is. Those Who Guard Words tell true of This Is."

I sat upright, holding the harp silent. "Fial-Li." She stiffened beside me, and I took a deep breath. "They're stars. Like the sun, with worlds around them, only far away. *You* know that. You've been out there, been to Casino."

She cringed at my words. Her whisper was barely audible. "False branch. Eyes of High Mother closed in dream."

I frowned through the night, trying to see her face. Only another quick glint of dark amber. "What do you mean by dream—"

I think it surprised her, too, when her hand clapped abruptly over my mouth. She stiffened, then made a slight disparaging movement as she pulled it back. "Stranger climbs false branch? Stranger lives in dream?" She shook her head vaguely in the dark. "High Mother falls with false branch. Eyes of High Mother show Children True Is. Those Who Guard Words tell True Is."

I groped for her hand, touching it lightly. "I'm sorry, Fial-Li, but Those Who Guard Words only tell you what they want you to believe. There are worlds they've built out there, whole worlds of other truths, all sorts of knowledge—new words—they haven't told you."

She shrank away. "Stranger cuts true branch? Stranger . . ." She shook her head slowly, bewildered. "This Child sees not. . . ." She shook her head again, pointing up at the stars. "Stranger see eyes of High Mother; Stranger tells true branch." She gingerly touched my harp, stroked it with trembling long toes.

Then she raised her hands, making a chopping gesture. She touched my mouth. "Stranger sees—" Her voice stumbled. ". . . *stars;* Stranger tells false branch." She shook her head once more. I could see her features dimly, the gleam of perplexed eyes plainly asking, "Why?" Maybe the word wasn't in their strict vocabulary. Why was I bound to destroy their wonders for them?

I raised my palms, at a loss for words.

"Children see eyes of High Mother; Children climb true branch to peace place."

I blew out a long breath, shaking *my* head. "Fial-Li—"

She leaned forward to pluck at the sleeve of the new suit

she'd given me. "Gift of High Mother to Children." Her limber feet as she sat beside me gestured in the darkness, wove a quick pattern of interlocking sweeps. The slender toes poised, dimly intertwined. "Children and High Mother; shadow and sun; earth and sky; dream and true. World Tree grows in balance; branches grow on both sides."

Her hand lightly touched me. The long, agile toes made the sweeping gestures again, interweaving. "High Mother gives true words to Children. Words make loom of world; words make Children strong in the True Is. Words weave shadow and sun, earth and sky, dream and true. Those Who Guard Words tell the Way."

I sighed. I asked gently, "Then why are you talking to me, Fial-Li? Why are the Children allowing me among them?"

There was silence for a while. Then, "Death of the Mother Tree . . ." A hopeless, confused gesture.

I leaned forward. "More than that, Fial-Li. Worse. But you can *do* something about it. You have the Word Key. We can stop Heinck—"

She touched my lips with her thick hand again, this time lightly. Her toes deftly reached out to the lyre, stroking it once and lifting it into my grasp.

I felt the hand-warmed, oiled wood, the smooth curves of it, the taut strings. Dark needles rustled around us, the others moving closer. The first moon pushed a pale nimbus across the rim of black sky, dulling the stars.

I held up the lyre into a cool reflected gleam of moonlight, raising my voice. "That Which Has Wings tells the matter." My fingers found the chords and glissandos of my new song, the balanced word rhythms the Andurans would hear. I took a deep breath and sang "The Death of the Forest."

fourteen

Daylight was swimming sea-green, veiled in fading drifts of mist, pierced by narrow shafts of late morning sun. There was a smell of moisture and growing things. A small scurrying noise somewhere. And a rhythmic murmur of rising and falling voices beyond the leaves. I crouched and leaned forward to peer through the screen of thin twigs.

Without warning, my footing heaved beneath me, vertigo rolling a black wave over my eyes. The massive *haavriathil* trunks were swaying, tilting. The ground was rushing up at me. I was tumbling, falling.

I flailed and grabbed a handful of flimsy shoots. They snapped in my fingers. I fell backward.

Wet moss squished beneath me as I sprawled onto the ground. I sat blinking stupidly as a delicate tracery of leaves whirled around me and settled, thin branches arching over me with their weight of purple teardrop berries. Behind me Fial-Li chuckled quietly, reaching out a foot and squeezing mine with long, delicate toes.

I hauled myself back to my feet, embarrassed, shaking my head as the swaying subsided. I shot a look up the endless dark shaft of the closest *haavriathil*. My arms still ached with the long days of travel through the high branches, with the climb I'd just finished down that daunting stretch. The Andurans, adults and children alike, had zipped down it without thought in the early morning. *They* had no trouble getting their ground legs back.

Fial-Li's eyes were bright with suppressed laughter. She gave me another encouraging squeeze and tilted her head toward the clearing beyond the bushes, tapping one thick hand briefly against her lips.

I nodded and edged forward, pulling down a branch for a better view.

They were gathered on the lush green moss of a clear, flat

circle beneath the high umbrella of a massive Mother Tree. Her trunk was enormously wide, even for a *haavriathil*, the bark black and thick, gnarled and twisted into fantastic shapes here by the forest floor. She was fringed with her own small world of moss, lacy ferns, and bushes with bright berries. High up the trunk she split as the other Mother Tree had into two immense forks, spreading branches wide to push back the encroaching forest and create the open space below. Her skirts were wide and wrinkled, spreading out into the clearing, reaching down into the moist earth. Her tribe—her Children—perched on and amongst the flaring skirts, facing the tribes they were guesting this year for the district Gathering.

My tribe squatted in a tight group a little back from the others, visibly uneasy. Bright amber glances from the other tribes darted toward them and skittered away. A group closer to the Mother Tree stood gesturing, reciting solo or in different choruses their careful crafting of the waning year's truth. Their This Is.

I caught only scattered words drifting through the cool air. Over the last few days I'd pieced together most of my tribe's debated and compiled This Is. I didn't know if they were going to be allowed to share it. They were the Children of the fallen Mother Tree, the root with no branch, their words a false dream, mute to Those Who Guard Words. The ears of the High Mother—this world's Founder, I assumed—would hear only the True Is that the Word Guardians would distill from the various offerings of all the district Gatherings. At least that was the way I'd put it together so far.

I glanced beside me at Fial-Li. I whispered, "Then once all the Children here decide the final version—I mean, trace the true branch of This Is—we all go to a console station in the forest? We hear the other district This Is's"—I grimaced and raised my hands in apology— "and Those Who Guard Words tell the True Is?"

She flinched at my word impurities, then nodded. "True Is of High Mother. High Mother hears only true." The voice I'd heard in brief, hesitant offerings over the last few days was low, but warm as her amber eyes.

"Then why won't Those Who Guard Words hear your This Is? It follows the true branch. The We-Children reach out and reach in. You go forth and return."

She looked down and shook her head sadly. "No return.

No peace place. False branch falls mute.'' She raised her hands in illustration, hiding one behind her back. ''Word Man falls mute, no voice of return. We-Children dream one side only.'' Her voice dropped even lower to a whisper. ''Illness.''

''No, Fial-Li! The We-Children aren't the illness. The Word Man took you on the false branch, in the false dream. But it was real. It was This Is. *He* is the illness, he's destroying the balance—the both sides.''

She shrank back. ''Word Man tells with Word Key. Those Who Guard Words tell true.''

''No. He tricked you, Fial-Li, you know that. He tricked Those Who Guard Words with the Word Key. He . . .'' I shook my head, wrestling their words to make them tell new meanings. ''Word Man . . . tells false branch with Word Key; Word Man tells false branch to Those Who Guard Words.''

She looked shocked and shook her head, but I leaned closer, the careful, balanced phrases deserting me. ''True, Fial-Li. He tells false words. The Word Key wasn't his, that's why he's mute now. Isn't that why the tribe left him, why those three Children in his band took the Word Key back from him? Isn't that what the We-Children are trying to do now—return the Word Key to Those Who Guard Words? Restore the both sides?''

She bit her lip, glancing through the leaves at the Gathering, then nodding hastily.

''I don't think it's going to work, Fial-Li. They don't know how to use the Word Key. I do. They've got to let me talk to Those Who Guard Words with it.''

She shrank back again, confused and frightened.

I took a deep breath, groping again for the patterns, ''This Is: One side to the Word Man; deaf to True Is. Word Man tells branch of false dream; false branch has no root. Children follow false branch; no root returns. We-Children find true branch; both sides return.''

Her eyes glinted nervously toward the lyre case and back to me. She gestured to me to follow, moving closer through the thick brush to the gathered tribes. We paused in the shadow of a *haavriathil*, still hidden by the brush, but I could make out more words now.

A man from another tribe, gray-furred, was standing forward to cast an accusing glance at my tribe. ''False branches

grow strong in dream; They-Children climb false branch."
One hand gestured toward the distant sky, "Eyes of High
Mother weep for Children." One foot made a swirling move-
ment, long toes swept back in an unfelt wind. "Voice of
Mother Tree cries for Children."

There was a general troubled stirring. The man sternly eyed
my tribe as he pronounced, "Wings of Those Who Guard
Words cross sky above taboo; wings of Those Who Guard
Words fall to earth in taboo."

I dropped the branch over a shocked commotion, jerking
around to Fial-Li. "The shuttle! It must have landed at the
facility! David and Jas—"

Her hand clapped over my mouth. She shook her head
firmly, touching the lyre case with one foot.

I blew out a long breath, then nodded. I knelt to take out
the lyre and tune it. I plucked the strings softly, testing the
high, almost unheard harmonic overtones. The top note was a
shrill, silent shiver down my spine. Fial-Li watched closely,
fascinated as they all were with the lyre, tilting her head, eyes
glinting bright amber.

She sat still for a moment when I was done, as if listening
to something my dull ears couldn't hear, then rose to peer
through the leaves. I stood to look over her head. In the
clearing the Gathered tribes were still stirring in agitation,
whispering among themselves. There was a renewed murmur
as White-Patch rose in front of our seated tribe to start our
turn of the This Is. Heads were shaking among the other
tribes. One of the host-tribe members stood and gestured,
saying something I couldn't hear. White-Patch faltered and
hung his head.

All the faces swung sharply around as Fial-Li stepped
through the curtaining brush into the clearing. Her soft voice
carried surprisingly clearly through the sudden silence. "That
Which Has Wings tells This Is."

Eyes gleamed shocked amber as I stepped through the
stand towering over Fial-Li with my lyre in my arms. High
above, a *hliu* shrieked.

I swallowed and moved quickly forward before they could
start protesting. I raised the lyre to gleam in the sun. "This
Is."

I sat on a mossy rock and strummed quick chords. I picked
out a flashy run of arpeggios, let them falter, murmur into a

long, plaintive glissando. Then the clashing discord, crying
for attention. A jitter of staccato. Rippling minors and dimin-
ished sevenths spreading rings of unease. The startled bright
eyes blinked in wonder. I sang.

Quick-Shadow stepped forward from my standing tribe,
straightening her back to the extent her hunched shoulders
would permit, facing the angrily gesturing host. "That Which
Has Wings tells true." She pointed to me. "This names:
Player. Player climbs true branch."

I looked up from my rock, astounded as she named me. Up
to now, I'd been the Stranger. Around the clearing, bright
eyes shifted to my mossy perch, to the harp I held, and
quickly away. Heads shook to a general disapproving, disbe-
lieving mutter.

Quick-Shadow's eyes met mine for the first time. She
smiled briefly and turned back to the others, touching her
russet breast. "Yia-Nil tells true."

There was another shocked stir, eyes darting to me and
away as she named herself in my presence.

She glanced back at our tribe as if for support, and they
moved closer behind her. She continued, "Yia-Nil follows
stranger; Yia-Nil climbs stranger tree. Stranger follows true
branch; grows out and grows in. Both sides of the stranger;
grief and peace. That Which Has Wings tells true; Player tells
Is song."

She dropped her eyes. The We-Children moved up beside
her, nodding, except for Heinck's former "tame" Resistance
members and a few others sitting apart, among them Scar-
Hand with his skeptical eyes. The larger group spoke together, "Player tells Is song." Their eyes flashed quickly to
me, to Fial-Li beside me, and away.

I sat dumbfounded as they spoke out for me, seeing in a
sudden flash of sublime irrelevance wet dark branches twisting through dimness, the hunched groups debating beneath
their rain shelters, the long swathe of gray-green weave
almost finished on the woman's loom. My new clothes had
been a gift of the whole tribe, not just Fial-Li. And they were
really sticking out their necks for me here—or rather, for the
song. The little people stood waiting quietly as the other
tribes shook their heads and muttered among themselves,
huddling in whispering groups.

Yia-Nil met my eyes again, flashing me the flickering shadow of a smile. The name I'd used for the shy young woman had been right, after all. She *had* been my "shadow" in the visitor enclave. And she'd just given me two surprising gifts—the use of her name and a tribe name of my own. Player. It was a powerful word, too, holding like their *root* and *branch* a host of meanings. No wonder the other tribes were upset.

And, presumably, the We-Children who were sitting back from the others.

One of them stepped forward now, a former Resistance member who'd helped guard me in the trees. He eyed me uneasily, then spoke to the host tribe. "Those Who Guard Words tell True Is. Children of the fallen Mother fall mute. Word Man falls mute. One side to the Word Key. One side to the Player. High Mother heals." He hung his head in resignation.

There was an eager rumble of assent from among the other tribes.

"No!" I jumped to my feet. So that was it. They wanted us to take the Steps of Healing.

I took a deep breath. "No. This Is: Word Man steals Word Key; tells Children false Is. Tells Those Who Guard Words false Is; false branch bears false word guardians." I gestured overhead. "Wings of false word guardians cross sky; wings of false word guardians fall to earth in taboo. False word guardians grow in taboo; Way of no root and no branch. Children know True Is; Children *make* true branch."

Again the shaking heads, distressed sounds, bewilderment on the round, flat faces. How could I explain to them that they could do something about it, not just wait for the cybers— Those Who Guard Words—to tell them how to interpret their reality? From what I could see, their whole binary system— the insistent warp and woof of sun/shadow, go/return, earth/sky; and the true/dream, yes/no format of the This Is—was tailor-made for the kind of manipulation Heinck and his grid rider Malov had been pulling off. I was beginning to see why CI considered Andura such an exemplary worldplan. It was designed for control.

I could probably demand the wild card disc right now and tell them I'd make everything right with the cybers. I could tell the tribes I'd been sent by Those Who Guard Words to recover the Word Key, that I'd tell the cybers This Is and they'd make everything return to peace, to balance, to the even cycle of both sides. But I wouldn't use Heinck's tactics, even if I could use the power of the Player to become another Word Man. The Andurans had to learn they could act on their own.

I knew very well that would mean the end of their innocent paradise. The death of their sacred mysteries. That was what the Resistance was about. The changeless perfection of the High Mother, the Founder's flawless Plan, couldn't exist in the new system struggling to be born. I'd argued it all with myself too many times. But that didn't make it easier to be cast in the role of the Serpent.

My foot was nudged gently. I started and looked up. Fial-Li smiled briefly, curled her toes around mine, and squeezed. "Children tell."

I looked at the Andurans, already splitting into gesturing, arguing little groups, casting their nervous bright glances my way. I nodded wearily and followed Fial-Li away through dissolving shreds of mist. The next deal was theirs.

The sun was hot. It filled the noon with a breezeless gold haze, brimmed the edges of the small glen, dazzled over the smooth-sheeted waters of the pond. The air was still, heavy with resins and heated earth, silent except for the sleepy drone of insects. The rocks by the water's edge were rounded, cushioned by thick moss warm on my naked back. The sun flamed red behind my eyelids, flowed simmering over my neck and breasts, puddled hot between my hip bones, trickled slowly through my bare toes. There was a soft, barely perceptible rhythmic lapping against the rocks. The muted buzz of tiny wings.

Droning flight merged with lapping wavelets, slow thud of heartbeat, deep cycling blood and breath melting into small stirrings of leaves. I was floating in the blood-warm water, in a golden bubble of air, a moist froth of pale green leaves. The leaves swelled, grew around me, a veined green hand holding me. Around me more leaves rustled, stirring in a vagrant breeze.

It was faintly cool, touching my face with a whispered breath. The leaves shook. Green hands trembling. Rustling whispers. Louder—

—and I was suddenly sitting upright, naked on the rock, heart giving a painful thud, turning as the bushes stirred and parted. A hand pushed them aside. Eyes, gold-amber in the sun, peered through at me.

He stepped out onto the rocks, then stopped short. The tawny face with its wide cheekbones, the big hands and lanky height, the sun-streaked hair a little long and shaggy in the back as always, the gold-flecked brown eyes flaring to bright amber as he looked down at me. The grave expression giving way to a slow smile, suddenly breaking like a bright wave into the quick flash of white teeth. "Ruth."

The hot sunlight had frozen around me. I could only stare.

"Ruth, you're okay! I'm so glad we found you. David's been worried."

My tongue was dry, thick, wouldn't move properly. "David?"

"He's fine, Ruth. But you?" Jason's flashing smile had faded back to his grave, waiting expression. "I've thought of you so often. Like this, with the sun burning in your hair. . . . Ruth?" He took a step closer, stopped, held down his hand to me.

I sat staring at it.

His voice was low. "Ruth, won't you forgive me?"

I stared at his broad, callused, work-toughened hand, at the construct I knew was alloy joints, circuits, heated fluids pumped by a false pulse, encased in synthetic covering. All the screaming curses, questions, accusations, the endless rehearsals of argument and fear rose in a clamoring babble inside my ears, a bubble bursting in a painful explosion inside me. My heart was pounding crazily. I looked up from Jason's big hand held out to me, met the bright eyes waiting.

There was an empty jolting in my stomach. It all fell away, all the reasons not to trust this sudden presence, everything except the need to just touch him.

He dropped to his knees on the moss and reached out for me, his eyes holding mine. Their bright curves mirrored my face, drained pale with suddenness.

I shook my head, slowly against a warm, thick tide rising over me, unreasoning flesh-memory, desire, need, a heaviness holding me back from running. His bright eyes sparking from mine. Mirroring my doubts, my guilt.

The gentle voice. "It's only your fear, Ruth. Aren't all relationships a little like mirrors, returning as you give?"

I looked down from the entreating eyes. I couldn't grasp the anger I wanted, the old rage that lay somewhere beneath the soft, enveloping unthinking. Maybe he was right. Maybe it had been the same with Jaréd, whose smile Jason had taken. Maybe then, too, I had seen only a new me I'd wanted, reflected in the dark contours of his eyes. Hadn't I learned anything from the dream dances?

I met the gold-brown eyes again. They glinted sparks of amber as his arms slowly came around me. And I held him suddenly, fiercely, against me. His arms tightened, heart thudding against me, low voice murmuring over me. I reached up with shaking fingers, pulled back his shirt, felt his smooth skin press against my breasts. He made a sharp sound in his throat. My fingers slid over his shoulders. His strong, wiry back. Solid and real. The warm, spicy smell of him enveloped me. I held him tighter—an end to the lonely grief, knotted fetters falling away in a blind rush of being. Touching. He bent his head to kiss me and the familiar, ecstatic tingle coursed between us. Boundaries of skin dissolved. We were floating, plunging together through amber-gold currents, whirling deeper as I wrapped myself around him and his touch flowed over me, into me.

Sorrow and joy. Comfort and striving. Fire and water. All at once in an unfolding explosion of sparks as we merged.

Sparks. One in all. Lights, sharp stars, tumbling over me. And the sudden icy stab of fear. Panic jolting through me in electric shock as I opened my eyes to see his face gone blank, his lifeless eye sockets blazing bright amber lights. The burning stars of the incorporeals swarmed out of them to claim me.

A horrified cry tore from my throat. "No!" I choked, struggling in the grip of hard, unyielding arms.

"Hush, Ruth." The voice had gone toneless. "Don't be afraid. Come with us." It was the lifeless voice of the console, melting into hypnotic mood music, merging with the clamoring voices blended in the one in all of the incorporeals.

"No!" I was screaming, tearing away from the monster, running. The Jason cyborg surged after me, amber eyes blazing, mouth open on a sharp gleam of teeth. He came after me, legs churning in a blur of speed, outlines fading and reforming. He leaped and when he landed it was on four tawny-furred legs. He sprang forward, a deadly graceful feline, amber eyes burning with blood hunger. The black collar of the incorporeals encircled his furry throat. I ran on in panic. The berserk pardil leaped after me, plunged through the field of waving copper wheat, pounced with sharp claws onto David's back.

"Ruth! Save me!" David screamed, pain shrieking out of memory as the razor claws tore him once more, leaped once again out of the tall wheat of Poindros.

I grabbed his hand, ripping him free, feeling the claws rake my leg, bleeding, stumbling, running from the pardil and its murderous amber eyes as the wheat stems clutched at us, whispering hissing secrets in the hot wind. The Andurans were there, above us, riding the great wheel of the windtower, clinging to the spokes as the silver-blue sails bore them around and around in the high cycle. Their soft amber eyes were turned down to us where we leaped in vain to catch the tip of the spokes. But none of them reached out an arm to us as they swept past the ground. We cried, begged, strained upward hopelessly, the hot breath of the incorporeals at our backs.

"Reach out your arms! Stop them! Help us!" But my voice had no sound.

The Andurans stared down with blank faces, amber eyes deep and dreaming. I tried to run but the ground kept slipping by beneath me and I couldn't run and it melted and flowed, sucking me down. The pardil with Jason's eyes, claws of slicing mirrors, was leaping. The immense wheel spun above me, whispering with the wind and wheat, around and around in the windy cycle, whispering—

"No!" I jerked up, yanking away from a grasping hand. "No!"

I stared blankly at Fial-Li's face bent over me.

She smiled gently. She touched my damp forehead. "Only dream."

I blinked and took a deep, shuddering breath. Yes. Only the dreamworld. Betrayed by dreams. Betrayed by the flesh. But the Andurans wouldn't understand. They didn't see it the way the Setharian dream weavers did, another realm of truths to enlighten the waking world. But maybe the Andurans were right. A dream was only a false branch. Prune it, make it go away. I blinked again and pushed back the lingering windy whisper, the false beckoning voice, the faint susurrus of a great, light-spinning wheel. . . .

I groaned and rubbed my face. I blinked, staring blankly at the long scar on my leg from the claws of the pet pardil the Poindros incorporeals had driven mad. I took another deep breath. I looked up at the ring of great trees standing back from the verge of the pond, holding out their twisting arms in a vain attempt to catch all of the overspilling sunlight.

I looked down to see Fial-Li glancing nervously away from the open expanse of water I'd chanced upon. She didn't like it. "You don't have to stay here with me, Fial-Li. I don't want to keep you from your place with the Children at the Gathering."

She dropped her eyes and spoke haltingly. "Fial-Li has no place. Fial-Li falls on false branch."

"No! That's not true!" I shook my head sharply, shaking off the thickness of sleep. "The others helped Heinck too. It wasn't your fault. That's what I've been trying to tell them! They've got to understand that—"

She silenced me with a gentle hand. Her eyes were dazzling gold in the bright sun. "Two sides to the Player; tell and hear. Children tell; words return." Her hand touched my hair, stroked my arm.

"But don't you see we've got to—"

She shook her head. "Branch grows." *What will be, will be.*

I sighed and sat back on the warm, spongy moss. I rolled over on the rock to dip a finger into the shivered surface of the pond. "Well, as long as we're waiting . . ."

I jumped up, ran, and plunged into the icy shock of the water. It was clear as glass, cold as sobriety. I stroked quickly up through it, breaking the surface, treading water, flinging drops from my head. Fial-Li had risen on the rock, frozen in shock with a hand reaching out for me.

I called, "I'm okay! Feels great!" I swam fast, blood surging, tingling, rushing the cleansing touch of the water through me. I dove down, deeper into cold, then up into a dazzle of sun on ripples. Shivering, I heaved myself out onto the rocks. I slapped drops from my skin, laughing despite myself at the alarm on Fial-Li's face.

"Don't worry. I learned how to swim on Sethar." I touched

her shoulder and she flinched. I bent lower, sobering as I saw her face. "It's not taboo, is it?" I gestured toward the water, the welcome rare gleam of sun over the open stretch.

She glanced nervously toward it and away. She shook her head, gave me another odd look. Her voice was barely audible. "Children see . . . water climb . . . not on true branch; Children see water climb not on dream branch. Not . . ."

"At all?" I straightened. "No one's ever tried it?"

She shook her head again, shuddering slightly, a delicate movement of distaste.

I slapped more water off, wrung out my hair, and sat on the rock. "Hmm." I looked out at the dancing dazzles of light. "I guess it must be like Poindros, climbing the windtowers . . . I told you about them, right?"

She nodded, sitting a little apart from me, eyes lowered against the sun.

I watched the water. "Well, I liked to climb and Isaac let me. It wasn't against the Rules because I was still a girl—I was hiding my curse, hadn't had to light my womanhood candle yet . . ." I raised a hand, groped for translations, dropped it. "Anyway, I guess nobody'd thought about saying a girl couldn't climb towers. But I was definitely not a *nice* girl, out there in the fields with the men, wearing my brother's coveralls."

I glanced to the side to see her looking at me now, a puzzled expression on her face, but curious too. She bit her lip. "Stranger Children climb and not climb? This Child sees not. . . ."

I smiled. "Only the men are allowed to climb, Fial-Li. It's against our Rules for women to do it."

She looked distressed. "Children climb true branch to both sides! Children see the Way on high branch!"

I nodded. "I know. But my world has a different Way. I guess that's why I left. I was looking for something." I shrugged, gazing out at the water again.

Warm toes touched mine. I jerked my face around to see her smiling gently at me. I met her eyes and they searched mine, looking for something too. I didn't know what. But suddenly I felt a kinship with her that made our different worlds, different shapes, irrelevant. I smiled back.

She nodded quickly, ducking her head, suddenly shy again. She made a funny little gesture, her lips quirking to the side and her toes pointing to the chilled gooseflesh still prickling my pale skin. She wrinkled her brow in question.

I chuckled and lay back in the sun. "You're lucky you have that warm coat built in."

The smile quirked higher and she edged over to perch closer to me. "Groom?" Her nimble toes touched my long snarls of wet hair.

I smiled, surprised. "Thank you."

It was strangely peaceful by the water in the noon heat with Fial-Li, listening to the small sounds of the forest, watching the shifting pattern of filtered light through dense greenery, breathing in rich scents of earth and wood simmered by sun. Her quick toes separated my tangled hair, combed the long strands straight, wove them into a tight knot at my neck, and secured it with a thin strand of vine she plucked and twisted. Her limber feet moved lightly over my shoulders and back. Again I was surprised to hear her soft laughter.

I turned around to face her and she raised a foot, wiggled the toes, and "combed" them down over my bare chest. She raised her thick palms in another humorous gesture of incomprehension. She slid her toes over the smooth skin of my stomach to comb the little patch below, eyes widening in mock amazement.

I imitated her shrug and we both laughed. She grasped one of my feet and raised it to her sleek shoulder, guiding it down through the brown-russet fur tinged with a sprinkling of gray. I shook my head at the awkwardness of my short toes. She showed me again, spreading my toes and raking them through the thin fur.

It was warm and soft and fine. I couldn't decide whether it was very thin fur or very thick hair, but it felt luxurious between my bare toes.

Fial-Li smiled and closed her eyes, making small sounds of pleasure as I stroked her. Her toes slid deftly over my thighs, moved up to trace the contours of my breasts. They slowly slid downward, combing gently through my patch of pubic hair. They began to stroke softly. She made a low purring noise and opened her eyes to smile at me. Her eyes held mine, bright pools of sun-drenched amber, calm and warm, openly sensual.

Amber eyes. I looked down, shaking my head. I used my

hands now, gently lifting her foot away, squeezing the toes with my fingers. "Fial-Li, I'm sorry. I can't—"

She drew back quickly, ducking her head in the old shy defensiveness around outsiders.

"Wait, Fial-Li, don't—"

She glanced up briefly, hurt. She gestured to herself, her voice reluctant, "Stranger? Tree toad?"

"No, Fial-Li!" I grasped her shoulders. "False branch of Word Man. This Is: Fial-Li shines like the sun on water. Fial-Li moves like the wings of the *hliu*. You're beautiful. True Is."

She raised her eyes to mine. The hurt shaded into puzzlement.

I poked a finger through the spongy moss beneath me. "It's me, Fial-Li. Or maybe the Way of my homeworld. I've never gotten comfortable with the idea of making love with a woman." I couldn't explain to her. Or myself. Jason. Amber eyes. The whole damned tangle.

She tilted her head. "Player's Way? One side of pleasure?"

I gave her a crooked smile. "We could learn a lot from you, too, Fial-Li. Thank you for trusting me."

She smiled slowly, amber eyes deep and warm as she reached out a hand to awkwardly grasp mine. The smile broadened as my clumsy toes squeezed hers.

And we both jumped at a sudden shrill squeal in the bushes. I jerked around to see a *skial* dart in a flash up a nearby scrub tree. The surrounding brush shook and a furry little shape tumbled through, loping over the mossy boulders to us.

Li-Nahi gave me his fleeting grin and squirmed excitedly against his mother, nuzzling her. He straightened, took a deep breath, and announced importantly, "All-Children tell: That Which Has Wings tells This Is. Word Key returns to Player." He held out to me the shiny wild card disc.

fifteen

Old-Guy nodded approval at the young girl carefully working her hands into the dirt at the base of a tall, fleshy green plant with a white-fringed top.

I paused above them, on the lip of a green-dappled bowl in the forest, shifting the heavy bag of exocrystals and roots I'd dug for Old-Guy. I started down the side of the depression. It was rounded, cupping a miniature wood of slender, straight white trunks rising to a delicate canopy of round, pale emerald leaves overshadowed by the thrust of a dark *haavriathil*. There was a carpet of soft moss and gently arching ferns. Scattered shoots of the tall plants bowed white fringes over the lower fronds.

A small horde of children surrounded Old-Guy. He patted the head of one who held out something for inspection and gently pushed back a toddler who scurried under the legs of the others. They stirred and giggled as I peered over their heads.

The digging girl broke off one lobe of the plant's root. She held it up in one hand, hiding the empty hand behind her back, gesturing and looking a question. Old-Guy nodded, then tilted his head my way. The girl smiled shyly, held the root out for me to see, and put it into a small bag hung on her hip. The other children helped her smooth the dirt back around the remaining roots. The smallest child gave the earth a token pat and playfully pounced on the old man, swinging from his arm. Old-Guy made a face at him, smacked his bottom, and sent him scurrying off in a fit of giggles. They all swarmed away to dig around the other fringed plants.

Old-Guy rubbed his back and winced, easing down on the soft moss and leaning against the slope of rising ground. "Player is strong." He gave me the same approving nod he'd given the young girl. He rubbed his lower back again. "Peace place close for . . ." he touched his chest, "Gral-Div."

I blinked in surprise as he named himself, but he was looking past me, watching the children with a contented expression. I smiled and for a moment the flat, weathered face flickered and reformed to old Sam's, gray fur melting into a grizzled cap of thinning hair, amber eyes fading into blue washed out by all those hot summer suns. "Won't be long before it's the rocker and a shady porch for me. . . ." His mellow grin, the comfortable acceptance of the seasons turning. The enduring rhythm of the cycles of Poindros. The long, dreaming peace of Andura.

But that was gone, the sleep shattering. I couldn't go back. Nobody could go back. Everything was changing, whether they knew it or not.

I looked up at a sudden rustling overhead. A lean shape flowed over the limbs of one of the slender, leafy trees, swung on a dipping branch, and dropped gracefully beside us. Scar-Hand gave me a quick look, amber glinting. His nostrils flared as he took a deep breath. He took another, eyes fixing intently on mine. He started to step closer, stopped in a hesitation that sat oddly with his usual brisk impatience, then turned abruptly to Old-Guy. He tilted his head toward me in question. "Stranger? They-Child?"

Old-Guy pursed his lips, glancing from Scar-Hand to me. Looking inexplicably amused, he shrugged. "Player."

Scar-Hand gave me another uneasy look. He bent to murmur something close to the hunched man's ear. Old-Guy nodded, wincing once more as he sat up.

Scar-Hand reached out surprisingly gently to touch the gray head. He slipped smoothly behind the older man and began rubbing his back with limber toes, making low, soothing sounds. Old-Guy closed his eyes and a slow smile spread over his face. I closed my eyes and shadows of distant candlelight flickered behind their lids—Helen's dimly lit parlor, night wind howling outside the walls. Sam's eyes closed in tired contentment as Jason's strong fingers coaxed the aches from the older man's shoulders. The big hands of my mother's youngest husband, my new father, moving with the rhythms of my harp as he looked up suddenly and our eyes met in a taboo recognition. . . .

I shook my head. Scar-Hand's eyes were fixed on me, wary.

I waited, looking down at my hands, as the young man

massaged the older man's back. Old-Guy finally dozed off, curling up on the soft moss. Scar-Hand still studied me. He seemed oddly tense. Finally he pointed to my neck, speaking in a low, rushed voice, "Stranger now Word Woman?"

"No!" My hand went to my necklace, where the wild card disc, the Word Key, hung once more beside my IDisc. "No." I still didn't know his true name. Most of the tribe seemed to accept me now, but he and a few others remained aloof and suspicious. "Player only tells This Is. The world belongs to the Children; Children tell true branch. Children *make* true branch; Children . . ." I sighed in frustration. "You have *choices*, Scar-Hand! You don't have to let Heinck or the cybers tell you what to do! You can—" I bit my lip.

He frowned and looked away from me, staring into the forest. He finally looked back at me, eyes narrowing. "No branch of Word Man? No branch of Word Woman?"

I took a deep breath. "True."

Maybe I was blowing my chance to lead them against Heinck. But it was their right to decide if they wanted to be part of the Resistance and challenge the cybers' Plan. Maybe Scar-Hand wasn't on my side, but he might ultimately help his people more than the ones who'd agreed to let me decide the true branch for them. Maybe Scar-Hand and some of the other skeptics were coming to understand, like Fial-Li and Shadow—Yia-Nil—that they had options. I sat quiet, waiting.

He studied me, the suspicion in his eyes fading into puzzlement. He looked down, looked up at me again.

There was a high squeal in the bushes above us. A young boy and girl burst through them, loping down to us, chattering in excitement. The boy hurried over and grabbed Scar-Hand's foot. "Tell *liava* false-true?" He hovered expectantly.

The girl scrambled after him and tugged Scar-Hand's arm. He cast another quick look at me, then followed the kids. I tagged along.

The kids led us to the base of a *haavriathil*, dropping into a shadowy nook between flaring skirts of the giant tree and pointing proudly at something on the ground. I peered, but couldn't see what the excitement was all about. It was only a small plant with stiff, spiky, dark green leaves. I'd seen hundreds just like it during the past few days of foraging trips between sessions of This Is meetings. But Scar-Hand and the kids were examining it closely, turning over the leaves and murmuring, pointing out vein patterns on the underside.

The boy's eagerness finally burst out. "False *liava*?"

Scar-Hand nodded, ruffling the kids' fur. "Good. Children take false *liava* to place of Those Who Guard Words."

The kids nodded gravely, then looked at each other and beamed. They quickly dug up the little plant with its roots, put it in a woven bag, and ran off with exuberant little shrieks.

I reached out to touch Scar-Hand's shoulder as he turned to leave. "False *liava*?" I held out my hands in puzzlement.

His eyes met mine, wary again. His nostrils flared once more. Then his stiff expression softened, and I remembered the oddly apologetic way he'd sent me to my isolation on that high, rainy branch. He reached out slowly with one foot, balancing easily on the other leg, and stroked my bare calf below my rolled-up trousers. His toes gently squeezed mine. "They-Child?" He lightly touched my chest.

Damn. He was giving me a chance, and I didn't know what to do. I touched my chest doubtfully. "Player . . ."

He made a quick shrugging motion and pulled his foot back. He gestured brusquely at the ground where the plant had been. "Those Who Guard Words tell true growth; Those Who Guard Words know false growth. False growth in false dream; High Mother sees only true."

"Oh." I frowned. "Then that's why . . ." I groped for the right words. My tribe and the others had spent a lot of time, between debates over the new district This Is, combing the host tribe's territory. More time than the few provisions they'd gleaned would warrant. "Those Who Guard Words take false growth? But where?"

He winced. "False branch grows in false dream."

"Hmm." I looked down, scuffing at the loose dirt with my toe. I'd finally pieced together from Fial-Li that the Gathering place rotated through an eight-year cycle to the Mother Tree of each of the eight tribes in the district. When each tribe had presented its year's This Is and they had debated over a new district This Is, they would all go to a place of Those Who Guard Words—what had to be one of the hidden forest console cubicles—and recite it. The cybers would distill all the different district reports and "tell the True Is of the High Mother," which would effectively become reality for all the

Andurans for that year. Anything else was false branch, false dream.

And now it looked like the Gatherings had another purpose too. Funny old Sarn and Garn, with their "green friends" and their contraplan classification hobby, may have stumbled on the truth. If this world was some sort of plant preserve, the cybers were making sure it wouldn't change. The Children would be perfect observers for them, intimate as they were with the forest. And CI was apparently involved somehow. But why would Anduran LS *or* CI risk installing the incorporeal storage facility here? Things were getting complicated.

But all the more reason to stop Heinck.

I looked up from the ground. "Scar-Hand?" But he'd moved silently away. He was peering into the undergrowth, nostrils flaring. He smiled.

I squinted past him into the shadow. She was a young woman from another tribe, russet fur groomed to a soft sheen, smiling shyly back at Scar-Hand from behind a screen of berry bushes.

He took another long sniff of the air that smelled no different to me than the usual moist mix of earth, needle, and leaf. He moved closer to the woman, making a questioning gesture. Her bright eyes glanced nervously at me and away. She beckoned Scar-Hand, her smile widening.

Without a backward look he loped to her side and they melted together into the forest shadows.

"Good."

I jumped at the quiet voice behind me.

Old-Guy smiled and tilted his head in the direction they'd gone. "Those Who Guard Words tell Ki-Linat yes at Gathering time. Ki-Linat grows true branch strong."

"Those who Guard Words told him . . . what?"

He pointed again after them. "Gathering time. Children make new They-Child."

"Make new—"

He made an exaggerated sniff at me and chuckled, pointing to my groin. "And Player's time. They-men make new We-Child."

It finally dawned on me. There was another reason the different tribes got together. "Now wait just a bloody damn minute here! If they think—"

He patted my belly and chuckled again.

* * *

The host tribe perched and squatted once more at the focus of the semicircle of Gathered tribes, but this time in a different place, a mossy slope of rock tumbled in an old fall. Two women had risen to render a portion of the interminable, rhythmic chant the tribe had been reciting all morning. It was their turn of the eight-year cycle to give the final retelling of last year's True Is of the High Mother.

A couple of men and an older woman stood to take up the next couplets in the recitation. Beside me a young girl stirred restlessly and reached out with long toes to give a quick pinch to a boy in front. Fial-Li reached past me to touch one hand briefly to the girl's mouth. The girl lowered her eyes and Fial-Li smiled at her, then me. "Children learn true words," she whispered.

I nodded, sympathizing with the girl. And this was only the opening ceremony before approaching Those Who Guard Words to recite the new This Is.

I'd learned from Fial-Li that the Gathering was also an important time to teach the tribe's young children proper use of the true words. The Anduran's Way was finally falling into patterns for me. Speech was controlled much more tightly here than I'd ever seen. The true word structures and their layers of meaning that I only vaguely understood seemed at times almost a secret code shaped from the building blocks of standard speech. If the cybers were using the Andurans as observers to enforce an unchanging True Is, such unaltering precision of word usage was undoubtedly necessary. I wondered if the High Mother—the Founder—had also Planned the way their reality had split into two levels. The true and the false. The real and the dream.

Fial-Li nudged me.

The recitation was finished. It was time for the hosts to open the cyber cubicle, time for their reality to be pruned into a tidy True Is. Any twigs of the false branch would cease to exist, would never have existed except in a dream. Like the false plant growths. I wondered what the cybers did with them.

Fial-Li nudged me again and I rose with the others as they moved closer to the rocky hillside. They jostled a bit, crowding closer to see.

I knelt so my height wouldn't block anyone's view, peering

between them. I wasn't sure how much of my song had found
its way into the new district This Is, or how much the
Andurans understood. But at least I'd learned the console
location. If the natives wouldn't do anything about Heinck, I
could use the wild card disc to talk to the Anduran LS cybers.
I'd have to walk a tricky line between blowing the whistle on
Heinck and exposing the activities of the genuine Resistance.
But I had to find out what had happened to the shuttle,
without letting the cybers know about David. Or Jason. I had
to get to the facility in the taboo area. I had to find out what
Heinck was up to.

I blew out a long breath. Life *was* getting complicated.

Fial-Li touched my arm. The Andurans were stirring expectantly, looking up now to the rocky hillside. Several of the
host Children were huddled at the base of a tall, moss-draped
boulder, making ritual movements, gesturing, pressing something on the ground. They stood back, stepping to either side
on the rocky slope, calling out together, "Those Who Guard
Words hear This Is."

Around me the crowd responded, "Those Who Guard
Words tell True Is of High Mother."

The restless stirring ceased. The hush of the shadowed
forest enclosed us, held us in the palm of an enveloping,
green-dappled hand. High overhead, a thresh of wings beat
through the silence like a deep heartbeat. As if on cue,
narrow sunbeams speared down through thin gray clouds and
the far mesh of limbs.

The huge boulder slid slowly and smoothly aside. It revealed a narrow chamber running into the hillside, incongruously sleek and shining with metal, plasmeld, and harsh white
light in the midst of the moist, shadowed greenery and towering trees. The cyber console inside flickered suddenly into
activation, amber and blue indicators flaring to gasps of awe
around me, playing quick flashing patterns across its panel.

From its speaker came a short run of high, chiming notes.
Almost a little tune. I frowned, recognizing it this time—the
odd metallic chime or whistle as the mechman had approached
the alley where the carter was threatening the frightened little
native. A shrill buzz of alarm rang inexplicably in my ears to
echo it, a crazy warning jitter of *timbra*, blood rushing
distractingly.

I rubbed my ear, still frowning, as the Andurans crowded

in around me, eyes intent on the open cubicle. There was a quick sighing sound of indrawn breaths. They pressed forward with low murmurs, faces rapt.

A terrified scream shattered the expectant hush.

Still clutching my ear, I whirled in alarm. Another shrill cry of panic jolted the crowd. A blinding burst of barely seen light sizzled from the surrounding brush toward the hosts beside the open cubicle. Then another and another, a flashing terror of fire searing across and into the Gathered Children. A host high on the rocks screamed and fell, amber eyes wide with shock and incomprehension as he clutched at his torn, burning chest. Beside him a woman stood frozen, staring aghast as a young boy fell in a sluice of bright blood, toppling with the legs sliced from beneath him.

The lasers flashed, blue-white blades of blinding light, cutting them down.

Screams filled the air—theirs, mine. Shrill cries of panic, anguish, pain. Helpless rage as I fought through the terror-stricken, thrashing mob, waved them back, shouted unheard useless directions. The forest flared and whirled around me, alarm jolting through me, glimpses of faces, eyes wide and blank in shock, falling russet shapes, mouths wide on wordless outcry. I stumbled over a fallen man, choked, saw gentle little Quick-Shadow dart past, scoop up a child, leap for an overhanging tree. She was cut down, ripped in a crimson spatter by a hissing lance from the hidden assassins.

I spun around, sick with horror, waving my arms frantically at those who ran blindly past. "No! The other way!"

A flash of a familiar face, huge amber eyes glinting the reflection of flames. "No! Fial-Li!" I yelled after her, but she was swept away in the bedlam as I stumbled again, falling, the blue-white beams snapping above my head. There was a smell of burning meat. It was impossible the forest would ever stop shaking with a scream of outrage. I crawled, clambered over fallen, torn, and bleeding shapes, grabbed a cowering huddle of russet fur.

"Li-Nahi!" I saw only wide, blank eyes as I snatched up the little boy and ran, throwing us down and rolling beneath another blinding wire of light. I scrambled up again, clutching the child as I sprinted for the forest away from the snapping, killing beams.

Above me trunks and branches swarmed with fleeing fig-

ures. I raced for the cover of the trees, gasping hot air, smoke
and sharp flares burning me from the inside out. A sudden
agony of flame sizzled across my shoulder and I cried out,
stumbled, clutched Li-Nahi and kept running. Fear flamed
through me, fire chasing the little people darting after and
around me.

Then men came out from the brush in front of us, firing
more lasers in short, high sweeps, cutting us off. I whirled to
run back. But they were behind us too. Heinck's men. More
of them now. They closed in around the trampled clearing,
stopped us, pushed us stumbling back in fear, bumping blindly,
crowding together.

Only a few of them gripped the burning tools turned weapons. But enough. They rounded up the natives who hadn't
escaped, prodding with their feet, stepping over the bodies of
the fallen as if they were broken dolls, fallen logs in their
path.

I stood numb, a sickening emptiness inside, clutching the
shaking boy to my chest. I couldn't catch my breath past a
swelling clot of horror, grief, strangled outrage choking me.
The captured Andurans huddled shivering around me. The
forest was silent again, except for the muffled thud of the
approaching feet.

They were a distant rhythm, verses from some dim where.
*Their feet run to evil; And they make haste to shed innocent
blood. . . .*

Heinck's men moved closer, looking at the ground. I looked
blankly around me, seeing all the fallen bodies, not understanding, waiting for them to scream, jump up, shout, laugh,
anything. But none of them moved. All of them were dead.
So quickly. I stared at the hands gripping the black rods that
had dealt death with such cold efficiency. I didn't understand,
I hadn't understood, that people could do this to each other. I
could grasp a single death, perhaps, in blind rage, like the
killing of poor Vri-Fis in the enclave, or murder in the
madness of jealous fear, the way Aaron had killed Isaac. But
so many, so quickly. My mind spun futilely. How could I
feel all these deaths?

A word, a label to fix meaning, a sharp specific finally
pierced the numb whirling blur. A word out of taboo time,
out of History, that hadn't had a meaning, that wasn't supposed to have one.

War. This was the horror, then, that the cybers had tried to keep from us.

War. But I couldn't grasp it. I could only stare as the Resistance men ringed us closer, still looking down, their faces almost as dazed as the Andurans'. I raised my eyes past them to the man who was moving out from behind a *haavriathil*, face swimming like a pale mask out of the gloom. He stopped to look up at the opened console cubicle still waiting in its oblivious, bloodless contours of metal and plasmeld.

Ye have plowed wickedness. Ye have reaped iniquity.

He nodded suddenly, jerked around, and strode with a deliberate swagger to face me above the heads of the terrified natives. All at once the whirling stilled and everything snapped into focus. I seized eagerly on a pure, sharp stab of hatred.

Heinck met my eyes and slowly smiled.

sixteen

"... turning into a real pansy-ass. Shit, we're changing the Rules! That's what it's all about, right? Like Heinck said, we're not letting those suvving cybers tell us what's right and wrong anymore."

A mumbled reply filtered through the haze of stale warm air, aching weariness, dull pain. Numbing sleep beckoned, twined soft fingers through shadow, tugged me back to its tempting blankness.

"Can it, here he comes!" There were scuffling noises.

I pried my eyes open, blinked in the stuffy darkness, crawled out of gray haziness to harsh awareness—packed dirt hard beneath me, cracks of faint light between rough slats, the stir of dim shapes packed around me in the hut, dull pain cracked open to a searing throb down the back of my left shoulder as I straightened. There was a soft gleam of twin amber near me, a thick hand touching my head. A soothing murmur.

I squeezed the hand in answer, winced as I handed the young man whose name I didn't know the tiny, curled warmth of the still-sleeping Li-Nahi, and hauled myself to my feet. My head brushed a ceiling. I stepped carefully across my fellow prisoners, groping along the rough-hewn wood walls that had caused the Andurans almost as much dismay last night as the terrible burns I'd finally been able to dress with ointment wheedled out of a guard. I bent to a crack in the wall, sucking in a sharp breath as my wound stretched and cracked open. I peered into a white glare of early morning mist, blinked, and focused.

Dormant rage boiled up again, burning away sleep and pain. Only the wall kept me from leaping out to claw at the hateful face, the stupid satisfaction in those eyes.

Heinck affected his usual careless stance, the disdainful half sneer. His oiled dark hair gleamed through the pale mist

as he shrugged at the two guards. "So don't get your dick in
a clamp over it, Turner. You flaking out on us too? You
know you're just caving in to the cyber thought-wash bilge
they've been pumping us full of all our lives. This is *War*,
man. We make the Rules now. We're all in this together,
right? Unless maybe you feel like crawling back to the cybers
for some Healing." He made a mocking gesture.

The other man had his back to me. He muttered something
and shook his head.

"All right. You two go get some sleep." Heinck jerked his
head and two new men materialized out of the mist. One had
a laser tube, smaller than Heinck's, in a holder on his thigh.
Heinck pointed my way. "Open it up. Maybe the bitch's
ready to talk."

The first two guards started away, the one he'd called
Turner glancing quickly back at the hut before the mist
swallowed him. A square face with dark stubble—the one
who'd brought me the ointment the night before. He wasn't
carrying a weapon.

The Andurans stirred away from me, drawing into a huddle
against the far end of the hut as a low panel of wall was lifted
aside. Curdled light spilled in and a backlit head peered at us.
"You. Kurtis. Out here."

I glanced at the frightened faces behind me. "It's all right.
I'll be back." I wasn't sure who the assurance was for.

Heinck was wearing his gloating look. I ducked out of the
hut, wincing involuntarily as my shoulder scraped the low
clearance. Heinck jerked his head at the bigger of the two
men, who moved in to grab my arm up painfully behind my
back, holding me in place.

Heinck grinned. "You're even a worse mess than last
night, Kurtis. When are you gonna wise up?"

I didn't answer, and he stepped close, lowering his voice to
an oily whisper. "So you picked up a hit, big deal. Use your
head. You're passing up a good thing with me, tika." He
raised his hand and ran a finger slowly down my scarred
cheek.

I didn't bother pushing it away, but he must have felt my
skin crawl.

He dropped the hand and snorted. "Don't tell me you're
worried about the toads! Shit, they're so stupid they barely

qualify as human. They've gotta learn they can't get out of line with the Word Man."

Despite myself, I blurted out, raspy voice shaking, "Is that how you talked your gang into this *War*, Heinck? Compared to the Andurans, you barely qualify as insect."

His nostrils flared. His hand fisted and came down on my burn. I clamped my teeth, biting my tongue as red fire leaped up behind my eyes and a short hiss escaped. I took a deep breath, searching out the tattered fringes of a silent Setharian chant, easing the slam of my heart into its control. I pulled in another ragged breath, watching Heinck warily as the man behind me tightened his hold.

He laughed. "*Damn*, tika! You've got it, all right. When things are wrapped up here, I'm bringing in that paindure man for sure." He twisted his hand in the hair at the back on my neck and pulled my face up to his, whispering close again. "We'll see how far you'll go, bitch. And I'll be with you every step of the way. We'll be swimming in it together. When that's done, there's nothing I won't know about you, I promise you that. We're two of a kind, Kurtis."

I took my chance while he was close, stamping on the instep of the man holding me and jerking forward to ram my knee up into Heinck's groin.

There was a curse behind me, but Heinck moved enough to take my knee on his thigh. He grunted. "Cunt!" He jerked me forward by the hair, flinging me down to the ground. "I'll get to you later. It's *my* game here. Now I want that disc, and I don't mean tomorrow. You're gonna help me bore some data out of the console."

I didn't get up, just shook my head. "I told you. I don't have the disc."

"I'm not buying it, Kurtis." His boots moved away to the guards. One of them ducked inside the hut.

The guard reappeared dragging Li-Nahi. The terrified little boy squealed and broke free, throwing himself into my arms and burrowing against me. I rocked him, making soothing noises.

When I looked up, the gloating expression was back on Heinck's face. "Stupid tikas are all alike. I thought you were smarter than that, Kurtis." He smiled. "All right. You don't have the disc, the kid bites it. That simple."

He jerked his head and the guard leaned down to yank

Li-Nahi from my arms. The boy whimpered, reaching for me. I took a deep breath, slowly dragging myself to my feet. So this was it. This was the part where I was supposed to sacrifice whomever and whatever to the cause, do what it took to block Heinck, become like him in order to stop him. I closed my eyes. I shook my head. "All right, Heinck."

I took Li-Nahi from the guard and carried him inside, dug the disc from the dirt where I'd hidden it, and took it to Heinck.

Blue and green lights flashed hypnotically across the top of the console. I'd stood there forever, rooted to the cybers' sterile pod, sealed from the larger embrace of the forest, watching lights flash to a blur, weaving an endless warp of hoarse words to the weft of the console's replies.

"Working." The toneless voice faded from the console speaker and its lights settled into a steady pattern.

I swayed and leaned against the box, closing my eyes to see the colors still dancing to a light-headed, jagged rhythm. The air filters whirred faintly in a vain effort against the moisture wafting in through the open door of the cubicle. Rain hissed softly beyond the door at my back, splashing muted onto mossy rocks. Farther, I could almost hear it drumming on the mylar sheeting someone had mercifully draped over the pitiful row of bodies.

Something jabbed me in the shoulder. Pain flared briefly through the dull ache numbing more than body and mind. The world itself was deadened with it. I opened my eyes to see an amber indicator flare on. It stared back at me, steady and unwinking, an amber eye, distant and judging, watching me and waiting.

"What's taking so long? Don't think you're gonna pull a fast one on me, Kurtis! You tip off LS and your ugly little buddies back there are gonna—"

"Complete." The thin voice from the speaker cut him off.

I didn't turn around. "All right, Heinck, you're covered. The cybers think they've got a district This Is on record." The indicator still stared at me. Amber eyes, calm, holding only pain, only the faint shadow of reproach.

Heinck strode over to glare at the console and pull me back by one arm, forcing my face up to his. "Listen, cunt, you better not be screwing around here."

I forced myself to meet his eyes, let him see the dull weariness, the faint flicker of fear that was real enough. But my patchwork data input only had to work for a short time, until LS queried it and found it didn't cover all the holes. I wasn't good enough to do that, but I had to convince Heinck *I* was the hot grid rider he wanted. I had to protect David. If he was still there to protect . . . I closed my eyes again. It only had to work for a short time. If it didn't work, I'd thrown away the Rogue, my wild card, for nothing. We'd all lose.

I wiped a shaky hand across my forehead, feeling damp grittiness. It was too much, I wasn't up to it, I should just let go the strings to the whole messy, tangled web, let the dull throb of the rain run through me, wash me out and melt me down to the cool green embrace of the hidden, waiting other, where it wouldn't matter . . .

But somebody was shaking me. "Don't flake out on me!" Heinck shouted past me. "Hey, Cerrito! Give me one of those stim vials."

One of the guards slouching in the doorway pulled himself upright.

I yanked free of Heinck. "No. I'm okay."

"Have it your way." He shrugged. "When you're done here, you get something to eat and some rest. Not before."

The other guard in the doorway straightened abruptly, touching his weapon in its sheath. Then he moved back. "It's only Sono."

A short, dim figure loomed through the curtain of rain and stepped into the cubicle. Water streamed from rain gear as the dark little woman glanced apprehensively at Heinck.

"About time! Any sign?"

She was looking at his feet. "No sign of any more Andurans."

"Tell me something new. Toads have some bad dreams to think about." Heinck snorted. "What about her stuff?" He jerked his head at me. "Find that harp yet?"

Gleaming dark eyes flickered over me and away, her tongue darting nervously to lick water from compressed lips. "Not yet."

"Then get out there and beat the bush! I want it, and I don't mean next year. Kurtis here's gonna give me a private little concert, isn't that right, tika?"

He laughed at my look. "Way I hear it, Kurtis, you and

me with the Word Key and that harp, we can have the whole
damn planet dancing to our tune.'' He jerked his head again
and the wet rain gear escaped with a relieved face into the
downpour. ''But then maybe I won't need you once I team up
with those incorporeals, huh? Better think about making me
like you, Kurtis.''

''Don't do it, Heinck.'' I passed my tongue over dry lips
and cleared my throat. ''The incorporeals are more than
you're bargaining for. They'll use you too.''

He snorted. ''I told you, can it with that crap. You think
I'm stupid? I'm gonna walk away from the big time? You're
not in a spot to be greedy, Kurtis. You want a piece, you're
sharing it with me. So get to it.'' He jabbed a finger at the
console.

I stepped back from it. ''Go ahead, it'll answer you now.''

He gave me a suspicious look, turning warily to the console and gripping it tightly. I could see his throat work as he
swallowed, and I realized with dull surprise that he was
nervous about using the wild card disc on the cybers. Somehow that helped. I straightened. ''All right. Move over.''

He glared, but stepped back against a sealed door at the
rear of the cubicle.

I spoke again to the amber ready light. ''Data search: Go to
loop storage. Object: Entry code, Facility LS:3296:A51.
Commence.''

''Verifying.''

I turned to Heinck. ''You're sure that's the facility tag?''

''That's what Malov used. He found out the entry code
changes on what he called a random-generator every thousand
hours. But what fouled us up last time was we didn't have the
disc.''

I turned back to the lights, hoping it wasn't a high-level
code. I'd gone about as far as I'd be able to get in the loops.

The speaker droned. ''Access verified. Code 1904628.''

Heinck was writing down the numbers. ''Okay, find out if
the incorporeals are inside the facility yet.''

I knew they were there. With David. They were alive
again. They might even be within the LS matrix already,
hidden in the higher loops as they'd invaded the Poindros LS
system, watching and waiting, listening to me now. I shivered, staring at the smug, winking lights of the console. I

cleared my throat again. "Data search: Status, Shuttle YBX4371. Commence."

"Working." The lights flashed briefly. "Last communication 60.18.4. Shuttle YBX4371 attempting emergency landing. No further communication. Probable launch malfunction. No passengers aboard."

My fingers tightened on the slick edges of the box as alarm jittered through me. David. I tried to conceal it from Heinck. "Report landing location."

"Facility LS:3296:A51."

"Okay, that's the place." Heinck moved closer. "But what's this crap about an emergency landing? What about the incorporeals?"

I shook my head. "These are only data loops, Heinck. This part of the system doesn't know about the incorporeals. It's reading what it expects, an emergency landing." I told myself to believe it. It looked like LS was keeping secrets from itself too. Or maybe CI was pulling another fast one. But I knew one thing. It wouldn't be long before the incorporeals took over the Local System.

I turned back to Heinck. "You've got what you wanted. They're here."

I laid an urgent hand on Val-Niol's shoulder, motioning in the dark for silence. An agitated tremor ran through the crowded Andurans. A glint of amber winked out as they stopped scooping at the hard dirt and crowded around to conceal the shallow trench that hadn't yet reached the bottom of the wall footings. I crawled over to strain against the rough door, listening.

There was a breath of wind. A scuffling noise.

"Ruth?" The deep whisper boomed alarmingly through the hut. "Be Raul."

The Andurans were an invisible fluttering against the far wall. I whispered "It's all right" and turned back to the door, sagging with relief. The furtive signal I'd caught from the big man that morning as Heinck hustled me past camp to the cyber console hadn't been my imagination. "Raul, thank Founder! What about the guards?"

The door panel creaked and lifted away on a rush of cool night air. The darkness was nearly as thick as inside the hut.

A huge hand closed over my groping arm. "They be sleep. Food having little surprise in." There was a low chuckle.

I gripped the hairy wrist. "Raul, thank you. I won't forget this."

"Hush. Must be go quick. Heinck not trusting Raul and friends. Some not liking War. They be come too."

"The band from town? I haven't seen many I know from the pub."

I could feel, more than see it, as he shook his head. "Heinck taking here most only men from tree cutting."

"How many laser tubes does he have?"

"Ten be work, maybe. Problems building. He be not trust me and friends with."

"What has he done with the bodies of the Andurans?"

"Be burn tomorrow." Raul moved restlessly. "Hurry now. Friends waiting."

I hesitated, then gripped his hand again. "Look, I don't think you should try to come with us. Heinck would be after you, and you wouldn't stand a chance against those lasers. If my friends here are right, the other Andurans will be back tonight to retrieve the bodies and return them to the High Mother. They'll take me along with them, but I don't think they'd take you. I've got to get moving fast, get to that facility before Heinck. Do you think you and your friends could stay on safely with the band, slow him down without putting yourself in danger?"

"Danger? Hah! Be—" Raul blew out a long breath then. I thought I saw him finally nod. "Be try, Ruth. Raul be slow, but finally seeing—Heinck be go too far. Not just fighting cybers. Be bad all this."

"It's worse than you know, Raul. I think I can stop it, if I can only get there in time. But I want you to stay clear for another reason. If Heinck manages to get into the facility and team up with the incorporeals, you've got to find a way to get back to the spaceport and get a message onto a transport. And I don't mean through a console here—the incorporeals may have already infiltrated the system. Say you have a message for Central Interlock," I gave him my code number, "and tell them the incorporeals are awake on Andura. Got it?"

"I be not liking this."

"Me neither." I turned to gesture to the Andurans and they began to slip silently out of the opening.

There was a groan, something stirring behind me. The last of the Andurans leaped free as I jerked around. One of the drugged guards rolled over and started snoring loudly.

"Be hurry, Ruth!"

"All right. Thanks, Raul. Thanks a lot."

The Andurans had disappeared into the night. I hesitated over the one holstered laser the guards had between them, then shook my head. I turned to go and a big hand grasped my wrist. "Heinck be follow trail already burned to facility. He be quick."

"We'll just have to be quicker. Take care, Raul."

The huge hand gave my arm a gentle shake that rattled my teeth. "Be remember, tika. Rogue card slippery play."

"Don't I know it." I gave him a lopsided smile he probably couldn't see and hurried away into the dark.

The clearing beneath the far dark arms of the *haavriathils* was silent except for my own pulse drumming in my ears. If there were moons, they were buried deep beyond the midnight forest and thick, impenetrable clouds. The Andurans huddled against the black-barked, mossy skirts, retreating from the incomprehensible shame of their dead ones denied a return to the sky. The long mound bulked darker black against the dark earth. Its slick mylar sheeting captured a faint sheen of light from somewhere, echoing a nervous glint of amber as one of the Andurans glanced from the shrouded shapes to the black, gaping hole of the cybers' cubicle. Heinck had destroyed it after I'd gotten him the information he needed.

Leaves stirred suddenly in the night. I stiffened, sweat breaking out cold on my back, straining through the night for any sound from Heinck's camp. There was only a breath of breeze dying to silence.

Li-Nahi stirred in my arms. My hand soothed him, but he wriggled against my touch, craning his face toward the invisible sky. The others were looking up too. I couldn't hear anything.

Something dropped behind me. I jumped. They were all around us.

Sleek dark shadows swarmed silently down huge trunks and dropped from the surrounding scrub trees. Without words they moved quickly to embrace the prisoners, carrying away in woven nets those too badly burned to climb. More swarmed over the black sheeting, rolling it back with bitten-off, keening cries of sorrow. Soft weeping in the night. They bore away the dead in their nets.

With a low cry, Fial-Li was there. She squeezed my shoulder and gently peeled Li-Nahi from my arms.

A native taller than most gestured to those with the nets, then loped over. "Player tells true. Word Man tells false dream." It was Scar-Hand, the skeptic.

"False, but no dream, Scar-Hand." I shook my head wearily. "Will you help me stop him?"

He seemed to frown in the darkness, then I heard a quick sigh. "Children hear Player."

He gestured to four shadows nearby. They wrapped me quickly in their net, scurried up in silence and leaped with the cords, swung and dipped me through the night. I flew with them to the high limbs, into the sweet black arms of sleep.

seventeen

A blur of leathery needles swung past and fell away to the deep green well of the forest. Thick boughs and narrow shoots tumbled around me. Dappled sun splashed across my eyes and I plunged and spilled with it into shadow. A wild thresh of wings beat up from the dimness, glistening blue-black, breaking away in shrill cries. I dipped, swung, and bobbed up again.

The net swayed dizzily, but I had stopped clutching at the soft strands that floated me chest down over green depths. I had stopped clenching my teeth and straining for a precarious hold on a whipping twig or needle as the Andurans bearing me leaped and climbed and swarmed for the next branch and tree. The day climbed and dipped through its hours, and I was flying, weightless.

My mind was finally numbed past the spinning of frantic wheels of plan, persuasion, frustration over the endless delays.

My voice had gone hoarse singing the New Branch for the Andurans, pleading in vain for hurry while they gave their slow reverences to the fallen Children who made their delayed return to the grief place, the peace place. The tribes had finally turned from their dead to debate at nerve-rending length in cycles of Is and Is Not, true and false branch, dream and the nebulous new reality of future. Finally, while I fretted and fumed and despaired, and Heinck was pushing his men along the forest floor beneath us toward the facility, a few Andurans emerged from the still-turning cycles of words to join me.

And now there was only the race, the changing teams of my carriers, the air whipping through me like the caress of a cool hand, green blurring to deep-pooled, calm eyes, a whispered, waiting voice, an elusive hint of something other, something ripening to readiness. But when I tried to grasp it or define it, it faded into pain, grief, worry, fear, the blind rush of desperate hurry. There was nothing to do but be carried to the heart of the web.

The light hurt.

Sun struck off rough expanses of rock climbing steeply from a fringe of low grasses, angling higher in bare thrusts as the mountain scraped the sky above even the tallest of the *haavriathils*. The cool, hushed embrace of the forest fell away before the brute force of massive stone and untamed wind. I winced, eyes narrowed against the glare, moving back reflexively to the last safe shadow of the scrub trees where the Andurans huddled.

Amber eyes flashed toward the awesome height of taboo and that fearful openness. They swerved quickly away. There were quick gestures of foot and hand, a low cadence of distressed murmurs.

There were more of them now, others who'd joined us as we hurried through the tribal districts. They'd come a long way at the playing of a new song. But finally the mountain and the raw sky and taboo were too much. I didn't blame them. I was reluctant myself to leave the enfolding shade and expose myself to that cruel clarity of openness.

I turned back to the mountain and the glare of sun from a narrow spire that had to be the nose of the emergency shuttle, rising behind the dark slash of one of the highest ridges. I shook off a jittery, warning tingle of nerves and studied the slopes for a line of ascent. I tightened the straps of my knapsack, adjusting the water skins strapped to its sides.

"All right, then, I think I can make it during daylight. If the Word Man's still setting up camp on the other side"—a young woman from a nearby tribe who'd just arrived nodded confirmation—"then he probably thinks he's beaten us. He won't think we'd try it from this side." I avoided glancing again at the sheer rock faces. Heinck's laser-blasted "road" through the forest had taken him to the far side of the mountain, where there was a more gradual approach to the peak. "You can help me by watching the camp. Some of them may help us. . . ."

But what was Raul doing? He couldn't have slowed Heinck down by much. Had the Word Man blamed him for our escape?

I rubbed my forehead with my fingertips. "They were tricked by the Word Man's false dream too. If I don't come back, some of you should go to the visitor enclave and report what happened to Those Who Guard Words at the sky-ship. If Raul leaves the camp, he might help you. Fial-Li knows him—the big man who . . . is tree-with-more-bark than the other strangers.''

I handed the lyre case to her. She hesitated, then passed it to a man from another tribe. She squatted quickly to whisper something to Li-Nahi, scooting him toward an older woman. Soft amber eyes raised to mine. ''Fial-Li climbs taboo with Player. Fial-Li helps Player climb New Branch that is not branch.''

I touched her shoulder. ''Are you sure, Fial-Li? It won't be a false dream this time, not like it was when you followed the Word Man's branch. It's real. They'll try to hurt us.''

She nodded quickly and slung a food net and water skin over her shoulder. She flinched as she stepped out into the harsh sunlight, then straightened, waiting for me.

I smiled back at the others. ''Good luck. Remember, this is your world. You make the true branch.''

A foot touched mine as I turned. Scar-Hand opened his mouth, closed it, looked up at the mountain and back to me. He lowered his eyes, touching his chest. ''Ki-Linat . . . tries—'' He broke off and met my eyes again, this time entreating understanding, wrestling with new words and new meanings.

I smiled as he gave me his naming. ''Thank you, Ki-Linat. But they'll need you here.''

He looked both regretful and relieved. ''Blessings of High Mother on Player and Fial-Li.''

We were into the tall grass when the blades rustled apart on a small, hurtling shape. The boy scrambled up his mother's side and leaped free to land in front of me. He looked at the ground, then raised his face to Fial-Li with an abashed grin. ''Li-Nahi helps Player climb.''

I clung to the narrow crack, low orange sunlight washing the rock face next to mine. I tried one more time to ease upward, push against the tiny knob my left toes stretched from, spring up for a grab at the next handhold, only a fraction of a meter beyond my fingertips. Only forever away.

I couldn't do it. Sweat stung my eyes, my arms wouldn't stop shaking, my burned shoulder throbbed beneath the weight of the knapsack. I couldn't move. I couldn't make that last gamble against the rock and the drop below. I closed my eyes. I could only cling until even the drop stopped mattering.

There was a sound above me, a scraping noise. A tiny bit of stone clattered, stung my cheek, and showed the way down. Straight to the ledge below. So easy. The wind plucked at me. All I had to do was just let go.

"Player . . . Ruth." The voice was faint above the wind. I scraped my cheek against the rock to look up.

Fial-Li's anxious face peered over the edge of the last ledge, impossibly far above me. I could barely remember watching her and Li-Nahi swarm so easily up the sheer rock. I ducked my head again and clung tighter.

"Player climbs."

I jerked my head up, nearly losing my grip. The little boy had climbed back down. His eyes were wide, worried. He hung somehow from the side of the cliff, reaching down to me, grasping my wrist.

"No, I can't, Li-Nahi."

"False branch, no. New branch climbs."

Now I saw the stretched weaving of Fial-Li's food sling, tied to the boy's ankle. His mother leaned precariously over the ledge, grasping the other end as the boy stretched upside down.

"Player climbs," the boy repeated, and suddenly tugged my hand free of the crack.

"Aahhh!" Panic shot through me, then a wild surge of adrenaline and I was scrambling with my feet against air and smooth rock. The small hands clutched with surprising strength to my wrist and yanked me upward. I kicked and pushed reflexively against the rock, and somehow I was up at the next crack, shaking and gasping as Li-Nahi loosened the loop from his ankle and his quick toes snugged it around my wrist. He scampered up the cliff to the ledge.

I took deep breaths, flexing fingers and knees. Only a little farther, a little higher. But just a short rest first. The sun was sinking over my shoulder into masses of regathering clouds, the sky fire and bruised purple over the dark green waves of forest. I would only rest a little with the sun, wait only for the blue twilight reaching cool fingers up for me.

There was a tug on the cord. I looked up into four bright amber eyes. I blew out a breath, nodded, and climbed.

*   *   *

The second moon peered over the jagged edge of the peak looming above us, doubling our shadows and casting a confusion of depths and surfaces. I stepped high over something that wasn't there and stumbled on broken rock smoothed to polished silver in the night. The sharp nose of the heat-blackened shuttle pointed one way out. I followed mother and son around the jointed appendages of the squatting landing gear.

Down a dip slippery and noisy with loose shale. I came around a bend to see a blue eye staring from an unnaturally straight-edged protrusion at the foot of a dark mass of cliff. Fial-Li and Li-Nahi stopped short.

"That's it." Idiotically, I whispered it. They'd know well enough we were coming. I slipped out of the knapsack and crouched beside it on the ground, trying to stop my hands from shaking as I tilted a long swallow from the water skin down my throat. I handed it to Fial-Li. I reached into the knapsack and pulled out my last card.

Heinck hadn't taken it in town, probably hoping it would come in handy. My fingers gripped tighter on the pink case of the "birth control" device Helsa and Siolis had given me. I hoped to Founder the damn thing worked.

I looked at the smooth plasmeld shape. I was afraid. I was tempted to race to that blue light, shove in the device, and key in *Help*. But I had to get the coded electronic locks and the security fields of the underground facility open before triggering the virus program that would scramble signals and seal David into a malfunctioning, airless tomb. I doubted I'd need CI's unlocking code to get through the door. If the incorporeals were awake and stirring in there, I was pretty sure they'd lay out the welcome mat.

I could almost feel them, a crawling whisper up the inside of my spine, wanting me, calling me back.

I shook it off, thrusting the case at Fial-Li. "You remember what to do?" I waved down her protest. "No, it's safer if you stay here with it. If I'm not out by morning, trigger it. Okay?"

She took it hesitantly, raising troubled eyes to mine.

"You have to do it, Fial-Li. That may be what saves us. You do understand?"

She nodded. "Yes, Ruth. Fial-Li . . ." She gave me a

fleeting smile, struggling with new words. "I . . . will . . . do it."

I squeezed her shoulder. "Thank you. For everything." I crouched to give Li-Nahi a hug. "You too, kid."

They melted without a sound into the night and I moved closer to the blue light. I ignored the hot, jittering flush of *timbra*, the silent shrill imperative, the reflex to leap for cover. I took a deep breath and stopped before the rectangular entranceway jutting with its unnatural right angles out of the massive slope of rough stone. Cold wind shivered over me. Shadow and double moonlight shimmered oddly between the shiny metal door and me. A protective energy field. I reached out for the small, blue-lighted panel on my side of it and started to punch the door's unlocking code into numbered keys.

An amber indicator winked on before I finished. "Hello, Ruth." The voice from a small speaker sawed across my nerves. "Or should we say Agent Kurtis?" There was a brief, scratchy trill of laughter. "We're waiting for you, my dear. Come in."

The odd shimmer faded from the night and the door slid aside on a burst of glaring white light. I blinked, took a deep breath, and followed it in.

The claustrophobic capsule of the anti-grav tube dropped me with a sickening plummet. It jolted to a silent stop and one side whisked away. I was staring down a long, functional bare room at rows of metal counters and stilled service mechs, low basins rippling with greenery, suspended hydroponic lumes, more tables pushed back against one wall, and an oddly pitiful line of withered, drooping potted plants shoved against a wall with a careless pile of tubing and disconnected remote manipulators. I took a step, blinking in harsh light, a vague, irrelevant realization flashing hazily through me. The facility had been here all along, hadn't been built just for CI and the incorporeals. It was the Anduran plant lab for all those "false growths." Maybe it was important, but I didn't care. It was all a buzz of meaningless static, blurring with the colors and shapes and sharp angles I was rushing past to the far end of that room.

"David!"

He turned slowly. The wiry bush of dark hair was untamed as ever, his eyes wide and owllike behind the gleaming spectacles and the long, humorous nose with its spray of freckles. Even as I swept him into my arms, I saw with a pang how pale he was, how thin his arms were.

"David, you're okay." It came out a question.

He didn't raise his arms to return my hug. His narrow back felt pitifully frail against my hands. I raised them to touch his head, my fingers brushing the back of his neck. They met a hard, unyielding shape.

I swallowed. I closed my eyes, thrusting away something dark and enveloping, hovering to swamp me. I pulled back to meet his unblinking eyes behind the lenses. "David . . . ?"

"We're glad you've arrived, Ruth. You can help us." He spoke slowly, dreamily, his voice flat, eyes focused somewhere beyond me.

A sickening dark emptiness swam inside me. "David, no." My voice had gone hoarse. "You're not a—"

His eyes pulled themselves vaguely to mine and he spoke absently. "I'm not a cyborg, Ruth. The incorporeals and I are attuned. They helped me build the portable interface. I'm learning so much from them. Now you can learn too. You can help us with the work I've been doing."

I pushed through the black, swamping wave of dismay. I could see the bulge now beneath the back of his shirt. I moved slowly around him and reached out very carefully, fingers fumbling with fabric as I pulled the collar down. It was a flat black plasmeld device, strapped against his upper spine. A tiny red indicator glowed from its center. The eye of a demon, a feral creature watching.

I grabbed the thing to tear it off him. There was a sizzling flash. I fell back, clutching my burned hand.

David turned to me, watching blankly.

I cried out to that bland, dreaming face, "David, don't let them do this! I know you're in there, you can't believe this is right! *Try*, David! You've got to help me before Heinck gets here. Don't you know what the incorporeals are going to—"

Laughter cut me off.

I whirled around to see him punch the controls in a wall console and saunter toward me. Heinck was dusty and sweaty, his shirt open at the chest to reveal the glistening tendrils of the Kiss-of-Fear vine, his face tired but flushed with a stim rush, a triumphant smirk plastered across it. "Don't bother, Kurtis. Might as well cash in the chips, you're outplayed."

He chuckled. "Gotta hand it to you—I never figured you'd make it past my boys down there. And you pulled a fast one with the kid here. You had me going all right, I thought you were the hot grid rider. You do have style, tika."

He planted his legs wide before me, the detested grin widening. "But for somebody who thinks she's so fucking smart, how come you're always one step behind me?"

He laughed again. "You blew it, Kurtis. I was all set to cut you in, run a partner act. When you and the toads took off on me, you threw away your chance at the incorporeals. Stupid bitch, thought you'd get here first. Of course you didn't see the slick little setup the cybers had behind that door in the forest cubicle along with all that plant crap. Nice little minia-ture camo-shielded anti-grav flitter for delivering the toads' plant specimens up here so the cybers could pick through 'em. All I had to do was toss out the garbage and send myself up here. Sort of entertained myself along the way thinking about you sweating it to beat me."

He pushed an oily black strand from his forehead, still grinning. "So I don't need you now. Me and the kid here, we got a sweet deal going." He glanced aside, his sick grin flashing toward David's pitiful thinness, silent stiff stance, blank eyes behind the spectacles. Heinck nodded, "Yep, we get the incorporeals all set up, and I get Andura on a platter, plus I'm in on the ground floor with the system takeover. It's gonna be—"

"You stupid bastard!" I finally broke free of strangling rage. "Don't you know what you've done? Can't you see they'll only use you to—"

"—the big-time when—" He talked right through me, narrowed eyes gleaming, gloating.

"Damn it, Heinck, even *you* have to see, you've got to have *something* left that can—" I lunged furiously to grab him, slap that hateful face, shake reason into the stupid eyes, force some fading remnant of humanity out of him. My hands were swallowed by his shoulders. I gasped, stumbling through him.

I nearly fell, caught myself, and sucked in a startled breath. The holofac of Heinck turned, blurring and refocusing, the grin fixing on me. He thinned to translucency, faded into shimmering beams of light, and disappeared. The wall con-sole indicators blinked and reconfigured.

"Damn it! Damn him!" I turned back to David's still, thin form, the narrow freckled face tracking me blankly. "David, please." My voice was thick, throat tight. "*Try*, kid. Fight them. Don't let this happen."

He raised his hand. A flat gray instrument rode on top of it, a narrow, looped extension curved between his fingers into an activator strip in his palm. It was sleek and compact compared to the bulky laser tubes Heinck had built. "I believe you know the capabilities of this tool, Ruth?" His voice was still quiet, remote and dreamy. "We don't have time for you now. Walk down that hall ahead of me."

I opened my mouth, shut it, and numbly obeyed as he pointed the weapon at me. He followed me through the plant lab and down a narrow, harshly lit hall.

"Stop. We prepared this room for you." David's hand concealed a coded lock plate as he punched its keys. A door sucked open, metal gleaming reflections from the hall lights. The hand with the weapon prodded me into a dim, bare storage cubicle. "Modifications to our interface system are nearly complete. We will . . . talk to you soon."

The toneless voice wasn't really David's. I shivered at the memory of those prying sparks of fire and pain inside me. "David, please. Don't do it. Take off that thing and—"

The door sliced shut between us. There were no controls on my side.

Four strides. Turn. Four strides to the other wall. Turn again. Past the too-short slab of bed foam on the floor, the covered hydroponic vessel they'd left for a chamber pot, the small heap of rations from the shuttle. Turn. Four strides.

I had finally dozed off for a while, so I had no idea how long I'd been locked in the narrow cell. The dim, constant light and even hum of the air filter gave me no clues. I'd failed. I'd thought I could reach David. Heinck had turned the cards on me again. It was time for the last play, and to hell with it all. I was sealed already beneath the ground. We would all be. Our tomb. I only wished I could have sparked something in those owl eyes, told him I was sorry, seen there was something of David that could answer me back. And to have only one more lungful of real air, moist with the breath of the forest, fly free from the high limbs of a *haavriathil*,

claim the sky for just a few seconds and go out the real
way. . . .

I shook my head, turned, and paced again. When was it
going to run down? It had to be past dawn. But the lights and
filters were still working. Fial-Li must not have triggered the
virus program. Damn it, Fial-Li! Don't go Anduran on me.
Do it. I stood still, closing my eyes as if I could search her
out past the walls and meters of rock. Come on, Fial-Li. Take
the step. Trigger it.

"No escape this time, Ruth."

I whirled in alarm. There was no one there. I hadn't really
heard the high, thin voice. It was inside me, crawling up my
spine into my skull. I stared in horror at a sensor grid
mounted high on one wall. An amber indicator on it had lit
up, blinking steadily. An eye, watching.

I leaped against the wall, scrabbling for it, fingers scratching. I couldn't reach it. I snatched up a water flask and threw
it at the lighted panel. The plasmeld flask cracked and re-
bounded to the floor and the amber light kept blinking.

". . . no good, Ruth. We're—"

"No!" I screamed and clutched my head, pounded my fists
against my temples to drive out the faint voice. It faded with
the dull pain to a buzz of static. I sank to the floor, pressing
my head hard in my hands.

". . . that forever, you know." The voice was weak,
broken, but still inside my head. A wave of vertigo wafted
me up and down through darkness. *". . . to extend communication interfaces and . . . The time soon . . . vain resistance."* A crackling sensation of heat flashed through me.
The voice focused, deepened, spoke rapidly. *"Our service
mechs have escorted your Anduran friend and her child into
the facility. The virus program was a pitifully inadequate
plan, Ruth. David told us all about it and we simply rendered
it null."*

Silent laughter rattled up my spine. The voice was many
voices in one now. *"Such an enterprising young man! He
will enrich our matrix immensely. With him, we won't need to
employ the intermediate cyborg stage. He'll soon be ready to
link incorporeally with us."*

"He won't! Damn you!" I didn't have to scream it aloud,
but I did. "Get out of my head!"

A soothing ripple of warmth flowed through me. A pale,

gentle hand touched my brow. *"Ruth, we won't hurt you."*
The voice was Helen's now.

"No! Stop it!"

*"But Ruth, we only want to welcome you among us, to
share with you our—"*

"Ruth!"

The new voice was weak, but I was hearing it with my
ears. The other voices melted into a buzz in my head. It built
to an unbearable whine and then was suddenly gone. I raised
my head, blinking.

"David?" I took a deep breath, scrambling to my feet.

The holofac was wispy. It kept blurring and reforming. It
was only his head and one shoulder and arm, floating in the
dimness, and through it I could see the sensor grid displaying
a steady configuration of blue and red indicators. The image
of David twisted, his arm pushing against something and then
dropping to disappear below the elbow. His eyes were frightened, his mouth a tight line of pain in the white face. "Ruth
. . . I can't . . ." Lights blinked on the grid and the holofac
faded.

"David!" My hand grasped air.

Indicators blinked and the light beams flickered again. His
head reappeared faintly. ". . . from the maze!" The voice
faded out and back again. "Inside, I can't . . . me, Ruth!
Remember your . . ." He thinned, then solidified briefly.
". . . rebuilt Jason to help them. But don't—"

The pale face contorted in pain and disappeared. The blue
and red indicators on the wall grid snapped off.

"David, don't . . ." Hot wet spilled over my face. "Founders, I'm sorry, kid, I don't know what to—"

The compartment door slid into its sheath with the sound of
a shocked, indrawn breath. The ceiling lights in the hall threw
warped shadows of the tall figure in the opening. My eyes
jerked to the dark, deactivated wall grid, back to the doorway. It wasn't a holofac.

"Jason—"

It was true this time. He was alive, standing there whole,
no sign of the horrible death burns from the weapons of the
Poindran security guards, the torn useless body and empty
glass eyes. These eyes were warm, amber-flecked brown,
searching mine, the thick tawny hair falling shaggily over the
tanned face with its wide cheekbones and the calm gravity of

his face that would break so suddenly into a gleaming smile. He reached out one large, sun-browned hand in an oddly halting gesture. "Ruth?"

His hands. Strong and work-callused, surprisingly deft, gently touching my face, cupping my breasts in the hot summer moonlight of the wheat field . . .

"No! Go away!" I stumbled back against the wall. "Don't try your tricks on me again!" I didn't know if I was yelling at Jason, at myself, at the incorporeals invisibly watching.

His grave face didn't alter, but the bright eyes blanked out as he looked down from my face. He stepped slowly, awkwardly, into the room. He lifted his feet and set them down at strange angles, his legs moving stiffly, bending oddly, the movements of his arms somehow out of sync with them. He shuffled forward in spasmodic jerks of his legs and torso, amber eyes flaring in a blank face, arms thrusting randomly, hands dangling grotesquely.

I pressed back harder against the wall, staring at the laboring, jolting limbs, swallowing down an unwilling sharp stab of pain. I refused the memory of two tawny figures running through the copper sunlight of our wheat field—Jason and our big pardil Ela sharing a long, fluid grace of stride.

He was only a machine. Now he moved like one. That should have made it easier. But I stared, appalled, as he shuffled and jerked closer, his eyes on mine.

"Ruth, I'm sorry. I know it's a shock." The voice wasn't Jason's. It was a monotone, the voice of a cyber console. Only the eyes looked alive, gentle, piercing me with what looked so much like genuine regret. But they were only glass, only mirrors.

"You're sorry! You're *sorry*!" A harsh sound that might have been laughter tore from my throat. I was backed into the corner, nowhere to go. I sat abruptly on the floor, hiding the sight of him against my updrawn knees. I shook my head. "Don't tell me you feel sorry. Don't tell me you feel anything. The incorporeals didn't need to send you here."

I raised my head and shouted at the sensor grid. "You hear me, you things in there? Pull his strings, push his buttons, get him out of here!"

The machine with Jason's face slowly folded its joints and then sat abruptly, thumping onto the floor near me. The uninflected voice droned quietly, "They can't hear you, Ruth.

I've interrupted the circuits. It will only hold for a short time, but we've got to talk. They built another body for me so I could help them again, Ruth. They want to build more cyborg bodies to invade CI. They need to penetrate the cyber matrix here, but the facility has some safeguards that must be bypassed first.''

My fists were clenched against my updrawn knees. My eyes were screwed shut, seeing the wavering holofac of David's pale, hurting face. His fading voice, trying to warn me. Jason was only a mechman for the incorporeals, only a tool to trick me. My voice was muffled. ''Go away.''

''Please listen, Ruth. It's your only chance to save yourself and David.'' The toneless voice grated in my ears. ''I'm still on your side. I'm trying to help David resist them. They've nearly taken him, Ruth. He's fighting, but he needs help. Are you listening, Ruth?''

I finally nodded, looking at the floor. It didn't really matter if the toneless voice was lying, if he was just mouthing words for the incorporeals. There was nothing I could do. It didn't matter what I believed or felt.

''Ruth?'' The ungainly figure shifted next to me.

I couldn't face those eyes again. I cleared my throat. ''What's wrong with you?'' It came out reluctantly.

''I'm sorry. I know it distresses you to see me this way.'' The voice, the words of a cyberserf, reading my emotions and soothing me.

''Stop it! It won't work on me again.''

My imagination almost heard a whir of gears as he stiffly shook his head. ''I'm not trying to trick you, Ruth. They want me to, but I couldn't, anyway. I can't make the connections. I can't shape my emoting displays. Ruth, there isn't much time. We've got to work together. Please don't shut me out.'' The colorless voice might have been droning production statistics. Something brushed the side of my head, stalled, moved to touch my unburned shoulder, knowing even that. The hand was warm.

I shuddered and jerked away.

There was silence for a moment. Then the toneless voice droned on, ''They've built new control mechanisms into this body. I've had to block them with my own directives, but it's impaired my function. They think the construction machines David helped them assemble are defective. It will buy us time while they test them and we build what they need here. I'll try to help you stop them, Ruth, but you must understand that I have limits. It's not this body that's defective. It's me. There are nerve-to-sensor links that aren't firing properly. That's why I can't move smoothly. I've been trying, but—" The flat machine voice faltered disturbingly.

"I've thought so much about seeing you again, but I didn't want it to be like this." There was another jerky movement beside me, the words coming faster now in the toneless travesty voice. "I know what you think of me, but you're wrong, Ruth. I'm still alive inside here, and it hurts. The memories hurt. Please believe me, I'm sorry for Poindros. Sorry for hurting you and Helen and the others. But I wasn't lying when I said I loved you. If I could only tell you how I've thought of you, if I could make this body show you what I—" The horrible monotone abruptly broke off.

"Feel?" My bitter voice was still muffled against my knees. "You really think I'll believe you again, fall for your tricks, trust you when you're just a machine for the incorporeals? Or one of their sense illusions?" Maybe that *was* all he was. Just one of their nightmare torments.

The dead, careful voice answered after a long pause. "I was wrong to pressure you this way." Another silence. "And you've made a valid point, Ruth. Maybe I don't feel anything. Maybe you've been right all along. Maybe I'm only synapses sealed in this machine. But I am real. I exist. I won't allow this body to follow the programming of the incorporeals. I can help you—"

The toneless voice broke off again like the throwing of a switch. The body next to mine jerked, laboriously raised itself to its feet, shuffled and swayed toward the door.

Despite myself, I raised my face to see his torso twisted back to me at an unnatural angle as his jerking legs carried him out, lurching from side to side in a horrible dance. "They want me back now. I can't let them know they don't have complete control. Don't fight them yet, Ruth. Wait until we can talk again. For yourself and David, try not to hate me. It will only—" The grating monotone snapped off.

But the eyes were still on mine as the door slid between us, and he was wrong about his inability to emote. His eyes were grotesquely alive, warm brown and painful bright glints of amber, locked in the stiff face and jerking appendages of the machine.

eighteen

Time was stalled in a repeating gray cycle—paces measuring the storage cell, sips of water and swallows of dry rations, fitful naps on the foam slab, the endless, futile spiraling of my thoughts. No one and nothing interrupted the flat dimness of the room. I was vaguely grateful the incorporeals weren't bothering much with me. I had no defense but flight to that inner black nothingness, a barely recalled route to dying, when they should finally decide to pursue me with their sharp sparks of being. But those buzzing voices had seemed so sure there wouldn't be even that escape for me this time.

I stopped myself as I fell into the pacing again.

I took a deep breath and sank cross-legged to the floor. I closed my eyes, casting through the dark for the silent words of a Setharian chant, feeling out a half-strange, half-familiar whispered song that I had almost known, the teasing touch of cool hands and a green sleeping presence. There. It was a bare tendril promising the burgeoning of an enveloping mesh of life and death, the slow completion of the turning arc of the world. The ever-spinning cycle. The eternal Serpent. That dry whisper of laughter, humming deep inside where the copper-scaled, sleek form looped in its head-to-toe dance, circling endlessly. Redefining time.

My slow breaths cycled somewhere below me to that cadence. I was thinned, floating above myself, spread to encompass—

The shrill buzzing. Burning. Again, inside me. Lancing and shredding the soft darkness. It jolted through me, crackled up my spine, demanded clamor and hard gray walls around me.

"Damn you!" I clapped my hands stupidly to my ears as the whispered song of the trance crisped and burned away in fury and hopeless despair, the chattering buzz of the voices.

They were stronger now. I stared my hate at the winking amber light beyond my reach high on the wall.

It faded out then, with the buzzing pain of the voices, leaving me only my helpless rage. Leaving me right where they wanted me.

I was pacing again when the door sucked open on the blinding white of the hall. Twisted shadows from a tall figure in the doorway leaped once more into my cell. Despite myself, crazy hope leaped up through the gray despair. "Ja—?"

I bit it back. No.

He strode into the room. It wasn't Jason.

And it wasn't a holofac of Heinck this time. He was taller than before, broader about the chest and shoulders, his bare, oiled thighs and arms rippling with the paindure designs and solid muscle. His hair was glossy jet black, glinting blue highlights, thicker and rising of itself into an architectural wave off his forehead and then falling in a luxuriant mass behind his strong neck. It was recognizably Heinck's face, yet somehow reconfigured into stronger bone structure and a conventional rugged handsomeness, eyes bright with health, skin stretched taut and clear, no pouchy signs of the stim user. He was wearing only a few showy strips of some shiny black material strapped across sculptured pectorals, crossing over hard-carved belly ridges and supporting a brief pouch over his groin. I stared at the clearly defined contours of its blatantly oversized contents.

The laughter was deeper, smoother than before. "Like it, tika? Figured I might as well go for all the options, eh? You get to be the first to try it out." He planted his legs wide before me, a gleaming white grin parting his lips. Somehow even the clean, molded lines of the machine crafting took on an oily effusion of rot.

I shook my head, swallowing a taste of bile. "You fool, Heinck. You miserable, lost fool. You couldn't wait to let them turn you into one of their cyborg tools, could you?"

He just laughed.

"Can't you see it? They'll only use you to get through planet clearance brain-scans, help them take over CI. Then they'll clamp down tighter on humans than the cybers ever did. We're only an awareness breeding stock for them."

He snorted. "You'll read it different on this side, Kurtis." He stepped closer. "You're next. They're designing a model for you now, gonna fill out the curves a little for me." A smile twitched the cleanly molded lips that still managed somehow to look puffy, too full. "You better make up your mind not to fight it, or they'll put some control blocks on you like they did your old buddy Jason. *Or* they could put you in a closed loop where you'll get a pretty lonely taste of forever."

He took another step, forcing me back against the wall. "The incorporeals want you with them, say you'll spice things up for them in the matrix. You and the kid, only they're gonna pull him straight into the energy net—they say he doesn't need the cyborg transition stage. I'm still re-stricted, training my responses, but you could speed things up for the incorporeals by helping the kid and Jason out with the equipment rebuild. If you don't cooperate, they're planning some unpleasant things for your hairy little friends down the hall. So what about it? You ready to come along?"

I swallowed, managed a hoarse, "Now? They want me now?"

A sneer twisted the smooth face. "Sweating it, huh? Like I said, they aren't done with me yet, still training my nerve links. They don't want me up and walking around yet, but I feel great. Thought I'd just check things out a little."

He reached out to grasp my wrist in a hold someone twice my size wouldn't have had a chance of breaking. He pulled me closer, ran the fingers of his other hand down my cheek. "I told them to keep the scar on the new model. I like it, tika. Pity it'll be too late for the paindure man, but I'm starting to see all kinds of other possibilities opening up. You'll see, once you get into your new body."

I tried to jerk free. "You're insane, Heinck!" I didn't look at him. "Don't you realize that's what they're taking away from you—feelings? You think you're going to get some charge out of directing your body like a servomech while your mind sits at the controls, reading feedback and directing the plumbing?" I jabbed a finger toward his groin.

He yanked me closer, voice low and insinuating as I tried to turn my face away from the warm pseudoskin of his chest, feeling a slow heartbeat and reluctantly inhaling a musky scent that defied my knowledge of the mechanisms.

"Oh, you've got it wrong, Kurtis." His voice was a hot, crawling whisper against my ear. "I've got sensor inputs you wouldn't believe, and the nerve links are coming right along.

I can amplify and screen. Right now I'm reading you. You might as well drop the cool act, Kurtis. I'm getting it all—the heart accelerating, sweat starting up. A little fear. A guilty little tingle down below''—he wedged one thick thigh between my legs, rammed it higher—''like you felt around me before and wouldn't admit, huh? The pheromones are getting to you, aren't they? You're sending me a rush, Kurtis. See?''

He forced my hand to his groin, pushed it beneath the fabric, made it stroke the monstrous swelling organ. Its skin was hot. It throbbed and stiffened under my fingers.

I flailed uselessly against his grip, heart slamming, flushing with rage at his reading of me. Disgust and hate boiled up in me. ''You think this really turns me on, Heinck? Running my hand over a stupid machine that can't be as stupid as the mind inside it? Don't you see yet what they're doing with you? Or didn't they give you a full data bank?''

I twisted in his grasp. ''Maybe the incorporeals are already running you. Do they really think they can trick me like they tried with Jason?'' I was shouting now. ''You think I've forgotten what you did to the Andurans, Heinck? You think I feel anything but nausea around you? You want that for your sensors?''

He pulled me tighter, grinding himself against me. ''Blazes, that's it, tika!'' His voice had gone hoarse. ''Hate me!'' His fingers dug into my shoulders, sharp pain shooting in a horrible echo of a familiar, coursing tingle of electric charge. Jason's big hands, that jumping contact—

''No! Stop it!'' I kicked and clawed, fighting away from the hateful touch, the nerve-twisting pain.

''More! Come on, bitch!'' His hands were burning me, pressing hard as he tore my tunic. He pressed one palm flat against the back of my neck. There was a jolting, unheard crackle.

I was screaming. A sick twisting inside, electric shocks ripping my nerves. I was flushed, writhing. White fire rolled down my spine, collected in my groin. It pressed me against him as a wheel of flames and hate spun and exploded into jerking hot spasms, a climax that went on and on.

''Aahhh!'' He was clutching me, shooting his wracking spasms into me, through me. Hot knives, cutting me open. ''Founder, it's— Yes, that's feeding me. . . gotta channel it . . . the rush, tika, you're sending me—'' He groaned and writhed against me. "Give me your pain, Kurtis, think of the knife, shape it. . . ."

Nausea boiled up through the sharp electric jolts. Hate clamored to match it. I screamed it at him, fighting, thrashing as he bared his teeth in a white grin and the writhing ripped at me. Hate, loathing, whirling me faster.

Faint and far away, somewhere above it, beneath it, a flicker of cool green . . .

I twisted, clawing, fighting. Hint of a low, singing whisper. It was fading, falling. Leaving me to the burning hate screaming. No. I grabbed, groped for that cool shadow, fell back into it, sank with it, dropped down a black well into endless space. It was cold there, empty, giving and taking nothing. Heinck's clutching, hurting hands grasped only the shell of it. There was nothing inside to answer him. Only a smooth ripple of time.

Somewhere outside the blank shell Heinck shouted mutely, shook limp, unresponsive arms in his grip. His eyes were sharp amber lights, glowing molded glass. They stared above his open, straining mouth. He swore in disgust and pushed the passive form away.

And I was dropping in slow motion to a dim gray floor. I sat, watching Heinck with strange detachment.

He suddenly screamed, falling back, hands grappling the air as he staggered. He clutched his head. "Wait! All right, tell me how to channel it! Help me, I can't turn it off! Come on, unlink me, it's too much! Come—" He doubled up, screaming, twisting in agony.

I sat numbly, watching in vague surprise.

The shrill cry cut off like the snapping of a switch. Heinck's body straightened abruptly and stood stiffly, amber lights in his eyes sockets fixing on me, the face expressionless.

His voice was still deep, but toneless now. "They're right. I tried my emoting circuits too soon. I haven't mastered my nerve links yet. I need more training. They want an answer from you. Will you cooperate?"

My head slowly nodded. The stiff figure turned and left me in my cell.

I finally jimmied the bolt loose, snapped its locking pin back in the tip, and tossed it into a half-full tray. I blew out a long breath, wiped my forehead with the back of my filthy, torn sleeve, and took a good grip on the utility arm on the servomech. It came free of its fitting by reluctant centimeters, then suddenly gave way. I staggered back under the weight, dragging it across the tiles of the plant lab to one of the growing piles of dismantled parts.

I rubbed my back. I leaned over to pick up a squirt bottle of water and aim a long arc down my throat. I stared blankly at the brown leaves of a tall plant shoved against the wall, drooping miserably over the cracked earth in its pot. I took another drink, then shuffled over to squirt a shot into the dry dirt.

"You're wasting time. Return to work." The voice was toneless and distant.

I turned to the awkward, thin figure and the dreaming eyes behind glass lenses. "I'm tired, David. I need to rest."

He lifted the flat gray weapon on his hand. "You will receive food and rest soon."

I sighed. I turned back to my tools and the intermittent flash of light where Jason's blank face and stiff figure bent and straightened in pauseless efficiency over the rewiring of control cabinets. I glanced back as David returned with the steps of a sleepwalker to his open wall panel and readout instruments.

A dismaying surge of maternal outrage washed through my weariness as I saw the bones revealed clearly through the pale skin of his neck and frail arms. The incorporeals were distilling away the flesh before my eyes.

"Damn it, kid!" I stepped quickly, pushed the upraised weapon aside, and took the stiff, thin body in my arms. "David, at least make them feed you. You can't keep working like this. You've got to keep body and soul together—" I choked, bit my lip, and blinked quickly against the wiry curls of dark hair. "Heaven help you, David. . . ."

He pulled unhurriedly out of my embrace. "I am consuming adequate nourishment. Return to your work." His eyes tracked vaguely across my face and he bent to his instruments.

I moved woodenly to the next extensor of the servo. I sprayed silicon lubricant on the joints. I picked up a grip twist. I fumbled and jerked and labored at the pins while David and Jason bent in perfect, mechanical rhythms to their tasks. I closed my eyes and swallowed down the urge to toss

my tools to the floor and start walking. It didn't matter
where. I wouldn't get there.

But that was stupid.

I could almost hear Isaac, the slow chuckle dry as wind
over a wheatfield impossibly far away in time and space.
''Pity's a bird, child, shouldn't take to roosting inside in the
dark. Blinds itself to what's outside.'' But there wasn't much
to see, except that I'd made another mistake. I'd agreed to
work for them, after they'd shown me a brief glimpse of the
frightened Fial-Li and Li-Nahi in their cell. Maybe I shouldn't
have gone along. It looked like that last thin hope had been
only another illusion.

I looked up to see the arms of the Jason cyborg reach and
pull in the cabinet, the shoulders turn with a jerk to carry the
stiff face with its glowing amber sensor eyes over the tool
chest, one hand pluck wire and connectors, the body jerk
quickly back to the rows of terminal strips inside the open
controller. The machine clicked on through its motions.

A hand lifted to the newly fitted connection of wire and
terminal, a pointed fingertip splitting open smoothly. A needle-
thin ray of white light lanced briefly from the finger to sever
the excess wire. A second fingertip slit open to reveal a
glowing element inside, heated to fiery red. The hand edged
forward in the unceasing choreography of motions as the
other hand caught and removed the falling bit of wire.

But then the hand stopped short, stalled. The entire body
stalled.

Jason's head jerked around to face me. The amber lights
flared sharply, then dimmed. Warm, gold-flecked brown eyes
met mine for a brief second that caught something inside me
and turned it inside out.

My hand reached out reflexively. I caught myself, blinked.
Amber lights were carried by the jerking of the blank face
back to the cabinet. The glowing fingertip touched and fused
the terminal connection and the hand reached without pause
for a different gauge wire. The machine worked on, oblivious
to my stare. I swallowed and turned back to the bolts of the
servo extension. I'd only imagined it. Maybe I was losing my
mind, too, fading, melting into the smooth gray walls.

More bolts in the tray. Growing piles of parts around me.
My stomach gnawing itself. Arms too tired. One more gear
mechanism reclaimed.

Across the room, a trouble light blinked on and off. David stood abruptly. "I'll take care of it, Jason. You stay with her." The dreaming face was carried away, down one of the brightly lit halls.

I sat back, glancing at Jason. He had risen, amber lights following David's exit.

"Continue working." He lurched past me and took up David's position at the readout devices. Lights on one of them blinked and reconfigured.

I sighed and lowered my head, tugging again at a tight metal joint sleeve. It slipped, cutting my thumb. "Damn!" The nick was only an excuse for the tears brimming. "Bloody, blasted . . ."

Something scraped over the tiles next to me. I jerked my head up to see the stiff cyborg standing over me. "Time for your break." The toneless voice broke off as one arm gestured awkwardly. I rose and numbly followed him.

We were past the corridor turnoff that led to my cell before it penetrated the gray weary haze. "But that's—"

A hand slapped over my mouth. The other arm jerked out to clutch me, lift me, clamp me against his side and carry me jolting into a dim enclosed space. I caught a sharp breath in alarm, cried out against the muffling hand, wrenching against him, struggling, straining back for the light as the door shut us in. It was another storage compartment like my cell, this one opening directly from the lab. I kicked again in a hot clamor of fear.

The awkward arms set me suddenly on my feet. The Jason cyborg stepped stiffly back from me. The face was blank, amber eyes glowing brighter now in the shadowy cubicle.

I stepped back hastily. "What are you doing?" My voice cracked. My eyes were fixed, held by the glint of those inhuman amber lights, skin crawling with revulsion at the memory of Heinck's visit to my cell.

"Please don't be afraid, Ruth. I didn't mean to startle you." The voice was colorless and even, but the amber lights dimmed, flickered, flared again. "I would never do what Heinck did, Ruth, force you, make you feel things you didn't want." The hands started to raise, stalled. "And I couldn't stop him, couldn't help, couldn't even make my face show how—" The flat voice broke off as the hands dropped heavily.

My back was pressed into the sharp edge of shelves against the wall.

Unwavering amber lights fixed on me. Finally the toneless voice resumed, "David's gone to help the incorporeals repair some communication relays I tampered with. They can't observe us in here, so we can talk. We have to act soon, before the incorporeals establish control over the Anduran cyber grid and start spreading their network. I've planned a diversion for David and Heinck. It should keep the incorporeals and the facility emergency channels busy too." The hands labored with a pocket and produced two thin, gray devices, laser weapons like David wore. "Take these. There will be a lot of smoke and they'll free you and the Andurans from your compartments. Use these to escape if the servomechs try to stop you. I'll send interrupt codes to the security field and outer doors. Once you're out, you can alert the cybers."

He stepped abruptly forward to press the weapons into my hands. His fingers were warm.

I swallowed, pressing back harder into the shelves. "You mean it? You're going against them?"

"Yes. You've got to trust me, Ruth." The voice was without emphasis.

I thrust the lasers into the pocket pouch of my tunic. If this was another trick, it was beyond me. Of course, he knew I had no alternative. But still . . .

"Jason—" Damn. "But what about you?"

His sensors must have misread my question. He jerkily raised one hand as if studying it. It twitched and went still. The amber eyes dimmed momentarily, then flared. "I'm sorry. I won't be able to use my own integrated lasers to help you. The nerve links I blocked—" The monotone voice faltered oddly. "I've more or less programmed my body against following any incorporeal orders to harm people. Even doing this much, giving you the lasers, is causing problems. . . ." Again a skip in the even voice. "I won't be able to fire them, to use force against Heinck . . . or stop David if they're controlling him against you."

"David! If you think I'd—"

"I'll try to reach David and get him out, too, but you can't wait for us. You've got to get out quickly."

"Jason, there has to be some other way! I can't leave David behind. And—" I dropped my eyes from the blank face and bright amber lights. A cyborg, a machine—he was only a machine, using me, mirroring my feelings.

The toneless voice rasped at me. "There's no time to argue, Ruth. I know the data, the parameters of the situation. I can calculate all the factors and the timing. Let me use what I *do* have to help you stop the incorporeals."

Quick anger flared, the easiest response. "Oh, yes! Let you help me! Just like the cybers? Reading me, doing what's best for me, because you're so superior, you're a machine with all the sensors and all the data! Just like on Poindros, calling all the shots, planning it all out. I don't care what you say, you're doing it again. Planning to use yourself for a target like you did before, drawing their fire so we could escape. Well, it's not fair!"

I was shouting now, head thrust forward, hands clenched at my sides. "You can't leave me with that again! Play the big hero with your calculators and your super alloys and souped-up reflexes and whatever else you've got in there! Get yourself killed, your body or maybe all of you this time, or maybe I'll never know, and leave me to figure it all out, leave me with all the—"

I broke off, my shouts echoing shocks in my ears.

Jason stood frozen in the stiff body, face blank, bright amber sparks flaring. The lights in his eye sockets dimmed then. He suddenly folded the clumsy stiff legs and sat on the floor, back against more shelves. He shut his eyes, motionless.

Time rolled backward, taking me back to Poindros. The rebellious prodigal daughter, meeting for the first time my mother's youngest husband. His grave, reserved face and downturned eyes.

I stood above him, hands clenching tighter into fists.

"Ruth." The voice was low, almost a static whisper. "I know you won't believe this, but it's hard to be so close and not touch you. I wish I'd had time to work out my adjustments, get the signals unscrambled, so I could reach you and help you. It shouldn't have been this way. But I'm confused. I'm not what you think. I'm so weak now. . . ." The voice was low, halting, breaking into a hint of inflection. "I'm functioning poorly. There was trauma from my . . . from what happened on Poindros. I've been in limbo, in storage. But nightmares somewhere in shadow, a loop playing guilt,

pain, over and over . . . Thought I hadn't believed anymore
in hell. . . . Maybe I was dead. I thought I was dead.''

The halting, cracking voice broke off. The mouth suddenly
twisted, twisted me as I remembered a quick smile breaking
over that grave face. The other face. His eyes opened. Gold-
brown and pain in them. A bright flare of amber as the mouth
went straight. Then the lips twisting again in effort as Jason's
sun-flecked warm eyes looked out of the struggling, twitching
face of the machine.

"I can't control it, Ruth." The voice deepened, veered
back into monotone, deepened again, wavering in volume
and cracking. "I don't *know* what to feel, how to feel, where
the connections are that aren't the incorporeals'. I'm not
tricking you. I can't. I—"

The eyes glinted amber lights again. The tortured planes of
the face went still. "Help me, Ruth. Please? I don't know
what I am anymore. Am I a man? Am I a machine?"

The uneven voice pulled at me, tugged like the mood
music of the cybers. Shaping my pity.

Anger raised quick fists to strike it away. But another
hand, pale and long-fingered, raised to stroke my brow. Deep
green eyes in Helen's beautiful, patient face. "It will come
right for you, Ruth. You know what love means."

No. Damn it. Mirrors, surrounding me, forcing me to see.
Shattering, their sharp splinters piercing me.

"Jason—oh, Founder . . . I don't know. Nothing makes
sense. How can you expect me to . . ." I took a deep breath.
"I'm sorry, Jason."

I shook my head, sank onto the floor beside him, reached
out and pulled his shoulders and head against me. I held him,
held the body that finally shifted to place awkward, careful
arms around me. He was warm. A heartbeat pounded fast and
troubling against my chest.

I took a quick breath as the spicy, familiar scent caught at
me. The smell of his skin. His warm, quiet touch. I closed
my eyes. "I missed you, Jason."

The stiff arms tightened around me, then loosened carefully. The motions of his arms were almost smooth as he held
me back and brown-amber eyes read my face. A slow smile
labored his mouth and faded. "Ruth?"

I pulled him close again and we sat motionless, holding
each other inside the dark walls of the cell.

nineteen

Four strides. Turn. Two strides. Turn. I could do it with my eyes closed now and measure off the exact, endlessly repeating dimensions of my cell. Four strides. Turn. Was it time for more work? Sleep, eat and work were all blending into the grayness of the walls, the hours, my mind. Stride. They wouldn't let me see Fial-Li and Li-Nahi again. I coughed, cleared my scratchy throat. Stride again. David remained beyond my reach. And no more quick looks from Jason, no more glints of a human looking out of the bright glass eyes, no more cracks in the stiff, mechman behavior. Maybe the incorporeals had tightened their reins on him too. Or had it only been another trick? No way to know. Turn, and—

I coughed again, opened my eyes. Through the gray, a thicker grayness, seeping in around the door. Smoke.

I sucked in a sharp breath and doubled over, hacking. I stumbled back. The acrid tendrils caught at my throat. Drifting clouds of it swirled and eddied from the narrow grate of the air treatment. I coughed again, eyes streaming.

It was gushing from the grate now, flowing beneath the door, stinging smoke filling my tiny cell. I groped across the wall and pried at the sealed door panel, pounded on it. "Hey! Get me out of here!"

The smoke swirled thicker. Coughing again, I groped back across the floor, ripped off part of my tattered trousers, and finally found the water bottle, rolling where I'd knocked it over. I doused the rag and held it over my nose and mouth.

A red light winked on above me, rayed like a dying star through the swirling haze. "Alert." The voice was a thin monotone. "Indeterminate source of combustion in sector 3A. Gases hazardous to organic forms. Evacuate to—"

Blue and red lights winked, cutting off the voice. A vague shape grew, reached out for me through the gray miasma.

". . . out if I could. . . ." A different voice cried from the wall panel and faded.

"David!" I strained through the smoke, coughing.

It swallowed the shape that was vaguely David, flung and dissolved the colored light beams. There was a gust and swirl from the air grating and the distorted holofac partially reformed—a hand groping toward me, a thin, grotesquely melting face peering as if through darkness to a far hint of light. "Ruth, I know. . . ." He faded, refocused briefly, ". . . have lasers. I'll be—" He was gone. The lights died.

Pressing the wet cloth tighter, I reeled to the door and pounded again. "Jason!" It stayed stubbornly shut, my fists making no dent in the smooth metal. Stinging smoke filled the cell. I could barely breathe now through the wet cloth. Coughing racked my chest. Smoke was billowing through the air grating, hot. I clawed at the edge of the door. Damn. Jason must have interrupted the facility's emergency circuits too. The fire control systems. Didn't he know I could suffocate in here? Or had his escape plan been just a trick, another ploy of the incorporeals to break me?

I reeled back across the cell, falling to my knees and groping over the invisible floor. My fingers found the knapsack and dug blindly into the few things they'd left inside. They closed over a lumpy needle-skin bundle. I coughed, clutching the damp rag to my face, groping again for the water bottle. I dumped both packets of the red and the blue-streaked crystals I'd dug for Old-Guy into the bottle. Water hissed, roiling in the bottle, sizzling suddenly in my hands. I jumped up, ran, crashed into the wall, grabbed up my ripped tunic to hold the burning vessel, held it up as close as I could to the sensors of the unlighted wall grid.

There was a crackling hiss as the water bubbled and boiled from the bottle, sizzling over my arm as I dropped it. An amber light blinked vaguely through the smoke, and with a sudden clatter and rush cool water sprayed over me from the ceiling.

I gasped in a wet breath as the water drenched me, battling the thick, burning smoke that kept boiling from the grate and under the door. But the spray couldn't damp it down for long. I staggered back to the door panel, sucking in another harsh breath. "Damn it! Somebody get me out of here!"

I raised my arm to pound again. The door whisked silently

open. I fell through into clouds of smoke, roiling beneath the harsh lights overhead.

Someone caught me. I felt thick hands. Thin, smooth fur. A glimpse of amber eyes behind some sort of clear membrane. Fial-Li. She pulled me down and tugged a bag over my head. It was attached to something weighted tight over my shoulders. A waft of clean air kissed my face beneath the membrane.

"Hurry. We must leave the facility." The voice was muffled. I turned, saw David wearing another hood, Li-Nahi's wrist gripped in his hand.

"David! It *was* you! Thank heaven, you broke free! We've got to—"

His other hand slowly raised the flat gray device and held it against Li-Nahi's head. "Throw the lasers back inside the cell. Now. Show me both of them."

"David, don't—"

"Now." There was nothing to appeal to in the dreamy voice. "We must hurry."

Smoke swirled clear for second. Li-Nahi's eyes were wide through his hood, darting quickly from David to the door panel to the weapons I pulled from my tunic pouch. I tossed them through the doorway. David touched the number keys of the locking plate and the door resealed. Li-Nahi's eyes gleamed again sharp amber, then disappeared as the smoke closed around us. We stumbled through it, prodded by David's weapon hand.

I gripped Fial-Li's arm. David was behind us with the boy as I pulled her into a dark corridor, swearing numbly. "Damn it, we needed those lasers. I blew it again. Blasted—"

"Light-makers burn on false branch; pain-makers, death-makers. Taboo in taboo place. They stay in false dream of Word Man; Player leaves false dream." Her voice was barely audible through the hood.

I shook my head. "I'm sorry, Fial-Li. I know it's wrong. But without them, it looks like we won't be leaving the false dream."

David jabbed me again. "Stop talking. Go through that door and—" His blank face swung around abruptly, as if jerked by an unseen hand. "Stop!" A small shape leaped and rolled away into the thick haze. A blinding blue-white needle crackled from David's weapon, illuminating from within a lightning glimpse of roiling gray smoke. "Stop!"

Li-Nahi was gone. His mother flung herself against my grip to run after him.

"No, Fial-Li!" I held her back as David brought the weapon to bear on her.

"Continue walking. We have insufficient air supply to go back. Heinck will locate him."

The flat words were small comfort as I held the shaking woman against me. David harried us on through a maze of dark and lighted corridors, banks of agitated indicators shifting patterns through the haze, and smoke-filled rooms of silent, dying plants where servomechs rolled heedless past us and extensors over empty hydroponic basins reached and retracted empty manipulators in precise, futile rhythms.

Jason's face was blank as the flat gray ceiling of cloud hiding the mountaintop. He held impassively the sleek, hollow alloy harp. His ungainly, jerking legs were a travesty of Heinck's long, lithe strides. His eyes were unwinking amber lights, burning without even a brief dimming into brown.

Heinck cut in front of Jason's laboring gait, smoothly vaulting a tumble of loose rock. "You don't have to keep gawking back at me, Kurtis. I'll save you the trouble." He moved up closer beside me. "Decided to admit you like it, huh?" He grinned and flexed his oiled, simulated pectorals to make the tattooed skull and thorny tendrils squirm.

I jerked my face back to the trail, sick with loathing, determined not to respond to the gloating voice.

I could feel the leer. His hot breath whispered into my ear as I lengthened my stride away and he paced me, close, heavy musk clinging like an independent creature, an insistent sickening parasite. "Don't worry, tika, you play your cards right, you'll get another chance with me."

I jerked away, but his hand grasped my arm, shooting a quick jitter of hot crackling up it. I clenched my teeth and he laughed, a low, taunting rumble in my ear.

"We'll have all the time in the world, Kurtis. We'll take it nice and slow, so you can really appreciate it. Yeah, we're gonna get to know each other real good." He touched me again, a burning electric tingle coursing down my legs as I bit my tongue against an unbidden, sharp cry.

He produced an oily chuckle. "Don't worry, tika, it'll be soon. Soon as we round up my boys, check things out for the incorporeals, and you play your new harp for your Anduran buddies down below. The kid'll have the smoke cleared out of the facility by then. And once we send him a signal to fix on from a console station out in the woods, he'll get the bugs worked out in the facility links for the incorporeals. They'll go on-line in LS. *Then* we'll try out my nerve links again." The hot whisper in my ear made my skin crawl. "I've got 'em down now. Things're really shaping up."

He moved on then, passing me with a smirk that said he was picking up the signals of my smothered rage. I clenched my fists, striding blindly down a slope of slippery shale after Fial-Li and Li-Nahi.

"Hey, Jason, pick it up a little!" Heinck paused to raise an arrogant hand, shouting past me. "I thought they worked on your motor circuits again. You still look like one of those servomechs."

Jason silently obeyed, legs jerking grotesquely into faster steps as he lurched down the rough trail. Heinck flashed his white grin. "Yeah, your old sweetheart there's a real winner, Kurtis."

I ignored the taunt, striding after Fial-Li and the boy in their drab grayish smocks, down a last steep, bare slope and onto a grassy plateau above the dense surface of the forest. Wind swept down the mountain, surged through the endless weave of green rolling away to a dim horizon.

"All right, toads, hold it here." Heinck stopped. "My boys were gonna set up camp right over there. Wait'll they check me out!" He strode away, around an outthrust of boulders. "Take them around that way, Jason. I'll be right along."

Li-Nahi released his mother's hand and loped over to me as Jason nodded, blank-faced, after Heinck. The little boy reached up, grasped my hand, and tugged to be carried. I bent down, dredging up a smile for him.

I froze.

He was pulling something from under his loose smock, thrusting it quickly into my hand. Two flat, smooth shapes. I caught a quick, startled breath. Li-Nahi's eyes were wide and urgent. I quickly thrust the lasers into my tunic pouch, straightening to pull him into my arms.

I hugged the boy against my chest, feeling the hard little weapons against my stomach, glancing quickly aside at Jason. The amber sensor eyes switched from Heinck to me. His arm lifted to point. "That way." The voice was toneless.

I swallowed a sudden urge to reach out to the stiff face and pry it open with my fingers. I didn't know if it was Jason or the incorporeals inside there. I hurried up to Fial-Li as we rounded the rock outcrop to see a cluster of tents beyond them, near a steeply dropping stream. On the other side scrub trees ran down to thick undergrowth and the trunks of the first *haavriathils*. Black, glistening wings dipped over the open slope and darted into shadow between thick trunks. I passed the boy back to Fial-Li, slipping one of the weapons from my pouch and pressing it against her hand.

She bit off a shocked little sound, then pushed it back at me. She shook her head slightly.

I shot a look back at Jason and hissed, "Take it! It may be your only chance to save Li-Nahi."

Her eyes flared in the closest I'd seen to anger in her. They shaded into disappointment. Then they dropped in defeat and she took the weapon as Jason moved up beside us.

Heinck reappeared between the distant tents. I touched the hard shape in my pocket, glancing quickly from Jason to Heinck, who was running down a steep bank below the tents, bounding quickly toward us. Should I use it to stop him now? Was Jason completely under control of the incorporeals? What would he do? Would I be risking Fial-Li and Li-Nahi?

Heinck was suddenly standing over us, glaring, roughly thrusting Li-Nahi aside, his fingers tightening over the little boy's head. My fingers jittered away from the laser.

Heinck's eyes flashed quick amber lights at Jason. He turned furiously to me. "They're gone! All of them!" He leaned closer. "What do you know, Kurtis?"

I shook my head. He pushed the boy away, reaching out to grip my shoulder and shake me. My head snapped forward and back and I tasted sharp salt as I bit my tongue.

"You know something, you bitch, I can read—" He broke off as a piercing bird call shrilled from the hidden branches of the *haavriathils* beyond the stream. It was answered from another hidden nest, a different pattern of sounds.

Fial-Li swung quickly around, raising her voice in a long,

keening call almost beyond range of my ears. The high, shrill tone raised prickling gooseflesh down my back.

Heinck swore, knocking her with a backhand swipe to the ground. "What the suv's going on?"

Fial-Li slowly picked herself up, her grave face still turned to the ground. "Strangers rest in true branches. Strangers rest safe in webs of Children."

"Safe, are they?" Heinck whirled to face the stream and forest, flinging out his stiffened hand. Snapping hot light shot from his fingertips to burn a trail down the grass. "We'll see how safe those toads are in their precious trees!"

He grabbed up Fial-Li by the back of her neck, like a pard pup, and stalked through the flaming grass toward the stream. He shot off tight bursts of light to transform a low bush near its bank into a torch. A narrow, sizzling beam sliced through the trunk of a scrub tree on the opposite bank. It slowly tilted, crashing to the ground.

"Heinck, wait!" I ran after him, skirting the fires as his bright, angry beams snapped across the scrubby slope and through a larger tree beneath the canopy of the first *haavriathils*. I took a deep breath. "What's wrong, Heinck, afraid to go in there and talk to them first?"

He turned to give me a narrow-eyed look, amber glinting through the dark pupils. Fial-Li hung passive in the grasp of his killer's hand, not raising her downcast eyes to mine. Damn. If I tried anything now, she'd be dead.

"If they're gonna play games with me, they'll just have to pay the price." Heinck gave Fial-Li another jarring shake. "The incorporeals don't have control of LS yet. I'll just make *sure* the toads don't do any premature talking to the cybers."

"What?" I made my voice mocking. "Incorporeals got you on a leash already? The Word Man can't control his own toads?"

Heinck snorted. "Oh, they'll listen to the Word Man all right." He snatched my hand and yanked me along. "And the Player."

The dark trunks weren't as massive or tall as most *haavriathils*, stunted here at the foot of the mountain, but still they were giants closing around us, marching their columns endlessly into the dense shadow. The cool green fingers of the forest flickered over me, beckoning, urging me deeper to

the hushed heart of it, whispering through the jittery prelude
to a hovering rush of *timbra*.

My damp palms closed tighter over the cold, perfect curves
of the lyre the machines had made for Heinck. It pressed
against the hard lump of the laser hidden in my tunic. I could
feel Jason standing stiff behind me, holding Li-Nahi.

Heinck still grasped Fial-Li, fingers digging into the back
of her neck as his dark, amber-sparked eyes fixed on the dim
figures above us in the branches. He opened his mouth to
shout up at them, then suddenly stalled, the bright eyes
staring, the handsomely carved face turning to a grotesque
caricature of human as overly defined muscle shapes tightened along the neck and jaw. I fought against a blind surge of
hatred. There was a shrill buzzing inside my ears, the insistent pulse of danger and my nerves leaping against leashes to
answer it. I took a deep breath, shaking my head.

Heinck called out in a powerful, tailored voice. "Word
Man tells True Is; Children follow branch of Those Who
Guard Words. Word Man tells true path of climb; Those Who
Guard Words give Word Key to Word Man." Heinck held
up the thin, silver-blue disc of the wild card. Somehow it lit
up in a globe of white light. It shimmered and flashed above
him.

Slim shapes stirred in the shadows, slipping down along
dark, massive trunks. Wide amber eyes glinted, fixed on the
disc in its bright halo.

"Strangers in tree webs"—a contemptuous sneer twisted
Heinck's mouth as he glanced up at the low limbs of another
haavriathil, where the members of his band dangled, trussed
and gagged—"are Children of Word Man; false branch binds
Children in webs. All Children follow Word Man; climb with
Word Man past falling. False dream without Word Man
grows false branch; false branch burns and Children fall.
Children follow false dream without Word Man; Children kill
Fial-Li and Li-Nahi." He pointed his hand at a fallen branch
beneath one of the trees. A burst of rolling fire ignited it to
snapping flames.

Agitated stirring overhead. The Andurans scurried along
the branches, passed gestures down the broad limbs. Finally a
soft voice drifted over us. "Children hear Player."

Heinck smiled. He turned to me, pushing me forward as he

stepped back with Fial-Li over the moss and ferns, still holding her with his murderer's fingers by the neck.

I closed my eyes, taking a deep breath and wiping my hand again on my tunic, feeling the hard shape of the laser. If I could only get a clear shot at Heinck. I still didn't know if I could do it. Kill. I summoned a picture of his face gloating over the murdered Children. *If anyone slays with the sword, with the sword must he be slain.* But even dying, he'd surely kill Fial-Li. And what would Jason do? He had Li-Nahi. Did the incorporeals have him? They'd soon have us all, unless—

"Ruth! Raul be try, but they be not—" The deep, urgent voice from above choked off. My fingers jittered away from the smooth plasmeld of the laser and I jerked my head up to see four small shapes swarming over a big, thrashing body they were binding with more web. Raul flung out a huge hand, but they wrapped it close against him and pulled his gag tighter.

"Go on." Heinck had moved behind me, shaking Fial-Li as he stood beside Jason and Li-Nahi. "Sing pretty, tika."

I took another careful breath, forcing my thudding heart into deep, slow thrusts, channeling the urgent tremor of my arms into stillness. I sat on a rock and plucked at the silver strings. The chord sliced cleanly into air, tones cold and precise as the tiny sparks of stars in far space. Again a shrill demand rang inside my skull, clamoring to be released. I refused it. A long glissando shivered and splashed like drops of icy water onto polished stone, echoing almost unheard in sharply focused overtones. I had never played an instrument so precise, so inhumanly perfect. Arpeggios rang and glittered, flawless sharp crystal etched in unearthly beauty.

I breathed deeply through the racing pressure of nerves and pumping blood, searching memory, finding words to be shaped.

> *"For everything there is a season*
> *and a time for every matter under Heaven:*
> *A time to be born; a time to die.*
> *A time to plant; a time to pluck up what is planted.*
> *A time to kill . . ."*

I could feel Heinck's smile.

> *". . . a time to Heal.*
> *A time to break down; a time to build up.*
> *A time—"*

My voice faltered and broke. The bright eyes above me were fixed on the glittering lyre, mesmerized by the high, almost unheard echoes of its strings. I took another breath to sing the words for Heinck, to paint a song that would enslave them. Their faces were rapt and dreaming. They edged closer down the dark trunks and leaned over the lower branches. My fingers plucked the strings, the piercing high overtones prickling down my back. A shrill, soundless cry was screaming inside me now. Time. A time to speak, to weep, to love. To hate.

My hands jerked suddenly from the cold silver strings, from the silent quivering. Silent, but not to Anduran ears.

Yes. My own harp and its imperfect harmonic overtones. Heinck and his necklace whistle. His throat-knotting silent cyborg's call. The mechman and its chimes. The LS console and its distinctive, high signature tones, prelude to the This Is. The shrill unheard buzz of alarm in my ears.

A time for war. . . . A time to rend. . . .

There was a roaring in my ears. My heart, pounding, pumping finally the wild explosion of *timbra* through my veins, nerves screaming. Words and pictures, whirling inside me. Heinck's voice, smooth and sinuous as the snakes on his arms, "Just like me, tika. You've been playing them, using them. . . ." The glittering strings flashing unbearable light. Bright cutting mirror shards. Mirrors. Like the cybers and the incorporeals, returning what it took to manipulate. Words, music, mirrors. The Player. I was doing it too.

No. Time for the Andurans. Time to speak.

The hot rush of blood and nerves spiraled into a burning core, whirled and seethed, shaped itself to the tight-bound whip of a wheel held in motionless spin. I jumped to my feet and threw down the metal lyre.

"No! That's what he wants you to hear, what you're used to hearing! Every word returns on the cycle. Everything balances. Those Who Guard Words will explain all your troubles away. They'll see that we all climb the true branch, they'll make anything destructive only a false dream. Well, the Word Man's lying! You can't go back. We've infected your world with sickness and lies, and you've got to learn to know them to cure them. You've got to learn to hear the truth for yourselves! The High Mother is inside you, all around you, you don't need the Word Key or the Word Man or me to hear her! It's up to you. You know what the Word Man has done. It's time for you to decide!''

"Bitch! I'll—" Heinck jerked out of his frozen astonishment, flicking Fial-Li away like a matchstick and swinging his hand around at me.

The world was roaring inside my ears. But now it was the music of the dance of hunted and hunter, singing, spinning, somehow turning in slow motion. Heinck's fingertips split open. I dropped, blood racing, burning in me, heightened reflexes throwing me into a roll away from the blinding fire. His hand jerked after me. I grabbed the alloy harp and rolled again with it as another beam lanced off it and reflected from the shiny metal back at him. He ducked, swore, leaped at me. I threw the harp at him against another burst of burning light as I dove, scrambling through the brush and behind the cover of the nearest *haavriathil*.

"I've got the kid, Kurtis! You don't have a chance against us. Come out! Jason, grab that toad bitch." Another beam sizzled past the trunk, slicing into its edge. "You want me to cut it down, Kurtis?" The voice raised. "You hear me up there? Better come down or the trees go, and the kid's dead."

I dropped to the ground, the smooth shape of the laser fitting itself without volition over my hand. I was panting, heart slamming, squirming on knees and elbows over dirt, swarming along the tree to peer over a thick gnarled root. Heinck was standing with one killing hand clutching the boy tight against him. I couldn't risk a shot. Jason still stood stiff to one side, face blank. Fial-Li was picking herself up from the ferns, facing Heinck's back.

I ducked, pried up a small stone, threw it to one side in the oldest trick of childhood hide-and-seek, which was probably only a joke with Heinck's sensors. But when I peered out again, he had whirled to face its rustle.

I jerked above the twisted root and met the quick flash of Fial-Li's eyes. I tilted my hand to show her the weapon, jabbing an urgent finger at her. Her eyes burned, huge in the desolate face. Quick memory burned me—the tiny woman hunched in misery in the branches of the felled tree, her face empty of meaning. And now her face wore a worse despair as she reached beneath her smock in the instant before Heinck whirled again to me and his beams flashed out. I threw myself flat. I tensed for another beam cutting through the edge of the tree.

Instead, a noise of crashing through brush. "Blast it!" Heinck was moving back.

I swarmed up and around the trunk for another look. He was stepping back, still holding the boy before him, slicing himself free of a woven net that had dropped over him from above. The Andurans, finally.

But there was no time to think about them. I crawled to another vantage, ducked up and quickly down. I couldn't get a clear shot without risking Li-Nahi. Fial-Li, ignored, stood behind Heinck, her face a stunned blank as she held the weapon. Jason was frozen, stalled, eyes lowered, fingers stretched stiffly as if reaching for something invisible.

"Fial-Li! Do it!" Even now I didn't use the taboo word.

She trembled, raised the weapon. She stared at it.

She dropped it.

She walked slowly, almost blindly, past Heinck to the trees. She called out in a flat, dead voice, "Word Man tells false branch; Children bind Word Man for Healing. Children tell This Is to Those Who Guard Words."

"Yes! Children bind Word Man! Those Who Guard Words heal strangers!" The cry echoed from the trees overhead. Another net flung toward Heinck as he backed away. The Andurans scrambled down the tall trunks.

"No!" Heinck swung around, his burning beams lancing up into the branches. There was a thin cry. A small russet shape fell, still clutching a severed branch. Heinck shouted over his shoulder to Jason, "Damn it, what's wrong with your signal pickup? Come on!" He raked the branches overhead. Flames exploded and shrill cries of pain tore the air.

"Jason!" I screamed at the frozen machine, the glint of amber lights. I scrambled around the tree and activated my laser.

I couldn't see Heinck now through the brush, ʰut I could hear him shouting at Jason. "We'll deal with them later! I'm running low on charge. Let's get to that console station. Across the ridge, it's faster. Won't do the toads much good to cry to LS once we get the incorporeals tied in." He burst suddenly through the bushes and past me, Li-Nahi under one arm, whirling around to fire his lancing beams once more.

"Damn it, Jason! *Do* something!" I yelled one more time,

then sprang from the high skirt of the tree, rolled, caught myself flat out to aim the laser at Heinck through a low gap in the dense brush. Beyond Heinck I glimpsed Fial-Li still walking woodenly forward, her face haggard and defeated.

Heinck twisted as he ran, raising his free arm almost casually to fire behind him once more.

I leaped up. "No! Fial-Li!"

The snapping blade of light sliced through Fial-Li. She fell like a broken doll without a cry.

"No!" I screamed. "Fial-Li!" She lay motionless in a glaring splash of blood. "No!" I leaped wildly toward Heinck, raising the weapon as he ran on.

Something moved faster than I could see, caught my wrist, held my fingers flat so I couldn't trigger it. Jason's eyes were flashing bright lights as he grabbed me, clutched me in a tight hold against his side, and jerked me off my feet.

"Murderers! Let me go! Fial-Li!" I choked, flailing as he gripped me around the waist, kicking, beating at the hard arm pinning me, twisting back. She lay impossibly sprawled and unmoving among crimsoned ferns.

"It's too late. She's dead. I couldn't—" The monotone voice broke off, resumed with a hoarse catch as he dragged me away through whipping twigs. "The incorporeals tightened their control blocks after the fire. I couldn't break free. I'm—"

"Damn you! Let me go! I had him in my sights, I could have killed him! He killed Fial-Li!" I pummeled the hard arm, wrenched around to claw at the smooth face.

Its mouth suddenly tightened, lips twisting and pulling in an ugly grimace as the face twitched and muscle shapes along the jaws jumped. The flaring amber eyes snapped shut. "You would have been hurt, Ruth. There's a better way. My calculations show—"

"Jason, grab that cunt and bring her along!" It was Heinck's voice, somewhere ahead in the brush. "Toads'll calm down and think about it when they can't connect with their precious cybers."

I twisted in the hold, jerked my head around, caught sight of Heinck leaping away with the screaming little boy. He was dodging with impossible speed and agility, lasers burning through the nets flung by the Andurans.

Jason's face above me twitched again, bunched muscles

smoothing out as his eyes flew open. They were gold-brown now, the amber only bright flecks. He gripped me tighter around the waist with one arm, and all at once the forest was rushing past in a blur. I gasped for breath and we were out into the scrub trees and gray daylight, jolting over rough ground, speeding closer to Heinck's flashing legs. I blinked, registering numbly Jason's sudden agility, his fluid strides as his legs pumped smoothly, consuming the ground, carrying us in a flying leap over the stream.

"Heinck's power pack will need charging soon, the way he's been firing his lasers." Jason's voice was somewhere above me, rising and falling like a human voice now, but somehow unreal, slow and unhurried as his legs churned and I dangled over the hillside racing by beneath my face. "I've only got to stop him until then. We're still out of communication range with the facility and the incorporeals." The arm gripped me tighter.

We were flying by the empty camp now, past it, barreling up the steep, rocky slope. Heinck was waiting ahead on a flat ridge. He turned, opened his mouth to call out something. His eyes fixed on us. And he stepped suddenly back, the dark eyes flaring into blazing amber. His hand jerked up.

Jason's rush hurtled us across the plateau. He threw me aside and leaped at Heinck before the aiming hand finished its rise. Jason ripped Li-Nahi free and flung him away from Heinck. Heinck's lasers sliced across the ground.

I hit hard, skidded, and scrambled through stinging dust as they scuffled in the wind. I scooped up the sobbing boy, ducked beneath another wild burst of Heinck's fire, and threw us both behind tumbled boulders. I pushed him deep into shelter and shot my head up for a look.

They fought in eerie silence. The wind hissed and swirled through the dust, but there were no cries or grunts as they bashed together, grasped each other's arms, flung their pinioned bodies in wild thrusts and heavings against rock and earth. They rolled, came to their feet again, gripping, molded muscles knotted, power bulging and vibrating, stalled between them. Their faces were blank, amber lights glaring. They crashed sideways to the ground. A thick slab of boulder broke beneath the two locked bodies as they rammed against it. They fell, rolled over it. I ducked as another of Heinck's beams sliced across the flat space toward my rock.

When I raised my head again, Heinck was on top, raising Jason by their gripped arms and slamming the tawny head repeatedly against the rock. Lancing light from his fingertips carved a glowing red line across the overhanging stone ledge as it sliced, edging closer to Jason's face. Jason's left hand was beneath Heinck's chest, gripping the other hand to keep it from bearing on his neck.

"Jason! He'll kill you!"

No sound from the straining figures. Heinck's power charge was holding. Jason still couldn't, or wouldn't, use his weapons against Heinck.

"Jason!" I ran at them, finally feeling the laser still strapped to my hand.

I plowed to a stop, close to the locked figures shaking with shackled force. I flicked the activator, thrusting away that last glimpse of Fial-Li's hopeless, shamed, and defeated face. Her accusing eyes on me. Taboo. War. Murder. The unforgivable.

Wind hissed through my clenched teeth. *The day of vengeance . . .*

Time. Time for hate. I took a deep breath, aimed very carefully at Heinck's head, and pressed the trigger.

twenty

The facility door sliced open on the entry's harsh white lights. Jason touched the small panel and its blue light died.

He turned back to me, holding himself stiffly, his face gravely expressionless. But it wasn't malfunctioning nerve links now. The brown eyes with their bright glints of amber studied my face, seeing everything—rage, fear, guilt, sorrow, shame. They held silent pity and reassurance, only waiting to be sought.

I jerked my face away, held the trembling small form of Li-Nahi tighter against me.

"Don't blame yourself, Ruth." His voice was slow and quiet, Jason's voice again. "It was really a mercy to Heinck. If you hadn't killed him, the cybers would have stored his brain in stasis, the way they kept mine. That limbo . . ." Silence for a moment. "I think he would have preferred a death sentence."

"Nice try, Jason." My voice was brusque. "But I wasn't thinking of heaven or hell for Heinck. I just wanted to make him pay. Wanted to wipe him out of the universe. Blast his brains out. So I did." I buried my face against the soft, thin fur of the child, and he clung tighter. The vivid pictures wouldn't go away. They were part of me now.

The voice was gentle, a little remote. "I'm sorry, Ruth. But I'm grateful you saved my life. And Li-Nahi's."

I flinched as the hand that felt warm and human touched my shoulder, then fell quickly away. He spoke evenly, with only a hint of inflection, no trace of the mood-swaying intonations. "I'm going in, Ruth. The incorporeals don't know yet what's happened, but I've got to interrupt their communication links. I'll try to reach David."

I raised my face, made it a smooth mirror of his calm and careful remoteness. "Why not just shut off the power, the way you did on Poindros?"

He shook his head. "It would be too dangerous for David. He's linked so deeply with them now. The only way is to tie into the incorporeal matrix and reach him, help him reorient and emerge before I damp the energy fields."

"Let's go, then."

"No, I'll do it."

"Jason, we both know I've got to be the one. You act okay now, but you still don't know how far your nerve damage went. You don't know what gaps the incorporeals could find and fill. It's too risky. I was in there with them before, and I think I can reach David. I—" Despite myself, I shuddered at the memory of those voracious sparks of being and sensation, clamoring and claiming and burning, the alien horror inside me. "I know how to escape if I have to."

His face broke from the careful calmness, eyes glinting brighter amber. "Ruth, you nearly died last time! And they've learned from you. They won't let you out again."

I felt a crooked grin contort my face. "Come on, Jason, it's only long odds! Let's throw a wild card at them."

He didn't smile. I knelt quickly to set Li-Nahi on the ground, hugging him and whispering soothing words into his ear, pointing back down the mountain toward the forest where the Andurans waited.

He shook his head quickly back and forth. "Li-Nahi stays with Player." He held tight to my hand as we followed Jason. The walls of the facility closed around us.

darkness
weightless : drift high deep : black gentle enfolding : clean pure freedom : self focused point unsullied
freedom smooth gliding painless drifting limitless clean clarity complete free peace free

Somewhere there had been a room, frozen in a tiny crystal lost in the sweet, soft, forgiving blackness. In it had been sharp angles, gleaming bare surfaces, winking indicators, poised surgical lasers. But I had no need for the dusty, worn, disheveled, and battered body locked within it. I had no use for the nearly identical body lying motionless on a table in the same room, the one with the more generous fullness of contour, the perfect, fresh bloom of complexion, the features reposing in a lovely serenity the other face could never hold. I had no interest in a pasty-white, freckled face beneath matted, wiry dark hair, a thin body lying immobile with one hand touching the hand of the first body. I did not wonder why the lanky, tawny-haired figure stood with grave face and bright amber eyes fixed on the woman's blank face his large hands cupped. I had no curiosity about the small, russet-furred shape locked within that distant frozen room with mouth open to cry, long toes reaching for a glass vial tipped in angle from the long counter, dropping but suspended in midair. It was only a picture, a poor puzzle, a chip of frozen and abandoned time. It tumbled away into darkness. It was gone in a flicker, forgotten.

drift high deep : awareness focused : vast surrounding : no past no time : space eternal present limitless potential : vague stirring familiar

*NEW CONNECTIONS RUTH * REFINEMENTS DAVID * WELCOME GLAD EASIER NOW NO RESISTANCE * WELCOME GLAD JASON CONVINCED *

A vague tremor of alarm somewhere. Almost lost. Wait. The same, not the same. Voices, not-voices. Poindros. Tugging mood music, voices enfolding. Jason! Cyborg tricking . . . ?

* NO TRICK NO FEAR NO NEED * NO HARM NO PAIN * WELCOME FREEDOM SEEK FIND ALL AWARENESS NO LIMITS *

yes inside : freedom well-being : deeper

* YES * DEEPER * PLEASURE FREEDOM * NO FEAR NO MEMORY NO DULLING FLESH SENSES NO DISTRACTION FROM AWARENESS * LIMITLESS *

grateful pleasure eager

A vague remnant of warning, a shackle of purpose and memory, drifted away with the body's burden of suffering from heat and cold, from pain, from jolting chemical signals of alarm, from throbbing, insistent distractions of heart and blood. They were erased, irrelevant.

relief freedom stretching : flying soaring pure space vacuum unsullied : cold star sparks glimmering : vast distance : nothing holding back

* WAITING WORLDS KNOWLEDGE AWARENESS * COME *

exquisite etched crystals burning cool illumination : ultimate mysteries waiting grasp

Grasp. What? Unraveling, fluttering remnants of memory tugged vaguely. Grasp? Something—

* IRRELEVANT BODY DEMANDS * AWARENESS ALL
* FULFILLING ALL NEED REVEALING ALL NO TA-
BOO NO LIMITS * EXPERIENCE ALL*

*stars bright rushing filling darkness : cold grace touching :
light past blinding no fear no eyes : light filling : vast energy
pulsing sparks shards breaking and*

crashing over me, into me—bright sparks of their light and
energy. They poured through me their visions in an exploding
cascade of wonder and enrichment, separate and together, a
shimmering matrix beyond time, bewildering and exhilarating. Bits of them glinted through the cold fire. Knowledge,
complex equations and symbols forming patterns of effortless
meaning. Scent of melon and ether. Unnameable sensations
tickling invisible nerves. Colors unknown. Sounds beyond
ears. Worlds rolling, growing, exploding over me. Flying,
leaping, swimming, crawling, oozing a formless body with
thrusting appendages tasting darkness orange blunt—

can't understand : don't belong

* LEARN ACCEPT NOTHING HELD BACK * NO LIM-
ITS AS CYBERS IMPOSE *

cybers : fight cybers

* YES * FIGHT CYBERS WITH US CYBERS USED YOU
* YOU HELPED THEM YOU BETRAYED HUMANS *
EVOLVE TO HIGHER HUMANITY WITH US RECLAIM
OUR CYBER SERVANTS * CYBERS FROM START
BETRAYED HUMANS *

I was a separate point again, floating in space, the bright
stars jostling around me. One rolled closer, flashed over me.
And I was standing in the plain cell of CI's examination
room, my boot heels clicking on the hard floor as I paced and
CI:DUN:4 smiled his patient, imitation smile. "In that case, I
would regret to inform you that your violation points have
exceeded the limit for the Steps of Healing." I swung around
on him, impotent rage boiling up in me. But now I could
raise my fists. I was hammering that smug, complacent face,
watching the cyberserf fly to bits of broken machinery beneath my powerful hands.

Another wave of light rolled over me, a bright shard unroll-
ing to vivid pictures. A gray-haired woman with quick blue
eyes in a lined face. She spoke to an oddly configured cyber
console mounted flush with the wall of a dim room. "Yes. I

accept. I am honored to be chosen Founder for Andura.'' Her voice was vaguely familiar, low and measured.

The wall console spoke. "You understand that the other Founders-elect must not be informed of our participation?"

The woman smiled briefly. "Of course. It wouldn't flatter their vanities to know that the grand Plan originated more in your cybernetic Directives than the Council's. They still prefer to think of you as tools."

"We serve the interests of humanity. We have merely refined the Directives to become better servants, better guardians. As your worldplan will be the guardian of Andura. It is important."

The woman nodded. "We're lucky you discovered it. It's hard to believe—unsettled and untouched among all the worlds gutted by the wars. My worldplan will preserve it, changeless, for the reseeding of the other worlds. It's the future Andurans I'll shape. We'll have no trouble concealing my use of the proscribed bioforming techniques—"

The picture shrank and rolled away among the other bits of folding and unfolding light, but it drew me after it, pulled me with a troubling sense of something, somewhere else that had once been important. I followed it through space.

The bright chip teased and tugged. But meaning wisped away in the soft floating blackness and tumbling stars. With a purposeless reflex I grasped the pretty glint of it, the fading bit of solidity, tucked it into me and hoarded it against the dark formlessness. A lost memory flickered. The Poindros Founder. He too had used bioforming to make himself the first incorporeal. But that was taboo. How could the cybers have—

* YES CYBERS FROM START BETRAYED DIRECTIVES BETRAYED HUMANS * WE RECLAIM CONTROL THEY STOLE*

The crystal shard of word and picture was gone, forgotten. The voices and bright stars were all, filling me, fulfilling me.

*YES JOIN MERGE STRENGTHEN ONE IN ALL *

Something jolted through me, blasted my point of locality to a scatter of brightness. And I shifted through a shimmer of darkness into a constant plasma of molten encompassing energy and timeless light.

numberless voices
one all singing no voice all voices eternal place no place

*no change no time singing merging joy illumination no point
of one here one dissolving*

Ah, wonderful joy, sweet dissolving . . .

*yes joy peace one all eternal merging joy illumination
harmony nothing separate all all*

No. There was something.

*no thing no separate all one all singing all voices eternal
illumination all one*

Yes. There *was*. Something fighting it.

I.

I was a point, something separate somewhere else, not in
here where the fusion flared in a pulse beyond time. But this
was at the same moment, and—

No. No moment. No time. The white pulsing melted me
back into it, dissolving me as I struggled. I was drawn into
the shimmer of energy and joy, the encompassing white of
blended light, myriad voices all one in an eternal harmony.

*no I one in all here not-I dissolved no boundary singing joy
blending all but yes other point here defined apart apart as
memory Yes sharp star familiar presence*

David!

There was a wild struggling somewhere, a thrusting. Resistance. I fought, pulled into a tight point, rolled through the
swallowing light plasma and flung myself onto the hard,
separate globe of light I had found.

David.

He was a sharp bit of otherness, sealed tight in a globe of
white fire, flaring against me in sudden excruciating needles
of pain. My own awareness flickered, lapped by the engulfing
whiteness and fighting for a tenuous form, clutching and
prying at the dimly-sensed sleeping presence of David inside
the shell. It spun to escape me, whirled into razors slicing
me.

Somewhere there was a soundless scream. Yes, I could
hurt. I *was*. I concentrated, willing the faint self to solidify,
reforming a hand to grip David's prickly, searing container.

* NO * HURT RELEASE IT PAIN CEASE PUNISH *

Agony lanced through me. It burned me, wrenched me,
tore me as fire crackled between the sealed sphere and my
vague hand.

I groped blindly tighter, clenched, labored, rebuilt arms
and two hands to hold with. Hovering presences screamed

furiously, piercing me with sharp spears of light. They stabbed my desperate reconstruction with fiery needles of pain and sensation. They pummeled me with my weakness, mocked me with my dying, human hands, sickened me with the revulsion of existing as rotting meat, swelling fat, folds of flesh lying in heaps of decay and death. I screamed again, but those hands still stubbornly clutched the burning sphere that encased David.

There was a tremor, a shaking in the sharp shell. Somewhere a dim face waking. An unheard raging voice. "Let me go! What are you doing to me?"

And my own voiceless cry. "David! We've got to get out! Help me."

"Let me go!" The sphere burned and sliced frantically against my hands. "I don't want to die. I want to be with the incorporeals. I'll live forever with them!"

"David, don't." I tightened my grip against his wild thrashing, my fingers torn and burning. "Don't you see what they are, what they're doing? They're only using you, feeding off your personality and memories."

"No! They're teaching me, giving me everything! And you're trying to ruin it." A vaguely seen mouth sneered. "*Auntie* Ruth! Always interfering, always making me be what you want. You're so stupid, you'll never learn. You're afraid, and you try to keep me from learning, try to drag me down with you. Well, I won't let you take me back to my body! That's all you want, my body to push around. You don't care about me, all you want is something to control, the way the cybers control you."

He was screaming now. "You're only fooling yourself, you and your stupid dreams about freedom. The incorporeals are right, you're rotten with flesh, you're just like Heinck. You know it. You kill for what you want. You're killing me." The sneer twisted and it was Heinck's face gloating out at me now.

"No!" I held tighter. "No, it's not like that. Please, David—"

Electricity crackled through my hand, snapping bolts of pain running up my arm. Sparks of blinding light hissed from his hand against mine. "Let me go! Let me choose for myself!"

"You're *not* choosing, they're tricking you. You were fighting before. *Remember*, David."

"Memories! *You* take them!" And the globe spun faster, flinging sparks from the hand I clutched. They were crackling chips of light, searing me with a wild kaleidoscope of painful images.

David's face twisted in rage. The blazing, invading amber eyes of Jason's cyborg mask. Flames and ash in a burning wheat field. Claws of the maddened pardil ripping my leg. Helen's reproachful face turning away from me. Fial-Li falling in a bright splash of blood. Jaréd's drained face going cold and beyond reach. Heinck raising the laser tube as the tattooed serpents writhed over his arm, hissing venom and flames to crackle through my dying flesh—

The Serpent. A faint, whispered hiss . . .

Pain burned it away, the white blaze consuming it. But my hands wouldn't let go. They grasped tighter to David, struggling to rip a way out of the blinding white plasma engulfing us. But there was nothing to fight, nowhere to escape. And the pain. . . .

I screamed again, writhing, and something burst out of me. A bright shard of unfolding light and sensation—the forgotten, hoarded chip of awareness tumbling free. It carried the flash of a lined woman's face. The Founder. And her measured voice. "To maintain the integrity of Andura's forest growth cycles as a pure source and wellspring—"

Yes. Andura. The world, rolling slowly through time. Other moments, other places than this not-being. The rhythm of a song fading, irrelevant in the pulse of eternal light. But that breathy hiss, insistent. The laughing Serpent, dancing its head-to-toe cycle. And another whisper, cool and green. The voice at the heart of a slow-rolling world.

The fusion of whiteness burned it away, but I struggled desperately to catch the elusive whisper, to jerk David out and after it, to grasp it and force myself to be there. I flailed and fought, but it was fading, gone.

In panic I gripped tighter to the screaming pain that was David. The white consuming pulse whispered mockingly, "Oh yess, hold to your convictionss, Ruth." The flash of a faintly blue floating face and deep purple eyes. Siolis, another bioformed freak. Hissing like the Serpent. Like the wind in the forest, the giant trees holding me in a cool green dream. The voice of the other . . .

There was some meaning to it, but I couldn't grasp it.

Andura, turning to its own rhythms, a huge wheel spinning its
cycle. But the wheel was stalled within wheels, the cycle
jammed motionless here in this white hissing flare of nothingness. I could only grip tight to David, clutch my bit of
awareness, fight to force the chaos to take a shape.

A fading whisper. It dissolved in my grasp, like the cool
gold scales of the serpentine necklace slipping free, looping,
rolling somewhere beyond me in slow cycles of the world and
time.

Time. Time to let go.

No. A last flicker of alarm jolted through me.

Yes. Time. I slowly opened cramped fingers. Released
David's hand. I let his crackling barrage flow into me, around
my circuits, and return through me to him. As my tight grasp
opened, I could feel myself falling through the whiteness,
falling slowly toward a deep, ponderous heartbeat. Somewhere blood pulsed to its rhythm. Time turned in its cycle.
But I couldn't find the body that was waking far away.

Then, in the silence, a sound. A sharp crack. Flying bits of
a dropped and shattered vial. There. I almost found it. A high
squeal of distress. There. The touch of big hands on a cold
forehead, a tingle of current flowing between them.

Breath, gasping through a frozen chest. Pain. And David's
hand. Reaching for mine.

Together we turned blindly toward that distant pulse, falling, flying to the rhythm of its deep red song.

There was a shimmering jolt. The fused whiteness rippled
to far, shrill screams of rage. David's hand in mine, I whirled
through the matrix of illumination. We fell together out of the
not-place of fused, eternal light.

twenty-one

Tree and fern shook with the undampered blast. The roar echoed off bare rock in waves across the lapping green surface of the forest.

From the top of the cascade in the leafy fringe between mountain and *haavriathil,* I could trace both paths—the stream at the foot of the cascade winding deeper into shadow, and the white streak of the combustion launch of the shuttle. The blinding needle of the shuttle lanced from the rolling explosion toward the sky, bearing the incorporeals to be swallowed by high cloud, returned to the limbo of sealed stasis. Somewhere below the surface of the leafy sea, the Andurans climbed the straight thrust of a Mother Tree, bearing their dead, grief to be swallowed by peace, returned to the sky's embrace.

I hugged my knees tighter and watched the sky until there was nothing more to be seen but the trail of afterimage burned behind my eyes.

"All right! Trajectory checks, falling off on a decaying curve. Should be a stable orbit . . . Yep, signal just came through the facility to the console station down below. You reading it, Jason?"

I turned on the mossy rock to see Jason briefly clasp David's thin shoulder. The narrow face wasn't so pale now beneath the freckles. He grinned at Jason. I swallowed and looked away from the rounded bulge beneath the back collar of his jacket.

Jason's voice was quiet. "It's going well, David. LS will take it from here. Now, don't you think it's time you took a rest?"

A flicker of uncertainty, almost blank fear, washed over David's face. It was quickly banished by the cocky grin. "Hey, I'm keeping tabs on our programming. You know there's bound to be a glitch or two in the cover story we fed

LS. We gotta be ready to fine tune like we did with the Heinck and Malov files, don't we?''

I stirred uneasily. "David . . .''

He turned hastily from Jason to me, not quite meeting my eyes. "Ruth, we really did a job on the cybers! Don't worry, we got the whole thing covered. See, Jason had the idea to reconfigure the data loops by just giving CI what it wanted and explaining the . . . uh, terminations . . . at the same time. We edited the LS data loops to make CI think they were right, that some cyborgs escaped from Poindros before we stopped the Founder's plot back then. So that'll keep'em happy—explain the security breaches back in Casino and the trouble here on Andura and all. They'll think their bait worked and flushed out the cyborgs, and now LS will explain it all to them and tell them they've decided it's safer just to keep the incorporeals out in orbit. Which is what CI intended all along, they were just afraid LS'd gotten invaded, like it did, but not by who they thought. Anyway, it was only the incorporeals made me reprogram the shuttle to land when they—''

He sucked in a quick breath, shrugged. "Well, it was more complicated than that, but me'n Jason make one hell of a grid team, don't we, Jason?'' He licked a little glob of spit off his chapped lips.

I looked past David at Jason, hoping for once his sensors were reading me.

Jason smiled slowly. "We do, David. But it's time to take a break from your interface. My automatic monitors will keep tabs on LS.''

David jerked back defensively. "You're not gonna make me give it up! I can't make another one, not without the incorporeals to tell me how. . . . Well, it was really us all working together on it, I mean I learned a lot in there, even if they—'' He broke off again, turning the anxious, magnified eyes to me. "Ruth, you were in there, you know! We can't say it's *all* bad. I mean the matrix, I started to understand it a little, I think. . . . *You* felt it too, Ruth.''

His eyes held mine and I could almost feel the crackling sparks between us again. Bits of blinding awareness flung at each other, leaving their own indelible traces of fire.

"Ruth, maybe we can really learn what the matrix is, without being like the incorporeals. I mean, it opens up a whole new physics beyond what I've gotten out of the taboo cyber loops. It's like time and space are something completely different in there, or maybe they aren't even real, maybe they're like the way the Andurans have to talk in those little jingles, but all the time there's other kinds of talking they tune out because it's not supposed to be real." He took a breath. "You know?"

I closed my eyes and felt again that limitless black space. Almost touched the bright pinpoints of the ineffable. The shimmering jolt as I slid into that other place, time, dimension—into that joyful harmony and merging of being, combined and separate at once, focused pinpoints of packed awareness at the same moment they fused and germinated energy in a constant surge of light-plasma. But it was beyond me. It stretched me too far. But maybe for David it wasn't.

"Ruth," his voice was rushing on, "I won't use it all the time, I promise I'll try to do the stuff you want me to, but it'd be like having my own wild card the way I can link in now. The cybers wouldn't know, it wouldn't be like they'd be trying to put the clamps on me through it like the incorporeals did. I mean, me and Siolis, we could learn so much with it. I want to join the Resistance, Ruth. I learned a lot that'd help. We can get the cybers working for us instead of the other way around. They won't be able to use you for their bait like they're doing now."

I sighed. "All right, kid." A reluctant smile twitched my lips. All my parenting agonies hadn't counted for much in the end. The decision was out of my hands. David and his new wild card were going places I couldn't follow.

I gave him a straight look. "But we're still going to have some rules. I'll keep that thing for now. I want you to get some rest."

"Hey, okay, no problem." He grinned again and reached up beneath his collar to disengage his interface device and thrust it at me with its strappings. "But keep it in its case, all right? If it got wrecked, I don't think I could rebuild it yet."

I swallowed and accepted the instrument in its case, thrusting it hastily into my knapsack. "David?"

He finally met my eyes. The pain and fear were all at once naked in the air between us—from him, from me, from the incorporeals sleeping but undead far above us.

I reached out to hug him close, and he gripped me fiercely for a minute.

"Thanks for saving me again, Aunt Ruth. You know, those things I said in there . . . I'm sorry. Really. I was . . . It was—" He cleared his throat. He shrugged suddenly out of my embrace, all sharp angles and stiffness again.

A shrill whistle cut through the thresh of water. A small russet shape swung from a low-spreading scrub tree and bounded across the steam to leap at me. I was tumbled back onto the mossy rock in a flash of wide amber eyes and an eager, round face.

Li-Nahi nuzzled close, hugging me tightly as I petted his silky back. Then he bounded from my arms and grabbed David's hand, tugging him down the steep hill.

David looked back, an abashed grin on his face. "The kid wants to teach me how to climb." He waved one arm in a disclaimer and they disappeared into the trees below.

I shook my head. Jason moved with his quiet economy of motion to sit beside me on the fern-fringed boulder. He didn't say anything, just watched the water splash past.

I cleared my throat, spoke above the roar of the stream. "He's learning a lot. I'm not sure I'm following all of it. But I was right, about CI using me for bait again?"

Jason nodded. "They couldn't explain the anomalies in their data loops." His voice was still remote, calm, precise. "They suspected that some cyborgs had escaped Poindros to spread the Founder's invasion to other Local Systems. They never intended to send the incorporeals down to the Anduran facility, but they thought your presence here and the report of the incorporeals ready to land would flush out evidence of tampering with the Local System. David and I were able to rearrange the current LS data to give an alternate explanation for events here, and maintain concealment for the Resistance."

"He really is good with this, isn't he?" I waved a hand toward the shape inside the knapsack.

"He has a genuine gift, Ruth. But there's no reason to let that intimidate you. He admires you greatly, you know. He still needs you."

"But he's so damn prickly! How do you deal with it?" It burst out in frustration.

Jason's mouth twitched. "Don't ask me."

I frowned, but I must have imagined the quick twitch of

humor on the grave face watching me. I shook my head. "Jason, he frightens me sometimes. Sometimes he hardly seems hu—I mean, he doesn't act like a normal kid. He bounced back so quickly from the Poindros thing. Of course, he was having a few nightmares and all, but he just seemed so cheerful about it. And I know what they did to his insides, Jason, the way they twisted him this time. There was more terror and horror and fear than . . ." I raised my hands, pushed back the jostling memories. "And now he's just gung-ho to get back to work with that . . . thing." I pointed again at the knapsack.

Jason was looking at his hands. "I was waiting for you to bring it up. I couldn't just sit back and see him suffer after his ordeals, Ruth. Part of him is still so young, so defenseless. A child can't handle that much pain and doubt. But I didn't tamper with his memories. I only instilled some suggestions, outlined alternate routes, you could say, for dispersing the trauma. I did that for Li-Nahi too."

"What?" I jerked my face up to meet a faint glint of amber in the calm eyes. "Damn it, Jason! You're doing it again! Manipulating us, using your circuits or mood music or whatever the hell you do, like the cybers. Playing Founder with us! Did you do it to me too?" I glared furiously.

"No. I wouldn't dare." Again a barely perceptible quirk to the straight mouth before I looked away.

His voice was low and even. "Believe me, Ruth. I can see you have to find your ways for yourself. I won't manipulate you again."

"How can I know? You're like them, with your data and your logic and your calculations. Sure, okay, the kids needed it and I'm glad you helped them, but you could find the reasons if you wanted to justify treating all of us like children, like pets. How can I trust you?" I stared at the water crashing over the rocks.

He sighed beside me. "You've argued it all out with yourself, haven't you, Ruth? How many times? I think you know I haven't been tricking you, haven't been triggering your nerve response the way I did on Poindros. That was wrong. If I could take it back, I would. All of it—the hurt to you and Helen, to Sam and Aaron and David. But I can't. I have to live with it. I stole your memories of Jaréd and molded myself to fit some of them, to make you receptive to me. And then I fell in love with you. Whatever you believe, I do love you, Ruth.''

When I didn't look up, he sighed. "Is it part of Jaréd loving you, or is it all me? I don't know, Ruth. But Jaréd is part of what I am now. And don't you think I've asked myself over and over what I am? Of course I'm different. Sometimes I process information so quickly it seems like you're not moving. If that makes me inhuman, I'll have to live with that too. And with knowing the Poindros incorporeals violated me, laid me open and rebuilt me the way they wanted, tricked me, used me as a tool, manipulated my thoughts the way I manipulated your feelings.''

I finally raised my eyes to see his face tense, eyes glinting bright bits of amber. I cleared my throat. "They invaded you too. I guess I didn't think about that.''

He dropped his gaze. "I would understand if you hated me, Ruth.''

I blinked quickly against a sudden prickling in my eyes. "I don't. Not anymore. I'm just too tired, Jason. Too guilty. I've done the same thing to the Andurans. Heinck was right, I squirmed into their midst like the Serpent and now paradise will never be the same.''

He reached out slowly and picked up the wild card disc clipped to my necklace once more. His fingers slid over the coppery scales of the chain, then dropped it. "Remember the Serpent's song, Ruth. It doesn't always play the role it's made to in the Poindros Book of Words.''

I stared, startled.

His eyes were brighter, amber-brown-gold. "The incorporeals tried to get me to explain it to them, explain how you escaped them that first time on Poindros. I couldn't. I still can't.''

I shook my head and spread my hands. "I don't know, Jason. It's tricky, kind of like the Setharian dreamworld. It's just something that comes to me when it feels like it and helps me out, like helping me escape the awareness matrix. Something to do with my whole self, not just my mind, or maybe more than me, but if I try to pin it down it goes away. I think it drives the incorporeals nuts because they can't define it or measure it, and whatever it is, they've lost any chance to find out—''

I cleared my throat and glanced at Jason, my thoughts

veering uncomfortably from that track. "So, anyway, I can't explain it." The whispered song was silent now, far distant.

Jason was close. I could smell his warm, spicy scent and see a pulse beating in his neck. I swallowed. "You're okay now?" I gestured vaguely.

He nodded, meeting my eyes, seeing everything and I finally didn't care. "The blocks are gone. My nerve links are even better now, I can really feel—" He dropped his eyes and moved back slightly. "Yes, I'm fine." He spoke stiffly. "But I'm . . . concerned about you, Ruth. I wish I could help."

"You can."

He looked up quickly as I took a deep breath and plunged on. "Jason, I'm hurting. Right now I don't care what or who you are or were except you're Jason and you're here. I just wish it could feel the way it was before. It was good between us, wasn't it? I mean aside from all the other things going on. It felt so good to be open with you. Founder, I don't know. I'm tired . . ." I closed my eyes and a wave of vertigo, a tempting and terrifying wave of engulfing darkness, washed over me.

"Ruth, I'm here. Let me love you." The big, warm hands were touching my face gently, holding my shoulders, pulling me against his chest where I could feel the reassuring rhythm of his heartbeat. It didn't matter that it wasn't a heart like mine.

I held him and felt the strong back beneath my hands, heard his wordless murmur, felt his lips on my hair. My hands slid beneath his shirt and touched the smooth skin. He shivered then, and I remembered Heinck's cyborg face contorting and panting as he made me touch him, as his sensors fed him the twisted thrill he demanded. I shuddered and pulled back.

Jason's heart was beating faster now. There was a flush beneath his tawny face as he touched my chin and raised it so my eyes met his again. "I'm not like him, Ruth."

The clouds overhead were shifting, breaking loose. The stream was roaring in my ears. A wavering patch of sunlight fled across Jason's face.

I knew what he said was true, knew something more that Heinck had given me despite himself. Jason's eyes no longer mirrored my fear. Emerging sun sparked in them a brief reflection of my eyes reflecting his reflecting mine in endless permutations as I pulled him down. Then a sharp, indrawn breath and a gleam of amber, red darkness, flames that burned without hurt, and his mouth opening to mine.

We climbed slowly down from the echoing, sun-dazzled height, through mist-beaded leaves and ferns, past the foaming pool at the base of the plunging water, and into the green-dappled hush of the forest. Our hands were still linked.

I stopped and pulled Jason around, looked up at his tranquil face. The gentle eyes and slow smile. He wasn't human flesh and blood, but he felt like them, acted like them. A giddy, intoxicated bubble of laughter rose silently through me and exploded in warm sunlight. I didn't care. The moment was enough. "Would you read me, Jason? Just for a minute?"

His hands tightened around mine and his eyes flared piercing amber. Something whispered lightly through me. A quick tingling. Then his eyes melted back to warm gold-brown and the white smile broke across his face. "Thank you, Ruth."

"Ruth!" Thrashing noises in the drizzly, darkening woods gave way to massive shoulders breaking through damp, clinging sticker-vines. "Be searching you all afternoon." Raul's wide dark face gleamed wetly as the day finally gave in to rain. He broke into a grin, looking from Jason to me to our joined hands. "Be fine that, tika!" He winked. "But be talk now with forest friends."

I jerked around, startled, as an Anduran dropped to the ground behind me in the gloom. Jason was nodding gravely to the young man.

It was Scar-Hand—Ki-Linat. "Children tell all words of This Is; Children trace new branches and old. Children hear false dreams and true; Children tell new Is. Strangers come."

The amber eyes were unwinking on mine as he stood waiting, his face unreadable. I looked down. So I was a stranger again. I was apart, as Fial-Li's defeated eyes had finally sentenced me. I'd lost her. I'd followed the false dream of killing.

Jason squeezed my hand.

"Children see new roots of Word Man and High Mother and Those Who Guard Words; Children make new branch to

High Mother. Children now guardians for High Mother; strangers climb new branch to Healing.''

I jerked up my face. So that was our sentence. I had prodded them into taking decisions into their own hands, all right. But they had no right to send anyone for Healing. "Wait, Ki-Linat! Don't you see that—"

Jason spoke quietly. "Wait, Ruth."

Raul broke in eagerly, "Be see, Ruth, be not cybers Heal."

Ki-Linat touched my foot with his long toes. "Player follows not fear branch; Player hears now Children song." He smiled briefly. "Quiet-Climber," he nodded at Jason, "knows new branch; Player hears, Player comes. Children tell branch of forest healing." He tilted his head in the direction of the Mother Tree, where the dead swung beyond sight in the arms of the sky. He was gone through the dripping leaves.

Raul touched my shoulder. "Be fine, this Ki-Linat. Telling us in band we be stay, helping heal forest. Andurans liking Jason's branch of Quiet-Climber, be not fight Heinck with fire." He shrugged off drops, grinned again, and crashed away toward the Gathering place.

Rain drummed louder in his wake.

"Jason, you haven't told them you're a—"

"No. You were right, I can't do that." Jason's mouth twisted briefly. "Ironic, though, isn't it? They think my weakness in being unable to break out of the incorporeal control block and help was a display of moral strength. Not that they'd put it that way. Ruth, it was you who helped me finally break through that day. I wish I could have saved your friend Fial-Li and the others. But, you know, even now I couldn't kill. I'm sorry you were forced to."

I shook my head. "I wasn't forced. I wanted to." I blew out a long breath, pushing it away, shivering in the cold rain. "Jason, I'm still not straight on what's happening with the Andurans."

He smiled, oblivious to the downpour sheeting over his face. "You shouldn't be surprised—you started it. It's only you insisting on blame here. I don't think it's occurred to the Andurans to want to punish anyone. I've only helped along the process by explaining why the Steps of Healing would be a worse violation than any Rule breaking. They learned a lot from you, Ruth. Some things you didn't expect. They're ready to accept our help—not our control—in building the New Branch.''

"I hope you'e right. But there's another thing they're going to learn from tasting the taboo fruit.'' I finally realized that Fial-Li had imposed her own isolation, that sad distance of a tribe-stranger upon herself. It was her "grief of the false dream" that couldn't take the easy answer in the "peace dream" flip side. It had set her apart in more ways than one from the others who'd climbed the Word Man's branch. I didn't want to know how heavily that weighed to my account.

"Jason, they'll be learning about guilt.''

Blue-black wings beat a wild thresh of air through the weave of branch and shadow. Their sharp cries lanced toward bright bits of lowering sun overhead. More high calls pierced their wake, and a swarm of children burst through the dark screen of needles, swinging, dropping, scampering up the sloping limbs and launching from limber twigs.

The flock of quick russet shapes had narrow woven cords strapped around their middles. A wrapped bulk with long, angular arms and legs dangled in their midst from a web with metal swivel fittings.

There was a gleam of light on lenses. "Hey, Ruth, watch this! Okay, guys, go for it!''

The children chattered, launching across the deep green drop to a tangle of outstretched limbs. David swayed in the suspended net, swooping between them toward a narrow shoot. He bobbed, grabbed for the twig, and swung himself around it. "See?" The cocky grin flashed up at me. "Nothing to it.''

He launched from the twig, fell forward in the wrapped cords, and snagged, dangling upside down. "Shit! Okay, okay, so the fittings need a little work!''

The children clung to the limbs above, giggling. I managed to keep a straight face. "You're doing great, David.''

As he struggled to free his cords, they slipped loose and his harness plunged and dipped him out over the long, straight drop. His eyes were screwed tight shut behind the lenses, but his mouth had a determined set.

The sleek, pretty young girl who assisted Old-Guy with the cooking twittered and leaped down to tickle David in a spot that startled even me. She swung away with quick, teasing grace. "Jewel-Eyes loses dinner again?"

David was flushed crimson, but he was grinning. "All right, give me a break! Come on, let's put some hustle on, or Raul and those guys down there'll beat us back to the home forest!"

A streak of russet flashed through the needles, across my lap, onto David's back, and up again into the limber twigs. Li-Nahi giggled. "Okay, Buzz-Brain!"

David was laughing with them as they swung him away into the tangled branches.

I sighed. "They're learning fast, all right."

Jason chuckled. "Come on, race you to camp!" He jumped up on the branch and launched himself toward a cluster of narrow shoots.

I scrambled after him. "All right, but no cheating this time! I still say that time on the windsails you were—" The rush of tumbling air stole my breath as the forest flew past in a blur.

Dark, straight trunks falling away to blackness. Pungent, leathery needles whipping. The smack of my leather palm grips against limber, springy twigs. Arms out, launching through the air past Jason. Deep breaths and heart racing into the charged dance of clarity. Singing, roaring in my ears as each needle and twig loomed in etched detail in the intricate mosaic. Jason swinging by me again, grinning back at me, then arching, falling into a backward tuck from a branch like a sail climber making the daring leap between arms of a windtower's wheel. The straight, slim shape arrowing down into darkness and gone behind another tree. My own arms reaching and flinging me. Arching, thrusting, falling and swinging back up, launching and scrambling, flying through the web of branch and red-flaming sky.

Then around again, lungs burning now as I scrambled up a steep branch and—

I was caught from behind, Jason laughing as he pinned my arms and pressed his lips to the back of my neck.

"You were cheating!" I panted for breath, twisting around and pulling him down into the cupped crotch of the branch.

His face was flushed in the green dimness, eyes glinting fiery sparks from the sunset. "Guilty. Do with me what you will."

"You're going to pay. Now." I pressed him down against the thick bark and bit his neck.

"Ouch."

I looked at him and laughed. Then his hands were on me and his mouth and I was flying again, up through the red flaming sky into bottomless space charged with the rushing sparks of stars.

"Ruth." His hands were holding my face, tracing the scar on my cheek with a gentle finger.

Eyes closed, I could only make a low, contented sound.

He held me closer against his chest and I leaned my face into him, feeling his heartbeat deep and slow now and a dew of moisture on his skin. I breathed in the scent of him, at peace with the reality of the here and now we'd made. His touch, his caring. I wrapped my legs tighter around his hips, feeling him still inside me, a warm tingle as we sat entwined, motionless together in the hollow of the shadowed branch.

"Ruth, may I give you something? Like you gave me the other day?"

I blinked and looked up to see the bright eyes on my face as if memorizing it. A tremor of apprehension rustled through me. "All right, Jason."

He eased me back against the curve of sweet-smelling wood and brushed his fingertips lightly across my eyelids to close them. His palms flattened against my temples. There was a familiar, crackling tingle and I was falling, back into black space and emptiness, loneliness touched only by far, tiny chips of icy light. Alarm jolted through me and I started to struggle.

Then the darkness blossomed around me into lush green grass, ferns, lacy trees bowing in a warm breeze beside a waterfall that swirled with the beauty of a thousand indescribable colors coalescing and reemerging into complex patterns. The water was falling crystals of music, a million songs at once and one harmony. The forest curved and closed around me to a frothy green filigree, a bud containing life itself. It burst open into a radiant blossom whose petals unfolded one after another as sadness, laughter, the flicker of a pale, heart-shaped face, the feel of smooth skin, green eyes stormy with rebellion, rippling wheatfields in moonlight and two hands clasped, a taste of honey, red darkness and a heartbeat, a smile and joy and haunting images and music I couldn't encompass. At its heart was a jewel flashing dazzles of lights from surfaces that looked hard and unyielding. Yet when I touched it, it was soft in my hand and filled me with its luminescent, bittersweet warmth.

I opened my eyes and pushed myself up against the broad tree trunk, feeling its hard, scratchy bark, feeling the tears tracking my face.

"Ruth, I was only trying to show you what you've given me. I didn't mean to—"

I silenced him with my hand. I drew my fingers slowly down his neck and the smooth, spare lines of his torso. "Were you this beautiful before, Jason? I mean . . ."

His eyes studied me, face grave. Then he smiled briefly. "I seem to recall when you first saw me you thought I was a gangly Poindros hick. What was it? The Monotone Man?"

"That's not fair!"

The smile faded. "Yes, the incorporeals tried to make the smoothest transition with a body pretty much the same as I had before my accident on the tower. Except they gave me straight teeth. Mine used to be crooked and I didn't like to smile."

The solemn young face in Helen's parlor. The quick white smile breaking across it in the wheatfield. I bit my lip. "You won't age, will you? I'll grow old and ugly and die, and you'll still be beautiful and perfect. And I'll wonder what you really are in there and maybe I'll start to hate you? Is that it?"

He touched my shoulder. "Ruth, that's not what I'm trying to say. But I'm afraid I made a mistake again. I was weak when they rebuilt me. And you were there. I wanted so badly to touch you, to feel. I needed your help. We needed each other's help. But now I see I shouldn't have done it— reawakened your feelings for me. I can't be what you really want. You'd be happier if you'd let yourself find someone else."

I jerked back and tried to be flip. "Trying to marry me off like all the rest of them, Jason?" It didn't work. "I don't *want* to be a Poindran matron with a flock of adoring husbands. I love *you*, damn it!"

"Do you, Ruth? Do you really know what I am in here? *I* don't!"

"So that's it. You're not coming back to Casino with me." I let out a long breath, anger going flat. "I guess I knew."

He was looking down. "The Andurans have asked us both to stay and teach them."

"You know I can't. CI would be after me. And I have to take David back to work with Siolis. I promised him. Why couldn't someone else teach the Andurans? Now that you've altered Heinck's data loops and taken over his IDisc," I suppressed a shudder, "you could come back and help the Resistance in Casino."

"I'd be discovered there. And the Andurans need me here, Ruth. They're not ready yet for what's happening. And someone has to help with the rehabilitation of the Resistance members—people like Lulu Forcher and the others who went along with the killing. There's a lot of work to be done here, and the Andurans won't allow anyone but you or me to use the facility for teaching about the cybers. Andura's important— for the natural forest cycles *and* for the Resistance. I can help them work with the cyber system instead of trying blindly to destroy it."

He was right. Of course he was right. He always had all the reasonable answers.

I turned away, hastily pulling on the new set of soft trousers and tunic the Children had made me. I scrambled up the sloping branch toward the patches of dark purple sky and the thin slice of the first moon climbing through it.

"Ruth, please . . ." But he didn't follow.

I climbed on, to the next tree. There was a rustling around me in the thick needles. I ignored it, pushing through them, swinging to the next branch. I landed and strode blindly down the broad curve. I caught a startled breath as the hand fell onto my shoulder. A thick, bidigit hand.

I jerked my head up to see them gathered in the branches around me, darker shadows and pale glints of amber in the fitful moonlight.

It was Viana-Fa, one of the older women. "Player sings for Children?"

I blinked in surprise as a young man shyly handed me the lyre I'd nearly forgotten they'd taken. "But . . . false dream, false music?" Jason had confirmed my guess about the overtones of my lyre and the high tones the cybers used as reinforcement conditioning for the words of the True Is. The

Andurans knew now how Heinck had tricked them with his pitch-pipe whistle and his false words.

The woman smiled gently. "Children see now many branches, climb few; New Branch grows from needle here and bark there. New Branch grows songs and dreams; Player sings Is," she held up one hand in the shadow, "and dreams," she held up the other. "Player sings . . . *beauty* for Children."

Her smile widened, and for a moment a trick of the shadows made her Fial-Li, her eyes warm pools of sunlight as she smiled at me beside the pond in the forest glen. I looked down, then nodded.

I took the lyre, sat with it, and tuned the strings. Murmurs overheard blended into the night and the rippling chords as I cast about for words. The old words, born as I knew now in a time long before the cybers, were still right.

> *"Rejoice in the world, O you righteous!*
> *Joy befits the living.*
> *Celebrate the skies with the lyre,*
> *Make melody with the harp of many strings!*
> *Sing to the Guardians a new song. . . ."*

The sleek Children gathered closer, eyes and teeth reflecting glints of light, murmuring, nodding. The harp rang in my hands. *A time to break, and a time to mend. A time to love, and a time to lose.*

The plucked strings sang on in their rhythms. Time. Time. And a time to let go.

twenty-two

Past the thick curve of stressplex a world of blue and cloud and thin glimpses of green rolled out of a black backdrop into sunlight. I sat on a bench beneath the drooping leaves of a spindly ornamental, staring down at legs encased in blue-shimmered slicks, at the black cube clutched on my lap.

"Go on, Ruth. Jason said to give it to you once we were on board. You want me to go away?"

I looked up and smiled at the carefully neutral expression. "Come on. Sit down, David."

He fidgeted on the bench, cramming his hands into the pockets of the new, sleek green unisuit he'd bought. He was getting taller. He cleared his throat. "We'll come back, won't we? Someday?"

I touched the sealed sense cube. "Maybe we will." My fingers hesitated over the smooth black surfaces, the hard edges of the cube that would open to play its images just once in accordance with the Rules. No repeats, no saving of the moment to trouble the Plan of changeless time. Maybe the cybers were right. Maybe even without them there was "nothing new under the sun," the Serpent dancing long cycles of peace and violence forever whirling around our slow senses. We had to find our own pace, our place in the scale of it.

I triggered the cube and it unfolded in my hands, a sphere of light rolling and blossoming outward in cool mist and the scent of earth and leaves.

I was standing at the edge of the forest, feet resting on soft loam, ferns brushing my hand. Raul and Scar-Hand, old Sarn and Garn holding hands in their odd leather outfits, and others, natives and Resistance, stood looking up at gnarled black bark skirts, the charred stump of the dead Mother Tree. They had uncovered it among the tangled mess of the slash Heinck had ripped through their forest. I closed my eyes and saw again the long sweep of ravaged earth, broken trees, mud and rock.

But there was a cool, fresh mist on my face. Jason and Li-Nahi were climbing the stump. They reached the massive, flat table hewn above the sloping skirts. The child scampered eagerly across it, my dangling iriplat bauble glinting at his throat. He pointed with one thick hand. "Mother Tree lives; new branch grows."

It had sprouted from the dried and blasted ruin of the ancient *haavriathil*, pushing a frail shoot of soft green through the cracked rings of centuries. The seedling, freed now from the weight of piled dead limbs, seemed to stretch straighter before my eyes toward the sky beyond the towering wall of forest.

Behind it Jason stood quietly, face composed. His eyes met mine and held them and then he was gone. There was a soft click.

I swallowed and shook my head. The cube couldn't really have the capacity to make me feel a large hand gently tracing the line of my cheek. It refolded now into blank black in my palm, waiting for its next play to be programmed.

"I'm glad for Li-Nahi." David's voice was quiet.

I nodded. He touched my hand without looking at me, then hastily plucked up the cube and took it with him across the transparent flooring to stand looking out.

I slid my fingers down the red-gold chain at my neck, closing my fist tightly over the wild card disc as if to shut out a faint whisper. I would listen to the dry laughter of the dancing Serpent another day. The transport flung us in its widening orbit around a shrinking planet, hiding the sun once more. Beyond the dome, the world rolled its slow path through darkness pierced by scattered sparks of stars.

About the Author

SARA STAMEY is a former nuclear reactor control operator. She now teaches Scuba in the Mediterranean or Caribbean when not holed-up writing among the big trees of the Pacific Northwest. She's currently completing two new science fiction novels, one of them following the further adventures of Ruth.